The Wizard of London

The Elemental Masters, Book Four

MERCEDES LACKEY

DAW BOOKS, INC.
DONALD A. WOLLHEIM, FOUNDER
375 Hudson Street, New York, NY 10014

ELIZABETH R. WOLLHEIM
SHEILA E. GILBERT
PUBLISHERS

DAW TRADEMARK REGISTERED

PRINTED IN THE U.S.A.

Dedicated to Elizabeth R. Wollheim.
Just 'cause.

1

ISABELLE Hellen Harton waited on the dock beside the gang-plank for the last of the steamer passengers from Egypt and Africa to disembark. She was not the only person waiting there; there were a number of friends and relations, eager to greet returning soldiers posted to distant climes, tourists, hunters, adventurers, businessmen, and assorted missionaries. But she was one of a small handful of quiet, soberly-dressed folk who were waiting for some very special passengers indeed.

The vast majority of the passengers had come from Egypt; it was a popular destination for those English who could afford it, especially in the winter. There were not many soldiers; they generally returned on troopships. Those who disembarked from this passenger liner were pale, thin, sometimes missing a limb or an eye; invalided out and sent home by the transport that they could get on first—or best afford.

For those who were returning under happier circumstances, there were the usual gay greetings, crowds swirled, made noise, and left. And at last, the final passengers made their solemn way down the gangplank.

A little gaggle of children, none older than ten, all very quiet and subdued, were accompanied by their guardians; three young English nannies, none pretty, all as subdued as their charges.

Isabelle fingered the letter in her pocket; she didn't have to read it again to know what it said. And what it did *not* say in words written on the page, but in those hopes and fears scribed between the lines, in thought and emotion.

Dear Mrs. Harton: As terrible as it is for us, we must send our daughter Sarah out of the dangers of Africa and back to the more healthful climate and safety of England. As we have no relatives with which to entrust our child, we cast about for a school, and yours has come highly recommended by those we trust. She is our only child, and very dear to us. We have been told that you are kind and caring, which speaks more to us than that you have French tutors and dancing masters.

Not mentioned, of course, was that the Harton School was not expensive either. A pair of missionaries would not be able to afford a great deal.

So—*I suspect they must have asked about a great many schools before they came to us.* There was a dusting, a faint glow of true Magic about the letter; not that Isabelle was a Magician herself, but she was sensitive enough to detect it in those who were. The writer was no Master of any Element, but was surely a practitioner of Earth Magic. Not surprising, in one who had gone to Africa to be a Healer and serve at the side of another.

And the father—Doctor Lyon-White—was he, too, Magician as well as Healer? That hadn't occurred to Isabel until now, and as she waited, she brushed her fingers across the surface of the envelope and under the first faint trace, discovered another, fainter still. Yes, another Earth Magician, and this one, a Master.

But if this little daughter had been so gifted, the parents would have sent her to another Elemental Mage to be schooled. *So as she is not an incipient Elemental Mage, and they have little money to afford the only school that has a reputation for training the otherwise gifted among the other Elemental Mages, they must have been quite desperate.*

Once again, it was what was not written in the letter that resonated to Isabelle's own finely-tuned—and "extra"—senses.

Sarah has gifts we cannot train, the letter whispered to her. *Nor can anyone we know. Those we trust tell us that you can—*

But they could not put that into words, of course; they were writing to a stranger, who might *not* be as they had been told, who might think them mad for saying such things. *Rumors of our special students at best among their set; and among missionaries and the like, only the assurance that we are kind and gentle.* They could only be sure of this: that those who ran this school would be good to a little girl who had been sent so far away from everything she knew and loved.

Isabelle wondered just what it was that little Sarah Jane *had* been gifted with, then dismissed it. Whatever it was, she would find out soon enough.

Down the gangplank at last came the line of little girls and boys, two by two, with one nanny leading and the other two following, all of them quiet and round-eyed and apprehensive, subdued, perhaps, by the gray northern skies, the smokes, the looming dark city that was so completely unlike Cairo or Timbuktu.

Isabelle had eyes for only one of them, a slender, big-eyed child in a shabby coat a little too large for her, who looked with reserve, but no fear, all around her. Not pretty, brown-haired and brown-eyed, a little wren of a child. This was Sarah Jane. She knew it, felt it, and felt something under that surface that told her that Doctor and Mrs. Lyon-White had been very wise in sending their child to the Harton School for Boys and Girls.

So it was Isabelle, of all of those waiting for their charges, who stepped forward first, and presented her credentials to the leading nanny. "I am Mrs. Harton, and I am here for Sarah Jane Lyon-White," she said in a firm voice as the nanny looked the letter over with hesitant uncertainty. And before the nanny could say anything more, she turned to the child she had singled out, and held out her hand, and put all of the welcome and love she could into her voice and gaze. "Come along, my dear. Your parents asked me to meet you."

The child's eyes lit up as she met Isabelle's gaze with her own. There was relief there, too, a relief that told Isabelle how lonely the poor thing had been on this journey, and how much she had hoped to find a friend at the end of it.

Without asking for permission, she left the group and took Isabelle's hand trustingly.

There was some fuss about getting the child's things sorted out from those of the rest of the children, and then a bit more nonsense with getting a cab. During the entire time, Sarah did not say more than ten words altogether, but she was good and patient, despite a growing fatigue that showed in her pinched face and shadowed eyes. Finally, they were settled in the cab, and alone at last. As the horses drew away from the curb, Isabelle put her arm around the child, and immediately felt the girl relax into the embrace. For her part, she felt her own heart respond without reserve to the trusting child.

"My dear, you are welcome with us," Isabelle said softly. "I won't insult your intelligence by saying I'll be like a mother to you, and that you'll never miss your home. You don't know me, and I don't know you. But in my school, besides learning our lessons, we set a great deal of store by taking care of each other, and being good to each other, and I *do* say that you'll have friends here. I hope you'll be happy. If you are not, it will not be because the rest of us have not tried to help you be as happy as you can be so far from home."

Sarah looked up at her. And hesitated a moment. "My mother said—" she began, then swallowed, and went on. "My mother said you might be able to teach me things. The kind of things M'dela was teaching me?"

With that name came a flash out of Sarah's memory, of a very black man with all the usual accouterments of a shaman . . . a man, as seen through Sarah's eyes, with an aura *and Talents* and possessed of great wisdom.

And Talents . . .

"Yes, my dear, I can." She tapped Sarah's nose gently. "And we will begin by teaching you how to keep your thoughts and memories out of other people's heads unless you *intend* for them to see such things!"

Sarah gaped at her a moment and then laughed, and Isabelle smiled. So. It was well begun.

❄

Isabelle sat in her office, reviewing the progress of each student in the day's lessons. The Harton School was not all that large, and she liked to know where each of her pupils stood in his or her studies on a daily basis, in no small part because if any of the teachers fell ill, it would be Isabelle who took over the class until the teacher was well again. She felt it, the moment her husband crossed the threshold, of course, the moment when everything inside her relaxed and said, "Yes, my other self, my other half, is at my side again." Her heart rose, as she looked up from her work, feeling him draw nearer with every moment.

Her door was open—it was never closed, unless she was having a private conference—and he limped in. Frederick Harton was a fine figure of a man despite his limp, with broad shoulders, the unruly wheat-colored hair of the Cockney street urchin he had once been, and merry blue eyes. "Well, my angel," he said, with that open grin she cherished, "How is your newest imp?"

"Not an imp at all," she replied, getting up and coming around to his side of the desk to nestle unself-consciously in his arms. "Truth to be told, she's a little dear. A touch of telepathy, both receptive and projective, I believe, and as young as she is, it may get stronger. I can't tell what else. She has the most remarkable set of tales about a pet of hers that she left in Africa that I hardly know whether or not to believe, however!"

At his look of inquiry, she told him some of the stories little Sarah Jane had imparted to her about her Grey Parrot. "I know *she* believes them to be true—I am just not certain how much of it is imagination and how much is real."

Frederick Harton looked down at her somberly. "This shaman gave her the bird in the first place, did he not?" he asked.

She nodded.

"And *he* said the bird was to be her protector?"

"He did. And I see where you are going." She pursed her lips thoughtfully. "Well, in that case, I think we should assume the tales are true. I wish she had been able to persuade her mother to allow her to bring the bird here."

"If the bird is meant to be with her, a way will be found," he replied, and kissed the top of her head. "And I believe if a way *is* found, little Sarah will prove to have more interesting Talents than merely a touch of telepathy!"

He let her go, and rubbed his hands together. "Now, I am famished, my love! I trust Vashti has prepared one of her excellent curries?"

She had to laugh at that and reached up to ruffle his hair. "How fortunate we are that your tastes are so economical! Yes, of course she has, and she is waiting in the kitchen to spoil her favorite man!"

❋

The object of their discussions was tucked up in bed in her own room, although it was a room that had another empty bed in it, feeling very mixed emotions. She was horribly homesick, and longed for her parents and her parrot, Grey, and her friends among the African tribe that had adopted the little family with an intensity that was painful—but she was not as unhappy as she had been on the journey here. In fact, there was a part of her that actually felt as close to happy as she had been since she left. Memsa'b Harton was everything Mummy and Papa had promised, and more, kind and warm and always with a comforting hug for anyone who looked in need of one. The journey from Africa to London had been sheer misery. Once alone with the children, the nannies had been horribly standoffish and cold, scolding anyone who cried or even looked as if they wanted to. The children had had to share the tiniest of cabins, two to a bunk. The food had been bland and mostly cold. The other children had not been particularly nice, and one of the boys, Nigel Pettigrew, had three older brothers who had made this trip before him and he was full of stories about "schools" and how terrible they were until all of the children were ready to weep with fear as they got off the ship.

For Sarah, at least, the nightmares had vanished like morning fog, and now she felt sorry for the others, who were not being sent to the Harton School, even though some of them had looked down their noses at her because she wasn't being sent to a "first-class academy."

When Memsa'b had determined that Sarah's tummy wasn't going to revolt, she'd done her best to give her a supper like the ones she was used to, the same as the grown-ups were getting. Most of the children and both cooks were from India rather than Africa, so it was, at best, an approximation, and she had milk for the first time in as long as she could remember (milk tended to go "off" very quickly in the Congo). She'd never had a "curry" before, but it all agreed with her, and if it tasted strange, it also tasted good, and didn't make her feel half starved like the watered-down tea and toast and thin broth and gruel which was all the three English nannies seemed to think suitable for children on the ship. Now she was in a soft bed, with enough blankets to make a tropic-raised child finally feel warm again, and with a little fire in the grate to act as a night light. She sighed, and felt all of her tense muscles relax at last.

For all of her nine years until this moment, Sarah Jane Lyon-White had lived contentedly with her parents in the heart of Africa. Her father was a physician, her mother, a nurse, and they worked at a Protestant mission in the Congo.

She had been happy there, not the least because her mother and father were far more enlightened than many another mission worker—as Sarah well knew, having seen others when she and her mother visited other mission hospitals. Her parents took the cause of Healing as being more sacred than that of conversion, even though they were technically supposed to be "saving souls" as well as lives. Somehow that part never seemed to take any sort of precedence . . . and they undertook to work with the natives, and made friends instead of enemies among the shamans and medicine people. Because of this, Sarah had been a cherished and protected child by everyone around her, although she was no stranger to the many dangers of life in the Congo.

When she was six, and far older in responsibility than most of her peers, one shaman had brought her a parrot chick still in quills; he taught her how to feed and care for it, and told her that while it was still an immature bird, she was to protect it, but when it was grown, it would protect and guide her. She had called the parrot "Grey," and the bird had become her best friend—and she missed Grey now more, even, than her parents.

Her parents had sent her to live in England for the sake of her health. Now, this was quite the usual thing. It was thought that English children were more delicate than their parents, and that the inhospitable humors of hot climes would make them sicken and die. Not that their parents didn't sicken and die quite as readily as the children, who were, in fact, far sturdier than they were given credit for—but it was thought, by anxious mothers, that the climate of England would be far kinder to them. So Sarah's Mummy had carefully explained to her, and explained that the climate of England would probably be bad for Grey, and so Grey would have to remain behind.

Though why, if the climate was supposed to be good for Sarah, it could be bad for Grey, Mummy had not been able to sufficiently explain.

"Perhaps if I'm good, Memsa'b will tell Mummy that Grey must come here," she whispered to the friendly shadows around her bed. Some of the other children already had pets—two of the boys and one of the girls had rabbits, one girl had a canary, and there were fine, fat, contented cats roaming about perfectly prepared to plop into any lap that offered itself, all of whom seemed to belong to the school in general rather than anyone in particular. So it seemed that Memsa'b was more than willing to allow additions to the menagerie, provided any additions were properly taken care of.

If there was one thing that Sarah was well versed in, it was how to take care of Grey, and she had already determined that the same vegetable-and-rice curries that the cooks made for the school meals would serve Grey very well. So food would not be a problem. And this room was warm enough. And Memsa'b had explained (and Sarah saw no reason to doubt her) that she had made it very clear to the cats that while they were welcome to feast on as many mice and rats and insects as they could catch, anything with feathers was strictly off-limits. So *that* was sorted. All she had to do, really, was figure out a way to ask Memsa'b to explain to Mummy—

And as she tried to puzzle out how to do that, the weariness of a journey that had been much too long and too stressful, and the release of discovering she was in a safe and welcoming place, all caught up with her, and she fell asleep.

❄

Sarah's first day had been good, but the ones that followed were better. Not that the other children were all angelic darlings who took her to themselves and never teased her—because they weren't. But bullying was not allowed, and teasing was met with remonstrations from every adult in authority, from the two Indian ayahs who cared for the babies to Memsa'b herself, so that it was kept to a minimum. And if Sarah didn't make any bosom friends (partly because she was more used to the company of adults than children), she at least got along reasonably well with all of the other children her own age and for the most part enjoyed their company. As far as schooling went, she was ahead of most of them in most subjects, since both Mummy and Papa had given her lessons, so that wasn't a worry. And it wasn't that she didn't make fast friends—because she did. It just wasn't another child.

The third day of her residence, she went into the kitchen in search of a rag to clean up some spilled water, to find a very slim, quite diminutive, very dark man in a turban sitting patiently at the table, waiting for tea. There was something about him that drew her strongly; perhaps it was that she could not hear his thoughts, and yet there was no sense that he was hiding anything, only that he had the kind of knowledge and discipline that Memsa'b was trying to train her in. He turned to look at her as she came in, and nodded to her, or she would not have said anything, but the nod seemed to invite a response.

"Hello," she said gravely, and offered her hand. "I'm Sarah Jane. I've just come. I'm from Africa."

He took it, and bowed over it. "I am Agansing," he told her, just as gravely. "I am from India. I am a Gurkha."

As it happened, there had been enough British military visitors passing through the Congo and taking advantage of the mission's medical facilities and hospitality that Sarah knew what a Gurkha was. In fact, she had seen some, and her Papa had told her about them; that they were exceedingly brave, exceedingly good warriors, and so trusted they had their very own regiment. She blinked. "Why are you here?" she asked boldly, because while many, many Gurkhas were in service to the Empire, once they retired, they always went home to the hills in Nepal rather than coming to England.

"I have no family, except Memsa'b and Sahib," Agansing said, without taking offense. "My family perished in a mudslide when I was younger than you, and I never had other family except my regiment and my sworn brother, Sahib Harton. When Sahib was to muster out, he offered me a home and work. It is also so with Selim and Karamjit, who are his sworn brothers as well. Karamjit is a Sikh. We three guard Sahib, Memsa'b, and you children, though I am usually with Sahib at his warehouse."

Selim, she knew from the name alone, was likely to be a Moslem, and her eyes went round. Many Indians came to Africa to become storekeepers and the like in the cities, and Sarah knew very well how unlikely it was that a Gurkha, a Moslem, a Sikh, and the other Hindu and Buddhist servants that she also knew were here would coexist amicably in the same household.

Agansing smiled at her surprise, and then smiled over her head. "Karamjit, my friend," he said. "Little Missy Sarah is come to us from Africa, and we surprise her."

Sarah turned; another surprise, because she could almost always tell when someone had come up behind her and she had not sensed—anything! There was a very tall, very dark man in a turban standing there regarding her with grave eyes. "Welcome, Missy Sarah," he said, holding out his hand. She shook it. "We are a surprising tribe here, I do think. Though you will not meet with Agansing and Selim often, you will see me. My duties keep me mostly here."

Though she could sense nothing from them, she had the feeling, a feeling so strong that she had never felt anything like it except in the presence of the shaman M'dela who had given her Grey, that she could trust these men with anything. And she gave Karamjit one of her rare smiles. "We need guarding, Mr. Karamjit?" she asked.

He nodded. "The leopards and tigers that prowl outside our gates are of the two-footed kind," he told her solemnly, "and the more dangerous for that. So you must not venture out of the garden, except with another grown person."

She nodded then hesitated, and looked from one to the other, for she knew, without knowing how she knew, that both these men had knowledge that she needed. "Can you—" she hesitated, then ventured it all. "Can you help me be quiet in my mind like you are?" she begged. "Memsa'b gives me lessons, but *you're* better than she is, because you're so quiet you aren't even *there*. And I know I need to be better."

The men exchanged a glance, and it was Karamjit who answered.

"I will, if it suits Memsa'b. If I do, you will pledge me the obedience that I gave to my master, for the teaching is not easy, and needs much patience."

And she knew at that moment that she had gained the respect and the friendship of both these men. "I promise," she swore.

She went and told Memsa'b what she had done at once, of course, in order to gain that permission, and as she had suspected, Memsa'b entirely approved. "Karamjit and Agansing both know meditation techniques that I never learned," she said to Sarah.

"And if you have the patience at your young age to learn them, they will be very good for you. You can use the conservatory; it's quiet, and you can tell Karamjit I have given you permission to do so, and thank him for agreeing to teach you."

That was an astonishing privilege, as children were not allowed in the conservatory, or "hothouse," as one of the boys called it, without an adult. This was in part because all the conservatory walls were glass, and children and glass walls usually do not coexist well. And in part it was because the adults used it as a refuge, since children were allowed to come and go in virtually every other room of the school, so having one place where there was some peace from childish racket was a necessary thing.

As Sarah now knew, the school had not originally been built for such a function; it had been converted from an enormous house and grounds that had once belonged to some very wealthy Georgian merchant (or so Memsa'b said) but which had been abandoned when the London neighborhood in which it stood began to deteriorate. Now it was a very bad neighborhood indeed, which was why Memsa'b and Sahib had been able to afford such an enormous place when they looked for a building to use as their school.

The bad neighborhood was one of the reasons why it was not a "first-class" school. "First-class" schools were situated outside of cities, far from bad neighborhoods, bad air, and the dangers and temptations of a metropolis. But the people who sent their children here, like Sarah's own parents, had very particular reasons for choosing it. Mostly, they only wanted their children to be cherished— but there were several other children here who also had what Memsa'b referred to as "Talents."

Now, Sarah had been *just* old enough, and just sensitive enough before she left, that she knew very well her parents shared M'dela's Magic, though she could not herself duplicate it. And she knew that though she did not have that sort of power, she had always been able to talk to Grey in her head, and she could often see the thoughts of other people—and these were things her parents could *not* do. As Mummy had told her, now that she was here, the peo-

ple at the school were going be able to help her sort these things
she could do out. Apparently other people knew that Memsa'b and
Sahib could do this, too, and probably those people felt that being
sorted out was the most important thing that their children could
learn.

So, "Thank you, Memsa'b," she said sincerely, dimly sensing
that Karamjit did not often offer his services in this business of
being sorted out, and that though this would be a great deal of
work, the reward was likely to be very high if she mastered what
he could teach. And that she had gained a very, very valuable
teacher, perhaps one of the most valuable she was ever likely to
have as long as she lived.

She went back to the kitchen where Karamjit was still waiting.
"Memsa'b says to thank you that you will teach me, and that we
can use the conservatory," she told him.

One dark eyebrow rose, but that was the only way in which
Karamjit showed that he found the second statement remarkable.
"Memsa'b is wise," he replied, and paused. "You have a question."

"Why are you quieter in your mind than Memsa'b?" she asked.

He pondered that for a moment, while Vashti, one of the cooks,
pretended to ignore them both out of politeness for what was a private conversation.

"Memsa'b believes that it is because of the way I was taught,"
he said finally. "This is only in part true. It is because of *what* I was
taught. Memsa'b has not learned this, because she cannot, not because of ignorance. It is—it is exactly that reason that you cannot
learn what your parents do. Memsa'b is not even truly aware that
I do this thing—that I become *not there* to all inner senses, unless
I wish to be *there.* Thusly—"

And suddenly, to her astonishment, she *sensed* him, just as she
could sense anyone else. Then, just as suddenly, he was gone again
except, of course, that he was still sitting right there.

"You and I are alike in this, Missy Sarah," Karamjit continued.
"Just as Agansing and Selim and I are. It is uncommon. Sometimes
it means that one is to be a kind of warrior, though not always."

She thought that over. "I don't feel like a warrior," she said truthfully.

He shrugged. "One need not have this to be a warrior. Sometimes it is a protection. Nevertheless. This is why Memsa'b cannot teach you. You must be very diligent, and very patient. It is a skill that takes years to learn and a lifetime to master, so you must not expect to be proficient any time soon."

She nodded. "Like being a doctor."

He smiled. "Very like. Now. Here is your first lesson in patience. I will undertake to begin your teaching only after I feel that you have settled well into the school. *I* will choose the time."

She sighed, a little disappointed, but knowing better than to argue—because M'dela had schooled her in much the same way.

And since that was clearly Karamjit's way of saying "you can go now," she excused herself.

Besides, it was teatime.

❄

Sarah was used to being taught in a very large class; she had been learning her letters along with the rest of the African children whose parents thought it wise to learn the foreigners' ways. Unlike some missions, there was neither bribery nor coercion involved in getting the African children to come to school, but Sarah's parents had pointed out that whether the natives liked it or not, the foreigners had the guns, the soldiers, and the big ships to bring more of both; that they were unlikely to be rid of them, and it would be a good thing to not have to rely on translators who might lie, and might come from another tribe altogether. And that it would be an even better thing to be able to read treaties and agreements for themselves, and not depend on someone else to say what was in such things. And it was the tribal chief who had thought it over, and decreed that those who were apt to the teaching should come.

There had been nearly thirty people in Sarah's class, and only one teacher. There were only six in this class, and she had three different teachers. To her mind, this was quite astonishing.

A tall thin woman, Miss Payne, taught Reading, Penmanship, Grammar, and Literature. She looked as if she was the sort who would be very cross all the time, but in fact, she was quiet and reserved, and when she got excited, her cheeks went quite pink, but there were no other signs of her state. Other than that, she was evidently someone Memsa'b trusted, and she always seemed to know when one of her students was having difficulties, because she always came right to the desk to help him or her out.

Professor Hawthorne, an old man who spoke very slowly and with great passion about mathematics, was in charge of teaching that subject, and Geometry as well. He did not have anything like the patience of Miss Payne, and if he thought a pupil was being lazy, he was able to deliver quite a tongue-lashing. "The ability to understand mathematics," he would say with vehemence, "is the only thing that distinguishes Man from the lesser animals!"

Sarah decided that she was not going to tell him that Grey could count.

Madame Jeanette taught French, Latin, and History. She spoke French with a Parisian accent, which she was quite proud of. She was also extremely pretty and young, and there were rumors among the boys that she had been a ballet dancer at the Paris Opera, or perhaps a cancan girl at the Moulin Rouge. Sarah thought that the boys would be quite disappointed if they learned the truth—a truth that Sarah had inadvertently "overheard" when Madame Jeanette was thinking very hard one day. The truth was simply that she was extremely well-educated, but that her family had fallen on hard times, and she had to go be a schoolteacher or a governess. After several wretched postings, a friend had directed her to England and Memsa'b. Memsa'b and Sahib placed no restrictions on her movements, did not spy upon her, did not forbid her to have beaus, and encouraged her to spend all the time she liked at the British Museum outside of lessons. The tiny difference in pay was far outweighed by the enormous difference in freedom, to her mind. And lately, there was a handsome young barrister who kept taking the carrel next to hers in the Reading Room. . . .

There were four other teachers, not counting the nursery teach-ers, but Sarah wasn't taking any classes from any of them.

Madame Jeanette was perfectly normal, but Professor Hawthorne and Miss Payne had—something—about them. Sarah didn't know just what it was yet, but she had the feeling there was a great deal more to both of them than appeared on the surface.

The other five children in her class were very nice, but—well, Sarah was just used to spending a great deal of time in the com-pany of adults, or people who acted like adults, and it didn't seem to her as if she had much in common with the others. They invited her to play in their games, but they seemed relieved when she de-clined. She was a great deal more attracted to some of the older children, but they ignored the younger ones, and she couldn't think of a good way to get their attention.

So, for the first month, she spent most of her free time alone, in the kitchen with the cooks and their helpers, or with Karamjit. Often she simply followed Karamjit on his rounds. He didn't seem to mind. In fact, when he wasn't busy, he would talk to her as if she were a grown person, telling her about his home in India, ask-ing her about Africa. And sometimes, he would drop little nuggets of information about the school, the teachers, and how it had all come to be.

It was all quite interesting, and during the daytime, enough to keep her from being at all lonely.

But at night—at night, she wished (for she wouldn't call it "praying," which she instinctively knew should be reserved for very special needs) for two things.

A friend, a real friend, another girl by preference.

And Grey.

2

Nan—that was her only name, for no one had told her of any other—lurked anxiously about the back gate of the Big House. She was new to this neighborhood, for her slatternly mother had lost yet another job in a gin mill and they had been forced to move all the way across Whitechapel, and this part of London was as foreign to Nan as the wilds of Australia. She had been told by more than one of the children hereabouts that if she hung about the back gate after tea, a strange man with a towel wrapped about his head would come out with a basket of food and give it out to any child who happened to be there.

Now, there were not as many children willing to accept this offering as might have been expected, even in this poor neighborhood. They were afraid of the man, afraid of his piercing, black eyes, his swarthy skin, and his way of walking like a great hunting cat. Some suspected poison in the food, others murmured that he and the woman of the house were foreigners, and intended to kill English children with terrible curses on the food they offered. But Nan was faint with hunger; she hadn't eaten in two days, and was willing to dare poison, curses, and anything else for a bit of bread.

Furthermore, Nan had a secret defense; under duress, she could often sense the intent and even dimly hear the thoughts of others. That was how she avoided her mother when it was most dangerous to approach her, as well as avoiding other dangers in the streets themselves. Nan was certain that if this man had any ill intentions, she would know it.

Still, as teatime and twilight both approached, she hung back a little from the wrought-iron gate, beginning to wonder if it wouldn't be better to see what, if anything, her mother brought home. If she'd found a job—or a "gen'lmun"—there might be a farthing or two to spare for food before Aggie spent the rest on gin. Behind the high, grimy wall, the Big House loomed dark and ominous against the smoky, lowering sky, and the strange, carved creatures sitting atop every pillar in the wall and every corner of the House fair gave Nan the shivers whenever she looked at them. There were no two alike, and most of them were beasts out of a rummy's worst deliriums. The only one that Nan could see that looked at all normal was a big, gray bird with a fat body and a hooked beak that sat on top of the right-hand gatepost of the back gate.

Nan had no way to tell time, but as she waited, growing colder and hungrier—and more nervous—with each passing moment, she began to think for certain that the other children had been having her on. Teatime was surely long over; the tale they'd told her was nothing more than that, something to gull the newcomer with. It was getting dark, there were no other children waiting, and after dark it was dangerous even for a child like Nan, wise in the ways of the evil streets, to be abroad. Disappointed, and with her stomach a knot of pain, Nan began to turn away from the gate.

"I think that there is no one here, Missy Sa'b," said a low, deep voice, heavily accented, sounding disappointed. Nan hastily turned back, and peering through the gloom, she barely made out a tall, dark form with a smaller one beside it.

"No, Karamjit—look there!" replied the voice of a young girl, and the smaller form pointed at Nan. A little girl ran up to the gate, and waved through the bars. "Hello! I'm Sarah—what's your name? Would you like some tea bread? We've plenty!"

The girl's voice, also strangely accented, had none of the imperiousness that Nan would have expected coming from the child of a "toff." She sounded only friendly and helpful, and that, more than anything, was what drew Nan back to the wrought-iron gate.

"Indeed, Missy Sarah speaks the truth," the man said; and as Nan drew nearer, she saw that the other children had not exaggerated when they described him. His head was wrapped around in a cloth; he wore a long, high-collared coat of some bright stuff, and white trousers that were tucked into glossy boots. He was as fiercely erect as the iron gate itself; lean and angular as a hunting tiger, with skin so dark she could scarcely make out his features, and eyes that glittered at her like beads of black glass.

But strangest, and perhaps most ominous of all, Nan could sense nothing from the dark man. He might not even have been there; there was a blank wall where his thoughts should have been.

The little girl beside him was perfectly ordinary by comparison; a bright little Jenny-wren of a thing, not pretty, but sweet, with a trusting smile that went straight to Nan's heart. Nan had a motherly side to her; the younger children of whatever neighborhood she lived in tended to flock to her, look up to her, and follow her lead. She, in her turn, tried to keep them out of trouble, and whenever there was extra to go around she fed them out of her own scant stocks.

But the tall fellow frightened her, and made her nervous, especially when further moments revealed no more of his intentions than Nan had sensed before; the girl's bright eyes noted that, and she whispered something to the dark man as Nan withdrew a little. He nodded, and handed her a basket that looked promisingly heavy.

Then he withdrew out of sight, leaving the little girl alone at the gate. The child pushed the gate open enough to hand the basket through. "Please, won't you come and take this? It's awfully heavy."

In spite of the clear and open brightness of the little girl's thoughts, ten years of hard living had made Nan suspicious. The child might know nothing of what the dark man wanted. "Woi're yer givin' food away?" she asked, edging forward a little, but not yet quite willing to take the basket.

The little girl put the basket down on the ground and clasped her hands behind her back. "Well, Memsa'b says that she won't tell Maya and Vashti to make less food for tea, because she won't have us going hungry while we're growing. And she says that old, stale toast is fit only for starlings, so people ought to have the good of it before it goes stale. And she says that there's no reason why children outside our gate have to go to bed hungry when we have enough to share, and Mummy and Papa say that sharing is charity and charity is one of the cardinal virtues, so Memsa'b is being virtuous, which is a good thing, because she'll go to heaven and she would make a good angel."

Most of that came out in a rush that quite bewildered Nan, especially the last, about cardinal virtues and heaven and angels. But she did understand that "Memsa'b," whoever that was, must be one of those daft religious creatures that gave away food free for the taking, and Nan's own mum had told her that there was no point in letting other people take what you could get from people like that. So Nan edged forward and made a snatch at the basket handle.

She tried, that is; it proved a great deal heavier than she'd thought, and she gave an involuntary grunt at the weight of it.

"Be careful," the little girl admonished mischievously. "It's heavy."

"Yer moight'o warned me!" Nan said, a bit indignant, and more than a bit excited. If this wasn't a trick—if there wasn't a brick in the basket—oh, she'd eat well tonight, and tomorrow, too!

"Come back tomorrow!" the little thing called, as she shut the gate and turned and skipped toward the house. "Remember me! I'm Sarah Jane, and I'll bring the basket tomorrow!"

"Thankee, Sarah Jane," Nan called back, belatedly; then, just in case these strange creatures would think better of their generosity, she made the basket and herself vanish into the night.

❋

Isabelle listened to Sarah's version of the meeting at the gate, and nodded gravely. She had already gotten Karamjit's narrative, and the two tallied. Both Sarah and Karamjit sensed nascent Talent in the child; this must have been the Talent that she herself had sensed a day or two ago, and had sent out a gentle lure for. It looked as if her bait had been taken.

Probably the little girl in question had very minimal control over what she could do; in her world, it would be enough that she had the sense of danger before something happened to her. That might well be enough . . . for the short run, at any rate. But her own husband had been a street boy collected from a sad and dead-end life by another Talented benefactor, and if this child was just as salvageable, Isabelle would see to it that she was taken care of as well.

"Thank you, Sarah," she told the child standing before her. "I'd like you to make friends with this little girl, if she will let you. We will see what can be done for her."

Sarah beamed, and it occurred to Isabelle that the poor little thing was very lonely here. So far, she had made no close friends. This chance encounter might change that for the better.

Good. There was nothing like catching two birds with one stone.

❋

Nan came earlier the next day, bringing back the now-empty basket, and found Sarah Jane waiting at the gate. To her disappointment, there was no basket waiting beside the child, and Nan almost turned back, but Sarah saw her and called to her before she could fade back into the shadows of the streets.

"Karamjit is bringing the basket in a bit," the child said, "There's things Memsa'b wants you to have. And—what am I to call you? It's rude to call you 'girl,' but I don't know your name."

"Nan," Nan replied, feeling as if a cart had run over her. This child, though younger than Nan herself, had a way of taking over a situation that was all out of keeping with Nan's notion of how things were supposed to *be*. The children of the rich were not supposed to notice the children of the poor, except on Boxing Day, on which occasion they were supposed to distribute sweets and whatever outworn or broken things they could no longer use. And the rich were not supposed to care if the children of the poor went to bed hungry, because being hungry would encourage them to work harder. "Wot kind'o place is this, anyway?"

"It's a school, a boarding school," Sarah said promptly. "Memsa'b and her husband have it for the children of people who live in India, mostly. Memsa'b can't have children herself, which is very sad, but she says that means she can be a mother to us instead. Memsa'b came from India, and that's where Karamjit and Selim and Maya and Vashti and the others are from, too; they came with her. Except for some of the teachers."

"Yer mean the black feller?" Nan asked, bewildered. "Yer from In'juh, too?"

"No," Sarah said, shaking her head. "Africa. I wish I was back there." Her face paled and her eyes misted, and Nan, moved by an impulse she did not understand, tried to distract her with questions.

"Wot's it loik, then? Izit loik Lunnun?"

"Like London! Oh, no, it couldn't be less like London!" Nan's ploy worked; the child giggled at the idea of comparing the Congo with this gray city, and she painted a vivid word picture of the green jungles, teeming with birds and animals of all sorts; of the natives who came to her father and mother for medicines. "Mummy and Papa don't do what some of the others do—they went and talked to the magic men and showed them they weren't going to interfere in the magic work, and now whenever they have a patient who thinks he's cursed, they call the magic man in to help, and when a magic man has someone that his magic can't help right away, he takes the patient to Mummy and Papa and they all put on feathers and charms, and Mummy and Papa give him White Medicine while the magic man burns his herbs and feathers and makes his chants, and everyone is happy. There haven't been any uprisings at our station for ever so long, and our magic men won't let anyone put black chickens at our door. One of them gave me Grey, and I wanted to bring her with me, but Mummy said I shouldn't." Now the child sighed, and looked woeful again.

"Wot's a Grey?" Nan asked.

"She's a Polly, a grey parrot with the beautifullest red tail; the medicine man gave her to me when she was all prickles, he showed me how to feed her with mashed-up yams and things. She's so smart, she follows me about, and she can say, oh, hundreds of things. The medicine man said that she was to be my guardian and keep me from harm. But Mummy was afraid the smoke in London would hurt her, and I couldn't bring her with me." Sarah looked up at the fat, stone bird on the gatepost above her. "That's why Memsa'b gave me that gargoyle, to be my guardian instead. We all have them, each child has her own, and that one's mine." She looked down again at Nan, and lowered her voice to a whisper. "Sometimes when I get lonesome, I come here and talk to her, and it's like talking to Grey."

Nan nodded her head, understanding. "Oi useta go an' talk t' a stachew in one'a the yards, till we 'adta move. It looked loik me grammum. Felt loik I was talkin' to 'er, I fair did."

A footstep on the gravel path made Nan look up, and she jumped to see the tall man with the head wrap standing there, as if he had come out of the thin air. She had not sensed his presence, and once again, even though he stood materially before her she could not sense anything like a living man there. He took no notice of Nan, which she was grateful for; instead, he handed the basket he was carrying to Sarah Jane, and walked off without a word.

Sarah passed the basket to Nan; it was heavier this time, and Nan thought she smelled something like roasted meat. Oh, if only they'd given her the drippings from their beef! Her mouth watered at the thought.

"I hope you like these," Sarah said shyly, as Nan passed her the much-lighter empty basket. "Memsa'b says that if you'll keep coming back, I'm to talk to you and ask you about London; she says that's the best way to learn about things. She says otherwise, when I go out, I might get into trouble I don't understand."

Nan's eyes widened at the thought that the head of a school had said anything of the sort—but Sarah Jane hardly seemed like the type of child to lie. "All roit, I s'pose," she said dubiously. "If you'll be 'ere, so'll Oi."

The next day, faithful as the rising sun, Sarah was waiting with her basket, and Nan was invited to come inside the gate. She wouldn't venture any farther in than a bench in the garden, but as Sarah asked questions, she answered them as bluntly and plainly as she would any similar question asked by a child in her own neighborhood. Sarah learned about the dangers of the dark side of London first-hand—and oddly, although she nodded wisely and with clear understanding, they didn't seem to frighten her.

"Garn!" Nan said once, when Sarah absorbed the interesting fact that the opium den a few doors from where Nan and her mother had a room had pitched three dead men out into the street the night before. "Yer ain't never seen nothin' loik that!"

"You forget, Mummy and Papa have a hospital, and it's very dangerous where they are," Sarah replied matter-of-factly. "I've seen dead men, and dead women and even babies. When Nkumba came in clawed up by a lion, I helped bring water and bandages, while my parents sewed him up. When there was a black-water fever, I saw lots of people die. It was horrid and sad, but I didn't fuss, because Nkumba and Papa and Mummy were worked nearly to bones and needed me to be good."

Nan's eyes widened again. "Wot else y'see?" she whispered, impressed in spite of herself.

After that, the two children traded stories of two very different sorts of jungles. Despite its dangers, Nan thought that Sarah's was the better of the two.

She learned other things as well; that "Mems'ab" was a completely remarkable woman, for she had a Sikh, a Gurkha, two Moslems, two Buddhists, and assorted Hindus working in peace and harmony together—"and Mummy said in her letter that it's easier to get leopards to herd sheep than that!" Memsa'b was by no means a fool; the Sikh and the Gurkha shared guard duty, patrolling the walls by day and night. One of the Hindu women was one of the "ayahs," who took care of the smallest children; the rest of the motley assortment were servants and even teachers.

She heard many stories about the remarkable Grey, who really did act as Sarah's guardian, if Sarah was to be believed. Sarah described times when she had inadvertently gotten lost; she had called frantically for Grey, who was allowed to fly free, and the bird had come to her, leading her back to familiar paths. Grey had kept her from eating some pretty but poisonous berries by flying at her and nipping her fingers until she dropped them. Grey alerted the servants to the presence of snakes in the nursery, always making a patrol before she allowed Sarah to enter. And once, according to Sarah, when she had encountered a lion on the path, Grey had flown off and made sounds like a young gazelle in distress, attracting the lion's attention before it could scent Sarah. "She led it away, and didn't come back to me until it was too far away to get to me before I got home safe," the little girl claimed solemnly, "Grey is very clever." Nan didn't know whether to gape at her or laugh; she couldn't imagine how a mere bird could be intelligent enough to talk, much less act with purpose.

Nan had breath to laugh with, nowadays, thanks to baskets that held more than bread. The food she found in there, though distinctly odd, was always good, and she no longer felt out of breath and tired all the time. She had stopped wondering and worrying about why "Memsa'b" took such an interest in her, and simply accepted the gifts without question. They might stop at any moment; she accepted that without question, too.

The only thing she couldn't accept so easily was the manservant's eerie mental silence.

But it didn't unnerve her as it once had. She wanted desperately to know *why* she couldn't sense him, but it didn't unnerve her. If she couldn't read *him,* she could read the way he walked and acted, and there was nothing predatory about him with regard to herself or Sarah.

Besides, Sarah trusted him. Nan had the feeling that Sarah's trust wasn't ever given lightly.

Or wrongly.

❆

"And how is Sarah's pet street sparrow?" Frederick asked, as Isabelle brooded at the window that overlooked the garden.

"Karamjit thinks she is Talented," Isabelle replied, watching Sarah chatter animatedly to her friend as they took the empty basket back to the kitchen in the evening gloom. "I don't sense anything, but she's quite young, and I doubt she can do anything much beyond a few feet."

Her husband sat down in a chair beside the window, and she glanced over at him. "There's something about all of this that is worrying you," he said.

"I'm not the precognitive, but—yes. We have a sudden influx of Talents. And it might be nothing more than that we are the only place to train young Talents, whereas there are dozens who are schooling their Elemental Magicians. Still, *my* training says that coincidences among the Talented are virtually unheard of, and an ingathering of Talents means that Talents will be needed." There, it was out in the open. Frederick grimaced.

"There's something in the air," he agreed. "But nothing I can point to and say—there it is, that's what's coming. Do you want to spring the trap on this one, or let her come to our hands of her own will?"

"If we trap her, we lose her," Isabelle told him, turning away from the window. "And while we are ingathering Talents, they are all very young. Whatever is going to happen will not happen this week, or even this year. Let her come to us on her own—or not at all."

❊

"How is your mother?" Sarah asked, one day as they sat in the garden, since the day before, Nan had confessed that Aggie been "on a tear" and had consumed, or so Nan feared, something stronger and more dangerous than gin.

Nan shook her head. "I dunno," she replied reluctantly. "Aggie didn' wake up when I went out. Tha's not roight, she us'lly at least waked up t'foind out wha' I got. She don' loik them baskets, 'cause it means I don' go beggin' as much."

"And if you don't beg money, she can't drink," Sarah observed shrewdly. "You hate begging, don't you?"

"Mostly I don' like gettin' kicked an' cursed at," Nan temporized. "It ain't loik I'm gettin' underfoot. . . ."

But Sarah's questions were coming too near the bone tonight, and Nan didn't want to have to deal with them. She got to her feet and picked up her basket. "I gotter go," she said abruptly.

Sarah rose from her seat on the bench and gave Nan a penetrating look. Nan had the peculiar feeling that the child was looking at her thoughts, and deciding whether or not to press her further. "All right," Sarah said. "It is getting dark."

It wasn't, but Nan wasn't about to pass up the offer of a graceful exit. " 'Tis, that," she said promptly, and squeezed through the narrow opening Karamjit had left in the gate.

But she had not gone four paces when two rough-looking men in shabby tweed jackets blocked her path. "You Nan Killian?" said one hoarsely. Then when Nan stared at him blankly, added, "Aggie Killian's girl?"

The answer was surprised out of her; she hadn't been expecting such a confrontation, and she hadn't yet managed to sort herself out. "Ye—es," she said slowly.

"Good," the first man grunted. "Yer Ma sent us; she's gone t' a new place, an' she wants us t'show y' the way."

Now, several thoughts flew through Nan's mind at that moment. The first was that, as they were paid up on the rent through

the end of the week, she could not imagine Aggie ever vacating before the time was up. The second was, that even if Aggie had set
up somewhere else, she would never have sent a pair of strangers
to find Nan. And third was that Aggie had turned to a more potent
intoxicant than gin—which meant she would need a deal more
money. And Aggie had only one thing left to sell.

Nan.

Their minds were such a roil that she couldn't "hear" any distinct thoughts, but it was obvious that they meant her no good.

"Wait a minnit—" Nan said, her voice trembling a little as she
backed away from the two men, edging around them to get to the
street. "Did'jer say Aggie Killian's gel? Me ma ain't called Killian,
yer got th' wrong gel—"

It was at that moment that one of the men lunged for her with
a curse. He had his hands nearly on her, and would have gotten
her, too, except for one bit of interference. Sarah came shooting
out of the gate like a little bullet. She body-slammed the fellow,
going into the back of his knees and knocking him right off his feet.
She danced out of the way as he fell, scooting past him in the nick
of time, ran to Nan, and caught her hand, tugging her toward the
street. "Run!" she commanded imperiously, and Nan ran.

The two of them scrabbled through the dark alleys and twisted
streets without any idea where they were, only that they had to
shake off their pursuers. Unfortunately, the time that Nan would
have put into learning her new neighborhood like the back of her
grimy little hand had been put into talking with Sarah, and before
too long, even Nan was lost in the maze of dark, fetid streets. Then
their luck ran out altogether, and they found themselves staring at
the blank wall of a building, in a dead-end cul-de-sac. They
whirled around, hoping to escape before they were trapped, but it
was already too late. The bulky silhouettes of the two men loomed
against the fading light at the end of the street.

"Oo's yer friend, ducky?" the first man purred. "Think she'd loik
t'come with?"

To Nan's astonishment, Sarah stood straight and tall, and even stepped forward a pace. "I think you ought to go away and leave us alone," she said clearly. "You're going to find yourselves in a lot of trouble."

The talkative man laughed. "Them's big words from such a little gel," he mocked. "We ain't leavin' wi'out we collect what's ours, an' a bit more fer th' trouble yer caused."

Nan was petrified with fear, shaking in every limb, as Sarah stepped back, putting her back to the damp wall. As the first man touched Sarah's arm, she shrieked out a single word.

"Grey!"

As Sarah cried out the name of her pet, Nan let loose a wordless prayer for something, anything, to come to their rescue.

She never would have believed that anything would—

Then something screamed behind the man; startled and distracted for a moment, he turned. For a moment, a fluttering shape obscured his face, and he screamed in agony, shaking his head, violently, clawing at whatever it was.

"Get it off!" he screamed at his partner. "Get it off!"

"Get what off?" the other man asked, bewildered and suddenly frightened, backing away a little from his agitated partner. "There ain't nothin' there!"

The man flailed frantically at the front of his face, but whatever had attacked him had vanished without a trace.

But not before leading more substantial help to the rescue.

Out of the dusk and the first wisps of fog, Karamjit and another swarthy man ran on noiseless feet. In their hands were cudgels which they used to good purpose on the two who opposed them. Nor did they waste any effort, clubbing the two senseless with a remarkable economy of motion.

Then, without a single word, each of the men scooped up a girl in his arms, and bore them back to the school. At that point, finding herself safe in the arms of an unlooked-for rescuer, Nan felt secure enough to break down into hysterical tears. The man who had her—*not* the silent Karamjit—patted her back awkwardly, then muffled her face against his coat. And for the first time since her granny had died, Nan felt safe enough to take advantage of the comfort offered; she clutched at him and sobbed until they passed through the gates of the school.

Nor was that the end of it; though she completely expected to be set on her feet and shooed away, she found herself bundled up into the sacred precincts of the school itself, plunged into the first hot bath of her life, wrapped in a clean flannel gown, and put into a real bed. Sarah was in a similar bed beside her.

It all happened so swiftly, and with such an economy of action, that she was hardly able to think until that moment. As she sat there, numb, a plain-looking woman with beautiful eyes came and sat down on the foot of Sarah's bed, and looked from one to the other of them.

"Well," the lady said at last, "what have you two to say for yourselves?"

Nan couldn't manage anything, but that was all right, since Sarah wasn't about to let her get in a word anyway. The child jabbered like a monkey, a confused speech about Nan's mother, the men she'd sold Nan to, the virtue of charity, the timely appearance of Grey, and a great deal more besides. The lady listened and nodded, and when Sarah ran down at last, she turned to Nan.

"I believe Sarah is right in one thing," she said gravely. "I believe we will have to keep you. Now, both of you—sleep."

The lady's eyes seemed to get very, very big. Nan's own head filled with peace, and she found herself lying down, obedient as a lamb. And to Nan's surprise, she fell asleep immediately.

❄

Isabelle Harton stood leaning against the doorframe of the girls' room for some time, feeling limp with relief. That had been a very near thing. If little Sarah had not been able to summon the spirit of her parrot—

She sensed her husband behind her, and relaxed into his arms as he put them around her, holding her with her back to his chest. "Well, my angel. I assume we are going to keep this ragged little street sparrow?"

"Sarah desperately needs a friend," she temporized.

"You don't fool me, wife," he replied, tightening his arms around her. "You would march straight out there and bring them all in if you thought we could afford to feed them. But I agree with you. Sarah needs a friend, and this friend is both clever and Talented. Karamjit says she is definitely a telepath, and possibly other things. We can't leave one of those wandering about on the streets. You wanted her to come to you of her own accord; well, here she is, and she doesn't look like she's interested in leaving. When she comes into her full power, she'd either go mad or become a masterful criminal of some sort, and in either case, it would be you and I who would have to deal with her."

"Or one of our pupils. But you're right, I would much rather salvage her now." She relaxed further, with a sigh. "Thank you for indulging me."

"No such thing. I'm indulging both of us. And it isn't as if the girl hasn't the potential to earn her keep. If she's any good with the infants, she can help the ayahs, and that will save us the expense of another serving girl or nursemaid in the nursery." He bent and kissed her cheek, and she relaxed a little more. He was right, of course. They needed another pair of hands in the nursery, particularly at bath and bedtime, and she had been worrying about how to pay for that pair of hands. This just might work out perfectly for everyone concerned.

"Then I'll ask if she wants to stay, and make her the offer tomorrow," she told him. "I doubt that she'll turn us down."

He laughed. "Not if she has any sense!"

❄

So ended Nan Killian's introduction to the Harton School. She joyfully accepted Memsa'b's offer of bed, board, and school in exchange for help with the babies, and within days, she was being idolized by the toddlers and fully accepted as the new pupil by the others. And best of all, she was Sarah Jane's best friend.

She had never been *anyone's* best friend before, nor had she ever had a best friend of her own. It was strange. It was wonderful. It gave her the most amazing feeling, as if now there was something she could always count on, and she hadn't had that feeling since her gran died.

But that was not the end to this part of the story. A month later, Sarah's mother arrived, with Grey in a cage, after an exchange of telegraphs and letters to which neither Sarah nor Nan had been privy. Nan had, by then, found a place where she could listen to what went on in the best parlor without being found, and she glued her ear to the crack in the pantry to listen when Sarah was taken into that hallowed room.

"—found Grey senseless beside her perch," Sarah's mother was saying. "I thought it was a fit, but the Shaman swore that Sarah was in trouble and the bird had gone to help. Grey awoke none the worse, and I would have thought nothing more of the incident, until your telegraph arrived."

"And so you came, very wisely, bringing this remarkable bird." Memsa'b made chirping noises at the bird, and an odd little voice said, "Hello, bright eyes!"

Memsa'b chuckled. "How much of strangeness are you prepared to believe in, my dear?" she asked gently. "Would you believe me if I told you that I have seen this bird once before——fluttering and pecking at my window, then leading my men to rescue your child?"

"I can only answer with Hamlet," Sarah's mother said after a pause. "That there are more things in heaven and earth than I suspected." She paused again. "You know, I think, that my husband and I are Elemental Mages—"

"As are a great many of my friends, which is why you got the recommendation for our school. I understand your powers, though Frederick and I do not share them." It was Memsa'b's turn to pause. "Nor does your daughter. Her powers are psychic in nature, as you suspected, though I have not yet deciphered them completely. She *is* being instructed, however, not only by myself, but by others who are even stronger in some aspects than I."

"Haha!" said the funny little voice. "There's a good friend!"

Cor! I wunner what this El'mental business is? Whatever it was, it was new to Nan, who was only now getting used to the idea that her "sense" was a thing that could be trained and depended on, and that she was most unusual for possessing it.

"Oh, bless!" Sarah's mother cried. "I hoped—but I wasn't sure—one can't put such things in a letter—"

"True enough, but some of us can read, however imperfectly, what is written with the heart rather than a pen," Memsa'b replied decidedly. "Then I take it you are not here to remove Sarah from our midst."

"No," came the soft reply. "I came only to see that Sarah was well, and to ask if you would permit her pet to be with her."

"Gladly," Memsa'b said. "Though I might question which of the two was the pet!"

"Clever bird!" said Grey. "Veeeeeery clever!"

Memsa'b laughed. "Yes, I am, my feathered friend! And you would do very well never to forget it!

3

A month had gone by since Nan was brought into the Harton School. Another child picked up food at the back gate of the Harton School For Boys and Girls on the edge of Whitechapel in London, not Nan Killian. Children no longer shunned the back gate of the school, although they treated its inhabitants with extreme caution. Adults—particularly the criminals, and most particularly the disreputable criminals who preyed on children—treated the place and its inhabitants with a great deal more than mere caution. Word had gotten around that two child procurers had tried to take one of the pupils, and had been found with arms and legs broken, beaten senseless. They survived—but they would never walk straight or without pain again, and even a toddler would be able to outrun them. Word had followed that anyone who threatened another child protected by the school would be found dead—if he was found at all.

The three fierce, swarthy "blackfellas" who served as the school's guards were rumored to have strange powers, or be members of the thugee cult, or worse. It was safer just to pretend the school didn't exist and go about one's unsavory business elsewhere.

Nan Killian was no longer a child of the streets; she was now a pupil at the school herself, a transmutation that astonished her every morning when she awoke. To find herself in a neat little dormitory room, papered with roses and curtained in gingham, made her often feel as if she was dreaming. To then rise with the other girls, dress in clean, fresh clothing, and go off to lessons in the hitherto unreachable realms of reading and writing was more than she had ever dared dream of.

She slept in the next bed over from Sarah's, in a room inhabited by only the two of them and the parrot, Grey, and they now shared many late-night giggles and confidences, instead of leftover tea bread.

Nan also had a job; she had not expected pure charity, and would, deep down, have been suspicious if she'd been offered this place for nothing. But Memsa'b had made it clear if she was to stay, she had to work, and Nan was not at all averse to a bit of hard work. She had always known, somewhat to her own bemusement, that the littlest children instinctively trusted her and would obey her when they obeyed no one else. So Nan "paid" for her tutoring and keep by helping Nadra and Mala, the babies' nurses, or "ayahs," as they were called. Nadra and Mala were from India, as were most of the servants, from the formidable guards, the Sikh Karamjit, the Moslem Selim, and the Gurkha Agansing, to the cooks, Maya and Vashti. Mrs. Isabelle Harton—or Memsa'b, as everyone called her—and her husband had once been expatriates in India themselves. Master Harton—called, with ultimate respect, Sahib Harton—now worked as an adviser to an import firm; his military service in India had left him with a small pension, and a permanent limp.

And now Nan knew why the Harton School was here in the first place. When he and his wife had returned, they had learned quite by accident of the terrible conditions children returned to England to escape the dangers of the East often lived in. Relatives exploited or abused them, schools maltreated and starved them, and even the best schools ignored homesickness and loneliness, insisting that the bereft children "buck up" and "keep a stiff upper lip" and above all, never be seen to shed a tear. Children who had been allowed by their indulgent ayahs to run the nursery like miniature rajahs were suddenly subjected to the extreme discipline of tyrannical schoolmasters and the bullying of their elders.

Originally, they had resolved that the children of their friends back in the Punjab, at least, would not have to face that kind of traumatic separation. Then, as their reputation spread, especially among those with a bent for the arcane, other children were sent to them. Now there was a mix of purely ordinary children, and those, like Nan and Sarah, with more senses than five.

Here, the children sent away in bewilderment by anxious parents fearing that they would sicken in the hot foreign lands found, not a cold and alien place with nothing they recognized, but the familiar sounds of Hindustani, the comfort and coddling of a native nanny, and the familiar curries and rice to eat. Their new home, if a little shabby, held furniture made familiar from their years in the bungalows. But most of all, they were not told coldly to "be a man" or "stop being a crybaby"—for here they found friendly shoulders to weep out their homesickness on. If there were no French dancing Masters and cricket teams here, there was a great deal of love and care; if the furniture was unfashionable and shabby, the children were well-fed and rosy.

And for a few—those with what the Hartons called "Talents"—there were lessons of another sort, and their parents would not dream of sending them anywhere but here.

It never ceased to amaze Nan that more parents didn't send their children to the Harton School, but some folks mistakenly trusted relatives to take better care of their precious ones than strangers, and some thought that a school owned and operated by someone with a lofty reputation or a title was a wiser choice for a boy child who would likely join the Civil Service when he came of age. And as for the girls, there would always be those who felt that lessons by French dancing masters and language teachers, lessons on the harp and in watercolor painting, were more valuable than a sound education in the same basics given to a boy.

Sometimes these parents learned of their errors in judgment the hard way.

※

"Ready for m'lesson, Memsa'b," Nan called into the second-best parlor, which was Memsa'b's private domain. It was commonly understood that sometimes Memsa'b had to do odd things—"Important things that we don't need to know about," Sarah said wisely— and she might have to do them at a moment's notice. So it was better to announce oneself at the door before venturing over the threshold.

But today Memsa'b was only reading a book, and looked up at Nan with a smile that transformed her plain face and made her eyes bright and beautiful.

By now Nan had seen plenty of ladies who dressed in finer stuffs than Memsa'b's simple Artistic gown of common fabric, made bright with embroidery courtesy of Maya. Nan had seen the pictures of ladies who were acknowledged Beauties like Mrs. Lillie Langtry, ladies who obviously spent many hours in the hands of their dressers and hairdressers rather than pulling their hair up into a simple chignon from which little curling strands of brown-gold were always escaping. Memsa'b's jewelry was not of diamonds and gold, but odd, heavy pieces in silver and semiprecious gems. But in Nan's eyes, not one of those other ladies was worth wasting a single glance upon.

Then again, Nan was a little prejudiced.

"Come in, Nan," the headmistress said, patting the flowered sofa beside her invitingly. "You're doing much better already, you know. You have a quick ear."

"Thankee, Memsa'b," Nan replied, flushing with pleasure. She, like any of the servants, would gladly have laid down her life for Memsa'b Harton; they all worshipped her blatantly, and a word of praise from their idol was worth more than a pocketful of sovereigns. Nan sat gingerly down on the chintz-covered sofa and smoothed her clean pinafore with an unconscious gesture of pride.

Memsa'b took a book of etiquette from the table beside her, and opened it, looking at Nan expectantly. "Go ahead, dear."

"Good morning, ma'am. How do you do? I am quite well. I trust your family is fine," Nan began, and waited for Memsa'b's response, which would be her cue for the next polite phrase. The point here was not that Nan needed to learn manners and mannerly speech, but that she needed to lose the dreadful cadence of the streets which would doom her to poverty forever, quite literally. Nan spoke the commonplace phrases slowly and with great care, as much care as Sarah took over her French. An accurate analogy, since the King's English, as spoken by the middle and upper classes, was nearly as much a foreign language to Nan as French and Latin were to Sarah.

She had gotten the knack of it by thinking of it exactly as a foreign language, once Memsa'b had proven to her how much better others would treat her if she didn't speak like a guttersnipe. She was still fluent in the language of the streets, and often went out with Karamjit as a translator when he went on errands that took him into the slums or the street markets. But gradually her tongue became accustomed to the new cadences, and her habitual speech marked her less as "untouchable."

"Beautifully done," Memsa'b said warmly when Nan finished her recitation. "Your new assignment will be to pick a poem and recite it to me, properly spoken, and memorized."

"I think I'd loike—like—to do one uv Mr. Kipling's, Memsa'b," Nan said shyly.

Memsa'b laughed. "I hope you aren't thinking of 'Gunga Din,' you naughty girl!" the woman mock-chided. "It had better be one from the *Jungle Book,* or *Just So Stories,* not something written in Cockney dialect!"

"Yes, Memsa'b, I mean, no, Memsa'b," Nan replied quickly. "I'll pick a right'un. Mebbe the lullaby for the White Seal? *You mustn't swim till you're six weeks old, or your head will be sunk by your heels*—?" Ever since discovering Rudyard Kipling's stories, Nan had been completely enthralled; Memsa'b often read them to the children as a go-to-bed treat, for the stories often evoked memories of India for the children sent away.

"That will do very well. Are you ready for the other lesson?" Memsa'b asked, so casually that no one but Nan would have known that the "other lesson" was one not taught in any other school in this part of the world.

"I—think so." Nan got up and closed the parlor door, signaling to all the world that she and Memsa'b were not to be disturbed unless someone was dying or the house was burning down.

For the next half hour, Memsa'b turned over cards, and Nan called out the next card before she turned it over. When the last of the fifty-two lay in the face-up pile before her, Nan waited expectantly for the results.

"Not at all bad; you had almost half of them, and all the colors right," Memsa'b said with content. Nan was disappointed; she knew that Memsa'b could call out all fifty-two without an error, though Sarah could only get the colors correctly.

"Sahib brought me some things from the warehouse for you to try your 'feeling' on," Memsa'b continued. "I truly think that is where one of your true Talents lies, dear."

Nan sighed mournfully. "But knowin' the cards would be a lot more useful," she complained.

"What, so you can grow up to cheat foolish young men out of their inheritances?" Now Memsa'b actually laughed out loud. "Try it, dear, and the Gift will desert you at the time you need it most! No, be content with what you have and learn to use it wisely, to help yourself and others."

"But card-sharpin' would help me, an' I could use the takin's to help others," Nan couldn't resist protesting, but she held out her hand for the first object anyway.

It was a carved beetle; very interesting, Nan thought, as she waited to "feel" what it would tell her. It felt like pottery or stone, and it was of a turquoise blue, shaded with pale brown. "It's old," she said finally. Then, "Really old. Old as—Methusalum! It was made for an important man, but not a king or anything."

She tried for more, but couldn't sense anything else. "That's all," she said, and handed it back to Memsa'b.

"Now this." The carved beetle that Memsa'b gave her was, for all intents and purposes, identical to the one she'd just held, but immediately Nan sensed the difference.

"Piff! That 'un's new!" She also felt something else, something of intent, a sensation she readily identified since it was one of the driving forces behind commerce in Whitechapel. "Feller as made it figgers he's put one over on somebody."

"Excellent, dear!" Memsa'b nodded. "They are both scarabs, a kind of good-luck carving found with mummies—which are, indeed, often as old as Methuselah. The first one I knew was real, as I helped unwrap the mummy myself, to make sure there was no unrest about the spirit. The second, however, was from a shipment that Sahib suspected were fakes."

Nan nodded, interested to learn that this Gift of hers had some practical application after all. "So could be I could tell people when they been gammoned?"

"Very likely, and quite likely that they would pay you for the knowledge, as long as they don't think that you are trying to fool them as well. Here, try this." The next object placed in Nan's hand was a bit of jewelry, a simple silver brooch with "gems" of cut iron. Nan dropped it as soon as it touched her hand, overwhelmed by fear and horror.

"Lummy!" she cried, without thinking. "He killed her!" She stared at the horrible thing as it lay on the floor at her feet.

Who "he" and "her" were, she had no sense of; that would require more contact, which she did not want to have. But Memsa'b didn't seem at all surprised; she just shook her head very sadly and put the brooch back in a little box which she closed without a word.

She held out a child's locket on a worn ribbon. "Don't be afraid, Nan," she coaxed, when Nan was reluctant to accept it, "This one isn't bad, I promise you." Nan took the locket gingerly, but broke out into a smile when she got a feeling of warmth, contentment, and happiness. She waited for other images to come, and sensed a tired, but exceedingly happy woman, a proud man, and one—no, two strong and lively mites with the woman.

Slyly, Nan glanced up at her mentor. "She's 'ad twins, 'asn't she?" Nan asked. "When was it?"

"I just got the letter and the locket today, but it was about two months ago," Memsa'b replied. "The lady is my best friend in India's daughter, who was given that locket by her mother for luck just before the birth of her children. She sent it to me to have it duplicated, as she would like to present one to each little girl."

"I'd 'ave it taken apart, an' put half of th' old 'un with half of the new 'un," Nan suggested, and Memsa'b brightened at the idea.

"An excellent idea, and I will do just that. Now, dear, are you feeling tired? Have you a headache? We've gone on longer than we did at your last lesson."

Nan nodded, quite ready to admit to both.

Memsa'b gave her still-thin shoulders a little hug, and sent her off to her afternoon lessons. Nan had finally learned to relax and enjoy hugs; she'd never gotten one from her mother and her gran had not been inclined to physical demonstrations either. Her cheeks flushed with pleasure as she went off to her lesson.

Figuring came harder to Nan than reading; she'd already had some letters before she had arrived, enough to spell out the signs on shops and stalls and the like and make out a word here and there on a discarded broadsheet. When the full mystery of letters had been disclosed to her, mastery had come as naturally as breathing, and she was already able to read her beloved Kipling stories with minimal prompting. But numbers were a mystery arcane, and she struggled with the youngest of the children to comprehend what they meant. Anything past one hundred baffled her for the moment, and Sarah did her best to help her friend.

After Arithmetic came Geography, but for a child to whom Kensington Palace was the end of the universe, it was harder to believe in the existence of Arabia than of Fairyland, and heaven was quite as real and solid as South America, for she reckoned that she had an equal chance of seeing either. As for how all those odd names and shapes fit together . . . well!

History came easier, although she didn't yet grasp that it was as real as yesterday, for to Nan it was just a chain of linking stories. Perhaps that was why she loved the Kipling stories so much, for she often felt as out of place as Mowgli when the human tribe tried to reclaim him.

At the end of lessons Nan usually went to help Nadra and Mala in the nursery; the children there, ranging in age from two to five, were a handful when it came to getting them bathed and put to bed. They tried to put off bedtime as long as possible; there were half a dozen of them, which was just enough that when Nadra and Mala had finally gotten two of them into a bathtub, the other four had slithered out, and were running about the nursery like dripping, naked apes, screaming joyfully at their escape.

But tonight, Karamjit came for Nan and Sarah as soon as the history lesson was over, summoning them with a look and a gesture. As always, the African parrot Grey sat on Sarah's shoulder; she was so well-behaved, even to the point of being housebroken, that she was allowed to be with her mistress from morning to night. The handsome bird with the bright red tail had adapted very well to this new sort of jungle when Sarah's mother brought her to her daughter; Sarah was very careful to keep her warm and out of drafts, and she ate virtually the same food that the children did. Memsa'b seemed to understand the kind of diet that let her thrive; she allowed her only a little of the chicken and beef, and made certain that she filled up on carrots and other vegetables before she got any of the curried rice she loved so much. In fact, she often pointed to Grey as an example to the other children who would rather have had sweets than green stuffs, telling them that Grey was smarter than they were, for she knew what would make her grow big and strong. Being unfavorably compared to a bird often made the difference with the little boys in particular, who were behaving better at table since the parrot came to live at the school.

So Grey came along when Karamjit brought them to the door of Memsa'b's parlor, cautioning them to wait quietly until Memsa'b called them.

"What do you suppose can be going on?" Sarah asked curiously, while Grey turned her head to look at Nan with her penetrating pale-yellow eyes.

Nan shushed her, pressing her ear to the keyhole to see what she could hear. "There's another lady in there with Memsa'b, and she sounds sad," Nan said at last. Grey cocked her head to one side, then turned his head upside down as she sometimes did when something puzzled her. "Hurt," she said quietly, and made a little sound like someone crying.

Nan had long since gotten used to the fact that Grey noticed everything that went on around her and occasionally commented on it like a human person. If the wolves in the *Jungle Book* could think and talk, she reasoned, why not a parrot? She accepted Grey's abilities as casually as Sarah, who had raised the bird herself and had no doubt of the intelligence of her feathered friend.

Had either of them acquired the "wisdom" of their elders, they might have been surprised that Memsa'b accepted those abilities, too.

Nan jumped back as footsteps warned her that the visitor had risen and was coming toward the door; she and Sarah pressed themselves back against the wall as the strange woman passed them, her face hidden behind a veil. She took no notice of the children, but turned back to Memsa'b.

"Katherine, I believe going to this woman is a grave mistake on your part," Memsa'b told her quietly. "You and I have been friends since we were in school together; you know that I would never advise you against anything you felt so strongly about unless I thought you might be harmed by it. This woman does you no good."

The woman shook her head. "How could I be harmed by it?"

she replied, her voice trembling. "What possible ill could come of this?"

"A very great deal, I fear," Memsa'b said, her expression some combination of concern and other emotions that Nan couldn't read.

Impulsively, the woman reached out for Memsa'b's hand. "Then come with me!" she cried. "If this woman cannot convince you that she is genuine, and that she provides me with what I need more than breath itself, then I will not see her again."

Memsa'b's eyes looked keenly into her friend's, easily defeating the concealment of the veil about her features. "You are willing to risk her unmasking as a fraud, and the pain for you that will follow?"

"I am certain enough of her that I know that you will be convinced, even against your will," the woman replied with certainty.

Memsa'b nodded. "Very well, then. You and I—and these two girls—will see her together."

Only now did the woman notice Sarah and Nan, and her brief glance dismissed them as unimportant. "I see no reason why you wish to have children along, but if you can guarantee they will behave, and that is what it takes you to be convinced to see Madame Varonsky, then so be it. I will have an invitation sent to you for the next séance."

Memsa'b smiled, and patted her friend's hand. "Sometimes children see things more clearly than we adults do," was all she replied. "I will be waiting for that invitation."

The woman squeezed Memsa'b's hand, then turned and left, ushered out by one of the native servants. Memsa'b gestured to the two girls to precede her into the parlor, and shut the door behind them.

"What did you think of the lady, Nan?" asked their teacher, as the two children took their places side by side, on the loveseat they generally shared when they were in the parlor together.

Nan assessed the woman as would any street child; economics came first. "She's in mournin' an' she's gentry," Nan replied automatically. "Silk gowns fer mournin' is somethin' only gentry kin afford. I 'spect she's easy t' gammon, too; paid no attention t'us, an' I was near enough t' get me hand into 'er purse an' she would never be knowin' till she was home. An' she didn' ask fer a cab t' be brung, so's I reckon she keeps 'er carriage. That's not jest gentry, tha's quality."

"Right on all counts, my dear," Memsa'b said, a bit grimly. "Katherine has no more sense than one of the babies, and never had. Her parents didn't spoil her, but they never saw any reason to educate her in practical matters. They counted on her finding a husband who would do all her thinking for her, and as a consequence, she is pliant to any hand that offers mastery. She married into money; her husband has a very high position in the Colonial Government. Nothing but the best school would do for her boy, and a spoiled little lad he was, too."

Grey suddenly began coughing, most realistically, a series of terrible, racking coughs, and Sarah turned her head to look into her eyes. Then she turned back to Memsa'b. "He's dead, isn't he?" the child said, quite matter-of-factly. "Her little boy, I mean. Grey knows. He got sick and died. That's who she's in mourning for."

"Quite right, and as Grey showed us, he caught pneumonia." Memsa'b looked grim. "Poor food, icy rooms, and barbaric treatment—" She threw up her hands, and shook her head. "There's no reason to go on; at least Katherine has decided to trust her two youngest to us instead of the school her husband wanted. She'll bring them to Nadra tomorrow, Nan, and they'll probably be terrified, so I'm counting on you to help Nadra soothe them."

Nan could well imagine that they would be terrified; not only were they being left with strangers, but they would know, at least dimly, that their brother had gone away to school and died. They would be certain that the same was about to happen to them.

"That, however, is not why I sent for you," Memsa'b continued. "Katherine is seeing a medium; do either of you know what that is?"

Sarah and Nan shook their heads, but Grey made a rude noise. Sarah looked shocked, but Nan giggled and Memsa'b laughed.

"I am afraid that Grey is correct in her opinions, for the most part," the woman told them. "A medium is a person who claims to speak with the dead, and help the souls of the dead speak to the living." Her mouth compressed, and Nan sensed her carefully controlled anger. "All this is accomplished for a very fine fee, I might add. Real mediums are very rare, and I know all of the ones in England by name."

"Ho! Like them gypsy palm readers, an' the conjure men!" Nan exclaimed in recognition. "Aye, there's a mort'a gammon there, and that's sure. You reckon this lady's been gammoned, then?"

"Yes, I do, and I would like you two—three—" she amended, with a penetrating look at Grey, "—to help me prove it. Nan, if there is trickery afoot, do you think you could catch it?"

Nan had no doubt. "I bet I could," she said. "Can't be harder'n keepin' a hand out uv yer pocket—or grabbin' the wrist once it's in."

"Good girl—you must remember to speak properly, and only when you're spoken to, though," Memsa'b warned her. "If this so-called medium thinks you are anything but a gently-reared child, she might find an excuse to dismiss the séance." She turned to Sarah. "Now, if by some incredible chance this woman is genuine, could you and Grey tell?"

Sarah's head bobbed so hard her curls tumbled into her eyes. "Yes, Memsa'b," she said, with as much confidence as Nan. "M'luko, the apprentice to the medicine man that gave me Grey, said that Grey could tell when the spirits were there, and someday I might, too."

"Did he, now?" Memsa'b gave her a curious look. "How interesting! Well, if Grey can tell us if there are spirits or not, that will be quite useful enough for our purposes. Are either of you afraid to go with me? I expect the invitation will come quite soon." Again, Memsa'b had that grim look. "Katherine is too choice a fish to be allowed to swim free for long; Madame will want to keep her under her control by 'consulting' with her as often as possible. And if she can, she will get Katherine to remain in England and become dependent on her."

Sarah looked to Nan for guidance, and Nan thought that her friend might be a little fearful, despite her brave words. But Nan herself only laughed. "I ain't afraid of nobody's sham ghost," she said, curling her lip scornfully. "An' I ain't sure I'd be afraid uv a real one."

"Wisely said, Nan; spirits can only harm us as much as we permit them to." Nan thought that Memsa'b looked relieved, like maybe she hadn't wanted to count on their help until she actually got it. "Thank you, both of you." She reached out and took their hands, giving them a squeeze that said a great deal without words. "Now, both of you get back to whatever it was that I took you from. I will let you know in plenty of time when our excursion will be."

It was past the babies' bedtime, so Sarah and Nan went together to beg Maya for their delayed tea, and carried the tray themselves up to the now-deserted nursery. They set out the tea things on one of the little tables, feeling a mutual need to discuss Memsa'b's strange proposition.

Grey had her tea, too; a little bowl of curried rice, carrots, and beans. They set it down on the table and Grey climbed carefully down from Sarah's shoulder to the tabletop, where she selected a bean and ate it neatly, holding in on one claw while she took small bites, watching them both.

"Do you think there might be real ghosts?" Sarah asked immediately, shivering a little. "I mean, what if this lady can bring real ghosts up?"

Grey and Nan made the same rude noise at the same time; it was easy to tell where Grey had learned it. "Garn!" Nan said scornfully. "Reckon that Memsa'b only asked if you could tell as an outside bet. But the livin' people might be the ones as is dangerous." She ate a bite of bread and butter thoughtfully. "I dunno as Memsa'b's thought that far, but that Missus Katherine's a right easy mark, an' a fat 'un, too. People as is willin' t' gammon the gentry might not be real happy about bein' found out."

Sarah nodded. "Should we tell Karamjit?" she asked, showing a great deal more common sense than she would have before Nan came into her life. "Memsa'b's thinking hard about her friend, but she might not think a bit about herself."

"Aye, an' Selim an' Agansing an' mebbe Sahib, too." Nan was a little dubious about that, having only seen the lordly Sahib from a distance.

"I'll ask Selim to tell Sahib, if you'll talk to Karamjit and Agansing," Sarah said, knowing the surest route to the master from her knowledge of the school and its inhabitants. "But tell me what to look for! Three sets of eyes are better than two."

"First thing, whatever they want you t' look at is gonna be what makes a fuss—noises or voices or whatever," Nan said after a moment of thought. "I dunno how this medium stuff is gonna work, but that's what happens when a purse gets nicked. You gotta get the mark's attention, so he won't be thinkin' of his pocket. So whatever they want us to look at, we look away from. That's the main thing. Mebbe Memsa'b can tell us what these things is s'pposed to be like—if I know what's t' happen, I kin guess what tricks they're like t' pull." She finished her bread and butter, and began her own curry; she'd quickly acquired a taste for the spicy Indian dishes that the other children loved. "If there ain't ghosts, I bet they got somebody dressed up t' look like one." She grinned slyly at Grey. "An' I betcha a good pinch or a bite would make 'im yell proper!"

"And you couldn't hurt a real ghost with a pinch." Sarah nodded. "I suppose we're just going to have to watch and wait, and see what we can do."

Nan, as always, ate as a street child would, although her manners had improved considerably since coming to the School; she inhaled her food rapidly, so that no one would have a chance to take it from her. She was already finished, although Sarah hadn't eaten more than half of her tea. She put her plates aside on the tray, and propped her head up on her hands with her elbows on the table. "We got to talk to Karamjit, Agansing, an' Selim, that's the main thing," she said, thinking out loud. "They might know what we should do."

"Selim will come home with Sahib," Sarah answered, "But

Karamjit is probably leaving the basket at the back gate right now, and if you run, you can catch him alone, and he can tell Agansing."

Taking that as her hint, for Sarah had a way of knowing where most people were at any given time, Nan jumped to her feet and ran out of the nursery and down the back stairs, flying through the kitchen, much to the amusement of the cook, Vashti. She burst through the kitchen door, and ran down the path to the back gate, so quickly she hardly felt the cold at all, though she had run outside without a coat. Mustafa swept the garden paths free of snow every day, but so soon after Boxing Day there were mounds of the stuff on either side of the path, snow with a faint tinge of gray from the soot that plagued London in almost every weather. Somehow, though, the sooty air never got inside the school. The air indoors, in all the buildings, was as clear as a spring day with a sea wind in the streets.

Nan saw the Sikh, Karamjit, soon enough to avoid bouncing off his legs. The tall, dark, immensely dignified man was bundled up to the eyes in a heavy quilted coat and two mufflers, his head wrapped in a dark brown turban. Nan no longer feared him, though she respected him as only a street child who has seen a superior fighter in action could.

"Karamjit!" she called, as she slowed her headlong pace. "I need t' talk wi' ye!"

There was an amused glint in the Sikh's dark eyes, though only much association with him allowed Nan to see it. "And what does Missy Nan wish to speak of that she comes racing out into the cold like the wind from the mountains?"

"Memsa'b asked us t' help her with somethin'—there's this lady as is a meedeeyum that she thinks is gammonin' her friend. We—that's Sarah an' Grey an' me—we says a'course, but—" Here Nan stopped, because she wasn't entirely certain how to tell an adult that she thought another adult didn't know what she was getting herself into. "I just got a bad feelin'," she ended lamely.

But Karamjit did not belittle her concerns, nor did he chide her. Instead, his eyes grew even darker, and he nodded. "Come inside, where it is warm," he said. "I wish you to tell me more."

He sat her down at the kitchen table, and gravely and respectfully asked Maya to serve them both tea. He took his with neither sugar nor cream, but saw to it that Nan's was heavily sweetened and at least half milk. "Now," he said, after she had warmed herself with the first sip, "Tell me all."

Nan related everything that had happened from the time he came to take both of them to the parlor to when she had left Sarah to find him. He nodded from time to time, as he drank tea and unwound himself from his mufflers and coat.

"I believe this," he said when she had finished. "I believe that Memsa'b is a wise, good, and brave woman. I also believe that she does not think that helping her friend will mean any real danger. But the wise, the good, and the brave often do not think as the mean, the bad, and the cowardly do—the jackals that feed on the pain of others will turn to devour those who threaten their meal. And a man can die from the bite of a jackal as easily as that of a tiger."

"So you think my bad feelin' was right?" Nan's relief was total; not that she didn't trust Memsa'b, but—Memsa'b didn't know the kind of creatures that Nan did.

"Indeed, I do—but I believe that it would do no good to try to persuade Memsa'b that she should not try to help her friend." Karamjit smiled slightly, the barest lifting of the corners of his mouth. "Nevertheless, Sahib will know how best to protect her without insulting her great courage." He placed one of his long, brown hands on Nan's shoulder. "You may leave it in our hands, Missy Nan—though we may ask a thing or two of you, that we can do our duty with no harm to Memsa'b's own plans. For now, though, you may simply rely upon us."

"Thankee, Karamjit," Nan sighed. He patted her shoulder, then unfolded his long legs and rose from his chair with a slight bow to Maya. Then he left the kitchen, allowing Nan to finish her tea and run back up to the nursery, to give Sarah and Grey the welcome news that they would not be the only ones concerned with the protection of Memsa'b from the consequences of her own generous nature.

❄

Sahib took both Nan and Sarah aside just before bedtime, after
Karamjit, Agansing, and Selim had been closeted with him for half
an hour. "Can I ask you two to come to my study with me for a
bit?" he asked quietly. He was often thought to be older than Memsa'b, by those who were deceived by the streaks of gray at each
temple, the stiff way that he walked, and the odd expression in his
eyes, which seemed to Nan to be the eyes of a man who had seen
so much that nothing surprised him anymore. Nan had trusted him
the moment that she set eyes on him, although she couldn't have
said why.

"So long as Nadra don't fuss," Nan replied for both of them.
Sahib smiled, his eyes crinkling at the corners.

"I have already made it right with Nadra," he promised.
"Karamjit, Selim, Agansing, and Memsa'b are waiting for us."

Nan felt better immediately, for she really hadn't wanted to go
sneaking around behind Memsa'b's back. From the look that Sarah
gave her, Nan reckoned that she felt the same.

"Thank you, sir," Sarah said politely. "We will do just as you say."

Very few of the children had ever been inside the sacred
precincts of Sahib's office; the first thing that struck Nan was that
it did not smell of tobacco, but of sandalwood and cinnamon. That
surprised her; most of the men she knew smoked although their
womenfolk disapproved of the habit, but evidently Sahib did not,
not even in his own private space.

There was a tiger skin on the carpet in front of the fire, the glass
eyes in its head glinting cruelly in a manner unnerving and lifelike.
Nan shuddered, and thought of Shere Khan, with his taste for man
cub. Had this been another terrible killer of the jungle? Did tigers
leave vengeful ghosts?

Heavy, dark drapes of some indeterminate color shut out the
cold night. Hanging on the walls, which had been papered with
faded gold arabesques upon a ground of light brown, was a jumble
of mementos from Sahib's life in India: crossed spears, curious

daggers and swords, embroidered tapestries of strange characters twined with exotic flowers and birds, carved plaques of some heavy, dark wood inlaid with brass, bizarre masks that resembled nothing less than brightly painted demons. On the desk and adorning the shelves between the books were statues of half-and fully-naked gods and goddesses, more bits of carving in wood, stone, and ivory. Book shelves built floor to ceiling held more books than Nan had known existed. Sahib took his place behind his desk, while Memsa'b perched boldly on the edge of it. Agansing, Selim, and Karamjit stood beside the fire like a trio of guardian statues themselves, and Sahib gestured to the children to take their places on the overstuffed chairs on either side of the fireplace. Nan waited tensely, wondering if Memsa'b was going to be angry because they went to others with their concerns. Although it had not fallen out so here, she was far more used to being in trouble over something she had done than in being encouraged for it, and the reflexes were still in place.

"Karamjit tells me that you six share some concern over my planned excursion to the medium, Nan," Memsa'b said, with a smile that told Nan she was not in trouble for her meddling, as she had feared. "They went first to Sahib, but as we never keep secrets from one another, he came to me. And I commend all of you for your concern and caution, for after some discussion, I was forced to agree with it."

"And I would like to commend both of you, Nan and Sarah, for having the wisdom to go to an adult with your concerns," added Sahib, with a kindly nod to both of them that Nan had not expected in the least. "That shows great good sense, and please, continue to do so in the future."

"I thought—I was afeared—" Nan began, then blurted out all that she'd held in check. "Memsa'b is 'bout the smartest, goodest lady there is, but she don't know bad people! Me, I know! I seed 'em, an' I figgered that they weren't gonna lay down an' lose their fat mark without a fight!"

"And very wise you were to remind us of that," Sahib said

gravely. "I pointed out to Memsa'b that we have no way of knowing where this medium is from, and she is just as likely to be a
criminal as a lady—more so, in fact. Just because she speaks, acts,
and dresses like a lady, and seeks her clients from among the gentry means nothing; she could easily have a crew of thugs as her ac-
complices."

"As you say, Sahib," Karamjit said gravely. "For, as it is said, it is
a short step from a deception to a lie, from a lie to a cheat, from a
cheat to a theft, and from a theft to a murder."

Memsa'b blushed. "I will admit that I was very angry with you
at first, but when my anger cooled, it was clear that your reasoning was sound. And after all, am I some Gothic heroine to go wide-
eyed into the villains' lair, never suspecting trouble? So, we are
here to plan what we all shall do to free Katherine of her dangerous obsession."

"Me, I needta know what this see-ants is gonna be like, Memsa'b," Nan put in, sitting on the edge of the chair tensely. "What
sorta things happens?"

"Generally, the participants are brought into a room that has a
round table with chairs circling it." Memsa'b spoke directly to Nan
as if to an adult, which gave Nan a rather pleasant, if shivery, feeling. "The table often has objects upon it that the spirits will supposedly move; often a bell, a tambourine, and a megaphone are
among them, though why spirits would feel the need to play upon
a tambourine when they never had that urge in life is quite beyond me!"

She laughed, as did Sahib; the girls giggled nervously.

"At any rate, the participants are asked to sit down and hold
hands. Often, the medium is tied to the chair; her hands are se-
cured to the arms, and her feet to the legs." Nan noticed that Memsa'b used the word "legs" rather than the mannerly "limbs," and
thought the better of her for that. "The lights are brought down,
and the séance begins. Most often, objects are moved, including
the table, the tambourine is played, the bell is rung, all as a sign
that the spirits have arrived. The spirits most often speak by means

of raps on the table, but Katherine tells me that the spirit of her little boy spoke directly, through the floating megaphone. Sometimes a spirit will actually appear; in this case, it was just a glowing face of Katherine's son."

Nan thought that over for a moment. "Be simple 'nuff t' tilt the chair an' get yer legs free by slippin' the rope down over the chair feet," she observed, "An' all ye hev t' do is have chair arms as isn't glued t' their pegs, an' ye got yer arms free, too. Be easy enough to make all kind uv things dance about when ye got arms free. Be easy 'nuff t' make th' table lift if it's light enough, an' rap on it, too."

Sahib stared at her in astonishment. "I do believe that you are the most valuable addition to our household in a long time, young lady!" he said with a delight that made Nan blush. "I would never have thought of any of that."

"I dunno how ye'd make summat glow, though," Nan admitted.

"Oh, I know that," Sarah said casually. "There's stuff that grows in rotten wood that makes a glow; some of the magic men use it to frighten people at night. It grows in swamps, so it probably grows in England, too."

Karamjit grinned, his teeth very white in his dark face, and Selim nodded with pride. "What is it that the Black Robe's Book says, Sahib? Out of the mouths of babes comes wisdom?"

Memsa'b nodded. "I should have told you more, earlier," she said ruefully. "Well, that's mended in time. Now we all know what to look for."

Grey clicked her beak several times, then exclaimed, "Ouch!"

"Grey is going to try to bite whatever comes near her," Sarah explained.

"I don't want her venturing off your arm," Memsa'b cautioned. "I won't chance her getting hurt." She turned to Sahib. "The chances are, the room we will be in will have very heavy curtains to prevent light from entering or escaping, so if you and our warriors are outside, you won't know what room we are in."

"Then I'd like one of you girls to exercise childish curiosity and go immediately to a window and look out," Sahib told them. "At least one of us will be where we can see both the front and the back of the house. Then if there is trouble, one of you signal us and we'll come to the rescue."

"Just like the shining knights you are, all four of you," Memsa'b said warmly, laying her hand over the one Sahib had on the desk. "I think that is as much of a plan as we can lay, since we really don't know what we will find in that house."

"It's enough, I suspect," Sahib replied. "It allows three of us to break into the house if necessary, while one goes for the police." He stroked his chin thoughtfully with his free hand. "Or, better yet, I'll take a police whistle; that will summon help in no time." He glanced up at Memsa'b. "What time did you say the invitation specified?"

"Seven," she replied promptly. "Well after dark, although Katherine tells me that her sessions are usually later, nearer midnight."

"The medium may anticipate some trouble from sleepy children," Sahib speculated. "But that's just a guess." He stood up, still holding his wife's hand, and she slid off her perch on the desk and turned to face them. "Ladies, gentlemen, I think we are as prepared as we can be for trouble. So let us get a good night's sleep, and hope that we will not find any."

Then Sahib did a surprising thing; he came around his desk, limping stiffly, and bent over Nan and took her hand. "Perhaps only I of all of us can realize how brave you were to confide your worry to an adult you have only just come to trust, Nan," he said, very softly, then grinned at her so impishly that she saw the little boy he must have been in the eyes of the mature man. "Ain't no doubt 'uv thet, missy. Yer a cunnin' moit, an' 'ad more blows than pats, Oi reckon," he continued in street cant, shocking the breath out of her. "I came up the same way you are now, dear, thanks to a very kind man with no son of his own. I want you to remember that, to us here at this school, there is no such thing as a stupid question, nor will we dismiss any worry you have as trivial. Never fear to bring either to an adult."

He straightened up, as Memsa'b came to his side, nodding. "Now both of you try and get some sleep, for every warrior knows that sleep is more important than anything else before a battle."

Ha, Nan thought, as she and Sarah followed Karamjit out of the study. *There's gonna be trouble; I kin feel it, an' so can he. He didn' get that tiger by not havin' a nose fer trouble. But—I reckon the trouble's gonna have its hands full with him.*

✳

"I'm glad you aren't angry with me—"

Isabelle and her husband had turned to each other and said virtually the same words at the same time. And now both laughed.

"Oh, we know each other far too well, my love." Frederick took her in his arms, and she laid her head contentedly on his shoulder. "Far too well. So, you were annoyed because I was being the warrior and not giving you credit for being one in your own right."

"And you were annoyed because I was planning on wandering off into danger without thinking," she said, ruefully. In hindsight, she had very nearly made a dreadful decision. And yet it had seemed harmless enough; the address of the medium was suitably genteel, no real harm had come to Katherine except to be fleeced of a few "gifts" in order to see what she thought was her son.

Isabelle now acknowledged that she just hadn't thought deeply enough.

"I would never have made that mistake in India," she admitted, "I would have assumed there was an entire clan of thieves behind the fraud. Or worse—"

Because there had been worse. It was not always money that was at stake in India, and there were worse fates than death.

"You were thinking of your friend—"

"And not of danger." She nodded.

"I think—" he paused. "I think danger here has become more subtle than when we first lived in England. The attacks are indirect."

She frowned a little. "I would have said, more petty. And that bothers me. We know there are great occultists with cruel agendas still living here. So where are they?"

"In hiding." He paused, and released her. She stood away from him a little, looking up into his face. "I wonder if they are not waiting for science to make people forget that they ever existed."

"So that they can return to prey on the utterly unwary?" She shivered. "An uncomfortable thought."

"But not one we need to confront tonight or tomorrow." He smiled down at her. *"Sufficient unto the day are the evils thereof."*

"True enough." She took his hand, and looked coyly up at him. "And since it happens to be night—"

He laughed.

※

The medium lived in a modest house just off one of the squares in the part of London that housed those clerks and the like with pretensions to a loftier address than their purses would allow, an area totally unfamiliar to Nan. The house itself had seen better days, though, as had most of the other homes on that dead-end street, and Nan suspected that it was rented. The houses had that peculiarly faded look that came when the owners of a house did not actually live there, and those who did had no reason to care for the property themselves, assuming that was the duty of the landlord.

Memsa'b had chosen her gown carefully, after discarding a walking suit, a mourning gown and veil, and a peculiar draped garment she called a sari, a souvenir of her time in India. The first, she thought, made her look untrusting, sharp, and suspicious, the second would not be believed had the medium done any research on the backgrounds of these new sitters, and the third smacked of mockery. She chose instead one of the plain, simple gowns she preferred, in the mode called "Artistic Reform"; not particularly stylish, but Nan thought it was a good choice. For one thing, she could move in it; it was looser than the highest mode, and did not require tight corseting. If Memsa'b needed to run, kick, or dodge, she could.

The girls followed her quietly, dressed in their starched pinafores and dark dresses, showing the best possible manners, with Grey tucked under Sarah's coat to stay warm until they got within doors.

It was quite dark as they mounted the steps to the house and rang the bell. The door was answered by a sour-faced woman in a plain black dress, who ushered them into a sitting room and took their coats, with a startled glance at Grey as she popped her head out of the front of Sarah's jacket. She said nothing, however, and neither did Grey as she climbed to Sarah's shoulder.

The woman returned a moment later, but not before Nan had heard the faint sounds of surreptitious steps on the floor above them. She knew it had not been the sour woman, for she had clearly heard those steps going off to a closet and returning. If the séance room was on this floor, then, there was someone else above.

The sitting room had been decorated in a very odd style. The paintings on the wall were all either religious in nature, or extremely morbid, at least so far as Nan was concerned. There were pictures of women weeping over graves, of angels lifting away the soul of a dead child, of a woman throwing herself to her death over a cliff, of the spirits of three children hovering about a man and woman mourning over pictures held in their listless hands. There was even a picture of a girl crying over a dead bird lying in her hand.

Crystal globes on stands decorated the tables, along with bouquets of funereal lilies whose heavy, sweet scent dominated the chill room. The tables were all draped in fringed cloths of a deep scarlet. The hard, severe furniture was either of wood or upholstered in prickly horsehair. The two lamps had been lit before they entered the room, but their light, hampered as it was by heavy brocade lamp shades, cast more shadows than illumination.

They didn't have to wait long in that uncomfortable room, for the sour servant departed for a moment, then returned, and conducted them into the next room. This, evidently, was only an antechamber to the room of mysteries; heavy draperies swathed all the walls, and there were straight-backed chairs set against them on all four walls. The lily scent pervaded this room as well, mixed with another, that Nan recognized as the Hindu incense that Nadra often burned in her own devotions.

There was a single picture in this room, on the wall opposite the door, with a candle placed on a small table beneath it so as to illuminate it properly. This was a portrait in oils of a plump woman swathed in pale draperies, her hands clasped melodramatically before her breast, her eyes cast upward. Smoke, presumably that of incense, swirled around her, with the suggestion of faces in it. Nan was no judge of art, but Memsa'b walked up to it and examined it with a critical eye.

"Neither good nor bad," she said measuringly. "I would say it is either the work of an unknown professional or a talented amateur."

"A talented amateur," said the lady that Memsa'b had called "Katherine," as she, too, was ushered into the chamber. "My dear friend Lady Harrington painted it; it was she who introduced me to Madame Varonsky."

Memsa'b turned to meet her, and Katherine glided across the floor to take her hand in greeting. "It is said to be a very speaking likeness," she continued. "I certainly find it so."

Nan studied the woman further, but saw nothing to change her original estimation. Katherine wore yet another mourning gown of expensive silk and mohair, embellished with jet beadwork and fringes that shivered with the slightest movement. A black hat with a full veil perched on her carefully coiffed curls, fair hair too dark to be called golden, but not precisely brown either. Her full lips trembled, even as they uttered words of polite conversation, her eyes threatened to fill at every moment, and Nan thought that her weak chin reflected an overly sentimental and vapid personality. It was an assessment that was confirmed by her conversation with Memsa'b, conversation that Nan ignored in favor of listening for other sounds. Over their heads, the floor creaked softly as someone moved to and fro, trying very hard to be quiet. There were also some odd scratching sounds that didn't sound like mice, and once, a dull thud, as of something heavy being set down a little too hard.

Something was going on up there, and the person doing it didn't want them to notice.

At length the incense smell grew stronger, and the drapery on the wall to the right of the portrait parted, revealing a door, which opened as if by itself.

Taking that as their invitation, Katherine broke off her small talk to hurry eagerly into the sacred precincts; Memsa'b gestured to the girls to precede her, and followed on their heels. By previous arrangement, Nan and Sarah, rather than moving toward the circular table at which Madame Varonsky waited, went to the two walls likeliest to hold windows behind their heavy draperies before anyone could stop them.

It was Nan's luck to find a corner window overlooking the street, and she made sure that some light from the room within flashed to the watcher on the opposite side before she dropped the drapery.

"Come away from the windows, children," Memsa'b said in a voice that gently chided. Nan and Sarah immediately turned back to the room, and Nan assessed the foe.

Madame Varonsky's portraitist had flattered her; she was decidedly paler than she had been painted, with a complexion unpleasantly like wax. She wore similar draperies, garments which could have concealed anything. The smile on her thin lips did not reach her eyes, and she regarded the parrot on Sarah's shoulder with distinct unease.

"You did not warn me about the bird, Katherine," the woman said, her voice rather reedy.

"The bird will be no trouble, Madame Varonsky," Memsa'b soothed. "It is better behaved than a good many of my pupils."

"Your pupils—I am not altogether clear on why they were brought," Madame Varonsky replied, turning her sharp black eyes on Nan and Sarah.

"Nan is an orphan, and wants to learn what she can of her par-

ents, since she never knew them," Memsa'b said smoothly. "And
Sarah lost a little brother to an African fever. The bird was her
brother's, and it is all she has of him."

"Ah." Madame Varonsky's suspicions diminished, and she gestured to the chairs around the table. "Please, all of you, do take
your seats, and we can begin at once."

As with the antechamber, this room had walls swathed in
draperies, which Nan decided could conceal an entire army if
Madame Varonsky were so inclined. The only furnishings besides
the séance table and chairs were a sinuous statue of a female completely enveloped in draperies on a draped table, with incense
burning before it in a small charcoal brazier of brass and cast iron.

The table at which Nan took her place was very much as Memsa'b had described. A surreptitious bump as Nan took her seat on
Memsa'b's left hand proved that it was quite light and easy to
move; it would be possible to lift it with one hand with no difficulty at all. On the draped surface were some of the objects Memsa'b had described; a tambourine, a megaphone, a little handbell.
There were three lit candles in a brass candlestick in the middle of
the table, and some objects Nan had not expected—a fiddle and
bow, a rattle, and a pair of handkerchiefs.

This is where we're supposed to look, Nan realized, as Sarah took
her place on Memsa'b's right, next to Madame Varonsky, and
Katherine on Nan's left, flanking the medium on the other side.
She wished she could look up, as Grey was unashamedly doing,
her head over to one side as one eye peered upward at the ceiling
above them.

"If you would follow dear Katherine's example, child," said
Madame, as Katherine took one of the handkerchiefs and used it to
tie the medium's wrist to the arm of her chair. She smiled crookedly.
"This is to assure you that I am not employing any trickery."

Sarah, behaving with absolute docility, did the same on the
other side, but cast Nan a knowing look as she finished. Nan knew
what that meant; Sarah had tried the arm of the chair and found
it loose.

"Now, if you all will hold hands, we will beseech the spirits to attend us." The medium turned her attention to Memsa'b as Katherine and Sarah stretched their arms across the table to touch hands, and the rest reached for the hands of their partners. "Pray do not be alarmed when the candles are extinguished; the spirits are shy of light, for they are so delicate that it can destroy them. They will put out the candles themselves."

For several long moments they sat in complete silence, as the incense smoke thickened and curled around. Then although there wasn't a single breath of moving air in the room, the candle flames began to dim, one by one, and go out!

Nan felt the hair on the back of her neck rising, for this was a phenomenon she could not account for—to distract herself, she looked up quickly at the ceiling just in time to see a faint line of light in the form of a square vanish.

She felt better immediately. However the medium had extinguished the candles, it had to be a trick. If she had any real powers, she wouldn't need a trapdoor in the ceiling of her séance room. As she looked back down, she realized that the objects on the table were all glowing with a dim, greenish light.

"Spirits, are you with us?" Madame Varonsky called. Nan immediately felt the table begin to lift.

Katherine gasped; Memsa'b gave Nan's hand a squeeze. Understanding immediately what she wanted, Nan let go of it. Now Memsa'b was free to act as she needed.

"The spirits are strong tonight," Madame murmured, as the table settled again. "Perhaps they will give us a further demonstration of their powers."

Exactly on cue, the tambourine rose into the air, shaking uncertainly; first the megaphone joined it, then the rattle, then the handbell, all floating in midair, or seeming to. But Nan was looking up, not at the objects, and saw a very dim square, too dim to be called light, above the table. A deeper shadow moved back and forth over that area, and Nan's lip curled with contempt. She had no difficulty in imagining how the objects were "levitating"; one by one, they'd been pulled up by wires or black strings, probably hooked by means of a fishing rod from the room above.

Now rapping began on the table, to further distract their attention. Madame began to ask questions.

"Is there a spirit here for Isabelle Harton?" she asked. One rap—that was a no; not surprising, since the medium probably wouldn't want to chance making a mistake with an adult. "Is there a spirit here for Katherine Boughmont?" Two raps—yes. "Is this the spirit of a child?" Two raps, and already Katherine had begun to weep softly. "Is it the spirit of her son, Edward?" Two raps plus the bell rang and the rattle and tambourine rattled, and Nan found herself feeling very sorry for the poor, silly woman.

"Are there other spirits here tonight?" Two raps. "Is there a spirit for the child Nan?" Two raps. "Is it her father?" One rap. "Her mother?" Two raps, and Nan had to control her temper, which flared at that moment. She knew very well that her mother was still alive, though at the rate she was going, she probably wouldn't be for long, what with the gin and the opium and the rest of her miserable life. But if she had been a young orphan, her parents dead in some foreign land like one or two of the other pupils, what would she not have given for the barest word from them, however illusory? Would she not have been willing to believe anything that sounded warm and kind?

There appeared to be no spirit for Sarah, which was just as well. Madame Varonsky was ready to pull out the next of her tricks, for the floating objects settled to the table again.

"My spirit guide was known in life as the great Paganini, the master violinist," Madame Varonsky announced. "As music is the food of the soul, he will employ the same sweet music he made in life to bridge the gap between our world and the next. Listen, and he will play this instrument before us!"

Fiddle music appeared to come from the instrument on the table, although the bow did not actually move across the strings. Katherine gasped.

"Release the child's hand a moment and touch the violin, dear

Katherine," the medium said, in a kind, but distant voice. Katherine evidently let go of Sarah's hand, since she still had hold of Nan's, and the shadow of her fingers rested for a moment on the neck of the fiddle.

"The strings!" she cried. "Isabelle, the strings are vibrating as they are played!"

If this was supposed to be some great, long-dead music master, Nan didn't think much of his ability. If she wasn't mistaken, the tune he was playing was the child's chant of "London Bridge Is Falling Down," but played very, very slowly, turning it into a solemn dirge.

"Touch the strings, Isabelle!" Katherine urged. "See for yourself!"

Nan felt Memsa'b lean forward, and another hand shadow fell over the strings. "They are vibrating . . ." she said, her voice suddenly uncertain.

The music ground to a halt before she took her hand away—and until this moment, Grey had been as silent as a stuffed bird on a lady's hat. Now she did something quite odd.

She began to sing. It was a very clever imitation of a fiddle, playing a jig tune that a street musician often played at the gate of the school, for the pennies the pupils would throw to him.

She quit almost immediately, but not before Memsa'b took her hand away from the strings, and Nan sensed that somehow Grey had given her the clue she needed to solve that particular trick.

But the medium must have thought that her special spirit was responsible for that scrap of jig tune, for she didn't say or do anything.

Nan sensed that all of this was building to the main turn, and so it was.

Remembering belatedly that she should be keeping an eye on that suspicious square above, she glanced up just in time to see it disappear. As the medium began to moan and sigh, calling on Paganini, Nan kept her eye on the ceiling. Sure enough, the dim line of light appeared again, forming a grayish square. Then the lines of the square thickened, and Nan guessed that a square platform was being lowered from above. Pungent incense smoke thickened about them, filling Nan's nose and stinging her eyes so that they watered, and she smothered a sneeze. It was hard to breathe, and there was something strangely, disquietingly familiar about the scent.

The medium's words, spoken in a harsh, accented voice, cut through the smoke. "I, the great Paganini, am here among you!"

Once again, Katherine gasped.

"Harken and be still! Lo, the spirits gather!"

Nan's eyes burned, and for a moment, she felt very dizzy; she thought that the soft glow in front of her was due to nothing more than eyestrain, but the glow strengthened, and she blinked in shock as two vague shapes took form amid the writhing smoke.

For a new brazier, belching forth such thick smoke that the coals were invisible, had "appeared" in the center of the table, just behind the candlestick. It was above this brazier that the glowing shapes hovered, and slowly took on an identifiable form. Nan felt dizzier, sick; the room seemed to turn slowly around her.

The faces of a young woman and a little boy looked vaguely out over Nan's head from the cloud of smoke. Katherine began to weep—presumably she thought she recognized the child as her own. But the fact that the young woman looked nothing like Nan's mother (and in fact, looked quite a bit like the sketch in an advertisement for Bovril in the *Times*) woke Nan out of her mental haze.

And so did Grey.

She heard the flapping of wings as Grey plummeted to the floor. The bird sneezed urgently, and shouted aloud, "Bad air! Bad air! Bad, bad air!"

And that was the moment when she knew what it was that was so familiar in the incense smoke, and why she felt as tipsy as a sailor on shore leave.

"Hashish!" she choked, trying to shout, and not managing very well. She knew this scent; on the rare occasions when her mother could afford it—and before she'd turned to opium—she'd smoked it in preference to drinking. Nan could only think of one thing; that she must get fresh air in here before they all passed out!

She shoved her chair back and staggered up and out of it; it fell behind her with a clatter that seemed muffled in the smoke. She groped for the brazier as the two faces continued to stare, unmoved and unmoving, from the thick billows. Her hands felt like a pair of lead-filled mittens; she had to fight to stay upright as she swayed like a drunk. She didn't find it, but her hands closed on the cool, smooth surface of the crystal ball. That was good enough; before the medium could stop her, she heaved up the heavy ball with a grunt of effort, and staggered to the window. She half-spun and flung the ball at the draperies hiding the unseen window; it hit the drapes and carried them into the glass, crashing through it, taking the drapery with it.

A gush of cold air, as fresh as air in London ever got, streamed in through the broken panes, as bedlam erupted in the room behind Nan.

She dropped to the floor, ignoring everything around her for the moment, as she breathed in the air tainted only with smog, waiting for her head to clear. Grey ran to her and huddled with her rather than joining her beloved mistress in the poisonous smoke.

Katherine shrieked in hysteria, there was a man as well as the medium shouting, and Memsa'b cursed all of them in some strange language.

Grey gave a terrible shriek and half-ran, half-flew away. Nan fought her dizziness and disorientation; looked up to see that Memsa'b was struggling in the grip of a stringy fellow she didn't recognize. Katherine had been backed up into one corner by the medium, and Sarah and Grey were pummeling the medium with small fists and wings. Memsa'b kicked at her captor's shins and stamped on his feet with great effect, as his grunts of pain demonstrated.

Nan struggled to her feet, guessing that she must have been the one worst affected by the hashish fumes. She wanted to run to Memsa'b's rescue, but she couldn't get her legs to work. In a moment the sour-faced woman would surely break into the room, turning the balance in favor of the enemy—

The door did crash open behind her just as she thought that, and she tried to turn to face the new foe—

But it was not the foe.

Sahib charged through the broken door, pushing past Nan and using his cane to belabor the man holding Memsa'b; within three blows the man was on the floor, moaning. Before Nan fell, Karamjit caught her and steadied her. More men flooded into the room, among them, Selim and Agansing who went to the rescue of Sarah and Grey, and Nan let Karamjit steer her out of the way, concentrating on those steadying breaths of air. She thought perhaps that she passed out of consciousness for a while, for when she next noticed anything, she was sitting bent over in a chair, with Karamjit hovering over her, frowning. At some point the brazier had been extinguished, and a policeman was collecting the ashes and the remains of the drug-laced incense.

It was a while before her head cleared; by then, the struggle was over. The medium and her fellow tricksters were in the custody of the police, who had come with Sahib when Nan threw the crystal ball through the window. Sahib was talking to a policeman with a sergeant's badge, and Nan guessed that he was explaining what Memsa'b and Katherine were doing here. Katherine wept in a corner, comforted by Memsa'b. The police had brought lamps into the séance room from the sitting room, showing all too clearly how the medium had achieved her work; a hatch in the ceiling to the room above, through which things could be lowered; a magic lantern behind the drapes, which had cast its image of a woman and boy onto the thick brazier smoke. That, and the disorienting effect of the hashish, had made it easy to trick the clients.

Finally, the bobbies took their captives away, and Katherine stopped crying. Nan and Sarah sat on the chairs Karamjit had set up, watching the adults, Grey on her usual perch on Sarah's shoulder. A cushion stuffed in the broken window cut off most of the cold air from outside.

"I can't believe I was so foolish!" Katherine moaned. "But—I wanted to see Edward so very much—"

"I hardly think that falling for a clever deception backed by drugs makes you foolish, my dear lady," Sahib said gravely. "But you are to count yourself fortunate in the loyalty of your friends, who were willing to place themselves in danger for you. I do not think that these people would have been willing to stop at mere fraud, and neither do the police."

His last words made no impression on Katherine, at least none that Nan saw—but she did turn to Memsa'b and clasp her hand fervently. "I thought so ill of you, that you would not believe in Madame," she said tearfully. "Can you forgive me?"

Memsa'b smiled. "Always, my dear," she said, in the voice she used to soothe a frightened child. "Since your motive was to enlighten me, not to harm me—and your motive in seeking your poor child's spirit—"

A chill passed over Nan at that moment that had nothing to do with the outside air. She looked sharply at Sarah, and saw a very curious thing.

There was a very vague and shimmery shape standing in front of Sarah's chair; Sarah looked at it with an intense and thoughtful gaze, as if she was listening to it. More than that, Grey was doing the same. Nan got the distinct impression that it was asking her friend for a favor.

Grey and Sarah exchanged a glance, and the parrot nodded once, as grave and sober as a parson, then spread her wings as if sheltering Sarah like a chick. The shimmering form melted into Sarah; her features took on a mischievous expression that Nan had never seen her wear before, and she got up and went directly to Katherine. The woman looked up at her, startled at the intrusion of a child into an adult discussion, then paled at something she saw in Sarah's face.

"Oh, Mummy, you don't have to be so sad," Sarah said in a curiously hollow, piping soprano. "I'm all right, really, and it wasn't your fault anyway, it was that horrid Lord Babington that made you and Papa send me to Overton. But you must stop crying, please! Laurie is already scared of being left, and you're scaring her more."

Now, Nan knew very well that Memsa'b had not said anything about a Lord Babington, nor did she and Sarah know what school the poor little boy had been sent to. Yet she wasn't frightened; in fact, the protective but calm look in Grey's eye made her feel rather good, as if something inside her told her that everything was going wonderfully well.

The effect on Katherine was not what Nan had expected either. She reached out tentatively, as if to touch Sarah's face, but stopped short. "This is you, isn't it, darling?" she asked in a whisper.

Sarah nodded—or was it Edward who nodded? "Now, I've got to go, Mummy, and I can't come back. So don't look for me, and don't cry anymore."

The shimmering withdrew, forming into a brilliant ball of light at about the level of Sarah's heart, then shot off, so fast that Nan couldn't follow it. Grey pulled in her wings, and Sarah shook her head a little, then regarded Katherine with a particularly measuring expression before coming back to her chair and sitting down.

"Out of the mouths of babes, Katherine," Memsa'b said quietly, then looked up at Karamjit. "I think you and Selim should take the girls home now; they've had more than enough excitement for one night. Agansing can stay here with us while we deal with the results of this night's adventure."

Karamjit bowed silently, and Grey added her own vote. "Wan' go back," she said in a decidedly firm tone. When Selim brought their coats and helped them to put them on, Grey climbed right back inside Sarah's, and didn't even put her head back out again.

They didn't have to go home in a cab either; Katherine sent them back to the school in her own carriage, which was quite a treat for Nan, who'd had no notion that a private carriage would come equipped with such comforts as heated bricks for the feet and fur robes to bundle in. Nan didn't say anything to Sarah about the aftermath of the séance until they were alone together in their room and Karamjit and Selim had returned to Memsa'b and Sahib.

Only then, as Grey took her accustomed perch on the headboard of Sarah's bed, did Nan look at her friend and ask—

"That last—was that—?"

Sarah nodded. "I could see him, clear as clear, too." She smiled a little. "He must've been a horrid brat at times, but he really wasn't bad, just spoiled enough to be a bit selfish, and he's been— learning better manners, since."

All that Nan could think of to say was—"Ah."

"Still, I think it was a bit rude of him to have been so impatient with his mother," she continued, a little irritated.

"I 'spose that magic-man friend of yours is right," Nan replied finally. "About what you c'n do, I mean."

"Oh! You're right!" Sarah exclaimed. "But you know, I don't think I could have done it if Grey hadn't been there. I thought if I ever saw a spirit I'd be too scared to do anything, but I wasn't afraid, since she wasn't."

The parrot took a little piece of Sarah's hair in her beak and preened it.

"Wise bird," replied Grey.

❄

Isabelle sat holding her friend's hand, as the police sergeant questioned her in a painstaking but ponderous manner. Isabelle felt obscurely sorry for Katherine; it was a difficult thing to have to admit that you had given your trust to someone who had then not only abused it, but done so in such a fashion as to make you look incredibly foolish. As Katherine reluctantly admitted the large sums of money she had pressed into "Madame's" hands—probably, Memsa'b reflected, with all the fervent devotion of a religious convert—she flushed and looked acutely uncomfortable until even the policeman noticed.

"Begging your pardon, mum," he said apologetically, "But we have to hev these particulars down in the report, or we can't prosecute the woman properly. This's theft, it is, and no two ways about it, as I'm sure the magistrate will say."

Well, while it might morally be theft, it actually was fraud under the law, and if Katherine hadn't been wealthy and highly connected, Isabelle very much doubted whether this police sergeant would be bringing it up to a magistrate on such charges.

But she was both of those things, and the upshot of that was that Madame—based on the amount of money she had taken—would probably be in prison for the rest of her life or, at least, would be transported to Australia.

Even more uncomfortable for Katherine was divulging the names of her other wealthy, titled, or connected friends who had been fleeced by this fraud. That was worse than embarrassment, it was very nearly social suicide. Katherine would have to live in India for another five years before people like Lady Harrington forgot who had been the cause of common police appearing at her door to question her—and the ensuing embarrassment on her part of discovering she had been taken in by such a fraud.

Still, there was nothing for it, and if Lady Harrington had been the one who had introduced Katherine to Madame in the first place, perhaps her annoyance would be tempered by guilt.

Finally, the police released them all, and Katherine fled to the safety and seclusion of her carriage, looking utterly shattered.

"She should have thanked you at least, Memsa'b," said Selim gravely, as the carriage rolled away into the darkness. Frederick had gone to look for a cab with Agansing, leaving her with the third of the guardians.

"Well, I can't say as I am surprised that she did not," Isabelle admitted. "She was one of the girls I went to school with, one in whom Elemental Magic burns very dimly. We tended to be thrown together within the group of the Gifted and the Talented on that account, you see; I had none of their Magic, and she had very little. But I did have *something* quite powerful that demanded a certain amount of respect. I may have been less than circumspect in my conversations about my powers, and as a consequence, I believe poor Katherine got some unrealistic notions about occult abilities."

"And yet Missy Sarah has them," Selim observed.

"Hmm." Isabelle's lips compressed. "I fear that if Katherine makes this known, the consequences will be some exceedingly intrusive and unwanted attention on all of us. There are many bereaved people in the world, none of whom really wishes to know that a loved one has moved on and left them behind."

"One cannot blame them," Selim replied. "But it would be hard on Missy Sarah to be the one to suffer at the hands of their need."

The sound that emerged from Isabelle's throat was of a laugh with no humor in it. "And there is not one in a thousand of them who will consider that asking a very young child to perform mediumistic work is both cruel and uncaring. Each of them is so enwrapped in her grief—for it is predominantly women who flock to mediums—that nothing else is of consequence."

"They would be better off seeking solace in the arms of their religion, and leave the child out of it." Selim's tone was grim.

"Well, they will be leaving the child out of it, because we are her guardians, and I have no intention of allowing her to do any such thing." Isabelle's tone was just as grim as Selim's. "Ah! Here is Sahib with our cab!"

The short journey back was conducted mostly in silence. It was Isabelle who finally broke it. "I know I thanked you all before—but now I have to thank you again, with the full knowledge of what foolishly rushing in to this situation could have brought me to." In fact, she felt a bit shaken and rather humbled at this point. It was painfully clear that at the least, she, the girls, and Katherine could have been harmed, and at worst—

"And who was it, Memsa'b, that kept me from believing I could brave the temple of Kali-ma alone?" asked Agansing.

"Or insisted that if I *would* go to meet that fakir, it would be while I was under the eye of my friends?" said Selim.

"Or told me to go direct to Bhurka Singh with my suspicions instead of allowing them to fester," added Karamjit, his teeth gleaming in a white smile in the shadows of the cab.

"Or kept me from rushing into a hundred foolish ventures," Frederick concluded, with his arms around her. "This is what it means to be human, as I quite recall you saying the last time I came home with a broken head. You succeed, you become a trifle overconfident, and at that point it is the duty of your friends to haul you back and point out the edge of the cliff at your feet."

"Well, nevertheless," she said, feeling a little better and a trifle less stupid. "Thank you."

"Nevertheless," said Frederick, with a squeeze, "You are welcome. Provided you continue to do me the same good turn, my love."

And somehow, that made her feel very much better indeed.

4

NAN sat on the foot of Sarah's bed, with her feet curled up under her flannel nightgown to keep them warm. Sarah Jane's parrot Grey lay flat on Sarah's chest, eyes closed, cuddling like a kitten. Warm light from an oil lamp mounted on the wall beside the bed poured over all of them. It wasn't a very big room, just room for Nan's bed and Sarah Jane's, a perch with cups screwed to it for food and water and a selection of toys hanging from it for Grey, and a wardrobe and chests for their clothes and things. If the wallpaper was old and faded, and the rugs on the floor threadbare, it was still a thousand times better than any place that Nan had ever lived in—and as for Sarah, well, she was used to a mission and hospital in the middle of the jungle, and their little room was just as foreign to her as it was to Nan, though in entirely different ways.

While only little Sarah had a pet from "home," there were plenty of pets acquired here in England for the other children. To make sure that the children never forgot those who had sent them here, other reminders of absent parents were encouraged here, and there was a supply of paper, ink, and penny stamps in each room. Most schools encouraged letters—so long as they were written in class where the teacher could ostensibly check for spelling, grammar, and penmanship, but in reality making sure nothing uncomplimentary about the school or the teachers went out through the mails. There was a great deal of laughter in the Harton School, and the lessons learned were all the surer for it.

And that was the least of the eccentricities here, in a school where not all of the lessons were about what could be seen with the ordinary eye.

Nan was alone in not wanting reminders of her family; she had no idea who her father was, and her mother had finally descended (last Nan had heard) to the lowest rung on the social ladder her type could reach, that of a street whore in Whitechapel. She roamed the streets now with everything she owned on her back, without even a garret or cellar room, or even an under-stairs cubbyhole to call her own, satisfying first her craving for drink, before looking for the extra penny for a bed or a meal. She would probably die soon, of bad gin, of cold and exposure, of disease, or of everything at once as her chronically-damaged body gave out. Nan had neither time nor pity for her. After all, it had been her gran that had mostly raised her, not her mam, who'd only been interested in the money Nan brought in by begging.

Sarah had a very special sort of bond with Grey—who Sarah insisted was a great deal more than "just" a parrot. Nan was in wholehearted agreement with that estimation at this point—after all, it was no more difficult to believe in than to believe that wolves could adopt a mancub, and Nan was convinced of the truth of Mr. Kipling's stories.

Sarah had a new set of lessons, now that they had learned she could on occasion, talk with, and see, the dead. This could be a very dangerous ability, so Memsa'b had told Nan, who had appointed herself as Sarah's protector.

Well, if Nan and Grey had anything to say about the matter, danger would have to pass through them to reach Sarah.

"Nan tickle," Grey demanded in her funny little voice, eyes still closed; Sarah was using both hands to support the bird on her chest, which left no hands free to give Grey the scratch she wanted.

Nan obliged by crawling up to the head of the bed, settling in beside her friend and scratching the back of Grey's neck. It was a very gentle scratch—indeed, more like the "tickle" Grey had asked for than the kind of vigorous scratching one would give a dog or a tough London cat—for Nan had known instinctively from the moment that Grey permitted Nan to touch her that a bird's skin is a very delicate thing. Of all of the people in the school, only Nan, Memsa'b, Sahib himself, and Agansing were permitted by Grey to do more than take her on a hand. Sarah, of course, could do anything she liked with the bird.

"Wish't Oi had a friend loike you, Grey," Nan told the bird wistfully, the remnants of her Cockney accent still clinging to her speech despite hours and hours of lessons. The parrot opened one yellow eye and gave her a long and unreadable look.

"Kitty?" Grey suggested, but Nan shook her head.

"Not a moggy," she replied. "Mind, Oi loike moggies, but—Oi dunno, a moggy don't seem roight. Not clever 'nuff."

Sarah laughed. "Then you must not be a witch after all," she teased. "A witch's familiar is always a cat, or a toad—"

Nan made a face. "Don' want no toads!" she objected. "So Oi guess Oi ain't no witch, no matter what that Tommy Carpenter says!"

Tommy, a recent addition to the school, had somehow made up his mind that she, Sarah, and Memsa'b were all witches. He didn't mean it in a derogatory sense; in fact, he gave them all the utmost respect. It had something to do with things his own ayah back in India had taught him. Nan had to wonder, given whom he'd singled out for that particular accolade, if he wouldn't be getting private lessons of his own with Memsa'b before too long. There was something just a little too knowing about the way Tommy looked at some people.

"But Oi still wisht Oi 'ad—had—a bird friend loike Grey." And she sighed again. Grey reached around with her beak and gently took one of Nan's fingers in it; Grey's equivalent, so Nan had learned, of a hug. "Well," she said, when Grey had let go, "Mebbe someday. Lots've parrots comes in with sailors."

"That's right!" Sarah said warmly, letting go of Grey just long enough to give Nan a hug of her own, before changing the subject. "Nan, promise to tell me all about the Tower as soon as you get back tomorrow! I wish I could go—maybe as much as you wish you had a grey parrot of your own."

" 'Course Oi will!" Nan replied warmly. "Oi wisht you could go, too—but you know why Memsa'b said not." She shuddered, but it was the delicious shudder of a child about to be regaled with delightfully scary ghost stories, without a chance of turning around and discovering that the story had transmuted to reality.

For Sarah, however, the possibility was only too real that, even by daylight, that very thing would happen. It was one thing to provide the vehicle for a little child ghost who had returned only to comfort his mother. It was something else entirely to contemplate Sarah coming face-to-face with one of the many unhappy, tragic, or angry spirits said to haunt the Tower of London. Memsa'b was not willing to chance such an encounter, not until Sarah was old enough to protect herself.

So the History class would be going to the Tower for a special tour with one of the Yeoman Warders without Sarah.

Sarah sighed again. "I know. And I know Memsa'b is right. But I still wish I could go, too."

Nan laughed. "Wut! An you gettin' t' go t' Sahib's warehouse an' pick out whatever you want, on account of missin' the treat?"

"Yes, but—" she made a face. "Then I have to write an essay about it to earn it!"

"An' we're all writin' essays 'bout the Tower, so I reckon it's even all around, 'cept we don't get no keepsakes." Nan ended the discussion firmly.

"I know! I'll pick a whole chest of Turkish Delight, then we can all have a treat, and I'll have the chest," Sarah said suddenly, brightening up in that way she had that made her solemn little face just fill with light.

Grey laughed, just like a human. "Smart bird!" the parrot said, then shook herself gently, wordlessly telling Sarah to let go of her, made her ponderous way up Sarah's shoulder and pillow, and clambered up beak-over-claw to her usual nighttime perch on the top of the brass railing of the headboard of Sarah's bed—wrapped and padded for her benefit in yards and yards of tough hempen twine. She pulled one foot up under her chest feathers, and turned her head around to bury her beak out of sight in the feathers of her back.

And since that was the signal it was time for them to sleep—a signal they always obeyed, since both of them half expected that Grey would tell on them if they didn't!—Nan slid down and climbed into her own bed, turning the key on the lantern beside her to extinguish the light.

✳

It was a gloomy, cool autumn day that threatened rain, a day on which Nan definitely needed her mac, a garment which gave her immense satisfaction, for up until coming to the school she had relied on old newspapers or scraps of canvas to keep off the rain. Getting to the Tower was an adventure in and of itself, involving a great deal of walking and several omnibuses. When they arrived at the Tower, Nan could only stare; she'd been expecting a single building, not this fortress! Why, it was bigger than Buckingham Palace—or, at least, as big!

Their guide was waiting for them under an archway with not one, but two nasty-looking portcullises—and the tour began immediately, for this was no mere gate, but the Middle Tower. The Yeoman Warder who took the children under his capacious wing was an especial friend of Sahib's, and as a consequence, took them on a more painstaking tour of the Tower than the sort given to most schoolchildren. He did his best—which was a very good "best," because he was a natural storyteller—to make the figures of history come alive for his charges, and peppered his narrative with exactly the sort of ghoulish details that schoolchildren loved to hear. Creepy, but not terrifying. Ghoulish, but not ghastly.

Nan was very much affected by the story of poor little Jane

Grey, the Nine-Days' Queen, and of Queen Anne Boleyn, but she felt especially saddened by the story of the execution of Katherine Howard, who had been rather naughty, but had been very young and pretty, and shackled in marriage to a King who was so fat he could hardly move on his own. No wonder she went after a bit of fun on her own! And the old King should have expected it!

They walked all over the Tower, up and down innumerable stairs, from the old Mint buildings, to the armory in the White Tower even to the Yeoman Warders' private quarters, where their guide's wife gave them all tea and cakes. Nan felt quite smug about that; no one else was getting tea and cakes! Most of the other visitors had to blunder about by themselves, accompanied with maps and guidebooks, or join a crowd of others being given the general tour by another of the Yeoman Warders, and dependent on their own resources for their refreshment. She tasted the heady wine of privilege for the first time in her young life, and decided that it was a fine thing.

But the one thing that she found the most fascinating about the Tower was the ravens.

Faintly intimidating, they flew about or stalked the lawns wherever they cared to; they had their very own Yeoman Warder to attend to them, because of the story that if they were ever to leave the Tower, it would be the end of England. But Nan found them fascinating; and kept watching them even when she should, perhaps, have been paying attention to their guide.

Finally Nan got a chance to watch them to her heart's content, as Memsa'b noted her fascination. "Would you like to stay here while the rest of us go view the Crown Jewels, Nan?" Memsa'b asked, with a slight smile.

Nan nodded; going up another set of stairs along with a gaggle of other silly gawpers just to look at a lot of big sparklers that no one but the Queen ever would wear was just plain daft. She felt distinctly honored that Memsa'b trusted her to stay alone. The other pupils trailed off after their guide like a parade of kittens following their mother, while Nan remained behind in the quiet part of the

Green near the off-limits area where the ravens had their perches and nesting-boxes, watching as the great black birds went about their lives, ignoring the sightseers as mere pointless interlopers.

It seemed to her that the ravens had a great deal in common with someone like her; they were tough, no nonsense about them, willing and able to defend themselves. She even tried, once or twice, to see if she could get a sense of what they were thinking, but their minds were very busy with raven business—status in the rookery being a very complicated affair—

Though the second time she tried, the minds of the two she was touching went very silent for a moment, and they turned to stare at her. She guessed that they didn't like it, and stopped immediately; they went back to stalking across the lawn.

Then she felt eyes on her from behind, and turned, slowly.

There was a third raven behind her, staring at her.

" 'Ullo," she told him.

"Quoark," he said meditatively. She met his gaze with one equally unwavering, and it seemed to her that something passed between them.

"Don't touch him, girl." That was one of the Yeoman Warders, hurrying up to her. "They can be vicious brutes, when they're so minded."

The "vicious brute" wasn't interested in the Warder's estimation of him. "Quork," he said, making up his mind—and pushed off with his strong, black legs, making two heavy flaps of his wings that brought him up and onto Nan's shoulder. "Awwrr," he crooned, and as the Yeoman Warder froze, he took that formidable bill, as long as Nan's hand and knife-edged, and gently closed it around her ear. His tongue tickled the ear, and she giggled. The Yeoman Warder paled.

But Nan was engrossed in an entirely new sensation welling up inside her—and she guessed it was coming from the bird; it was a warmth of the heart, as if someone had just given her a welcoming hug.

Could this be her bird friend, the one she'd wished for?

"Want tickle?" she suggested aloud, thinking very hard about how Grey's neck feathers felt under her fingers when she scratched the parrot.

"Orrrr," the raven agreed, right in her ear. He released the ear and bent his head down alongside her cheek so she could reach the back of his neck. She reached up and began a satisfying scratch; she felt his beak growing warm with pleasure as he fluffed his neck feathers for her.

The Yeoman Warder was as white as snow, a startling contrast with his blue-and-scarlet uniform.

The Ravenmaster (who was another Yeoman Warder) came running up, puffing hard and rather out of breath, and stopped beside his fellow officer. He took several deep breaths, staring at the two of them—the raven's eyes were closed with pure bliss as Nan's fingers worked around his beak and very, very gently rubbed the skin around his eyes.

"Blimey," he breathed, staring at them. He walked, with extreme care, toward them, and reached for the bird. "Here now Neville, old man, you oughter come along with me—"

Quick as a flash, the raven went from cuddling pet to angry tyrant, rousing all his feathers in anger and lashing at the outstretched hand with his beak. And it was a good thing that the outstretched hand was wearing a thick falconer's gauntlet, because otherwise the Warder would have pulled it back bloody.

Then, as if to demonstrate that his wrath was only turned against those who would dare to separate him from Nan, the raven took that formidable beak and rubbed it against Nan's cheek, coming within a fraction of an inch of her eyes. She, in her turn, fearlessly rubbed her cheek against his.

The Warders both went very still and very white.

"Neville, I b'lieve you're horripilatin' these gennelmun," Nan said, thinking the same thing, very hard. "Would'jer come down onta me arm?"

She held out her forearm parallel to her shoulder as the Warders held their breath.

"Quock," Neville said agreeably, and stepped onto her forearm. She brought him down level with her chest and as he rested his head against her, she went back to scratching him in the places where she was now getting a sense that he wanted to be scratched. He was a great deal less delicate than Grey; in fact, he enjoyed just as vigorous a scratching as any alley cat.

"Miss," the Ravenmaster said carefully, "I think you oughter put him down."

"I c'n do that," she said truthfully, "but if 'e don't want to leave me, 'e'll just be back on my shoulder in the next minute."

"Then—" he looked about, helplessly. The other Warder shrugged. "Miss, them ravens belongs t' Her Majesty, just like swans does."

She had to giggle at that—the idea that anyone, even the Queen, thought they could own a wild thing. "I doubt anybody's told them," she pointed out.

"Rrrk," Neville agreed, his voice muffled by the fact that his beak was against her chest.

The Ravenmaster was sweating now, little beads standing out on his forehead. He looked to his fellow officer for help; the man only shrugged. " 'Ollis, you was the one what told me that Neville's never been what you'd call a natural bird," the first Warder said judiciously, and with the air of a man who has done his best, he slowly turned and walked off, leaving the Ravenmaster to deal with the situation himself.

Or—perhaps—to deal with it without a witness, who might have to make a report. And what he didn't witness, he couldn't report. . . .

Nan could certainly understand that, since she'd been in similar situations now and again.

Sweating freely now, the Ravenmaster bent down, hands carefully in sight and down at his sides. "Now, Neville," he said quietly, addressing the raven, "I've always done right by you, 'aven't I?"

Neville opened one eye and gave him a dubious look. "Ork," he agreed, but with the sense that his agreement was qualified by whatever the Ravenmaster might do in the next few moments.

"Now, you lissen to me. If you was to try an' go with this girl, I'd haveta try an' catch you up. You'd be mad an' mebbe I'd get hurt, an' you'd be in a cage."

Nan stiffened, fearing that Neville would react poorly to this admission, but the bird only uttered a defiant grunt, as if to say, "You'll catch me the day you grow wings, fool!" The feathers on his head and neck rose, and Nan sensed a sullen anger within him. And the fact that she was sensing things from him could only mean that as the Warder had said, Neville was no "natural" bird.

In fact—he was like Grey. Nan felt excitement rise in her. The fact was a tough bird like a raven suited her a great deal more than a parrot.

But the Yeoman Warder wasn't done. "Now, on t'other hand," he continued, "If the young lady was to toss you up in th' air when you'd got your scratch, and you was to wait over the gate till her an' her schoolmates comes out, an' then you was to follow her— well, I couldn't know you was missing 'till I counted birds on perches, could I? An' then I couldn't know where you'd gone, could I? An' this young lady wouldn't get in no trouble, would she?"

Slowly, the feathers Neville had roused, flattened. He looked the Warder square in the eyes, as if measuring him for falsehood. And slowly, deliberately, he nodded.

"Quok," he said.

"Right. Gennelmun's agreement," the Warder said, heaving an enormous sigh, and turning his attention at last to Nan. "Miss, I dunno what it is about you, but seems you an' Neville has summat between you. An' since Neville's sire has the same summat with the Ravenmaster afore me an' went with 'im to Wight when 'e retired, I reckon it runs in the family, you might say. So."

Nan nodded, and looked at Neville, who jerked his beak upward in a motion that told her clearly what he wanted.

She flung her arm up to help him as he took off, and with several powerful thrusts of his wings, he took off and rowed his way up to the top of the main gate, where he ruffed up all of his feathers and uttered a disdainful croak.

"Now, miss," the Yeoman Warder said, straightening up. "You just happen to 'ave a knack with birds, and I just give you a bit of a talkin'-to about how dangerous them ravens is. An' you never heard me talkin' to Neville. An' if a big black bird should turn up at your school—"

"Then I'll be 'avin' an uncommon big jackdaw as a pet," she said, staring right back at him, unblinking. "Which must've been summun's pet, on account uv 'e's so tame."

"That'd be it, miss," the Warder said, and gathering his dignity about him, left her to wait for the rest of the class to come out.

Memsa'b, Nan was firmly convinced, knew everything. Her conviction was only strengthened by the penetrating look that her teacher gave her when she led the rest of the Harton School pupils out to collect Nan. Since the Crown Jewels were the last item on their programme, it was time to go—

"How did you get on with the ravens, Nan?" Memsa'b asked, with just that touch of irony in her voice that said far more than the words did. Could someone have come to tell her about Neville being on Nan's shoulder? Or was this yet another demonstration that Memsa'b knew things without anyone telling her?

Nan fought hard to keep her accent under control. "I'm thinkin' I got on well, Memsa'b," she said, with a little smile.

Memsa'b raised an eyebrow. If there had been any doubt in Nan's mind that her teacher might not be aware that there was something toward, it vanished at that moment.

She raised another, when, as they made their way down the broad walk away from the Tower, a black, winged shape lofted from the gate and followed them, taking perches on any convenient object. For her part, Nan felt all knotted up with tension, for she couldn't imagine how the great bird would be able to follow them through London traffic. It seemed that the Ravenmaster hadn't yet got around to trimming Neville's wing feathers, for he had them all but two, so at least he wasn't going to be hampered by lack of wingspan. But still . . . how was he to get from here to the Harton School?

They boarded a horse-drawn omnibus and—since it wasn't raining yet—everyone ran up the little twisting staircase to the open seats on top. After all, what child cares to ride inside, when he can ride outside? They were the only passengers up there due to the chill and threatening weather, and Nan cast an anxious look back at the last place she'd seen Neville—

He wasn't there. Her heart fell.

And right down out of the sky, the huge bird landed with an audible thump in the aisle between the rows of seats, just as the 'bus started to move. He folded his wings and looked about as if he owned the place.

"Lummy!" said one of the boys. "That's a raven!" He started to get out of his seat.

"No it isn't," Memsa'b said firmly. "And no one move except Nan."

When Memsa'b gave an order like that, no one would even think of moving, so as Neville walked ponderously toward her, Nan crouched down and offered her forearm to him. He hopped up on it, and she got back into her seat, turning to look expectantly at Memsa'b.

"This is not a raven," their teacher repeated, raking the entire school group with a stern glance. "This is an uncommonly large rook. Correct?"

"Yes, Memsa'b!" the rest of Nan's schoolmates chorused. Memsa'b eyed the enormous bird for a moment, her brown eyes thoughtful. Memsa'b was not a pretty woman—many people might, in fact, have characterized her as "plain," with quiet brown hair and eyes, and a complexion more like honest brown pottery than porcelain. Her chin was too firm for beauty; her features too angular and strong. But it was Nan's fervent hope that one day she might grow up into something like those strong features, for to her mind, Memsa'b was a decidedly handsome woman. Right now, she looked quite formidable, her eyes intent as she gazed at Neville, clearly thinking hard about something.

"Bird—" she addressed the raven directly. "We are going to have to go through a number of situations in which you will not be welcome before we get home. For instance, the inside seats on this very 'bus—since I think it is going to rain before we get to our stop. Now, what do you propose we do about you?"

Neville cocked his head to one side. "Ork?" he replied.

Now, none of the children found any of this at all peculiar or funny, perhaps because they were used to Memsa'b, Sarah, and Nan treating Grey just like a person. But none of them wanted to volunteer a solution either if it involved actually getting near that nasty-looking beak.

"Oi—I—can put 'im under me mac, Memsa'b," Nan offered.

Their teacher frowned. "That's only good until someone notices you're carrying something there, Nan," she replied. "Children, at the next stop, I would like you to divide up and search the 'bus for a discarded box, please—but be back in a seat when the 'bus moves again."

Just then the bus pulled up to a stop, and slightly less than twenty very active children swarmed over the vehicle while passengers were loading and unloading. The boys all piled downstairs; they were less encumbered with skirts and could go over or under seats quickly.

The boys hadn't returned by the time the 'bus moved, but at the next stop they all came swarming back up again, carrying in triumph the very thing that was needed, a dirtied and scuffed pasteboard hatbox!

As their teacher congratulated them, young Tommy proudly related his story of charming the box from a young shopgirl who had several she was taking home with her because they'd been spoiled. Meanwhile, Nan coaxed Neville into the prize, which was less than a perfect fit. He wasn't happy about it, but after thinking very hard at him with scenes of him trying to fly to keep up, of conductors chasing him out of the windows of 'buses, and of policemen finding him under Nan's mac and trying to take him away, he quorked and obediently hopped into the box, suffering Nan to close the lid down over him and tie it shut. Her nerves quieted down at that moment, and she heaved a sigh of very real relief. Only then did she pay attention to her classmates.

"I owes you, Tommy," she said earnestly. "Sarah, she said last night she was gonna get a chest've Turkish Delight from Sahib's warehouse for her treat and share it out. You c'n hev my share."

Tommy went pink with pleasure. "Oh, Nan, you don't have to—" He was clearly torn between greed and generosity of his own. "Half?" he suggested. "I don't want to leave you without a treat, too."

"I got a treat," she insisted, patting the box happily. "An' mine'll last longer nor Turkish Delight. Naw, fair's fair; you get my share."

And she settled back into her seat with the pleasant, warm weight of the box and its contents on her lap, Memsa'b casting an amused eye on her from time to time. Neville shifted himself occasionally, and his nails would scrape on the cardboard. He didn't like being confined, but the darkness was making him sleepy, so he was dozing when the box was on her lap and not being carried.

There were no difficulties with the rest of the journey back to the school; no one saw anything out of the ordinary in a child with a shopworn hatbox, and Neville was no heavier than a couple of schoolbooks.

They walked the last few blocks to the school; the neighbors were used to seeing the children come and go, and there were smiles and nods as the now-thoroughly-weary group trudged their way to the old gates, which were unlocked by Memsa'b to let them all back inside.

True to her word, Sarah had gotten the sweets, and when the others filed in through the front door, she was waiting in the entrance hall, with Grey on her shoulder as usual, to give out their shares as soon as they came in. Nan handed hers over to Tommy without a murmur or a second glance, although she was inordinately fond of sweets—Sarah looked startled, then speculative, as she spotted Nan's hatbox.

"Sarah, you just gotter see—" Nan began, when Memsa'b interrupted.

"I believe that we need to make a very careful introduction, Nan," she said, steering Nan deftly down the hall instead of up the stairs. "Sarah, would you and Grey come with us as well? I believe that Nan has found a friend very like Grey for herself—but we are going to have to make sure that they understand that they must at least tolerate one another."

There was a room on the first floor used for rough-housing on bad days; it had probably been a ballroom when the mansion was in a better neighborhood. Now, other than some ingenious draperies made out of dust sheets, it didn't have a great deal in it but chests holding battered toys and some chairs pushed up against the walls. For heat, there was an iron stove fitted into the fireplace, this being deemed safer than an open fire. This was where Memsa'b brought them, and sat Sarah and Grey down on the worn wooden floor, with Nan and her hatbox (which was beginning to move as a restless raven stirred inside it) across from her.

"All right, Nan, now you can let him out," Memsa'b decreed.

Nan had to laugh as Neville popped up like a jack-in-the-box when she took off the lid, his feathers very much disarranged from confinement in the box. He shook himself—then spotted Grey.

Grey was already doing a remarkable imitation of a pinecone, with every feather sticking out, and growling under her breath. Neville roused his own feathers angrily, then looked sharply at Nan.

"No," she said, in answer to the unspoken question. "You ain't sharin' me. Grey is Sarah's. But you gotter get along, 'cause Sarah's the best friend I got, an my friend's gotter be friends with her friend."

"You hear that?" Sarah added to Grey, catching the parrot's beak gently between thumb and forefinger, and turning the parrot's head to face her. "This is Nan's special bird friend. He's going to share our room. But he'll have his own food and toys and perches, so you aren't going to lose anything, you see? And you have to be friends, because Nan and I are."

Both birds clearly thought this over, and it was Grey who graciously made the first move. "Want down," she said, smoothing her feathers down as Sarah took her off her shoulder and put her down on the floor.

Neville sprang out of his hatbox, and landed within a foot of Grey. And now it was his turn to make a gesture—which he did, with surprising graciousness.

"Ork," he croaked, then bent his head and offered the nape of his neck to Grey.

Now, in Grey's case, that gesture could be a ruse, for Nan had known her to offer her neck—supposedly to be scratched—only to whip her head around and bite an offending finger hard. But Neville couldn't move his head that fast; his beak was far too ponderous. Furthermore, he was offering the very vulnerable back of his head to a stabbing beak, which was what another raven would have, not a biting beak. Would Grey realize what a grand gesture this was?

Evidently, she did. With great delicacy, she stretched out and preened three or four of Neville's feathers, as collective breaths were released in sighs of relief.

Truce had been declared.

✳

Alliance soon followed. In fact, within a week, the birds were sharing perches (except at bedtime, when each perched on the headboard of their respective girl). It probably helped that Grey was not in the least interested in Neville's raw meat, and Neville was openly dismissive of Grey's cooked rice and vegetables. When there is no competition for food and affection, alliance becomes a little easier.

Within a remarkably short time, the birds were friends—as unlikely a pair as the street brat and the missionary's child. Neville had learned that Grey's curved beak and powerful bite could open an amazing number of things he might want to investigate, and it was clear that no garden snail was going to be safe, come the spring. Grey had discovered that a straight, pointed beak with all the hammerlike force of a raven's neck muscles behind it could break a hole into a flat surface where her beak couldn't get a purchase. Shortly afterward, there had ensued a long discussion between Memsa'b and the birds to which neither Nan nor an anxious Sarah were party, concerning a couple of parcels and the inadvisability of birds breaking into unguarded boxes or brightly-wrapped presents. . . .

After the incident with the faux medium and the spirit of the child of one of Memsa'b's school friends, rumors concerning the unusual abilities Sarah and Nan possessed began to make the rounds of the more Esoteric circles of London. Most knew better than to approach Memsa'b about using her pupils in any way—those who did were generally escorted to the door by one of Sahib's two formidable school guards, one a Gurkha, the other a Sikh. A few, a very few, of Sahib or Memsa'b's trusted friends actually met the girls—and occasionally Nan or Sarah were asked to help in some occult difficulty. Nan was called on more often than Sarah, although, had Memsa'b permitted it, Sarah would have been asked to exercise her talent as a genuine medium four times as often as Nan used her abilities.

One day in October, after Memsa'b had turned away yet another importunate friend and her friend, a thin and enthusiastic spinster wearing a rather eccentric turban with a huge ostrich plume ornament on the front, and a great many colored shawls draped all over her in every possible fashion, Nan intercepted her mentor.

"Memsa'b, why is it you keep sendin' those ladies away?" she asked curiously. "There ain't—isn't—no harm in 'em—least, not that one, anyway. A bit silly," she added judiciously, "but no harm."

The wonderful thing about Memsa'b was that when you acted like a child, she treated you like a child—but when you were trying to act like an adult, she treated you as one. Memsa'b regarded her thoughtfully, and answered with great deliberation. "I have some very strong ideas about what children like Sarah—or you—should and should not be asked to do. One of them is that you are not to be trotted out at regular intervals like a music-hall act and required to perform. Another is that until you two are old enough to decide just how public you wish to be, it is my duty to keep you as private as possible. And lastly—" her mouth turned down as if she tasted something very sour. "Tell me something, Nan—do you think that there are nothing but hundreds of ghosts out there, queuing up to every medium, simply burning to tell their relatives how lovely things are on the Other Side?"

Nan thought about that for a moment. "Well," she said, after giving the question full consideration, "No. If there was, I don't s'pose Sarah'd hev a moment of peace. They'd be at her day an' night, leave alone them as is still alive."

Memsa'b laughed. "Exactly so. Given that, can you think of any reason why I should encourage Sarah to sit about in a room so thick with incense that it is bound to make her ill when nothing is going to come of it but a headache and hours lost that she could have been using to study, or just to enjoy herself?"

"An' a gaggle of silly old women fussing at 'er." Nan snorted. "I see, Memsa'b."

"And some of the things that you and Sarah are asked to do, I believe are too dangerous," Memsa'b continued, with just a trace of frown. "And why, if grown men have failed at them, anyone should think I would risk a pair of children—"

She shook herself, and smiled ruefully down at Nan. "Adults can be very foolish—and very selfish."

Nan just snorted. As if she didn't know that! Hadn't her own mother sold her to a pair of brothel keepers? And Neville, perched on her shoulder, made a similarly scornful noise.

"Has he managed any real words yet, Nan?" Memsa'b asked, her attention distracted. She crooked a finger in invitation, and Neville stretched out his head for a scratch under the chin.

"Not yet, Memsa'b—but I kind uv get ideers about what he wants t' tell me." Nan knew that Memsa'b would know exactly what she was talking about, and she was not disappointed.

"They say that splitting a crow or raven's tongue gives them clear speech, but I am against anything that would cause Neville pain for so foolish a reason," Memsa'b said. "And it is excellent exercise for you to understand what is in his mind without words."

"Quork," said Neville, fairly radiating satisfaction.

❉

After that, Nan put her full attention on the task of "understanding what was in Neville's mind without words." It proved to be a slippery eel to catch. Sometimes it all seemed as clear as the thoughts in her own mind, and sometimes he was as opaque to her as a brick.

"I dunno how you do it," she told Sarah one day, when both she and Neville were frustrated by her inability to understand what he wanted. He'd been reduced to flapping heavily across the room and actually pecking at the book he wanted her to read, or rather, to open so that he could look at the pictures. She'd have gone to Memsa'b with her problem, but their mentor was out on errands of her own that day and was not expected back until very late.

Grey cocked her head to one side, and made a little hissing sound that Nan had come to recognize as her "sigh." She regarded Nan first with one grey-yellow eye, then with the other. It was obvious that she was working up to saying something, and Nan waited, hoping it would be helpful.

"Ree," Grey said at last. "Lax."

"She means that you're trying too hard, both of you," Sarah added thoughtfully. "That's why Grey and I always know what the other's thinking—we don't try, we don't even think about it really, we just do. And that's because we've been together for so long that it's like—like knowing where your own hand is, you see? We don't have to think about it, we don't even have to try."

Nan and Neville turned their heads to meet each other's eyes. Neville's eyes were like a pair of shiny jet beads, glittering and knowing. "It's—hard," Nan said slowly.

Sarah nodded; Grey's head bobbed. "I don't know, Nan. I guess it's just something you have to figure out for yourself."

Nan groaned, but she knew that Sarah was right. Neville

sighed, sounding so exactly like an exasperated person that both of them laughed.

It wasn't as if they didn't have plenty of other things to occupy their time—ordinary lessons, for one thing. Nan had a great deal of catching up to do even to match Sarah. They bent their heads over their books, Nan with grim determination to master the sums that tormented her so. It wasn't the simple addition and subtraction problems that had her baffled, it was what Miss Bracey called "logic problems," little stories in which trains moved toward each other, boys did incomprehensible transactions with each other involving trades of chestnuts and marbles and promised apple tarts, and girls stitched miles of apron hems. Her comprehension was often sidelined by the fact that all these activities seemed more than a little daft. Sarah finished her own work, but bravely kept her company until teatime. By that point, Nan knew she was going to be later than that in finishing.

"Go get yer tea, lovey," she told the younger child. "I'll be along in a bit."

So Sarah left, and she soldiered on past teatime, and finished her pages just when it was beginning to get dark.

She happened to be going downstairs to the kitchen, in search of that tea that she had missed, when she heard the knock at the front door.

At this hour, every single one of the servants was busy, so she answered it herself. It might be something important, or perhaps someone with a message or a parcel.

Somewhat to her surprise, it was a London cabby, who touched his hat to her. " 'Scuze me, miss, but is this the Harton School?" he asked.

Nan nodded, getting over her surprise quickly. It must be a message then, either from Memsa'b or Sahib Harton. They sometimes used cabbies as messengers, particularly when they wanted someone from the school brought to them. Usually, it was Sahib wanting Agansing, Selim, or Karamjit. But sometimes it was Nan and Sarah who were wanted.

"Then Oi've got a message, an Oi've come t'fetch a Miss Nan an' a Miss Sarah." He cleared his throat, ostentatiously, and carried on as if he was reciting something he had memorized. "Missus Harton sez to bring the gur-rels to 'er, for she's got need of 'em. That's me—I'm t'bring 'em up t' Number Ten, Berkeley Square."

Nan nodded, for this was not, by any means, the first time that Memsa'b had sent for them. Although she was loath to make use of their talents, there were times when she had felt the need to—for instance, when they had exposed the woman who had been preying on one of Memsa'b's old school friends. London cabs were a safe way for the girls to join her; no one thought anything of putting a child in a cab alone, for a tough London cabby was as safe a protector as a mastiff for such a journey.

Nan, however, had a routine on these cases that she never varied. "Come in," she said imperiously to the cabby. "You sits there. Oi'll get the gels."

She did not—yet—reveal that she was one of the "gels."

The cabby was not at all reluctant to take a seat in the relative warmth of the hall while Nan scampered off.

Without thinking about it—she suddenly knew exactly where Sarah and Grey and Neville were; she knew, because Neville was in the kitchen with the other two, and the moment she needed them, she'd felt the information, like a memory, but different.

Stunned, she stopped where she was for a moment. Without thinking about it— So that was what Grey had meant!

But if Memsa'b needed them, there was no time to stand about contemplating this epiphany; she needed to intercept Karamjit on his rounds.

He would be inspecting the cellar about now, making certain that no one had left things open that should have been shut. As long as the weather wasn't too cold, Memsa'b liked to keep the cellar aired out during the day. After all, it wasn't as if there was fine wine in the old wine cellar anymore that needed cool and damp. Karamjit, however, viewed this breech in the security of the walls with utmost suspicion, and faithfully made certain that all possible access into the house was buttoned up by dark.

So down into the cellar Nan went, completely fearless about the possibility of encountering rats or spiders. After all, where she had lived, rats, spiders, and other vermin were abundant. And there she found Karamjit, lantern in hand, examining the coal door. Not an easy task, since there was a pile of seacoal between him and the door in the ceiling that allowed access to the cellar.

"Karamjit, Memsa'b's sent a cab t'fetch me'n Sarah," she said. "Nummer Ten, Berkeley Square."

Berkeley Square was a perfectly respectable address, and Karamjit nodded his dark head in simple acknowledgment as he repeated it. "I shall tell Sahib when he returns from his warehouse," Karamjit told her, turning his attention back to the cellar door.

He would; Karamjit never forgot anything. Selim might, if he was distracted or concentrating on something else, but Karamjit, never. Satisfied, Nan ran back up the stairs to collect Sarah, Grey, and Neville—and just for good measure, inform the two cooks of their errand. In Nan's mind, it never hurt to make sure more than one person knew what was going on.

"Why do you always do that?" Sarah asked, when they were both settled in the closed cab, with Grey tucked under Sarah's coat and Neville in his hatbox.

"Do what?" Nan asked, in surprise.

"Tell everyone where we're going," Sarah replied, with just a touch of exasperation. "It sounds like you're boasting that Memsa'b wants us, and we're getting to do things nobody else in the school gets to."

"It does?" Nan was even more surprised; that aspect simply hadn't occurred to her. "Well, that ain't what I mean, and I ain't goin' ter stop, 'cause summun oughter know where we're goin' 'sides us. What if Memsa'b got hurt or somethin' else happened to 'er? Wouldn' even hev t'be anything about spooks or whatnot—just summun decidin' t'cosh 'er on account uv she's alone an' they figger on robbin' 'er. What're we supposed ter do if that 'appens? 'Oo's gonna lissen t'couple uv little girls, eh? 'Ow long'ud it take us t'find a perleeceman? So long's summat else knows where we've gone, if there's trouble, Sahib'll come lookin' fer us. But 'e can't if 'e don't know where we are, see?"

"Oh." Sarah looked less annoyed. "I'm sorry, I thought you were just—showing off."

Nan shook her head. "Nah. I show off plenty as 'tis," she added cheerfully, "But—well, I figger around Memsa'b, there's plenty uv things t'go wrong, an' why make it worse by bein' stupid an' not tellin' where we're goin'?"

"Clever bird," Grey said, voice muffled by Sarah's coat.

"Quork," Neville agreed from within his box.

Sarah laughed. "I think they agree with you!" she admitted, and changed the subject. "I wonder why Memsa'b sent for us."

"Dunno. Cabby didn't say," Nan admitted. "I don' think 'e knows. All I know's that Berkeley Square's a respect'ble neighborhood, so it might be one of 'er fancy friends again. Not," she added philosophically, "that ye cain't get coshed at a respect'ble place as easy as anywhere's else. Plenty uv light-fingered lads as works Ascot, fer instance."

"Do you always look on the bright side, Nan?" Sarah asked, in a teasing tone of voice that told Nan she was being twitted for her pessimism.

Nan was just about to let her feelings be hurt—after all, just how was someone whose own mother tried to sell her to a brothel keeper supposed to think?—when her natural good humor got the better of her. "Nah," she said dismissively. "Sometimes I get pretty gloomy."

Sarah stared at her in surprise for a moment, then laughed.

It was fully dark when they arrived, and the cabby dropped them off right at the front door. "The lady sed t'go on in, an' up t' the room up there as is lit—" he told them, pointing to an upper room. Light streamed from that window; very much more welcoming than the rest of the darkened house. Before either girl could ask anything further, he snapped the reins over the horse's back, and drove off, leaving them the choice of standing in the street or following his directions.

Nan frowned. "This don't seem right—there aughter be servants about—"

Sarah, however, peered up at the window. "Memsa'b must be with someone who's hurt or ill," she said decisively. "Someone she doesn't dare leave alone." And before Nan could protest, she'd run up to the door and pushed it open, disappearing inside.

Bloody 'ell. Nan hurried after her, with Neville croaking his disapproval as his box swung beneath her hand. But she hadn't a choice; Sarah was already charging up the staircases ahead of her. Something was very wrong here—where were the servants? No house in Berkeley Square would be without a servant to answer the door! And as she rushed through the door, she noticed something else. There wasn't any furniture or pictures in the front hall either—and that was just wrong all over.

She raced up the stairs, with her feet thudding on the dusty carpet covering the treads, aided only by the light from that single door at the top. She wasn't in time to prevent Sarah from dashing headlong into the lit room—so she, perforce, had to follow, right in through that door left invitingly half ajar. "Memsa'b!" she heard Sarah call. "We're here, Mem—"

Only to stop dead in the middle of the room, as Sarah had, staring at the cluster of paraffin lamps on the floor near the window, lamps which had given the illusion that the otherwise empty room must be tenanted.

There was nothing in that room but those four lamps. Nothing. And more importantly—no one.

"It's a filthy trick!" Nan shouted indignantly, and turned to run out—

Only to have the door slam in her face.

Before she could get over her shock, there was the rattle of a key in the lock, and a further sound as of bolts being thrown home. Then they heard the sound of footsteps rapidly retreating down the stairs.

The two girls looked at each other, aghast.

Nan was the first to move, because her immediate thought was that the men she'd been sold to had decided to collect their property and another girl as well for their troubles. Anyone else might have run at the door, to kick and pound on it, screaming at the top of her lungs. She put down the hatbox and freed Neville. Even more than Grey, the raven, with his murderous claws and beak, was a formidable defender in case of trouble.

And Neville knew it; she felt his anger, and read it in his ruffled feathers and the glint in his eye.

Grey burst from the front of Sarah's coat all by herself, growling in that high-pitched, grating voice that she used only when she was at her angriest. She stood on Sarah's shoulder, every feather erect with aggression, and wings half-spread.

Nan growled under her breath, herself, and cast her eyes about, looking for something in the empty room that she could use as a weapon. There was what was left of a bed in one corner, and Nan went straight to it.

"Sarah, get that winder open, if you can," she said, wrenching loose a piece of wood that made a fairly satisfactory club. "Mebbe we can yell fer help."

She swung the bit of wood, feeling the heft of her improvised club. With that in her hand, she felt a little better—and when whoever had locked them in here came back—well—they'd get a surprise.

"Nan—there's something wrong—"

At the hollow tone in Sarah's voice, Nan whirled, and saw that she was beside the window, as white as a sheet.

"Nan—I don't think a stick is going to be much use now—" she faltered, pointing a trembling finger at the lamps.

And as Nan watched, the flames of the lamps all turned from yellow to an eerie blue. All Nan could think of was the old saying, *flames burn blue when spirits walk.* . . .

Nan felt every hair on her body standing erect, and her stomach went cold, and not because of some old saying. No. Oh, no. There was danger, very near. Sarah might have sensed it first, but Nan felt it surrounding both of them, and fought the instinct to look for a place to hide.

Neville cawed an alarm, and she turned again to see him scuttle backward, keeping his eyes fixed on the closed door. The lamp flames behind her dimmed, throwing the room into a strange, blue gloom. Neville turned his back on the door for a moment, but only long enough to leap into the air, wings flapping frantically, to land on her shoulder. He made no more noise, but Grey was making enough for two. His eyes were nothing but pupil, and she felt him shivering.

"There's something outside that door," Sarah said in a small, frightened voice.

"And whatever 'tis, locks and wood ain't goin' t' keep it out," Nan said grimly. She did not say aloud what she felt, deep inside.

Whatever it was, it was no mere ghost, not as she and Sarah knew the things. It hated the living; it existed to feed on terror, but that was not all that it was, or did. It was old, old—so old that it made her head ache to try and wrap her understanding around it, and of all that lived, it hated people like Sarah the most. That thing out there would destroy her as casually as she would swat a fly—but it wanted Sarah.

Grey's growling rose to an ear-piercing screech; Sarah seemed frozen with fear, but Grey was not; Grey was ready to defend Sarah with her life. Grey was horribly afraid, but she was not going to let fear freeze her.

Neither was Neville.

And I ain't neither! Nan told herself defiantly, and though the hand clutching her club shook, she took one step—two—three—

And planted herself squarely between whatever was behind the door and Sarah. It would have to go through her, Neville, and Grey to reach what it wanted.

I tol' Karamjit where we went—an' when Memsa'b comes 'ome wi'out us—

She knew that was the only real hope, that help from the adults would come before that—Presence—decided to come through the door after them. Or if she could stall it, could somehow delay things, keep it from actually attacking—

Suddenly, Grey stopped growling.

The light from behind her continued to dim; the shadows lengthened, collected in the corners and stretched toward them. There was no more light in here now than that cast by a shadowed moon. Nan sucked in a breath—

Something dark was seeping in under the door, like an evil pool of black water.

The temperature within the room plummeted; a wave of cold lapped over her, and her fingers and toes felt like ice. That wave was followed by one of absolute terror that seized her and shook her like a terrier would shake a rat.

"Ree—" Grey barked into the icy silence. "Lax!"

The word spat so unexpectedly into her ear had precisely the effect Grey must have intended. It shocked Nan for a split second into a state of not-thinking, just being—

Suddenly, all in an instant she and Neville were one.

❋

Knowledge poured into her; and fire blossomed inside her, a fire of anger that drove out the terror, a fierce fire of protectiveness and defiance that made her straighten, take a firmer grip on her club. She opened her mouth—

And words began pouring out of her—guttural words, angry words, words she didn't in the least understand, that passed somehow from Neville to her, going straight to her lips without touching her mind at all. But she knew, she knew, they were old words, and they were powerful. . . .

The light from the lamps strengthened, and with each word, she felt a warmth increasing inside her, a fierce strength pouring into her. Was it from her feathered companion, just as the words were? Or was it the words that brought this new power?

No, it wasn't the light behind her that was increasing! It was the light around her!

Cor—

A golden halo of light surrounded her, increasing in brightness with every word that spilled from her lips. And now Grey joined in the chanting, for chanting it was. She caught the pattern now, a repetition of some forty-two syllables that sounded like no language fragments Nan had ever heard. She knew what Italian, Hebrew, and Chinese all sounded like, even if she couldn't speak or understand them, for folk of all of those nationalities thronged the slums where she had lived, from Whitechapel to Limehouse. She knew what Latin, Greek, and French all sounded like too, since those were taught at the School. This language definitely wasn't any of those. But when Grey took over the chant, Nan stopped; she didn't need to speak anymore. Now it was Grey who wove an armor of words about her—and a moment later, Sarah's voice, shaking, faltering, but each syllable clear, if faint.

Then—she went all wobbly for a moment. As if something gave her a good cuff, she experienced a sort of internal lurch of vision and focus, a spirit earthquake. The room faded, thinned, became ghostly. The walls receded, or seemed to; everything became dim and gray, and a cold wind buffeted her, swirling around her.

On the other side of that door, now appallingly transparent, bulked an enormous shadow; that was what was oozing under the door, reaching for them, held at bay by the golden light around her. The shadow wasn't what filled her with horror and fear, however—it was what lay at the heart of it, something that could not be seen, even in this half-world, but which sent out waves of terror to strike devastating blows on the heart. And images of exactly what it intended to do to those who opposed it—and the one it wanted.

Now the shadow was on their side of the door, and there was no getting past it. The shadow billowed, and sent out fat, writhing tentacles toward her.

But Nan was not going to break; not for this thing, whatever it was, not when her friend needed protecting from this horror that was going to devour her and take her body for its own!

She brandished her club—and as the weapon in her hand ripped through the thick, gray tendrils of oily fog the thing sent toward her out of the shadow, she saw with a shock that she no longer held a crude wooden club. Not anymore—

Now she held a shining sword, with a blade polished to a mirror finish, bronze-gold as the heart of the sun. And the arm that swung the blade was clad in bronze armor.

She was taller, older, stronger; wearing a tunic of bright red wool that came to her knees, a belt of heavy leather, her long hair in a thick plait that fell over one shoulder. And Neville! Neville was no heavier than he had been, but now he was huge, surely the size of an eagle, and his outspread wings overshadowed her, as his eyes glowed the same bronze-gold as her sword and the golden aura that surrounded them both.

But the form within the shadow was not impressed.

The shadow drank in her light, swallowing it up, absorbing it completely. Then it began to grow. . . .

Even as it loomed over her, cresting above her like a wave frozen in time, she refused to let the fear it wanted her to feel overwhelm her, though she felt the weight of it threatening to close in on her spirit and crush it. Defiantly, she brandished her sword at it. "No!" she shouted at it. "You don't get by!"

It swelled again, and she thought she saw hints of something inside it . . . something with a smoldering eye, a suggestion of wings at the shoulders, and more limbs than any self-respecting creature ought to have.

She knew then that this was nothing one single opponent, however brave, however strong, could ever defeat. And behind her, she heard Sarah sob once, a sound full of fear and hopelessness.

Grey and Neville screamed—

And the ghost door burst open behind the horror.

In this strange half-world, what Nan saw was a trio of supernatural warriors. The first was a knight straight out of one of her beloved fairy books, broadsword in hand, clad head to toe in literally shining armor, visor closed—though a pair of fierce blue eyes burned in the darkness behind the visor with a light of their own. The second bore a curved scimitar and was wearing flowing, colorful silken garments and a turban centered with a diamond that burned like a fire, and could have stepped out of the pages of the *Arabian Nights,* an avenging jinn.

And the third carried not a sword, but a spear, and was attired like nothing Nan had ever seen except in a brothel or a filthy post-card—in the merest scrap of a chemise, a bit of draped fabric that scandalized even Nan, for inside that little wisp of cloth was—

Memsa'b?

The shadow collapsed in on itself—not completely, but enough for the knight to slam it aside with one armored shoulder, enough for the jinn and Memsa'b to rush past it, and past Nan, to snatch up Sarah and make a dash with her for the now open door, with Grey flapping over their heads in their wake.

Nan saw the shadow gather itself, and knew it was going to strike them down. *"Bloody hell!"* she screamed—or at least, that was what the words that came out of her mouth meant, although she certainly didn't recognize the shape of the syllables. And, des-perate to keep it from striking, she charged at the thing, Neville dove at it, and the knight slashed frantically upward.

Again it shrank back—not in defeat, oh, no—but startled that they had dared to move against it.

And that was enough—just enough—for Memsa'b and the jinn to rush past bearing Sarah, for Nan and Neville and Grey to follow in their wake, and for the knight to slam the door shut and follow them down the stairs—

Stairs which, with every footstep, became more and more solid, more and more real, until all of them tumbled out the front door of Number Ten, Berkeley Square, into the lamplit darkness, the perfectly ordinary shadows and smoke and night sounds of a Lon-don street.

Neville fluttered down, panting, to land on the ground. Sahib slammed the front door shut behind them and leaned against it, holding his side, and breathing heavily. Gone were his armor, his sword—he was only ordinary Sahib again, with a cane to help his bad knee. Selim—and not the jinn—put Sarah down on the pavement, and Grey fluttered down to land on her shoulder. Neville looked up at Nan and quorked plaintively, while Memsa'b, clad in a proper suit, but with her skirt hiked up to scandalous shortness, did something that dropped her skirt from above her knees to street length again.

"Are you two all right?" she asked anxiously, taking Sarah by the shoulders and peering into her face, then doing the same with Nan.

"Yes'm," Nan said, as Sarah nodded.

"Faugh," Sahib coughed, as he straightened. "Let's not do that again any time soon, shall we? I'm getting too old for last-minute rescues."

Last minute rescues—'cause we went off alone, like a pair of gorm-less geese! "Oh, Sahib—Memsa'b—" Nan felt her eyes fill with tears, as it suddenly came home to her that her protectors and benefactors had just put themselves into deadly danger to save her. "Oh, I'm sorry, I didn' mean—"

"Nan, Nan, you aren't to blame!" Sahib said immediately, putting one strong arm around her shoulders. "You did nothing that you shouldn't have done, and if you hadn't been so careful, we wouldn't have known where you were until it was too late! No, it was our fault."

"It certainly was," Memsa'b said grimly. "But it was someone else's as well . . . and there is going to be a reckoning when I find out who. But let's get away from here first. I don't altogether want to find out if the bindings keeping that thing confined to this house will hold under provocation."

Sahib took Sarah's arm, giving her Grey to tuck inside her coat, and Selim offered a hand to Neville, who was so tired he hopped onto it without a protest, and then lifted the raven onto Nan's shoulder. As they walked quickly away from the building, Memsa'b continued.

"Someone came to me a few days ago with a story about this place, how some haunt was making it impossible to rent out and he was in dire difficulty because of it. He wanted Sarah, or me, or both of us together to lay the spirit—but I have heard all of the stories about this address, and I knew better than to try. Something came to dwell there, over a hundred years ago, and it is not a thing to be trifled with. Men have died here, and more than one, and many people have gone mad with fear. Whatever that thing was—"

"Is old," Nan put in, with a shudder. "Real, real old. I dunno how it got 'ere, but it ain't no spook."

"Well, evidently this person decided to force our hand," Sahib said thoughtfully—and as Nan looked up when they passed under a streetlamp, she saw that both his face and Selim's were grim. "I believe that I will have a private word with him."

"As will I—although I am sorely tempted to tell him that his devil has been laid, and suggest he spend a night there himself," Memsa'b said, with deep anger in her voice. "And from now on, we will contrive a better way of bringing you girls if I should need you."

"Please," Sarah said, in a small voice. "What happened to Nan and Neville? And you and Sahib and Selim?"

Sahib cleared his throat awkwardly; Selim just laughed, deep in his throat. "You saw us as we seem to be—"

"Are," Sahib corrected dryly.

"Are, then—when we are Warriors of the Light," Selim concluded.

"Though how Nan happened to slip over into a persona and power she should not have until she is older—much older—I cannot imagine," Memsa'b added, with a note in her voice that suggested that she and Nan would be having a long, a very long, talk at some point in the near future. Then she sighed. "Pray heaven I will not need to begin teaching you ancient Celtic any time soon."

But, for now, Nan was beginning to feel the effect of being frightened nearly to death, fighting for the life of herself and her friends, and somehow being rescued in the nick of time. She stumbled and nearly fell, and Sahib sent Selim in search of a cab. In a good neighborhood like this one, they were not too difficult to find; shortly, both the girls were lifted in to nestle on either side of Memsa'b, birds tucked under their coats with the heads sticking out, for Nan had left Neville's hatbox and was not at all inclined to go back after it. And in the shelter of the cab, Neville providing a solid oblong of warmth, and the drone of the adult voices above her head, safe at last, she found herself dropping off to sleep.

But not before she heard Memsa'b saying, "I would still like to know how it was that the child came into her Aspect without any training—and where she found the Words of Power for invoking the Holy Light."

And heard Grey answer.

"Smart Neville," she said in her sweetest voice. "Very smart Nan."

❋

The children and birds were tucked up safely in their beds, and Sahib had gone out for that "private word" with the one who ostensibly owned Number Ten. He had taken both Selim and Agansing with him, leaving Karamjit and Isabelle herself to stand watch over the house. Karamjit had made the rounds, reinforcing his shields and wards, and she had gotten out the set of Elemental Wards given to her a long time ago, before she had left for India, and placed them at the cardinal points of the grounds. She had no way of knowing on her own if they were still powerful, those little four-colored pyramids of stone and glass, but she had faith in the friends who had given them to her. She had seldom had to use them, twice in India, once in England, but never since her return.

The troubling thing about this was that she was not altogether certain the incident had been one man's ill-conceived attempt to clear his property of the evil that haunted it. In fact, the more she thought about it, the less likely that seemed. She sat in her favorite chair beside the fire, and though the fire was warm, her spirit felt chilled by the prospects of *that* eventuality.

"Karamjit?" she said to the shadow standing at the window. "Are you as uneasy about this evening as I am?"

"At least, Shining Star," he replied grimly. "We have not ended what this night began. And the thing behind that door may be the least and most obvious of the evils we face. Sahib is returned."

She leaped to her feet as the front bell rang, and with Karamjit behind her, hurried to the front hall.

"Not here," Frederick said, *sotto voce,* as he handed his hat, coat, and gloves to Sia to take away. She nodded, and all five of them returned to the warmth and privacy of his study.

"The bird," he said succinctly, as he settled into his chair, "has flown. Not only that, but he was a bird in false feathers. I am reliably told, and Selim has verified, that there was no deception on the part of our quarry's servants, that Mister Benson has not been resident in his townhouse for a month. He has been salmon fishing in Scotland, and knowing the gentleman's sporting reputation, that is not an opportunity he would have forgone even for a death in the family. So whoever it was that *called* himself Benson had no right to that name and no *financial* interest in the property." He grimaced. "We have, as young Nan would say, been gammoned."

Isabelle took a deep breath. "Which leaves us with the question of why someone would lure those two children there. If Nan had not told Karamjit where she was going—we would not have known where they were until they were found."

"Which would not have been until morning." Frederick's eyes were dark with rage. "And we know what state they'd have been in at best. If they had lived. At least four people who remained overnight in that room have died, and several more have gone mad. *Someone* wanted those two children dead or insane. Specifically those two children, and not you as well, my heart, because the cabby was sent at a time when you were away from the school."

Isabelle felt her eyes widening, and a cold rage welling up in her heart. "So we have two linked mysteries to unravel—who and why."

He nodded. "And when we have those answers, we need something more. We need to know what we are going to do about it."

A deep growl, like that of an angry lion, interrupted him. "Only let me have my hands upon the dog, Sahib," said Karamjit.

"And I," added Selim darkly. "The Prophet does not forbid—"

"Peace," Agansing said unexpectedly. "This has a larger shape than someone who wishes harm to our children. Perhaps it is not what they *are,* but what they may *become* that is at issue here. That they may be a great threat in the future. Perhaps we should first see if other such children have been—negated—of late. If so, then we deal with someone who takes the long view, and is willing to eliminate opposition before the opposition is more than a potential."

Isabelle wrinkled her brows. "But how can we possibly discover that?" she protested. "It would be like trying to find footprints after the tide has washed them away! Even if children have been—murdered—how could we find out who they were and what they could have been had they grown up?"

Agansing raised an eyebrow. "There is one here who can discover that, Memsa'b."

Frederick's eyes widened, and Isabelle's hand came involuntarily to her throat.

"Sarah," they said, at the same time.

Agansing nodded. But it was Karamjit who raised the objection they all felt. "Not until all other ways have been tried," he said, in that tone that meant he would not countenance any other course of action.

"Peace," Agansing said again, this time with a suspicion of a twinkle in his eye. "We are your Long Friends, Lion. When have you known us to do otherwise?"

Karamjit visibly relaxed. "Never," he admitted. "It is my anger speaking, not my reason."

Isabelle closed her eyes a moment, then said, reluctantly, "This does tend to point in the direction of Magic, rather than the Esoteric, you know."

Frederick raised an eyebrow, then sighed. "And you, my heart, are the only one of us with contacts in those circles. I am loathe to ask it of you, but I can only suggest that you will need to pursue them." Then he shook his head and added with a smile, "It could be worse. It could be the Esoteric rather than the Magic. And some of our friends are a trial even to my patience."

Isabelle thought over the last party they had attended, when Aleister Crowley had swept in wearing a flamboyant scarlet cape, circled the room without saying a word to anyone, then swept out again, and as a few people bristled, assuming insult, Beatrice Leek had announced in a voice loud enough to be heard in all parts of the room, "Don't mind Aleister, darling, he's just being invisible again."

Trying to get any two of that lot to move in the same direction was like trying to train cats to pull in a tandem harness. "You're right, as usual, my love," she said and put her hand to her temple. "In the meantime, I am exhausted, and so should the rest of you be. If we sleep on the problem, we may be given some direction."

At least, that was something she could always hope for.

5

THE next day, everything was pretty much back to normal, which was both a relief and a bit of a vexation for Nan. For Sarah, it was unalloyed relief; she had confessed to Nan last night that she never, ever wanted to see or even think about "that Thing." But Nan, like the Elephant's Child, was full of " 'satiable curiosity" and like Rikki-tikki-tavi, if she could not get the answers immediately, she was bound and determined to "run and find out."

So when her hour with Agansing came around, before he even opened his mouth to begin her breathing exercise, she forestalled him with, "Master Agansing, what *was* that 'orrible Thing?" And for a very long moment, there was no sound in the Conservatory but the hiss of the steampipes and the drip of water.

Now, at the Harton School it was the policy of the adults to be as absolutely honest with the pupils as they could. Sometimes the answer to a question was "I don't know." Often, it was, "I know, but I want you to go find out for yourself, and I will help you." Very rarely it was "I don't think you are old enough to need that answer, but I promise when you are, I will tell you." This last was seldom if ever invoked for Nan; as a streetchild, there was very little she was "too young" to know, and most of the things under that heading she probably knew already, anyway. The main use for that particular answer to Nan was to let her know as subtly as possible that *she* was not to impart that information either, if one of the other pupils asked her.

So Agansing merely sighed for the disruption of his lesson, and answered, "I do not know, Missy Nan. I know that it is old, and we are of the opinion that it is a thing more of Magic than of spirit."

Now, this would be the first time—ever!—that Agansing had used that word with reference to things Nan's gran would have labeled "uncanny." He had always spoken of "mental discipline" and "the full use of all of the senses" and "transcending the physical" and the like. She looked at him uncertainly.

"Thoughtcher said there ain't no such thing as magic," she retorted.

"I said nothing of the sort," Agansing replied with unruffled dignity. "I said that *we* do not use such a thing, nor use that name. I never said it did not exist. There are two sorts of ways in which one can manifest Power," he continued. "One is to use the Power that is within us all, which is what we do here, myself, Karamjit, Selim, Sahib, and Memsa'b. And you, and Missy Sarah, and some of the other children, of course."

Odd. He never had come out to tell her *which* of the other children had Talents. For that matter, neither had any of the other adults. Briefly, she wondered why. Was this one of those things she was supposed to find out for herself? Or was this a reflection of the careful way in which the adults guarded the privacy of all the children?

"The second way, however, is to use the Power that exists around us, often through an intermediary creature, either by means of its cooperation, or its coercion. *That* is Magic. *That* is what Missy Sarah's parents can do, though we cannot."

She gaped at him. "They can?" This was news to her. She wondered if it was news to Sarah.

"But they cannot teach Sarah in the use of her Talents, nor do they have any understanding of them. This is why she is here." He shrugged. "At any rate, we believe that creature is a twisted creature of Magic, something called an Elemental, although which it could be, or what Element it owes its form to, we are not equipped to tell. This is why it is not like an ordinary haunting, which we could banish, with some work. But since it is clearly a creature either powerful enough, transmuted enough, or both, for ordinary mortals to see and be affected by, it is quite beyond us to do anything about it. And I can tell you nothing more on that subject, and very little on the subject of Magic. You must ask Memsa'b, though she may not answer you. And now, you will assume the position of meditation."

Her mind buzzing, she obeyed. And despite her curiosity eating at her, she kept her mind on her lessons, enough so that Agansing gave her a "Well done, under the circumstances. You may go."

The next lesson was History, and after that, she helped the ayahs get the little ones down for a nap. But she kept thinking about Magic. . . .

Now, given what she had already been learning, she was quite prepared to believe that the sort of Magic you found in fairy tales was real. What she had difficulty in grasping was that there was something that Memsa'b and Sahib *couldn't* master.

After some consideration, she decided that she wouldn't ask Memsa'b about it. Not just yet. Last night had been hard on everyone; it might be best to let things settle for a bit before she started asking questions. Especially since there was no telling just where those questions might lead, because it might be to a place where she really didn't want to go.

❋

Isabelle was paying a call on an old acquaintance, and she wasn't entirely certain what her reception would be.

It was an acquaintance she had last seen before she had left, brokenhearted (or so she had persuaded herself) for India. Somehow, in all the years she and Frederick had lived in London, she had not been able to bring herself to renew those old friendships. The one or two from those days who *had* sought her out had made the first overtures, not she.

But after all, she was in a very different social circle from theirs, and far lower in class, as merely the daughter of a country vicar. She had been out of their social class back then, too—but she had deluded herself for a while that social distinctions did not matter. The vicar and his family were always welcome in the homes of the ennobled and wealthy—provided, she *now* knew, that they did not overstep their place, nor (in the case most especially of a daughter) dare to think they could actually fit in. . . .

❄

She felt the old bitterness creeping into her thoughts, and ruthlessly throttled it down. *Don't be a fool,* she scolded herself. *If you were to ask most of them if they would trade places with you, if they were honest with themselves, they would.* How many of those girls she had once called "friend" were now shackled in loveless marriages to men whose sole qualification for the position of husband was a pedigree, wealth, and the interesting distinction of being an Elemental Mage? Half, surely. Among the Elemental Masters, there was the commonly-held sentiment that if one was not wedded for family or love by the time one reached the age of twenty-one, the best one could do would be to at least marry someone appropriate, of the right breeding, from whom one would not have to conceal one's magic, even if you scarcely knew the prospective spouse, and had less in common with her than an Oxford don with an Irish bricklayer.

Yes. And I was common as dust and without a penny to my name, and no Elemental Magic. Small wonder. . . . She stifled the rest of the bitter thought.

It had taken Isabelle part of the morning and a steady perusal of the present and past editions of *Burke's Peerage* to find out what had become of Beatrice DeLancy. She was now Lady Beatrice—or rather, as etiquette would have it, Lady *Nigel*. Lady Nigel Lytton, to be precise. And since *Lord* Nigel had figured nowhere in Bea's adolescent daydreams, it was probably safe to assume she could be counted among those who held with the philosophy of "marry appropriately."

Isabelle mounted the steps of the elegant townhouse, after paying the cabbie, and was let in by a faintly contemptuous butler. *I have faced down psychic vampires, old haunts, and dacoits, my lad. You do not frighten me a bit.* She sent in her card, with the added words, *née Carpenter* neatly printed after "Harton." But she was damned if she was going to be ashamed of the address of *Harton School for Boys and Girls* on it, nor was she going to pretend she was anything other than what she was. She'd tried to do that once . . . and look where it had gotten her. If this meant she cooled her heels in the hallway, only to be told that "My Lady is not at home," so be it. One snub was not going to kill her, and Beatrice was by no means the only name on her list.

In fact, she had gotten herself so completely prepared for rejection, that when Bea came flying down the stairs in her soft pink morning wrapper (much to the horror of the supercilious butler) her hands outstretched in greeting, it took her so much by surprise that for a moment she simply gawked at her old friend, dumbfounded.

Fortunately the moment didn't last; she was too used, after all these years, to thinking on her feet.

So it was to her feet that she jumped, and the two of them met in an embrace which wiped out all of the years in between their last meeting and this one, after which Beatrice drew her up the stairs and into her dressing room.

"The Harton School! Now that is the last place I would have expected to find you, so no wonder I had no idea you were in London! Who *is* this mysterious Harton?" Bea asked in teasing tones, as she settled Isabelle in a comfortable chair and handed her a plate of sugar biscuits. "He must be something remarkable to have turned you into a schoolmistress! I thought you were going to go become some sort of female *guru* amongst the Hindus!"

"Frederick is rather more than remarkable," she replied, noting with amusement, that, aside from a slight fading of the yellow-gold of her hair and a slightly plumper figure, Bea hadn't changed a bit. "I could equally ask you who Lord Nigel is."

Bea shrugged, dismissed her maid with a little wave of her hand, and picked up the teapot. "Nigel isn't the love of my life, but he doesn't bore me to death either. We both had to marry or our families would have nagged us to death about it, and at least we were friends. But you, Belle—who *is* this Harton fellow? Did you meet him in India? Tell, tell, tell!"

"There isn't that much to tell," she replied. "He was with the Army; he's common as clay, God bless him, and straight from the streets of this very city, but a very kind and childless gentleman recognized him for what he was, saw to his education and bought him his commission—"

"Ah, another paranormal like you, then?" Bea asked shrewdly.

"Something like, though his Talent lies in clairvoyance and clairaudience rather than telepathy and psychometry," she admitted with a slight smile.

"Well, being able to see what was going on over the next hill would be quite useful for a soldier, I would think!" Bea chuckled, pouring her a cup of tea. "A good thing he had a mentor, though!"

"A very good thing. His mentor owned a bookshop here in London specializing in rare and Esoteric volumes as you might expect—and I am sure you will be unsurprised to learn that I frequented the place. By that time, Frederick was already in India and had earned his way up the ranks. When this gentleman discovered I was determined to go to India, he sent me with introductions to some teachers of his acquaintance, and that was where I met Frederick." All perfectly true so far as it went—though her explanation did not go nearly far enough—

"And you are leaving out all the good parts, I am sure," Beatrice retorted, wagging a finger at her. "Curses and dacoits, phantoms and secret societies, and all manner of dreadful menaces that the

two of you faced, which you are sworn not to tell anyone because
it all involves occult oaths."

She had to laugh, because Bea was actually far too close to the
truth! "Something like that, yes. With the one detail that I *can* tell
you, that it was love at first sight for the two of us and when he
was discharged, we—and some fellow native occultists—decided
to come back here to put up the school, so that children with psychical talents would have somewhere to go to learn how to manage themselves." She sighed. "And a school that would care
properly for the poor little dears who might not have such Talents,
but who still were being shipped back to England. There are more
bad schools than good, I fear. And it is useful for anyone dealing
with even ordinary children to have some occult talent."

"Fellow occultists!" Beatrice's eyes sparkled. "This becomes
more interesting all the time! Hindus?"

"One Gurkha, one Sikh, and one Moslem," she replied. "And a
motley assortment of our old servants from India, so we do have
some Hindus among us. And Buddhists." She thought for a moment. "I am reasonably sure there are no Sufis, Jainists, or Farsi,
but I would not be willing to swear to that."

"Good heavens, Belle, you brought back the entire cross-section
of the subcontinent!" Bea seemed delighted. "At some point I am
going to have to visit—and now that I know your school exists, I
have somewhere to refer children who are Talented rather than
Magicians. That is exceedingly useful. I know I can count on you
to be practical and caring, and too many of these people *mean*
well, but haven't the common sense of my canary."

"Your canary has rather more common sense than some of
them," Isabelle said dryly. "At least the Elemental Mages are more-
or-less levelheaded and disciplined, which brings me to the reason
I wanted to talk to you. If I were going to find the person who was
the closest thing to a leader in your Esoteric circle, who would
that be?"

And Beatrice hesitated.

That was distinctly peculiar, and not at all like Beatrice.

"In terms of being a leader, in virtually all ways," she said slowly, "I would have said Alderscroft. *Lord* Alderscroft, now; his father died two years ago, poor man. He's immensely skilled, and quite eclipses most of the other Elemental Masters hereabouts. They're calling him the Wizard of London, now, and the Young Lion."

Isabelle managed a slight smile, although it gave her a pang to think of how well that name suited him. "I can see how that would please him," she said, in as neutral a tone as possible. "He always did enjoy being the recipient of accolades if he thought he had earned them."

Bea nodded. "Don't men always? Nigel is just as susceptible. But Alderscroft does have power and skill, and it's not just Esoteric power either; he's gotten political, and he has connections. He's talking about finding a sympathetic Minister, revealing what we can do to him, and making the Elemental Masters into an adjunct arm of the War Department. He says that we will have to reveal our powers to someone eventually, so it ought to be on our terms, so that we are the ones negotiating from a place of strength. . . but. . . ."

"But?" Isabelle prompted.

"But—he's just so cold. Which is an odd thing to say of a Fire Master, I know, but he *is* and he gets worse every time I meet with him. Even Nigel remarked on it, and when it comes to commenting on the foibles of his fellow man, Nigel simply doesn't." She smiled, slightly, "He has a terribly sweet temper, does my Nigel, which I thought was a decent reason to marry him. Earth, of course, which is why I am here and he is not, he cannot abide even this little clean area of London for more than a week at a time. But at any rate, Alderscroft began getting distant just before you left, and he would be a hermit, I think, if he didn't have to interact socially with the rest of us to herd us in the direction he wants. Or—" She wrinkled her brow—"He wouldn't exactly be a hermit, because he is everywhere, socially. One can't go to a party without seeing him. But he might as well have an invisible barrier about him." She shook her head. "I'm doing a very bad job of explaining myself. I suppose you would have to see it for yourself."

That's hardly likely. Isabelle hesitated a moment, then asked the loaded question. "Is Lady Cordelia still his mentor?"

"Oh, Her Ladyship is very much present in his life, I assure you." Bea pursed her lips and looked wise. "If she weren't such a pillar of dignity, chastity, and sanctity, one would assume all manner of goings-on, but I cannot imagine Her Ladyship removing so much as a glove in the presence of a man." She sighed. "One *wants* to like her. After all, it isn't as if there were that many female Elemental Magicians in London, much less another Air Mage. But that off-putting manner . . . it's as bad or worse than that barrier Alders-croft has about him."

Isabelle nodded, understanding all too well. She was more than halfway convinced that Lady Cordelia Bryce-Coll was at least par-tially, if not fully responsible for that final snub on Alderscroft's part that had sent Isabelle off in tears. But, of course, the woman had been as sweet and smooth as honeyed cream in public, and had even sent a little bon voyage gift, so there was no way to prove anything. Lady Cordelia never gossiped, never said an unpleasant word about anyone in public. Back in her girlhood, Isabelle and her friends had formed the habit of referring to Cordelia as "the nun," both from her penchant for dressing all in ice-blue or white, and her demeanor. Even *thinking* improper thoughts about her was impossible. To this day Isabelle, who had spent so many years in the sensuous East and been exposed to things that would send most English women reeling back in a dead faint if even *hinted* at, could not imagine Cordelia Bryce-Coll in any state other than fully clothed, ramrod straight, and cool and calm as the marble image of a saint.

"You know," Bea said thoughtfully. "I always thought it was her fault that Alderscroft snubbed you."

Isabelle gazed at her friend in astonishment. "Whatever makes you say that?" she asked.

"Well, who else would it have been? After that incident at Vesuvius, his father wasn't capable of putting two sentences together, and besides, the old lord *liked* you. If his mother had been alive, there might have been trouble, but I can't think of anyone else who would have wanted to meddle." Bea shook her head. "No, it was Delia, I would stake my diamonds on it."

Isabelle made herself shrug with feigned indifference and sipped her tea. "It doesn't matter, really, now does it? It's all in the past. But I think I would rather not consult with Alderscroft about this, especially not if *she* is still hanging about him."

"Well," Bea said slowly, winding a strand of hair around her finger. "You might tell me what this is all about. I know practically everyone in Elemental circles, at least in London, these days. I might be able to help."

Since Isabelle could not imagine anyone she would rather talk to, she launched into her narrative with a will. She began all the way back at the point when little Sarah and Nan joined the school—because Sarah and Nan were so integral to the story—

"Though I can't in all honesty call Nan a charity case, when she more than pays for her way with all of the hard work she does—"

Then she went on to the phony medium, Sarah's true mediumistic abilities, all the inquiries about the girls—and went from that to the incident in Berkeley Square. Bea listened intently to every word.

"Well, I must say, I wish Nigel was here. That *sounds* like an Earth Elemental to be sure, but I don't know enough to make an identification." She frowned. "And I don't imagine that an Earth Master gone wrong is going to identify himself to the rest of us."

"Probably not," Isabelle agreed, and sighed. "Still, if one of you could look into the situation—"

"That, my dear, is a given," Bea told her, raising her head with a determined set to her chin. "We simply can't have something like that loose, even if it *is* confined to a single building. Someone could be hurt. If we haven't dealt with it by the time Nigel returns,

I'm sure he'll banish it, but I suspect I can find a Water Master to get rid of the vicious thing."

Isabelle sighed, and nibbled a biscuit for the sake of politeness. "This was deliberate, you know. Whoever did this intended to frighten or harm my charges. I'd like to know who set it." She braced herself, knowing she was unlikely to get an answer to that statement that she would like.

"Well—this is really something that the Elemental Masters should deal with, Belle," came exactly the reply she had expected. "We do try to police our own."

Run along, little girl, and don't bother your pretty head about it. The old Isabelle would have snapped something rude at her old friend. Over the years, although diplomacy did not come naturally to her, she had been forced to acquire it.

"It isn't precisely an issue internal to the Elemental Masters anymore, Bea," she said gently. "Whoever did this mounted an attack on Talented children. My charges and my charges specifically were lured there and locked in to be attacked. Someone sent a cabby to the school to ask for them by name. Two boundaries have been violated, the one that says that the Masters are not to attack the Talented and vice versa, and the one that holds that children are off-limits. At the very least I would like to know why, if not who. There may be more such attacks, and I am the protector of these children; I have the right to know who I am protecting them against."

Bea had the grace to flush. "That's true enough," she admitted. "I'll see that you're told whatever it is you need."

Whatever you think it is I need. Still, it was the biggest concession she was going to get out of them. She nodded, and changed the subject to that of her old schoolmates. She needed to find out what they were up to anyway.

❄

She stayed through luncheon at Bea's insistence. It was definitely a treat; it wasn't as if the Harton School could afford the sorts of dainties Lady Nigel could put on her table.

She had arrived by cab; she went home in Lady Nigel's carriage. The congested streets that slowed the carriage's pace to practically nil allowed her to sit back against the velvet cushions and think about her old friends, the young—now, not so young—women she had gone to school with.

That school was home to mostly young ladies of rank and privilege. She had, in fact, been given a scholarship, or her family never could have afforded it. Her benefactress had been a Talent of no mean ability herself, and knowing that there was no school for Talented girls had found and sent her to the next best thing. Presumably, the idea had been that she would get the sort of education fit to make her a governess, but whatever had been in the donor's mind, Isabelle had found herself in the company of those who also recognized her Talent for what it was, and shared with her the secret of their own powers. For the first time she had found herself among girls from whom she needed to hide nothing, for she had been sent to a school populated entirely by, and taught by, the daughters of Elemental Masters and Magicians. There was only one other school like it, and that one was for the sons of these same families. She was not the only girl on scholarship there; nor was she the only one who did not share a spot in *Burke's Peerage*. But she was the only one of the less-privileged lot who was comfortable around the titled, the legacy of hundreds of tea parties, tennis parties, and dinner parties accompanying her father to "the Great House" since her mother was no longer alive to do so. In English polite society, the vicar was the one man who was welcome in the drawing rooms of the rich and the front stoops of the poor, and Isabelle was well used to accompanying her father to both venues. Had it not been for her limited and modest wardrobe, she could not have been told apart from any of the girls of rank and title.

Isabelle had a knack for making friends, for being a warm and caring companion, and for acting as both a sounding board and a peacemaker. Once again, of course, such traits were invaluable to the daughter of a vicar. As she had soothed tempers around the tea table of the Lady's Friendly Society, she now soothed ruffled feathers at the school, and was accepted as a friend by all. As a consequence, she was brought along on every possible excursion, and if her wardrobe was lacking, the clothes' chests of all the other girls were flung open and at her disposal.

And that, of course, was how the trouble really started. There was no way for David Alderscroft to have known that she was *not* in his social circle. Her (borrowed) clothing did not betray the fact, nor did her manners. Whenever there was a party that was a girl short, Isabelle, with her wonderful manners, got an invitation, since the parents in question would always think, "Ah, now she's not an Elemental Mage, nor has she independent means, she'll be no competition for *my girl.*" And it was true enough that she should not have been—most of the young men in question already knew of her and her status, and while they laughed and flirted with her, it was lightly, and with no intent on either side.

Not so David Alderscroft. He had no idea she was only a vicar's daughter; he had been schooled at home, by private tutors, and was not privy to the crucial information that she was, in the delicate terminology of his class, "not quite up to the mark," at least in the sense that a marriage to her for any of the scions of these noble houses would have been a marriage far beneath them.

But she had flattered herself, when he began to pay her attention, that perhaps she was not so "ineligible" as all that. After all, although she was not a Magician, she did have arcane abilities of her own, inherited from both sides of the family. Her father, the vicar, was sensitive to spirits and to the emotions of others. Although she barely remembered her mother, her older sisters hinted that Mariana Carpenter had been even more Talented than Isabelle was. And vicar though he might have been, her father saw to it she was properly trained in the use of her unusual abilities, and looked the other way when that teaching skirted close to things that might be called "pagan." He himself did not have the strength of Talent to become a Warrior of the Right-hand Path and a Light Bringer, but he was terribly proud when she proved to have that level of ability. By the time she was enrolled in Madame Grayson's Academy, in her late teens, she had already achieved that accolade, and it was one acknowledged by the Elemental Masters as well as the Talented. The families of the Elemental Masters themselves were known to acquiesce to marriage across class boundaries, so long as both parties were Masters, and surely the title of Light Bringer was the equivalent. So there was every reason for her to consider herself David Alderscroft's equal and carry herself that way.

As for David, as Bea had said, his father approved of her entirely, though His Lordship was a tragic case. He and a handful of other Elemental Masters had been forced to deal with an occult circle led by a renegade Fire Master, and as Isabelle understood the story, he had stepped in between the Master and his own men, and absorbed most of the power of an awakening Phoenix himself. He had not been the same man afterward; he acted like one lightning struck, with tremors, facial tics, and an inability to speak clearly. But he was able to convey to David that he approved of Belle.

Probably because I read him newspapers and books for hours on end.

Of course, she and Bea could both have misread the poor man. Maybe he thought David was planning to engage her as a companion, and not that David was interested in making her his wife. . . .

She stared at her hands, fingers entwined in her lap, and sighed. No. No, she was sensitive enough to know, although she had not actually read the poor man's mind on the subject, that the late Trevor, Lord Alderscroft had liked her for herself, and would have been perfectly happy to see her take a wife's place beside his son.

No, she didn't think old Lord Alderscroft had anything to do with what happened after Lady Cordelia appeared on the scene. . . .

Without his father, David had had no one to properly train him. There was no truly strong *male* Fire Master in that part of the country. But Lady Cordelia was one of those rare creatures that though she was a Master of Air also had just enough of Fire to do as a teacher, and *she* volunteered to train David the day he turned eighteen. David's father must have consented to the plan, for Lady Cordelia was soon a long-term guest at Harwinton House, the Alderscroft ancestral home—when she wasn't living in her own town house in Cambridge.

None of this, however, filtered down to the girls at Isabelle's school, nor even to Isabelle. All she had known at the time was that David had just begun his university education. David was attending Cambridge, most of the girls' brothers were either going into the military as officers, too young or too old for university, or going to Oxford. David himself never wrote to Isabelle—after all, it would hardly have been proper, and any letters from a young man not one's brother would have been confiscated by the headmistress. There should have been no reason for anyone to inform Isabelle about anything having to do with David Alderscroft.

Isabelle brooded out the carriage window, staring at nothing. That, of course, was the official version. The unofficial version was that she and David had come to what was known as an "understanding." Or at least, she had thought so. He had said, and more than once, that he was going to speak to her father when she came of age. If he had meant the comment in jest, she thought she would have sensed that. She'd had every reason to think he regarded her with deep affection, even love, and she had certainly felt the same. She had dreamed, not of what life would be like as Lady David, but of what life would be like as an occultist Warrior of the Light and a Master, working together.

I honestly don't recall ever thinking much about the prestige, or the money, or the title. She sighed, and closed her eyes, leaning back against the seat cushions. The carriage was stalled in traffic, and had this been a cab it would have been a great deal less pleasant. It would have been even worse in a 'bus. This made a good place to think about the past, truth to tell. Surrounded as she was by the noise of traffic, she was conversely as isolated as if she had been on top of a mountain, or sitting in splendid silence in a deserted temple in the jungle.

No, it wasn't that the money and the title meant nothing, it was that she didn't regard anything above and beyond what constituted a "comfortable" life as being terribly important. Pleasant, yes, but not vital. So far as her ambitions, well, they had always been centered on the realms of the Esoteric rather than the mundane, and she really, truly, did not think she had thought covetously about what being married to one of the wealthiest peers in the county would have meant.

If her memories were correct, the largest part of the equation had been that she felt very strongly about David—and if it was, perhaps, "only" first love, it was still the most powerful emotion she had ever experienced at the time. True, they had done nothing except walk and talk together for hours at a time. But that was far more than many of their contemporaries ever did. The "understanding" that they had was something she had clung to, dreamed about, and cherished. She had been so certain that the bond between them was such that she didn't need letters to know how he felt, nor to confirm the depth of his feelings toward her.

Ah, but understanding or not, that all changed the moment Lady Cordelia came into his life.

The next time she saw him, at a shooting party, he was literally a different person. When he greeted her, although it was polite enough, there was no mistaking his tone of detachment. He treated her exactly as he treated all the other girls insofar as affection went—but insofar as the level of courtesy—

To her utter shock he had added to his demeanor with her a touch of arrogance that clearly said, "You are tolerated here because you are polite and well-mannered, but you do not, and never will, *belong*."

And that was that.

His attitude clearly surprised and puzzled the other girls, but they said nothing. Perhaps they assumed he and Isabelle had had some sort of lovers' quarrel. At any rate, it was one of those situations where nothing was *said*, but everything was *understood*.

And the moment when Isabelle first saw Lady Cordelia, she had known deep in her heart who was to blame.

You could not have said that David danced attendance on Her Ladyship, because he did not. And there was nothing remotely loverlike about the way he treated her. If anything, his attitude was of deference, as of the disciple to the great teacher, as if she were conveying some great favor to him by giving him her attention. It was the sort of attitude one would expect if she had been a great and wise philosopher of the sort that Isabelle eventually found in India. . . .

But the pupils of those great and wise teachers grew more humble in their attitudes toward others, not more arrogant.

The abrupt change in David's attitude was, perhaps, the worst and most painful experience of Isabelle's short life. Perhaps it was just as well that the encounter had occurred at teatime; she had been able to plead a headache and retreat to her room, not to emerge even for dinner. The headache had been real; she had cried for hours, until her eyes were swollen and her head pounding. And, fortunately, the friend that had invited her in the first place quickly took pity on her and arranged for her to return to the school the next morning so that there were no more such encounters.

She never accepted another invitation again; instead, she concentrated on her studies, both academic and occult, and set her eyes on the goal of leaving the country altogether and somehow getting to India. Since that had also been a longtime ambition of her benefactress, they had arranged for a trip for the two of them, with Isabelle as the lady's companion. Her father had been bewildered, but accepted it. Her friend, the London bookshop owner, gave her people to contact.

And when she had met Frederick—everything changed for the better.

"Well," she said aloud. "Now I know that my memory of things matches Bea's."

That, too, had emerged from their morning of "catching up." She had *not* been mistaken, everyone around her had assumed that she and David Alderscroft were going to make a couple as soon as she came of the proper age to do so. She was not the only one who had been shocked by his change of attitude.

But perhaps most importantly, there had been one fundamental mistake that she *had* made. Her immediate circle of friends did not condone David's behavior toward her, much less share it. Now, there probably were some girls at the school, and there were *certainly* some young ladies in the exclusive social circle in which David resided, who applauded what he had done and felt that Isabelle had been pushing herself in where she did not belong. But her real friends, though she had been blind to it at the time, were incensed by his treatment of her. Their doors were still open to her, just as Bea's had been.

And that was of vital importance, for she was going to have to try to find some way of discovering who had set the trap for Sarah and Nan without the aid of the tacit leader of the Elemental Masters hereabouts.

She laughed aloud, remembering what Frederick had once said to her. *When you want something done, you ask a man. When you want it done quietly and without any fuss, you ask a woman.*

Perhaps a circle of old friends wasn't a bad place to start.

6

DAVID Alderscroft looked out over the tree-shaded boulevard in front of his town house and frowned. Too many people, too many untidy people, clattering back and forth along the pavement. A nurse pushing a pram, some wretched boy running an errand, two carriages, and a tradesman's van—too many people. How much better it would have been had there been no one out there, the pavement spotless, the street silent—

Better still had it been winter. Everything lightly coated in snow, all the imperfections invisible beneath the frozen blanket. That would be ideal—

It would be so tidy if winter remained year round. No mess, people properly remaining inside their own four walls, tradesmen keeping to their proper place in the alleys. He entertained himself with a vision of the frozen city for a moment, everything as pure and white and clean as new marble, with nothing to mar the shining perfection of it.

He shook his head slightly. He shouldn't be obsessing over such trifles. He had some serious campaigning to do, if he was going to penetrate the circle surrounding Her Majesty, Queen Victoria.

It wasn't a circle he would normally have entrée to. The Queen was very particular about those she allowed near her. He wasn't a family man, nor was he particularly fond of children. Her Majesty was not noted for her partiality to *young* men, nor was she inclined to put her trust in them. But she was susceptible to men in general, in the sense that she tended to rely heavily on them, and to be manipulated by them—not easily, but when you knew what to say to her, when and how to say it, she tended to defer to your judgment, over and above her own.

David didn't know what those things were, nor when and how to say them—but Lady Cordelia did. So if he did his job correctly, and managed to get into that magic circle, the rest would be easy. So she had told him, and he believed her. Nothing she had told him thus far had ever been wrong.

He turned back to his desk, and the frown smoothed. Here, in his office, everything was precisely as it should be. The books had all been shelved in their proper place along the walls, his massive mahogany desk was dustless and polished until one could see one's face in it. The Turkey carpet was newly swept, the ashtrays washed, the two leather chairs on the far side of the desk the exact distance from the desk that he favored. The blotter was precisely in the middle, and his pens, pencils, paper and ink right where he wanted them. This was more like it. Here was order, everything properly arranged and tidy. He glanced at his pocket watch, saw that it was precisely ten o'clock, and sat down to begin his correspondence for the day.

Parliament would not be in session again until October; there would be nothing to occupy him there until the summer recess was over, but that did not mean that he would not be planning for the opening.

Politics was something of a new field for the Alderscrofts. His father had taken no interest in his seat in the House of Lords and neither had his grandfather, but David had, on Lady Cordelia's advice, been active since before his father died. He had been taking his seat nearly every day when Parliament was sitting for the past three years, and had been making a quiet name for himself there, in the cleverest way possible—as a voice of moderation. No one expected a young man to be the voice of moderation; he was attracting attention for that reason. It was good attention, too; the Queen approved.

He worked steadily until luncheon; his secretary James came in twice, quietly and unobtrusively removing what he had finished with and bringing him new correspondence to deal with. Some of it was political, much was social, a very little was business relating to the running of the estate. He spent very little time there, since his father had died; the old manor troubled him in a way he could not define. Perhaps it was simply that there were too many memories there. In any event, he left most of that business in the hands of his estate manager. "Pay competent people who know the job," Lady Cordelia had said. "Do not try to attempt things you are not expert at and do not care for." Good advice, and he had gratefully left the estate in the hands of Colin Foxward. The report was good, neither too much rain nor too little, crops looking favorable, and he dismissed the estate from his mind with a feeling of relief. It was more of a burden than a blessing, so far as he was concerned—except, of course, for the income. And these days no one held it against a gentleman if his income derived from investment rather than land. If it were his choice . . . but it wasn't. And besides, the old place was useful in the shooting season. Near enough to London to take the train, far enough for good hunting, and his gamekeeper did a fine job in making sure there were plenty of pheasant, duck, and quail. It was useful socially, and would become more so as he rose in social circles.

At noon, precisely, he rose from his desk. He did not need to call for his carriage, for his household knew his habits; it was waiting at the door to take him to his club, where he lunched. He then spent precisely three hours making social calls, not returning home until teatime. He couldn't abide taking his tea as a social call; difficult enough to make calls on ladies when they were merely receiving, for at least then one could escape when the level of chatter grew too high. One was trapped at tea, and the clatter of china was only eclipsed by the chatter of gossip. Lady Cordelia was the only female of his acquaintance who eschewed gossip; she was the only female of his acquaintance who showed any sense about the matter. Now that he was not busy with politics until the October opening, she had resumed his lessons in Elemental Magic; she would be here for tea, and then, a lesson.

Precisely on time, no more than ten minutes after he had arrived, he looked out of the window to see her carriage roll up to the front entrance. It was a distinctive vehicle; most carriages in London were black or dark shades of red, green or blue. Hers was white, trimmed in light blue, and it was probably the entire job of one servant to keep it clean and shining in the filthy air of the city. Her horses were matched grays; her coachman's livery was light blue. A moment after the carriage rolled to a halt, the footman opened the door, and Lady Cordelia, dressed in her customary colors of pale-blue and white, descended from the carriage. She moved with a cool grace he had never seen in any other woman; she glided as if she was on wheels.

She was curiously ageless; her hair so white a blond that it was not possible to see any silver or gray in it, her face as smooth and unwrinkled and serene as if carved from alabaster. Her eyes were a pale blue-gray, her form as slender as a young birch, but as erect and straight as a wand of silver, and all in all, there could not possibly have been a more perfect physical representation of an Air Master. There was nothing about her of the occasional giddiness or spontaneity of an Air Master and no sign at all that she had a touch of the passionate Element of Fire in her.

But Lady Cordelia had too firm a grip on the reins of her character and her Element to allow passion to come into play. In fact, she had taught David that passion, especially when dealing with Fire, was dangerous. She had instilled in him a discipline and control he had no notion existed before she began teaching him, and taught him to keep his Elemental creatures under firm control and tight rein

She had also taught him something else, something he had never seen nor heard of before. The absence of fire was cold; she taught him how to harness his Element in a way that allowed him to create an arctic chill instead of furnace heat.

And there were Elementals that thrived in that atmosphere, odd creatures of negative Fire, if that was possible. Strange little Ice Fey and Frost Fey; a kind of counter-Salamander, creatures of snow and glacier, and—or so she claimed—even the famous Yeti, though it was highly unlikely he would ever see one of those in England. They were utterly obedient to his will, never fighting him, as opposed to their flame-driven brethren. Perhaps this was why he liked them so much, preferring them over the common aspect of his Element. One would have thought that water, in the form of snow and ice, being inimical to his Element would have made these creatures just as hostile. But in fact, this was Water locked away in a crystalline form that rendered it unreachable by Water Elementals. In a sense, this was where Fire conquered Water.

Sometimes, though, he looked back on the days of raw power, of careful negotiations with a Phoenix, with nostalgic longing. Still, those were the days when he was very young, childish in fact. Only children preferred chaos over order, uncertainty over certainty. Children did not understand control and self-control. Cordelia had set him straight on that path.

There was a crystalline order to cold that appealed to him as well. As every snowflake was an orderly lattice, mathematical and precise, so was the matrix of spells that controlled the cold. The only flaw in the situation, and it was a small one, was that the Elemental creatures he had so far encountered were inferior in power to those of Flame. Still, it wasn't as if he was going into Duel Arcane any time soon. *Those* unhappy days were over.

Cordelia entered the drawing room, followed immediately by the maid with the tea cart, and he advanced to greet her exactly as always, the comfort of well-rehearsed pathways making him feel settled. She extended a kid-glove-clad hand for him to shake, he took it, squeezed it once, and released it. She smiled faintly.

"My dear David," she said, taking her place in her favorite chair, and motioning to the maid to begin serving, "I am given to understand you have been exceptionally busy this afternoon. Following up on an invitation to meet with the Prime Minister, no less! I am impressed by your progress."

He no longer wondered how she knew these things; her sources of information were logical. They were in the same circle of friends, she would have been told of the invitation at some point during her morning calls, and it was beyond the realm of possibility that he would *not* have been putting great thought into the exact wording of his acceptance this afternoon. "It's only a large dinner party," he replied, hastily making it clear that although he had managed this himself, it was an inferior achievement to those things she could do for him. "I doubt very much that I will be able to get more than a word or two with him."

"But that will be several words more than you have gotten heretofore," she countered, with no sign of disapproval. "Congratulations."

He felt a little glow at her praise, and indeed, he *had* worked hard to get this invitation. He suspected that he had ultimately gotten the invitation because he was an eligible bachelor, and the lady of the house had two unmarried daughters to dispose of. Not that he would even consider either of them.

He had higher ambitions, and any wife he took would have to fit those ambitions. Neither of the two hapless daughters fit that mold, but of course, she would not know that. You manipulated people by knowing their weaknesses and exploiting them in such a manner that they did not actually feel exploited. Best of all was if you could exploit them in such a manner that they felt an obligation to accommodate you, or a desire to fulfill your desire.

He had never met anyone quite as skilled at doing this as Cordelia. She could extract nearly anything she wanted from someone, and leave him (or her) with the feeling that it was Cordelia who had been conferring the favor.

And yet, this approach failed regularly with Elemental Masters, who seemed impervious to her charms. David found that something of a puzzle.

Perhaps it was only that she was a mere female. While men as a whole were susceptible to womanly wiles, Elemental Masters took a longer view of things, and were inclined never to make hasty decisions when it came to matters of Magic. So although they might smile and nod and be charmed while Cordelia was with them, they would commit to nothing without first taking time to think it over. Without Cordelia *there,* her propositions often seemed less attractive, and even reasonable suggestions coming from a woman appeared to be trivial matters. Even a woman like Cordelia.

"The most that I hope for is to be memorable in a positive sense to the P.M.," he told her. "Anything beyond that is less than likely, but the next time I stand to speak, if the P.M. has some recollection that I appeared to be a grave, sensible fellow, he is more likely to note my speech."

Her faint smile bestowed her approval on him. "I wish that all my protégés could have been as wise as you," she replied. "Those of Air could never achieve a proper understanding of how a serious approach to all things is of great benefit, and those of Fire never would understand that the discipline of the opposite aspect of Fire allows one to impose control on every aspect of Fire."

He did not allow her rare praise to go to his head; instead, he turned the subject to commonplaces things; the invitations he had accepted or declined, whether he intended to go to the country at all this summer, and some initial planning for the first shooting party of the season. She no longer gave him daily instruction in the control of his Element; only if he found himself at an impasse did he ask for her help. And that, only rarely; she was more likely to direct him to certain volumes in her esoteric library, or his own.

She left at six precisely; they both had social obligations, which often, but by no means always, overlapped.

Tonight, he had nothing; a rare evening to stay at home. Not that it would be a leisurely evening; he had reading to catch up on.

Yet, when the house was silent, the servants all safely "below-stairs," and only the ever-present hum of London a steady back-drop to his thoughts, he found himself paying very little attention to the book in his hand. Instead he found his eyes straying to the greenery outside the window, and his thoughts back to a time be-fore he had ever met Cordelia. . . .

Belle.

The memories of his first love? No, say "infatuation," rather, since it was obvious from the first how unsuitable the attachment had been, had he only been sensible enough to acknowledge the fact. The details of her face had become hazy over the years, but certainly Belle had never been the sort of striking beauty that Cordelia was even to this day. Fine eyes, though, really her best feature.

Odd, he hadn't thought of her in years.

Shame he'd had to snub her the way he had, but Cordelia had been right. It was the only way to effectively put the girl in her place and show her that her foolish dreams were only that; dreams, and no more substantial than air.

Some of the other girls in her set had initially come over a bit nasty to him afterward. He'd been forced to make his indifference to their anger clear, and after all, they were only schoolgirls, they couldn't possibly have understood that romance had no place in the alliances of their class and their Calling. A word or two by Cordelia in certain parental ears had cleared all that up. After all, if the Masters were to start indulging in the foolishness of roman-tic attraction when it came to marriage, well! The next thing you knew some duchess' daughter would go running off with the dust-man or the chimney sweeper.

Still, the hurt that had been in those eyes—

He shook his head to rid it of the unwanted thought. It was not as if he had plunged a dagger into her! It was nothing more than something she should have expected from the beginning. It had been no worse a tragedy than a child denied a sweet it ought not to have been promised nor craved in the first place.

It was her own fault anyway. She had brought all the hurt on herself, with her silly lending-library romances and the friends who had done her no favors by allowing the country vicar's daughter to think she was the social equivalent of the rest of them.

It had been on a night exactly like this one; a summer house party, the first of the summer after the end of the Oxford term. Probably that was why his thoughts had wandered in this unpleasant direction. A breath of breeze holding more than usual of the scent of blossoms, perhaps, or a momentary lull in the sound of the traffic that triggered memories best forgotten.

Memories of startlingly intelligent conversation; of learning, with some fascination, about the world of those whose Talents had nothing to do with Magic. Sometimes, just listening to the stories of life in a small village, so different from his own childhood.

He shook his head again. What was wrong with him? This was ridiculous. Yes, the girl had been vaguely attractive, had a certain intelligence, and a naïve charm, but that was all! She certainly didn't warrant more than a passing thought!

Still . . . he wondered what had become of her. She had vanished from the party, had not come down to dinner, and the next day there had been some specious story about being taken ill and going back to school—if the girl really *had* been ill she wouldn't have made a journey all the way back to a school that was ninetenths empty over the summer recess. And after that, nothing, except for a rumor she had gone to India.

Probably chased down some poor officer and married him before anyone got a chance to object. The women that went out to India alone, or as someone's companion, were generally husband hunting. There were a great many unattached officers in India, and very few unattached British women. Isabelle was probably over there now, queen of a bungalow, having snared herself a captain.

His mind began to complete that picture—except that the bungalow began to shape itself into his drawing room, and the Hindu servant into his own parlor maid, and that was when he resolutely, and with an unwarranted feeling of anger, set his mind to reading that damned book

❋

It was a small room, and austere, but exquisite in every detail. The floor, of the finest white Carerra marble, was polished to a mirror gleam. The walls were likewise of the same marble—which was a little unusual, and gave the room the look of a cube made of snow. The ceiling was made of glass panels, but not clear; they were opaque glass, swirled whites and pale, pale blues, leaded into a pattern that teased at the mind, because it *almost* looked like a great many things, but it was not possible to say precisely what it was. The effect was slightly disturbing.

There were no windows. Light came from four lamps of opaque white glass, standing on four metal, marble-topped tables, one in each corner. There was something odd about those lamps. The light they gave off was dim and blue, not the yellow of an oil-fueled flame. It could have been gas, turned down until the flame was blue, but there was no evident gas pipe, and at any rate, a flame like that should have been too hot for a glass shade.

And in an era when people crowded furniture into their rooms until there was scarcely space to turn, this room had only the four small tables, and in the center, a very strange chair and a fifth table. The chair, a single solid piece of quartz crystal, looked like something carved out of ice. The table, identical to the four in the corners of the room, held, at the moment, nothing.

The chair, however, held Lady Cordelia.

Her eyes rested on the empty surface of the table and there was a frown of concentration on her face. And only when a puff of mist and a breath of cold manifested on the tabletop did she stop frowning. "Speak," she said.

The mist curled into the shape of a tiny, wingless dragon, that seemed to be made of transparent crystal. This was an Ice Wurm, the Elemental opposite of the Salamander yet, strangely, controlled by Fire.

"The children are now further protected," it hissed. "By Earth and Air, by Fire and Water—as well as by Spirit. The woman has new allies."

Cordelia frowned again. "Powerful allies?" she asked, but the Ice Wurm did not reply, as it would not if it did not know the answer. So, "Show me the woman," she demanded. She had viewed the face of her enemy in the past, but only briefly, to assess and dismiss her. It seemed further examination was in order.

The Ice Wurm breathed on the tabletop, and a mirror of ice formed at its feet. Cordelia leaned forward and stared into it, pondering the rather uncompromising features of the woman shown there. As she stared, she tapped one perfectly manicured fingernail on the tabletop. She ignored the simple gown, which was perfectly in keeping with a schoolmistress of modest means. This woman was far more than she seemed on the surface, and gowns were irrelevant—a mistake in assessment that Cordelia had already made with her.

She had begun to form the reluctant conclusion that this unprepossessing woman was the same forgettable girl with whom David had formed an inappropriate relationship years ago, just as she herself had come on the scene. She thought the chit had been properly dealt with then, but—there was an echo of that girl there. And how many female occultists in London had attained the levels to which this woman had risen?

And yet, it seemed the height of improbable coincidence that it should be she. There was no reason for their paths to cross at this point, much less their swords. The girl had vanished from polite society, as was only proper; no mere vicar's daughter should have been pushing herself into Elemental Master circles, much less the social circles in which Cordelia was a leading light. Cordelia had not even troubled herself to discover where she had gone; it was fruitless to attempt to hunt down the fly one has swatted away so long as it does not return. David had seen the error of his ways, and it was unlikely in the extreme that he would ever encounter the girl again.

But—the given name was the same, Isabelle. And—the child had formidable psychical powers, even back then. She would not have been in the school she had been attending, if she had not. The features were similar enough, at least insofar as Cordelia's vague memory of the girl went.

Cordelia's frown deepened. This was more than mere coincidence. The longer she stared, the more convinced she became. This woman *was* the older version of that child she had sent packing. How else would she have gotten Magicians of all four Elements to protect her charges? Certainly not by recruiting from occult circles, which contained, by and large, people with no Elemental Power worth speaking of.

The mere existence of those children could be detrimental to her plans for David Alderscroft. There were just not that many genuine mediums around, and certainly none of the power the younger of the two children possessed. Elemental Magicians, of course, while they could certainly *see* spirits, were disinclined to do anything much about them. If there was a particularly troubling Revenant, one might send it on its way, of course, but for the most part, Elemental Mages considered the realm of the spirits to be something in which they did not meddle. Renegade Earth Masters could and did use them as weapons, but they were generally not terribly effective against another Master in full possession of his or her powers. It was rather like trying to use a swarm of bees to kill a horse. It could be done, of course, but the horse would have to face a swarm of immense numbers, be unaware of the attack until it was too late, and be unable to run once the attack began.

Cordelia—took a different tack.

It had begun much longer ago than she cared to think about, when the Honorable Cordelia Westron had made the Grand Tour with a number of her schoolmates. They had found themselves locked into one of the finer resorts in Switzerland by an unseasonable spate of blizzards, and while the rest of her party amused themselves with cards and dancing, flirting with the young men similarly stranded, and complaining about the conditions, Cordelia had decided to take up a guide's offer to walk to a glacier. After all, she was an Air Master; in her opinion, there was nothing that mere weather could do to harm her.

With her own powers keeping her much more comfortable than the shivering guide, she found the landscape utterly fascinating. There was something very attractive to her in those vast stretches of pure white snow and ice and stark black rock; a Spartan beauty that was very appealing, especially after being locked in an overheated hotel, smelling of rich food and perfume, with a lot of chattering magpies.

And when she found the ice cave, despite the guide's remonstrations, she insisted on going in. The blue stillness drew her, the silence in which she and the guide were the only living things, the purity of it, the hygienic sterility—

And then, suddenly, the guide became very quiet.

She had turned, to find him as frozen in place as any statue; she had tried to shake him, then slap him out of his stupor, but nothing broke the spell. She had been about to invoke the Element of Air to wake him, when a flat sheet of ice formed between her and him, the ice took on a mirror sheen, and she found herself staring at herself—or rather, a reflection of herself.

Pretty mortal child, a voice in her head had crooned. *So strong in her Element!*

She had looked wildly about for the source of the internal voice, but had seen nothing.

A pity such beauty is mortal, too, the voice continued, and as she watched in horror, the image before her aged, aged rapidly, until what stood before her was a hideously distorted reflection of an old, senile and withered crone wearing her clothing, which sagged and bagged on the shrunken, bent body. With a gasp, she had stepped forward and involuntarily touched the mirror.

You do not like what you see? The voice had been sardonic. *Oh, of course not. You silly mayfly mortals, who do not understand preservation, only consumption. You devour in moments what has taken long years to produce, then wonder why everything about you withers, including yourselves. Look at yourself! You who are the very epitome of the eroding property of Air, instead of the slow preserving of Ice. You could remain ageless in your beauty, and instead, you fling yourself headlong into the Abyss to whirl yourself away to nothingness.*

That had caught her attention, but she was cautious enough not to grasp for what the voice had hinted at. Instead, she had stepped back. "You imply a great deal," she had said boldly. "But Ice is only the other side of the element of Fire. I am a Master of Air, and even if I do not yet know how to control you, whoever you are, I have the means to destroy you."

A silent laugh had been her only answer. And the mirror dispersed into icy mist again, the guide woke from his frozen state without knowing he had ever been in it, and the two of them left the ice cave.

But she had come back . . . oh, yes. She had come back again, this time alone.

This time determined to have some answers.

She had gotten them, too. Some of them, anyway, though she was still not entirely sure what the creature of the ice cave called itself. Possibly an Ice Dragon; it was more powerful than any Phoenix or Firebird she had ever encountered, and the only Elemental of the flame aspect of Fire that was more powerful was an avatar of a fire god, or a dragon. In return for subjugating her Power of Air to the Power of Ice, she would be granted a force far more effective than that of Air alone. It didn't matter to Cordelia; she had gotten what she wanted, and near as she could tell, the only thing the entity wanted in return was for more control to be exerted in the world by Ice. Sometimes it was difficult to fathom the motives of Elementals; by definition they didn't think like humans.

But that was not pertinent to the moment; at this juncture, she faced an obstacle in her path, in the form of a child medium and the woman who guarded that child.

The other Masters who had taught her made little or no use of

Revenants and other lingering spirits, either from foolish sentimentality, or the mistaken conviction that they were by-and-large
powerless. And that might well be true of those that had been created of random tragedy, or out of their own will and reluctance to
leave the earth.

But at the promptings of the Elemental in the ice cave, Cordelia
had done some specific and very secret research. She learned it
was not true of those who were created and bound from the beginning . . . and though the power was subtle, it was sure, when
properly guided. Cordelia had been creating such servants for
decades now, a few at a time.

In any time and place, there were always the poor, and in any
given time and place, three-fourths of the poor were children. Now,
setting aside the difficulties inherent in their immaturity, children
were the best and easiest human beings to manipulate, and thus
the best subjects for someone looking for immaterial servants.
They were used to obeying orders without question, they would
believe anything told them with authority, and they were disinclined to rebellion. They were trivially easy to lure away from parents who had little time for them anyway at best, and at worse
were brutish and brutal. Cordelia exploited all of these aspects of
childhood.

First, she found children with a certain amount of Elemental or
psychical power. Then she lured them into the hands of one of her
agents with the promise of food and shelter; using "agents" who
were not much older than the children themselves. Where street
children were wary of adults, they were often inclined to trust one
of their own. With great care and subtlety, she gradually introduced them to herself as the authority figure to which they owed
everything. And when they were accustomed to obeying her orders, even those which seemed odd or even bizarre, she killed
them.

Quietly. Peacefully. So that they were not even aware that they
were dead. A dose of morphia in their evening meal, and then,
cold that enveloped them, stilled their hearts, their breathing, their

lives. Painlessly, without trauma, they "woke" when she called them and went about the business she sent them on, and even when they eventually realized what had happened to them, it took weeks, months, years before they had that revelation. By then, of course, they were used to their situation. In many ways it was an improvement over their old life. They were no longer hungry, cold, or in need, and none of those Cordelia selected were acquainted enough with Christianity or any other religion to have any expectation of a joyful afterlife. Most, in fact, had been told repeatedly that they were destined for hell, and were not in any hurry to proceed on the next leg of that journey. They had each other for company, and in the endless twilight of their new existence, without the powerful and developed personality that an adult would have to hold them together, they gradually faded into passive, obedient wraiths, all looking very much alike.

So they served her. And the few that rebelled, she was able to control despite their willfulness.

And this was what they could do.

They slipped inside the thoughts of the unwary.

They drifted into dreams, whispering whatever message Cordelia wished the victim to hear. They hovered, waiting for the right moment, to murmur Cordelia's words when there was a flash of doubt. They could, and did, haunt individuals tirelessly, relentlessly, feeding them what Cordelia wanted them to think until the victim became convinced that Cordelia's thoughts were his own. Not even Elemental Masters were immune to this, for it was not an attack, and the wraiths drifted in past the shields and protections effortlessly.

So Cordelia had won higher title, then position, then property. So she had won social status in the highest of circles, and amusingly enough, only the fact that she did not want the position, and in fact had worked tirelessly to prevent anyone from offering it, had kept her from being appointed one of the Queen's ladies-in-waiting. Firstly, she found Victoria herself to be a terrible bore, with her obsession with her dead husband and her living children and complete lack of understanding of politics both domestic and international. And secondly, it was an appointment with less than no power. So one child spirit was assigned permanently to the Queen, murmuring that Lady Cordelia was an admirable woman, perfect in all ways . . . that Victoria herself was not really interesting enough to be worthy of Lady Cordelia's friendship . . . that Lady Cordelia already had so many good works in hand that Victoria would be imposing to offer her the position . . . that other honors would certainly be much more appropriate. . . .

There really was only one group standing in the way of Cordelia's ambitions.

Men.

The world was owned and ruled by men. Women were distinctly second-class citizens; cherished pets at best, or chattel at worst. Men maneuvering for positions of power who listened to the advice of women were thought weak. Only the artistic could grant status to women, and the artistic had no power except in their own circles. No matter what she did, no matter how many little whisperers she created, she would never have the position of power she required. Men were particularly resistant to those whispers of self-doubt that were so effective against women.

The day that Cordelia had finally given in to that truth had been one of the few times she had indulged herself in rage. But she had not permitted the rage to last long. Instead, she had gotten down to work, and knowing that she would never have the secular power she craved in her own name, she had set about finding a proper vehicle to be her puppet.

David Alderscroft had not been the first, but he had proven to be the most malleable. Unlike many, he was susceptible to those whispers of negativity, especially when he began his University studies, left the relative isolation of tutors and small private academies, and found himself no longer the leading light of his group.

Once he accepted that, and once he accepted her as his mentor in Magic, he was hers. There had been the small diversion of that girl, but it, and she, were easily dealt with.

Or so Cordelia had thought.

She pursed her lips. Bad enough that there was a true medium in London now who was strong enough to hear her whisperers and free them, but that this child was being guarded by the same person Cordelia had separated from David—that smacked not of coincidence, but of the intervention of something or someone.

"You may go," she told the Ice Wurm, who vanished, taking its mirror with it.

To say this was displeasing was an understatement. But it was by no means a major setback.

Yet.

Patience. That was the byword here, patience and vigilance. She would have to make sure that her control over her whisperers was absolute, and make certain the child in Isabelle's custody never got the opportunity to spot one of them. She would also have to investigate Isabelle Harton and her school, looking more thoroughly for chinks in the armor, weaknesses to be exploited, ways to bring the school into disrepute, perhaps.

Or put them on ground of Cordelia's choosing. It would be enough merely to drive the school and the woman into the countryside, for instance. Or perhaps not even "drive"—perhaps, if she could manipulate matters, the offer of a suitable building would suffice. A building of Cordelia's selection, of course, and one in which any number of accidents could happen should it become necessary to try and kill the child again. But the main thing was to be patient and enterprising—and no more use of intermediaries. That mad Irish anarchist Earth Master had managed to get himself shot by the police only just in time to keep the others from tracing him back to Cordelia.

The first step: investigation, this time as thorough and as exacting as even the fictional Sherlock Holmes would appreciate. That was one thing she had truly learned back there that day on the ice: there was never enough time to rush into something, because the amount of effort you would spend undoing hasty mistakes would more than exceed the time you spent doing things carefully. Thus was the path of the glacier: slow, relentless, unstoppable.

She left the room to itself, closed the hidden door behind her, and set her mind on that path.

7

NAN and Neville held themselves very still in the darkness of the closet. This was no time for the adults to discover her listening post. Neville did not so much as flick a feather.

Memsa'b was pacing, and Memsa'b never paced; Nan recognized the quick light sounds of her footsteps going up and down, up and down the room. Sahib was not pacing, but Memsa'b was restless enough for both of them.

And Memsa'b was not at all happy. The mysterious friends of hers who were going to find out who had lured Nan and Sarah into the clutches of that horrible haunt had found out the "who"—but not the "why." And as for the "who," well, he was, in Nan's cynical mind, all too conveniently dead. In Nan's world, when you wanted to make sure no one spilled a secret, you made him a "grave" man.

"There are more things left unanswered than answered," she complained, an edge of anger to her voice. "Why would an Irish anarchist who had only been in London for two months set a trap to harm or kill two obscure British children?"

That was a very good question. The only Irish Nan knew were not the sort to use a haunt to get revenge when a boot to the head was so much more immediate and satisfying. And she rather doubted Sarah knew any Irishmen at all.

"The workings of a damaged mind?" asked Karamjit, doubtfully. Memsa'b tsk'ed.

"And he came to learn of them, how?" replied Agansing. "An Elemental Master was he, not in psychical circles. And why? This makes no sense, even for a madman. Madmen follow their own logic, it is true, but it *is* logic. The children could have been of no threat, no rivalry to him, no real interest. He could have made no use of them, and their harm would not help him in any way."

"He was working for someone else, obviously," replied Sahib. "Someone who does see one or both of the girls as a potential threat, now or in the future. We'll never know who, now. And having gotten their immediate answer, the Masters are disinclined to look further into the matter. Sometimes, my dove, these people make me very annoyed."

Memsa'b sighed. "Trying to get them to work together is, as Bea says, like trying to herd cats. Not that our kind is very much easier, but at least we are a bit more inclined to gather in groups than they are, and to think on the larger scale than personal rivalry and alliance. I wish David Alderscroft joy of them."

"Hmm. One hears that he has succeeded in reviving a Master's Circle from the days of Mad King George," said Agansing. "With some success, if rumors I have heard are true. He and his followers have laid some troublesome things to rest."

Memsa'b sniffed. "It is a men's club in fancy dress," she said dismissively. "It is even headquartered *in* his club. They admit no women, thus halving their available resources, and few commoners, thus further depriving themselves of power. And they admit none who are not white British at all. If I were to revive a Master's Circle I would do so in the country, where one could find Earth Masters, and I would scour the countryside for Masters and Mages of both sexes. While I was at it, I would see to it that foreigners were welcome, because there is foreign magic in England now, like it or not, and it would be much wiser to have the weapons to counter the misuse of it in hand before there is need for them. *That would be effective.* And it's not to the point, except insofar as it was the Master's Circle who discovered who was responsible, but only *after* Bea's husband confined the Earth Creature for them."

Nan made notes in her head. *Master's Circle. David Alderscroft.* Memsa'b might dismiss both, but at least they had found out something. That counted as a partial success at least, which was more than Sahib and Memsa'b had. Nan got a feeling there was something about this Alderscroft fellow that Memsa'b didn't like—

The moment she thought that, from his perch on her shoulder, Neville rubbed his big, warm beak against her cheek to get her attention. She closed her eyes and consciously relaxed.

The image she got from him was set in bird terms, of course, and seemed to be a mate squabble, two females competing over the same male. Ravens were monogamous, keeping to one mate their whole life barring accident, so such things were comprehensible to a raven. Neville was much better at picking up feelings and the images called up by those feelings, than Nan was. And now, with much practice, he was better at projecting them to Nan.

So Memsa'b and some other skirt got into it over this Alderscroft . . . Another quick rub of Neville's beak, and the impression that the winning rival was much older than the younger "bird" confirmed that. *Must've been way before Memsa'b went to Indja, an' met Sahib. Cor. That 'splains a lot.* No young woman in Nan's circle was ever graceful in romantic defeat.

Well, now, that was interesting. So Memsa'b was probably going to dismiss this Alderscroft fellow right out of hand, which in Nan's estimation was a mistake. All the signs were pointing at an Elemental Master being the one who wanted Sarah gone. It just made sense to go to the Elemental Masters about it, preferably the fellow on top—but it appeared that the fellow on top was someone Memsa'b wanted to see only the back of.

"We have, thanks to your lady friends, protection against all four Elemental magics on the girls, and on the school," Sahib pointed out. "Nothing is going to get past those without at least giving up some warning."

"Which still leaves perfectly ordinary attacks as a possibility, leaving aside the fact that my friends are not the most power Elemental Masters in London," she replied, with a stubborn tone to her voice. "I am not convinced that this is over by any means."

"Nor I," Selim put in, as Nan kept her breathing as still as she could in order to catch every word. "I am far more convinced there is something about young Sarah's powers that is a threat to someone in this city. I do not anticipate that unknown person would lightly give up his attempt to rid himself of that threat."

"I agree with Selim," said Karamjit firmly.

Me, too! thought Nan.

"Time—" began Agansing.

"Are you willing to wait to see what time will bring, when realistically speaking, it could bring a threat from an unexpected quarter?" Memsa'b demanded. Nan could picture her whirling and fixing Agansing with a gimlet stare.

"But running off blindly serves no purpose either." Agansing was silent for a moment. "The wise warrior examines all possibilities. We have a possibility before us. And we have many possible responses to it. We can hunt down the one who is responsible and confront him. We could ignore this, and hope that the threat will fade or go away. We could move the school. Once removed from London, perhaps the unknown assailant will conclude the children are no longer a threat."

"Retreat?" Karamjit sounded aghast. "Never!"

"If we were all warriors here—but we are not. These are children," Selim said reluctantly. "They can hardly defend themselves, and they are not old enough to be required to do so."

"Moving from our stronghold into unknown territory would be a grave error," Karamjit growled. "We have a fortified home here. It will take very long before a new place is as well suited."

"Moving at all is out of the question," Memsa'b replied flatly. "In the first place, all of our available monies are sunk into this building and its grounds. And in the second, even if someone were to offer us as good or better a place elsewhere, we haven't the money to make such a move. There are resources we can draw on to help educate the children that we cannot find elsewhere. And in the third place, although this is a relatively trivial concern, outside of London there are no places where most of the foodstuffs you all favor can be easily obtained."

"Ah," said Selim. There was a note to his voice that made Nan smile. *Trust a feller to think of his stomach,* she thought wryly. *An' trust Memsa'b t' think he'd think of it.*

Nan distinctly heard Sahib stifle a chuckle, so she wasn't the only one with that particular thought.

"I see no reason to leave permanently," Sahib said firmly. "However, an interesting offer has come my way, by way of a holiday for the school. The gentleman who actually owned that cursed property wishes to offer the use of his country home near Windsor to the school for a summer retreat. It seems, my dear, that you know him peripherally as he is in some of the saner occult circles. He is going to France for next month. It is not that far from London, but the property includes a small home farm as well as a pond and plenty of parkland to romp in. He feels very much responsible for what happened, and wishes to make some sort of amends." He paused. "This would remove the children from London and potential harm temporarily, and perhaps that would be enough. If the perpetrator sees the school standing empty, he might believe we had gone."

"Only a month, you say?" Memsa'b replied dubiously, as Nan held her breath. She had never been outside of London in her life. And London in June could be stiflingly hot. The country was something she had only read about; the wildest place she had ever been were the overgrown parts of the school garden.

"Possibly more, if the situation works to everyone's advantage; a summer holiday would be good for all concerned. Everything needed could be brought down in a couple of cartloads," Sahib said coaxingly. "It would be very good for the children. No lessons, fresh air, country food. Think how they would blossom."

"And let them run wild for a month?" Memsa'b countered. "In someone else's home? I am not sure I would care to take responsibility for that."

"There's a nursery," Sahib replied. "A proper nursery, big enough to hold all the infants and toddlers twice over. The place is a vast barn, from what he tells me. He has autumn shooting parties for up to fifty there, but there's no fishing, no adult amusements, and he's a bachelor. Outside of hunting season and some lazing about in summer, he never uses the place. He says it would be a good thing for the house and the servants to have someone there to look after over the summer."

A house that big an' 'e never uses it? Cor! Nan thought with raw envy. *Must be nice to be rich!*

Strange how her vision of "rich" had changed. Not that long ago, she had thought Memsa'b and Sahib were "rich"—and of course, by the standards of poverty in Whitechapel, they were. But now she was privy to the economies of running a school, the compromises Memsa'b had to make, had seen both Memsa'b and Sahib consulting over the bills and working out what could and could not be done. Nothing here was ever wasted, not a stitch of fabric, not a bit of space, not a scrap of food. It might be given away in charity, but it was never wasted.

"And how would his servants feel about an army of children descending?" Memsa'b countered. "I have no wish to suffer the vagaries of a staff full of resentful servants, and neither will our own people. And as to our own people, I also do not wish to subject them to the rudeness and prejudice of those who are not prepared to welcome them as equals and superiors."

"He says he believes there will be no problem." Sahib paused. "But I see your point. Let me explore this further; I'll even visit the place with Selim and we will sound out the servants. But if there is no problem?"

Memsa'b sighed. It sounded reluctant. "Then I agree, it would be a good idea. But there will be *half* holidays only. I do not want the children to get out of the habit of the discipline of lessons."

❄

It took every bit of "discipline" in Nan's body to keep quiet about the promised treat. For one thing, she didn't want to disappoint anyone if it turned out not to come to pass. She'd had far too many disappointments of her own, things her mother promised in the euphoria of gin that never happened, or promises that sounded enticing that turned out to be traps set by unscrupulous adults eager to take advantage of a child. For another, if she revealed it, they'd *know* she had a listening post, and then there would go the source of information.

So she kept her lips firmly shut, and went on with life as usual. Not that it was unpleasant! Far from it. There were a great many "school treats" in these summer months, as she came to learn. There were trips by omnibus to the zoo, to the many parks, to the British Museum. There were Sunday School treats for parish children, not only for churches in *their* parish, but for others nearby, that Memsa'b, with her clever ways, managed to get them all invited to. Sahib somehow contrived a boat ride on two canal barges, one going upriver, and another back down for the return trip, that took them through Camden Lock; a fascinating thing for Nan and even more fascinating for the boys.

Many of these occasions involved ice creams, a treat Nan had never before encountered, which left her wondering what possible reward could be in heaven if Earth was able to provide ice creams.

Well . . . perhaps if heaven included ice creams for breakfast, luncheon, tea, and dinner. . . .

Neville and Grey came along on these excursions, of course. One of the problems of taking Grey had been completely negated by the presence of Neville; there was not a bird in the sky that would dream of attacking Grey with the enormous raven flying escort, nor was anyone likely to try stealing the parrot with Neville flashing a wicked eye and nasty beak nearby. Only once was there any trouble, when a bully of a lad at Hyde Park tried to make a grab at Grey. Neville dove down out of a nearby tree and made a slashing stab at his clutching hand, coming so close to actually connecting that neither the boy's governess nor the now-hysterical boy himself could be convinced he hadn't until the intact fingers were displayed for the policeman who intervened. By then, Neville had wisely taken himself back up into the tree again, so there was nothing to prove that the raven even belonged to anyone in the school party but hearsay witnesses.

"Sounds to me like you been aggravatin' all the birds hereabouts," the bobby said, having had just about enough of both boy and governess by then. "If I was you, I'd go hop over to the Museum. Birds are all stuffed there. You can't aggravate 'em, they can't harm you."

While Nan hadn't completely forgotten the conversation, she had just about convinced herself that the summer could hold no better joys than this continuing series of excursions, when one night, Memsa'b called for silence just before dinner was served.

Since these wildly infrequent occasions always meant some grand surprise—she always saved bad news for morning assembly—she got instant quiet.

"A very kind gentleman has offered the school the use of his country home for the month of June," she said, and quelled the uprising before it started with a single look. "There will be rules; this is *not* our home, and we will take as much care of the things in it as we would the things in the museum, Tommy."

Tommy, who had very nearly caused an incident over his desire to drop into an enormous jar at the British Museum and leap out again, like the thieves in Ali Baba, hung his head. Nan stifled a grin.

"You will treat his servants with respect, as you treat your teachers and my helpers here at the school," she continued. "You will obey them when they ask you to do something or refrain from doing something, you will refer to them as 'Miss,' 'Mrs.' and 'Mr.' and you will not play the Little Sahib and Missy Sahib with them. If you are good, there will be half holidays in the week, and Saturday and Sunday will be full holidays. If you are not, we will pack up and return here."

The silence remained unbroken, but the children exchanged looks of delight. Even Grey mantled her wings and pinned her eyes, though Neville contrived to look bored.

"Tomorrow will be free of lessons as you pack up your belongings for the month," Memsa'b continued. "And the day after tomorrow, we will all take the train to Highleigh Court."

Only now did she smile, as whispers began. She said nothing more, though, merely sat down as the signal for serving to begin. All the children ate together except for the few in the nursery, at four big tables arranged down the dining room. One teacher sat at each table, while Memsa'b, Sahib, and the other teachers sat at a fifth table.

Sarah leveled grave eyes on her friend. "You knew about this, didn't you?" she whispered, as she passed the bowl of boiled carrots to Nan, who served herself and passed it to Amanda Truitt. Sarah handed a piece of carrot to Grey, who took it and held it in one claw while taking neat bites out of it.

Nan nodded, just a little. Sarah smiled. "It's all right," she continued. "I know why you didn't tell."

Of course she did; she had listened in that same closet herself, more than once. But Nan was relieved that she didn't take it amiss.

It was hard to sleep that night, knowing that the treat really was in store. Nan expected she would be quite busy the next day, not with her own packing, but with helping to pack up the little ones' things. It wasn't as if she had much of her own, after all.

But at midmorning she got a surprise, as Memsa'b took her away from folding little pinafores and pressing small shirtwaists, to go back to her own room where Sarah was packing. There was an enormous stack of clothing on her bed.

"I have several friends with little girls a bit older than your age, Nan," Memsa'b said without preamble. "So I canvassed them for outgrown clothing for the summer. Some of it won't fit, of course, and some will be unsuitable, but we should find some things in these piles that will do. So let's begin trying them on you."

Some of the clothing made Nan blink. She could not ever imagine herself in a dress so covered with frills she thought she looked like a right Guy in it, nor in the item of embroidery and lace so delicate she was afraid to touch it, lest her rough hands snag on it. But a fair amount fit her reasonably well, and was tough enough to survive her, for when Nan played, she played hard, and with the determination of someone who had the fear she might never be allowed to play again. She played cricket with the boys as often as dolls with the girls. When they were through, Nan had a wardrobe only a little less extensive than Sarah's.

After she had packed up these new things, she returned to help with the littlest ones, and the next day, when they all filed out to take the omnibus to the train station, with a cart to follow with all of their luggage, it was with startlement that she realized she had just as much as anyone else.

Neville had something new as well, a fine new round cage to travel in with a handle on top, as did Grey. Both cages had cloth covers over them, more to prevent the curious from looking in and poking at them, than to prevent the birds from doing anything or seeing things that might affright them, as there wasn't much that would frighten either of them. Grey settled onto her perch with a sigh of resignation, but Neville grumbled.

"They won't let y' on the train loose, Neville," Nan explained to him with patience. "Look! Grey knows, and she's bein' good!"

Grey gave Neville the same look Memsa'b gave naughty boys. Neville bristled for a moment with resentment, then shook himself, hopped onto the perch, and muttered once more as Nan closed the cage door and dropped the cover over the top.

The omnibus ride to the station was uneventful except for the excitement of the children. Sahib had closed the warehouse for an hour or two and brought his workers down to help with the luggage at the station. He and Selim would remain living at the school with two of the servants to tend to them and keep the school up; he would only be coming down on the weekends. Seven pushcarts heaped with luggage were all duly checked in and tagged with their destination, and the children all filed into

the bright red railway carriages practically vibrating with anticipation. The birds, of course, came in the carriage; one conductor looked as if he might demand that they ride with the
luggage, but a gimlet stare delivered by Memsa'b made him
change his mind.

The seats right next to the windows were the most desired, but
no one disputed the right of the girls and their birds to have two
of them. Sitting across from one another on the high-backed
wooden benches, with the cages held on their laps, Nan and Sarah
pulled up the covers on the window side of the round brass cages
so that the birds could see out.

The train pulled out of the station with a metallic shriek of
wheels, the final warning hoot of the whistle, and a lurch. It
quickly picked up speed to the point where Nan was a bit uneasy . . . she had never traveled this fast before. She hadn't known
you could. She wasn't entirely sure you ought to. She had to keep
glancing at Memsa'b, sitting beside Sarah, calmly reading a book,
to reassure herself that it was all right.

The city gave way to the suburbs, houses each with its own
patch of green lawn, set apart from its neighbors rather than
crowded so closely together that the walls almost touched, or actually did touch. And then, out of the suburbs they burst, into
green space that Nan immediately and automatically identified as
"park," except that it went on as far as the eye could see, it was
somewhat overgrown, divided by fences, walls, and hedges, and—
and there were animals in it. Herds of sheep, of placid cows, even
of goats. All of them browsing, or occasionally raising their heads
to watch the train pass.

Nan was beside herself; this was the first time she had ever seen
a cow, a sheep, or a live goat. Until this moment, they had only
been images in a picture book. She was surprised at how big the
cows were, and when she saw the woolly sheep with their half-
grown lambs frisking alongside, her fingers itched to touch them.
Horses, of course, were everywhere in the city and she knew
horses quite well, but it was the first time she had ever seen a foal,

and the lively awkward creatures made her exclaim and forget her fear of how fast they were going.

Grey was excited and interested; atypically, she said nothing in *words,* instead, "commenting" on the passing scenery with little mutters, whistles, and clicks. Sarah, too, kept her attention riveted on the landscape, which surprised Nan, considering how far her friend had traveled, until Sarah said, in a surprised voice, "This is nothing like Africa—"

"It ain—isn't?" Nan replied.

Sarah shook her head. "The trees are different; the leaves are smaller, the trees aren't as tall or as green. There are big vines with huge leaves everywhere in the jungle. The bushes are different, too. Even the cattle are different; the cattle in Africa are leaner, with longer horns. We don't have sheep. The goats are the same, though."

Grey whistled.

Neville yawned, doing his best to look blasé. Nan laughed.

"Nothing flusters his feathers," Sarah said fondly. "You'd think he journeyed by train every day."

"Well, he has done just about everything else," Nan replied reflectively. "An' it's not as if he don't know what countryside looks like. Reckon he's flown out to look at it a time or two."

All four of them continued to watch the landscape fly past with great interest. Nan wondered fleetingly what a longer trip would be like; they were due to arrive, so Memsa'b said, before noon, and would be at Highleigh Park by that hour at the latest. Did you eat on the train? She supposed you could sleep on it, the seat was more comfortable than many other places she had slept. But what did you do about a loo? Did the train stop so that everyone could traipse out, use one, and come back aboard?

This was not a "special," and it made several stops along the way. The little towns and villages surrounding the railway station were picture-book perfect, so far as Nan could tell; so perfect it was hard to believe people actually lived in them. She wondered what life would be like in one, so small that everyone knew everyone else, and all about everyone else's business, too.

Finally, at just about the point where she was beginning to wish she could get up and move about, the conductor announced their village. "Maidenstone Bridge. Maidenstone Bridge!" And to Neville's disgust, Nan dropped the cover over him again and prepared to leap to her feet to get out, for she had a sudden panicked image of herself *not* managing to disembark before the train pulled out of the station, and the train leaving with her trapped on it.

She needn't have worried. The train remained in the station for a good long while after they all poured out and their luggage was sorted out and piled, once again, on pushcarts. But as Nan surveyed the quiet village street, without seeing a sign of an omnibus, she had another feeling of repressed panic. Now what? Were they supposed to walk to this place pushing the handcarts before them?

That was when the first of the wagons came around the corner.

There was a veritable parade of them, big commodious farm wagons, and when the first driver hailed Memsa'b, it became clear the carts had come for them. One came with an empty bed for the luggage, and the rest had been padded with a thick layer of hay for the children to sit on. With the wagons came a set of burly farm workers, smelling of tobacco, horse, and hay, who tossed the children up into the back of the wagons as if they weighed nothing. When they came to Nan and Sarah, they lifted each of them, cage and all, over the back of the wagon to settle at the rear. A more dignified charabanc had been provided for Memsa'b, the teachers and some of the servants, though the ayahs were happy enough to be helped in alongside their small charges in a third wagon just for the little ones.

Wisely, the farmers had separated the boys and the girls into separate wagons. They boys were able to tumble about in the hay and roughhouse as much as they pleased without getting into too much trouble over it.

In Nan's opinion, they were missing the best part of the journey with their skylarking. There was so much to look at, she felt as if her whole body was filling up with new sights. It was all like something out of one of her books; all those things that had been described in words now suddenly had *things* attached to them. The lane they traveled down, with thick hedgerows on either side, was nothing like the thoroughfare called a "lane" in London, and now she understood, really, how one could get tangled in a hedgerow and be unable to get through it. When they traveled down a part of the lane where the trees formed a dense green archway above it, so it was as if they were traveling in a long, living tunnel, she was practically beside herself with pleasure as she recalled just such a description in another book. The horses' hooves had a different sound on the soft dirt of the road than they did on the paved streets of London, and the scents! She had never smelled so many wonderful things! Flowers, and new-cut hay, a fresh green scent of water utterly unlike the smelly old Thames, wood smoke and things she couldn't even begin to identify. Birds sang and twittered everywhere, the hedges were alive with little birds, and there were rooks twanging in trees everywhere. Even Neville forgot to look bored.

And then, they found themselves passing beside a wall, a very tall cream-colored brick wall topped with an edge of white stone, exactly like the one around the school, except this went on for a very long distance. It was covered in ivy, and craning her neck, Nan saw a gate in the wall, a gate made of wrought iron like the one at the school. The charabanc ahead of them turned and went into the gate, as a man stood there holding the gate open. Right inside the gate there was a house of black timbers and white plaster with a thatched roof, and at first Nan was horribly disappointed, wondering how all of them were supposed to fit into that house, because it didn't look as if it had more than two or three bedrooms at best—

But the charabanc and then the wagons kept going, and that was when the word "gatehouse" connected in her mind with the house at the gate, and she stared at it in awe, realizing that here was a house *just* for a man and his family to live in so he could *tend the gate*. And that was *all* he did!

The cavalcade continued on up a twisting lane that led through wooded and meadowed land that looked exactly as well groomed as a park, and then turned a corner—

And there it was, and Nan blinked in surprise and even shock at the place that would be their home for the next month.

It was a chaotic, glorious pile of a place, a mishmash of styles and eras, and if Nan could no more have named those styles and eras, she could certainly tell that the blocky stone tower with its slitlike windows that anchored the left was nothing like the mathematical center of more cream-colored brick and tall, narrow windows, which was in turn, nothing at all like the florid wing thrown up on the right. The only unifying force was that except for the square tower, it was all built of the same mellow cream-colored brick of the wall, and that was all.

And it was *enormous*. Easily three times the size of the school.

Nan looked around her, and so did the rest of the children, eyes as wide as they could stretch—at manicured parkland that could easily hold three Hyde Parks and then some—at the huge pile of a building, that promised endless opportunities for exploration—at the glimpse of gardens in the rear, and beyond that, a hint of water. And for the first time they all understood that all of this was, within reason, *theirs* for the month, to run in, play in, explore, hide, make up stories in and act them out—

And it was Nan who summed up all their feelings in a single word.

A word which burst out of her like a cannonball out of a gun.

"Cor!" she shouted in glee.

Memsa'b, being handed down out of the charabanc, merely looked up and smiled.

8

MUCH as he admired and depended upon Lady Cordelia, there was some relief for David Alderscroft in being in a place to which she could not go. Here in his club, surrounded by men and the things of men, with not even a hint of women about (the few maidservants kept themselves discreetly out of sight as best they could), there was a sense that one could let down one's guard and relax.

Not that Cordelia was like most women, but still . . . here, one didn't have to be so terribly careful of manners and speech, and if one made a faux pas, a man would simply wave it off, where a woman would stew about it for hours. Women were grand ornaments to life, but even the best of them forgot that a man needed to be a man among men on a regular basis.

Small wonder that many men all but lived at their clubs even when they did not have rooms there. Even working men knew the pressure of too-attentive female companionship, and had their pubs and their coffeehouses. He never felt quite so comfortable as when he was at the club, with women restricted to the Visitors' Parlor and Visitors' Dining Room—and if there were females in a

resident member's rooms, well, that was his business and had
nothing to do with the rest of the members. One could have sisters
and a mother, after all. And aunts. And if they were deuced attractive sisters and aunts, who might or might not have careers on
the stage, well, such things happened. So long as they did not in-
trude on anyone else, it was none of his business. Here, not only
were the members incurious about who came in and out, so long
as it was discreet, they were incurious about what came in and out,
and a phenomenal number of them were Elemental Mages, occultists, or had had brushes with the uncanny. Here, they knew
how to keep secret and silent when odd things happened. And here
he had chosen to make the headquarters of his new incarnation of
a much older Elemental Masters' Master's Circle.

The Master's Circle, or White Lodge, was an ancient magical
tradition, created for the purpose of self-policing one's own kind,
as it were. Originally intended to hunt down and destroy the enemies of the members, it had evolved to the more civilized function
of ensuring that no Elemental Master within its jurisdiction attacked another, or attacked those not blessed with magic.

It had been at its most active during the Regency, when the no-
torious Hellfire Club (which actually had very little in the way of
true Magical power) and those modeled after it (some of which
did) had flourished. Since that time, it had declined to little more
than a social group that occasionally did some investigative and
disciplinary work. One of the most recent had been the ill-fated,
though ultimately successful, attempt to track down and bring to
heel a wayward Fire Master—the attempt that had cost David's
own father so much. It had been David's idea, not Cordelia's, to re-
vitalize the lodge and make it more effective. In this, he flattered
himself, he had been quite successful—enough so that he heard
that he was being called the "Wizard of London" now.

Truth to tell, Cordelia did not much like the Circle. He suspected that she resented the fact that she was not permitted inside
the club and had not been invited to join, but really, a woman had
no real place in a Master's Circle—

Well, *most* women. There were a few, a very few, who like the few neck-or-nothing riders in his Hunt Club, could keep up in terms of energy and sheer instinct for the kill with the best of the men, but they were rare indeed. He could not imagine Lady Cordelia in such a position, with her cool, calm demeanor and immaculate manners. She would regard much of what the Circle did with distaste, as "dirtying her hands." For heaven's sake, he couldn't even imagine her on the back of a horse in hunting dress, much less traipsing across the countryside in search of a rogue magician!

So he ignored her obvious disdain for the work of the Circle, as he ignored nothing else she said or did, and went early to the meetings of the Circle so he could enjoy the masculine ambience of the club before he picked up his arcane duties.

This particular Master's Circle had been the one to which his father had belonged, and it had been when his father had been unable to muster an adequate hunting party and had been injured that had made David take notice. He had decided then that the situation simply would not do, and began rectifying it.

Now it was a matter of sending a few messages across the city to muster a full-strength hunting party within the hour, and within three, a Circle of Initiates could be assembled.

There were, in fact, enough Mages and Masters in the group to gather a Circle Trine if the need arose, and *that* had not been the case since the Circle had first been formed. Possibly the fact that the Circle had been moved to London, where most of the members at least had town homes, had made the difference. Perhaps it was because in London there simply were so many people it was not at all difficult to find enough Mages. Perhaps it was because it was in a men's club; it was easy to give the wife the excuse that one was going to one's club in order to slip out. Granted, Mages usually married Mages, but women with the Talent were still women, and inclined to favor commitments to dinner parties over commitments to the Master's Circle—and were equally inclined to be both far too curious and far too suspicious when a gentleman had to be evasive about where he was going and what he was doing.

Nor could they manage to keep the secrets secret.

But a man could say, "I'm going to the club," and a woman would nod and think nothing more of it.

And perhaps that was the main reason for the success of the Master's Circle. A man could come here, do the Work of the Circle, and return home late, and the spouse would ask why so late a return, and a man could say "Oh, Lytton went off on one of his shooting stories and we lost all track of time," or "A billiard game turned into a match, you know how it is," and if there were no signs of inebriation or the presence of floozies, there would be no further questions.

Yes, that might be the best reason for success of all.

Tonight would be routine, a follow-up meeting of the key members of the Circle to find out the disposition of a little problem Nigel Lytton had reported, a matter of an Elemental Magician gone wrong in London itself. It was fairly trivial as such things went, and a preliminary report had stated that the miscreant in question had already passed the jurisdiction of mortal justice, but Alderscroft liked to have things properly neatened up in the wake of the resolution of any situation.

And besides, it was as good an excuse as any to take supper here.

Although his cook—his chef, rather—was good, he was also French, and it was a secondary relief to enjoy simple English fare once in a while as well. It had occurred to David, and more than once, that perhaps he ought to sell or close up his town home, take up residence here, and a great many aspects of his life would be improved. There would be no more servants' crises, for instance; those details were taken care of invisibly by the club staff. Normally such things were handled with equal invisibility by one's wife or mother, but David had neither, and had to deal with staff upheavals himself.

But no, Cordelia would not be able to go past the Visitors' Parlor room, which would mean that to get further lessons from her, he would have to come to her home, and something about that made him feel rebellious. Silly, perhaps, but nevertheless such a feeling would be counterproductive to actually learning anything.

He took the steps of the club briskly and nodded to Stewart, the doorman, as that worthy held the portal open for him. The familiar and comforting aroma of tobacco and brandy, books, and newspaper struck him as he entered, and he headed straight for the Members' Dining Room without a pause. The savory scent of good roast beef met his nose as he entered, which cemented what his selection would be in his mind before he even sat down.

Scotch broth, to begin, and oysters, then roast beef and potatoes, Yorkshire pudding, new peas, and an apple tart . . . wonderful. He savored his brandy and a cigar afterward, and wondered why his expensive chef could not understand that plain food was just as good as, if not superior to, the fancy sauces of French cooking. And it made him think, fleetingly, of their good old cook, back at the manor, who had made it very clear that she would *not* be moving to London.

But no. The disadvantages of life there so far outweighed the advantages that there was no comparison. He was not, and never had been, the sort to enjoy country life. Nor was Cordelia, really. Now Isabelle—

With a faint oath, he forced the thought of Isabelle from his mind. What was wrong with him anyway? Time and time again, he found himself thinking of the silly girl, someone he had given no thought to whatsoever for years!

It was enough to put him right off enjoying his brandy and cigar, and with irritation he extinguished the latter and left the table to go up to the top floor of the club, where the rooms reserved for the Master's Circle were located.

The top floor was called the Founder's Suite, and had once been the residence of the founder of the club who had himself been an Elemental Master. It had been vacant for years; no one had the temerity to consider taking over the space that had once housed so formidable a personality. But a good half the space was taken up by a Meeting Room and a Working Room, and when David had brought the Master's Circle to his club, it had been with the idea in mind of using these rooms.

That Founding Member in question had been an Air Master, and the light blues and whites with which the area was decorated had not fared well over the years. By the time he got permission to use the rooms, the whites had yellowed and the blues gone to muddy blue-gray. The net effect was of ingrained grime. At his own expense, David had arranged for it all to be redone in Turkey red, ocher, and other colors he found comfortable. No one seemed to object, though he suspected one or two of the others found it amusing that the place was clearly a haven for a Fire Master. But he consoled himself with the knowledge that the colors were practical, unlike lighter tones that honestly would not survive a winter of soot and pea soupers.

There should be no work tonight, so he went straight to the Meeting Room. Deliberately, with the vague idea that King Arthur's Round Table was a good idea to establish equality among peers, there was no "head" or "foot" to the square table in the middle of the room, and no difference in the quite comfortable chairs. As he had requested, the gaslights had already been lit; he brought in a newspaper and settled down to read it until the rest arrived.

It would not be a full meeting tonight by any stretch of the imagination, so as the others trickled in, they all clustered at the end of the table where he was. When they were all assembled, he rang for the servant, who brought the decanters of port and brandy and glasses, and left. As was their custom, they served themselves; the brandy had been supplied by David from his father's private stock, the port by Atherton Crey. Both liquors were over a hundred years old. The pouring of the drink signaled the start of business.

"So, Nigel," David said, cradling his snifter in his left hand to warm the contents and release the aroma. "Give us the full report on that anarchist incident."

Nigel, Lord Lytton, was an Earth Master, and as such acutely uncomfortable in London, where so much of the soil was covered over, poisoned, or both. He always looked half-choked whenever he came into town, and today was no exception. His long, solemn face looked even longer than usual, and was certainly several shades paler than it ought to be. "If you don't mind, I'll begin this where I think it ought to start, and not with that rogue Talent, Connor O'Brian," he said, passing his hand over his thinning, nondescript brown hair. "And that is with a little girl. Two of them actually, since they seem to be inseparable, but the one that concerns us is already a powerful medium, and she's barely ten."

David, who knew some of this already, merely nodded, but the others looked variously surprised or impressed, depending on their natures.

"There's a lady and her husband who have a school for the Gifted children of expatriates mostly posted in India," Nigel continued. "Not all the children are Gifted, of course, but this is where they're sent if their parents know of the place. Harton School. Isabelle and Frederick Harton; she met him in India, where they picked up some more Gifted servants from among the natives there. My wife knows the woman; old school friend of hers that went off to India once her school days were over."

The name "Isabelle" had struck David Alderscroft with the force of a blow, and to hear that the woman was a school friend of Nigel's wife only made it worse. To sit there and listen to a description of a woman that he was more convinced with every word was "his" Isabelle took all his strength of will. It took a great deal of effort to wrench himself out of his numb shock to listen, even with half an ear, as Nigel explained how the little girls had been lured to the building in question and shut in, while an Earth Wight specially conjured and bound to an existing spirit that already haunted the place there was loosed on them. He wasn't the least interested in two little girls, no matter what their plight had been—

He managed to get his attention back on the subject as Nigel described capturing the creature, then interrogating it as to who had brought it there, then banishing it. It was a strong Elemental; it had taken Nigel and three friends to do the job.

"It didn't know the Master's real name, of course, but what it knew led us to O'Brian who was, by that time, dead," Nigel concluded. "The problem with all of this is that those little girls, *obscure* little girls, with no enemies, were without any shadow of a doubt, the real targets of the attack. Alderscroft, that makes no sense. Killing them would accomplish nothing, get no notoriety for his cause. Unless—"

"Unless what?" asked Crey.

"Unless he—or someone using him—wanted to be rid of that specific little girl." Nigel pinched the bridge of his nose, probably to relieve a headache. "That she is already a powerful medium could make her dangerous to someone."

"Who?" demanded old Scathwaite—old in years and experience, but keen in mind and as agile in body as some of David's contemporaries.

"I would say, ask that of those in psychical circles," David said slowly, slowly getting control back over his runaway emotions. "Especially those who claim mediumistic powers and have none. They have the most to lose, and are the most threatened by a real medium. And if you wanted to hide what you were in order to prevent being caught by your own kind, what better than to hide behind an Elemental Master?"

"By heaven, David, you may be right!" Nigel sounded surprised and relieved at the same time. "It's the psychical ones who knew about the girl in the first place. All right, I'll go back to Mrs. Harton and suggest that if she hasn't checked her friends and acquaintances for someone willing to use anyone and anything to further his own ambitions, she ought to. Then see if any of *them* can be traced back to a contact with O'Brian."

"The simplest solution is often the right one," David replied, and shrugged. "Of course the simplest solution is usually something not very palatable."

He had managed, by dint of great effort, to shove his emotional reactions off to the side, and cool masculine logic had reasserted itself.

"The point is, *our* involvement in this distasteful incident is fundamentally closed," agreed Thomas Markham, a viscount. "It seems clear to me at least that it is wildly unlikely that the instigator is one of ours. The Harton woman should definitely be encouraged to look among her own kind for the enemy. Heaven knows there are more than enough unstable types in psychical circles to account for an attack on those poor little children."

"And Bea has made sure that the children and school are protected from all sorts," Nigel put in eagerly—no doubt thinking with relief that now he would be able to go back to his country estate and escape the miasma of London again. "I think everything has probably been done now."

Nods all around the table. David smiled. "Good!" he said. "Now, I would like to discuss some of our tentative plans for becoming more involved with those in political office who are at the moment unaware we even exist . . . ."

✳

Nan had decided that if heaven was anything like Highleigh Park, she was going to have to put a lot more effort into being good so she could end up there.

There had been some initial reserve on the part of the servants about a horde of strange children running loose; not that Nan blamed them, no, not at all. They all got rooms in the area that held the nursery, which also held the rooms for the servants of visiting guests.

That was not at all bad; the rooms were plain and they had to share, but the rooms at the school were also fairly plain and they had to share. The littlest children, too young for lessons yet, got the best of it, Nan thought, because the nursery and schoolroom were both enormous, and the nursery was full of old, worn, but perfectly good toys from previous generations or left by visiting children. All the toys were new to the Harton School toddlers, of course, so they were very happy.

The first of the children to get into trouble was, predictably,

Tommy, who seemed to gravitate toward trouble the way a moth was attracted to flame. They had all had their luncheon and most of them had gone off in little groups to explore the parkland, except for Tommy, who had gone off by himself.

Nan and Sarah were—with Grey and Neville's assistance—investigating a charming but neglected little stone building, when suddenly there was a great crash from the direction of the manor house, followed by a veritable chorus of barks and howls. Sarah and Nan exchanged a glance.

"Tommy," they said as one, as Grey and Neville exchanged a glance of their own, then flew in the direction of the noise.

By the time they all got there, the howling and barking had subsided, and Tommy was in the custody of the Master of the Hounds, for it appeared that Highleigh Court was home to a foxhound pack, and Tommy had decided the half-grown pups were irresistible. Unable to get into the locked kennel, he had climbed the fence around the pens, fallen off, and landed among the hounds, who reacted with confusion and startlement. Once he had fished Tommy out of the pen and ascertained he was not seriously hurt, the Master of the Hounds was pink with anger.

By this time, most of the children from the school had arrived, and so had most of the servants who could spare a moment. The Master had Tommy by one ear and looked as if he was going to haul the boy up in front of some authority but hadn't yet figured out who that was.

As Nan and Sarah hid, Memsa'b appeared, and the stormy expression she wore did not bode well for Tommy. The Master of the Hounds misinterpreted it, however.

"Now see here, Missus!" he began to bluster. "This boy of yours—"

"Has been getting into where he had no business being," Memsa'b said, interrupting, her voice stern. "I know this because your master told me that the kennels are kept locked. Tommy knows this because he was told not to attempt any place that was locked up. So what do you suggest his punishment should be? On the whole, I am against whipping or caning, but a good spanking would not go amiss."

For one long moment the Master of the Hounds stared at her, mouth agape, as Tommy hung limp with resignation in his grasp. "Ah—" the man began. "Don't much care for beating a boy myself. Beating never helped boy nor dog to my knowledge."

Memsa'b raised an eyebrow. "Perhaps, then, you could put him to some useful work instead? Since he seems so determined to see the dogs, he could help your underlings clean the kennels?"

Now taken even more aback by the suggestion that Tommy should do manual labor reserved for menials, the Master began to stammer. "Ah—Missus—what would his parents—"

"His parents have left his discipline in my hands," Memsa'b replied, "And I think he will come to far less harm having a set down to his dignity by learning how much work a servant must do, than he would by a caning. Perhaps afterward he will be more considerate of his servants when he is grown."

With a silent and astonished audience of manor servants listening raptly, the Master and Memsa'b worked out a compromise that kept Tommy in the kennels, helping to water and feed the dogs and other chores with the hawks and horses until just before suppertime, giving him just enough time for a bath and a change of clothing. Nan couldn't help but grin; not because Tommy was one of the few who would have been inclined to play Little Sahib over the manor servants, but at the reaction of those servants themselves.

"They're all on Memsa'b's side now, aren't they?" Sarah whispered, as a chastened Tommy was shooed into the precinct which he had but a few moments ago so much desired to get into. Nan nodded, feeling gleeful. She'd known she could count on Tommy to get into something that would put him at odds with the manor staff, but she hadn't thought he'd do so that quickly.

And Memsa'b cemented that, by turning to her audience—an audience which others in her position might have ignored—and addressing them. "If any of the children get into mischief that discommodes you or violates one of the house rules, I would appreciate it if you would bring your complaint and the child in question directly to me, at once," she said. "Thank you."

The servants went back to their work, and the rest of the children went back to their explorations, and Tommy put in a much-scrubbed appearance at dinner in an interesting mood—chastened by the amount of hard work he'd had to put in, but very full of information about foxhounds, rat terriers, and the huge mastiffs that the caretaker and gamekeeper used to help them guard the place.

The next day, and the day after that, passed with only minor incidents—the head cook found three of the boys investigating the cellars looking for a dungeon, and one of the housemaids discovered a toddler who was supposed to be napping running gleefully naked down the portrait gallery.

But the next incident, alas, was all Nan's doing.

She was passing the kitchen door, when a heady aroma seized her and dragged her inside. It was a scent she had whiffed only once before, and then she'd had no possibility of trying the product, and furthermore, on that occasion she had been literally starving and the aroma had nearly driven her out of her head with longing and despair.

Strawberry tarts. Fresh strawberry tarts. Her mouth watered and the hunger of that long-past day came back quite as strongly as if she had not been eating well and steadily for the past several months.

Perhaps if anyone had been in the kitchen, she would simply have begged a tart from the first servant that looked kind. But the kitchen was momentarily empty, and the tarts were all set out in rows on the big table to cool, and the temptation was too much to resist. She seized as many as she could carry and scurried out with them, to hide (she thought) in a little nook and share them with Neville.

But an alert kitchen maid not only saw that the tarts were missing, but thought to look in the kitchen garden and spotted Neville with half a tart in his beak, and traced his path back to Nan's hiding place. Found with crumbs on her face and surrounded by empty tins, her guilt had been clear.

Hauled up to Memsa'b with a full belly and just a twinge of regret, she found it hard to look completely repentant.

Memsa'b shook her head and sighed. Without even asking Nan if she was guilty—though of course the sticky fingers were mute evidence of that—she turned to the kitchen maid.

"Who of the kitchen-staff did the preparations for the tarts?" she asked, surprising the maid. "The cleaning and hulling and so forth."

"Ah, that'd be me, Ma'am," the maid stammered.

"Then you have charge of her. She's no stranger to hard work, though you might have to show her what to do. She is yours for the remainder of the day, only see that she gets luncheon and is free in time to clean herself for dinner." And with that, Memsa'b consigned her to her fate.

So she suffered through the hard work of a day in the kitchen under the direct supervision of the kitchen maid, who took immense and vindictive satisfaction in giving Nan all the most tedious jobs, and Nan discovered at firsthand how much work went into feeding a vast, and now augmented household like the one at Highleigh Park. Worst, probably, had been that she had been denied Neville's company the entire afternoon of her incarceration, only getting free to scamper outside and try to explain it to him at luncheon. Neville did not entirely understand how doing something so natural as raiding a ready food supply of delicious treats was a bad thing. Nan got the feeling that he comprehended that *people* thought it was a bad thing, but he still didn't grasp the reasoning behind that attitude. However, though Nan was incarcerated for the day, there was plenty for *him* to do, and he simply accepted it phlegmatically.

Two days later, Nan was still debating whether or not the pleasure of stuffing herself with strawberry tarts had been worth the pain of kitchen duty.

By that time the half holiday here was enough to make her giddy with happiness. She could have spent days merely exploring and observing the little lives in the brook that ran through the grounds. The home farm was near enough to run over to, and lambs were just as delicious to pet as she had imagined. There were half a dozen orphaned or rejected little things and extra hands to help bottle nurse them were always welcome.

This was when Tommy, who was now on good enough terms with the Master of Hounds to be allowed inside the kennel to play with puppies, discovered the home farm. Now, he had been utterly forbidden to even consider trying to ride any of the great high-bred horses in the stable, even though the grooms, who were not a great deal older than he, did so regularly to exercise them. There were no ponies there, as there were no children in the household, and he was mad to try and ride something.

And there, lord of the flock of sheep in the pasture nearest the manor, was a great big ram, relatively placid in nature and inclined to accept graciously any tidbits and scratches that came his way.

The combination was as irresistible for Tommy as strawberry tarts had been for Nan.

Nan and Sarah had been bottle-feeding lambs when shouts from the pasture made them and the farm manager come running. By that time, so she later learned, Tommy had already climbed the fence, jumped aboard, and had managed to stay on the ram's back long enough to get halfway across the pasture before the offended animal bucked him off.

They arrived just in time to see Tommy trying to run—then see Tommy flying through the air when the ram administered his own form of punishment.

He picked himself up again, and the ram repeated the procedure. One more time as he tried to scramble over the fence that divided the pasture from the goose pond sent him sailing into the midst of the geese, who had half-grown goslings with them and were not inclined at all to take this interloper lightly.

The geese decided to compound the retribution. Mister Thackers, in charge of the farm, was by this time laughing so hard that tears were running down his face, and waded in to Tommy's rescue.

"Oh, my lad," he said, as Tommy tried very hard not to cry, but was clearly in no little pain, "You're one of those, ain't you? Come along of you. I think you've learned more than enough of a lesson for one day, without me taking you to your mistress."

At that point, he took Tommy off to the farmhouse. Nan lingered, as she and Sarah soothed the ram's anger and indignation, and Sarah wordlessly promised him that no one would try that trick on him again. When Tommy came out again, this time alone, he was walking a bit easier and smelled strongly of horse liniment.

Memsa'b found out about it, of course, but other than a single pointed remark at dinner, nothing more ever came of it.

Neville was in heaven, too; here he had an entirely new set of interesting things to get into and investigate than in London. Memsa'b had gotten him to tolerate a set of bright red glove-leather leggings before they left, carefully fitted to and sewn onto his lower legs, and the gamekeepers and farmers were under strict orders not to shoot the raven with the red legs, so even an incident of egg eating at the home farm was let off with a scolding. Fortunately, the number of eggs a raven could eat at a sitting was far less than the number of strawberry tarts that could be consumed by an active girl at one go. When it was made clear to him that while pigeon, pheasant, quail and chicken eggs were strictly off-limits, rook, starling, sparrow and crow nests were fair game, he was a much happier raven.

As for Sarah and Grey . . . there was no doubt in anyone's mind that both were as happy as they could be outside of being home again. Grey, like Neville, managed to get into a great deal of mischief with her curiosity and her prying beak. Unlike Neville, she was sneaky about it and never got caught.

Like Neville, however, she brought back all manner of curious objects for Sarah, and their little treasure boxes were filling fast. Neville found a great deal of trash and treasure in his raids on the nests of rooks and crows. Some were clearly valuable; a silver locket, for instance, and a broken rosary of delicate gold wire and blackened seed pearls that looked extremely old indeed, and a small hoard of coins. Memsa'b always made sure there were no existing claimants for such finds before allowing the girls to keep them. Some were merely interesting; odd pebbles, pot-metal charms, tiny faded pottery figurines and three small dolls of the sort called "Frozen Charlottes" because they were all one solid piece. Some were just trash: horseshoe nails, bits of ribbon and string, unidentifiable pieces of china and metal. Those, the birds kept, in their own little "treasure boxes," a couple of old tea chests they could open themselves and poke about in.

Memsa'b's plan for lessons every day was not as onerous as it had sounded. One morning was completely devoted to splashing about in the pond and learning about aquatic life, and similar mornings were spent exploring other parts of the home farm, gardens, and parkland. On rainy days, the servants would open older parts of the building and they would examine history in context as they looked at antique furnishings, pictures, and the rooms themselves. They spent whole evenings learning about stars and planets, and the myths behind the names of the objects in the night sky. There was a daily lesson in gardening, and when the mood was on her, the cook would even give lessons in plain cookery. There was a trip to the forge to learn about metal working, right down to the chemistry of it, and another to the mill to study the mechanics of turning flowing water into something that could grind grain into flour and run other machinery. The French teacher took them out on walks, taught them the French names of things, and required that they converse in that language the entire time. Memsa'b did the same in Latin.

Another set of lessons was that they were going to perform a play, Shakespeare, *A Midsummer Night's Dream*. They were having to make the costumes and props, learn their speeches by heart, and were also learning what some of the odd things they were saying meant. In Nan's opinion, none of it was really lessons at all, just a way for Memsa'b to say she was giving lessons without really doing it.

But there were two places where neither Nan nor Sarah felt the least urge to go; two places that made them both feel strange, uneasy and acutely uncomfortable. One was an old dry well that the servants called a "wishing well," though no one ever made any wishes there, nor in fact, ever seemed to visit. It was in the back of the kitchen garden near the oldest part of the manor. No bird or animal could be persuaded to approach it, and even Tommy, after one curious toss of a pebble into it to see how deep it was, left it alone.

The other was the bridge over the river on the road that led to the next village, a place none of the children had visited yet. Nan and Sarah had followed the road on a long walk one afternoon out of pure curiosity to see where it went.

They came to a signpost, eventually, which at least told them that they had come a half mile from the Highleigh Park gate, and that some place called "Shackleford" was another mile farther on. At this point, the wall of the park ended. The road continued on, as far as they could see, cutting through farm fields. In the far, hazy distance was a church steeple, presumably marking the village.

"Go on, or go back?" Nan asked.

Sarah shrugged. "They didn't say we couldn't." she pointed out. "They just said not to get lost. We can't get lost if we stick to the road."

Nan nodded, and they went on.

But they could not have gone more than a quarter mile before they came to a bridge over a substantial river. There was nothing remarkable about the bridge itself; it was built of the same brick and stone as the manor, and was in good repair. Yet the nearer they drew to it, the more uneasy they became—very much like the feeling they had at that dry well, though not quite as strong. As they paused about ten feet from it, Neville circled overhead, croaking that he did not like Nan getting so near to the structure, and Grey fluttered down from where she usually flew beside him, landed on Sarah's shoulder, and growled.

That settled it. Without a word, they turned, and made their way back to the manor. But both situations had the effect of, not rousing Nan's curiosity, but cooling it. She did not want to know why the bridge and the well made her feel so uneasy, and even felt a reluctance to discuss it with Sarah, or anyone else.

Finally, she decided that it was a natural reaction, after that encounter with that horrible Thing in Berkeley Square.

"Leave well enough alone," she told herself, and made an effort to put both of them out of her mind.

For now, at least.

9

DAVID Alderscroft descended from his carriage at the gate of a long-forgotten manor at the edge of some of the least-desirable real estate in London. Though the building itself was substantial, surrounded by an impressive wall and seemed to be in reasonable repair, he could not imagine anyone in his set willing to admit they owned it, much less live in it. He hesitated a moment—surely this could not be the correct address!—but the inscribed brass plaque inset into the right-hand gatepost assured him that this was, indeed, the "Harton School for Boys and Girls."

So this was where Isabelle, his Isabelle, had come!

With a stern mental hand he shook sense into himself. Isabelle Harton, if indeed she was the same person as the girl he had once been acquainted with, was not, and had never been "his" Isabelle. Not that he couldn't have had her, had he wanted her! Possibly even, in the crudest and most Biblical sense, had he put his mind to it. But of course, such an action, besides leaving him open to all manner of unpleasant repercussions, was unworthy of him and unworthy of the name he wore.

And, he reminded himself yet again, he had not wanted her.

Well, except during the first flush of infatuation. But Cordelia had persuaded him to responsible behavior, and that flush had cooled under the harsh light of reason.

Even assuming she and the headmistress of this school were one and the same. That was by no means certain, despite the name, and the fact that Nigel's wife had known the woman in school—that was why he was here, after all, to find out the truth of the matter.

He rang the bell, and while he waited, contemplated the gardens just visible inside the walls. Though not showing the hand of a professional gardening staff, they were not as overgrown and neglected as he would have thought. The plants growing here were all hardy things, sturdy specimens that could tolerate a little neglect and a great deal of London's bad air. Not manicured, but at least, trimmed and contained.

It took a very long time for someone to answer, long enough that he was about to give up and assume that there was no one in residence, when he became aware with a start that he was no longer alone. A tall, swarthy fellow in a coat of faintly military cut and Indian antecedents had come up soundlessly while he stared at the hostas and ivies through the bars of the gate. It startled him, actually; how long had the fellow been there? How had he managed to slip up so quietly?

"May I help you, sir?" The tones, flavored with a faint accent, were as cultured as his own.

He coughed, momentarily taken off-guard. "I would like to speak with Mrs. Isabelle Harton, please," he replied after a pause.

"I am devastated that we cannot meet your request, sir," came the immediate reply, followed by his own surge of anger and disappointment, both quickly repressed. "The headmistress has taken the pupils to the country for a holiday. May I conduct you to Master Harton instead?"

Suddenly he found himself hoist on his own petard. He had *wanted* to see this woman for himself, and if he discovered that she was the girl of his youthful infatuation, use her current state to destroy any lingering, sentimental memory of that girl. After all, the years were generally not kind to poor vicars' daughters, and he was certain they would not have been kind to her. One look at a prim-faced, stern-eyed creature in the severe, dark, unfashionable gown that seemed to be the universal garb of all schoolmistresses, and he was sure the soft, pastel-colored memory of that girl would be burned from his mind. The last thing he wanted to do was to confront her husband.

But there seemed no way that he could avoid such a confrontation now. If he declined to meet with Mr. Harton, there would be questions as to *why* he had turned up, and why he wanted to meet with Mrs. Harton and not her spouse, questions he did not want to have to answer. Nor did he want the absent Mrs. Harton to have to answer an interrogation about his presence later either—whoever she was.

"Yes," he said simply, if reluctantly, "Master Harton will suffice."

The servant bowed, unbolted a little postern door on the left side of the gate, and let him inside the walls. Silently, the man led the way to the front door, and with continued silence, brought him into the vestibule from there into a small parlor.

"If you will wait, sir, I will summon the Master," the servant said, taking his card. "It will be no more than a few minutes at most."

In fact, it was less than that. David had no time at all to look at most of the souvenirs of India displayed on the walls and tables of the parlor. The servant's steps had hardly faded when a different set of footsteps, with a limp this time, heralded the approach of someone new.

David rose and turned toward the door.

Standing in the doorway was a middle-aged man—a gentleman, in fact, who was probably no more than five or six years older than David—with the physique of someone considerably younger than his apparent age. David was immediately conscious that he was not nearly so robust as this fellow; jaunts in carriages around London did not lend themselves to looking as if one hiked six miles through the jungle before breakfast. In coloring, he was ordinary enough, brown of hair and eye, though there was a set to his jawline that suggested toughness and a hint of a smile that suggested sardonic good humor. The hair itself was just a little long and carelessly untidy, as if the wearer had put off seeing a barber for a little. The eyes were frank, honest, and appraising. David had expected a military bearing, given the servant, but there was less of it than he would have anticipated.

He stepped forward, holding out his hand.

The other clasped it, a good, strong handshake, warm, dry and firm. "David, Lord Alderscroft," David said, wondering what the other made of his own grasp. The man chuckled.

"Plain Frederick Harton, and pleased to meet you. I had been hoping to make your acquaintance, since my wife and I had a bit of a problem with an Elemental Master not long ago."

David tried not to blink; the fellow certainly did not beat about the bush!

"Erm, yes," he temporized. "But the problem seems to have solved itself, more or less."

"So I've been told," came the noncommittal reply. "Would you care to come to my office? You might find it more comfortable than this parlor."

David had intended to say, "No," intended to claim he had only stopped to let the Hartons know that the problem with the renegade had been disposed of, but found himself saying instead, "Yes, thank you."

The man led the way to a small room just off the parlor, lined with books, displaying more exotica, and quite comfortable in that shabby, well-worn way that the lounges of the adventurers' clubs often looked. Without being asked, Frederick Harton poured and handed him a brandy. Wordlessly, David accepted it, and took a seat in a handsome, if slightly battered, leather chair that accepted his weight and embraced it. He also hadn't intended to drink what he had been handed, but a whiff and a cautious taste proved it was not an inferior product.

On the wall over the fireplace was a photographic portrait of the Hartons, presumably made in India, since the woman was wearing a white gown suited to the tropics.

And there was no doubt; the woman was "his" Isabelle. Nor did that sepia photograph do anything to erase the memories from his mind. Though looking grave and serious, and certainly as if she had seen many things and perhaps endured many trials, Isabelle Harton looked considerably less aged than the face that gazed back at David's from his mirror every morning. The years, which had not been kind to him, had laid a light hand on her.

"I hope you understand that while we are grateful for your attention, we are not entirely convinced that the threat has ended with the death of your miscreant," Frederick Harton said, as he seated himself behind his desk.

"Ah, well, that is what I came here to speak to Mrs. Harton about," David replied, grateful for a chance to turn the tide of conversation in his own favor. He drew himself up a little and gathered all of his authority about himself. "You see, Mr. Harton, my associates and I think you would be doing better to look among the ranks of the psychical set for your enemy, if indeed there is one."

He rattled on, repeating all the arguments made in advance, to an attentive, but neutral Frederick Harton, until at last he ran out of arguments.

"I see," Harton said, sounding unconvinced. "These are all good arguments, to be sure, but it does not answer *how* such presumed enemy contacted an Elemental Master in the first place, nor how he or she convinced said Master to work for them in the second place. It is a conundrum that has as yet to be addressed."

Drat the man! Why did he have to be so intelligent and thoughtful? David had hoped to find a stereotypical retired Colonial soldier, rigid and uncomfortable with matters nonmilitary—or else a moony mystic, easily persuaded by a stronger personality. He found neither. Instead, he discovered he was facing an intellect as powerful as his own; he had literally met his match. If this man did not lead a psychical Master's Circle, it was because he felt enough of them existed that he did not need to create one.

"Unfortunately," he replied, setting down the empty glass and rising, "The one person who can answer that has gone beyond the reach of our justice, so we shall never know, I expect. Good evening, Mr. Harton. I hope your school continues to flourish with an absence of incident."

"Oh, where there are children there will always be incidents," came the ironic reply, as Harton rose and shook his hand. "One simply hopes to keep them confined within the four walls of the school."

David Alderscroft took his leave, and his carriage, feeling that somehow, though swords had never been crossed in the meeting, he had come off second-best.

❄

Props and costumes for the play had mostly been constructed, and still the full cast had not yet been chosen. Nan and Sarah were to be Helena and Hermia, the two friends whose tangled affairs formed the bulk of the play—a natural choice, though Nan was a little disappointed, as she had hoped to be Hippolyta the Amazon Queen. She rather fancied herself in armor.

But Memsa'b and Sarah had convinced her that the semicomic role of Helena suited her better, and after studying the text with Memsa'b's help, Nan agreed. Anna Thompson, a girl tall for her age and rather angular, would be Hippolyta; the role was not precisely a demanding one, when it all came down to it, and Anna would fill it well enough. Almost all the other roles had been filled, except two of the most crucial: Bottom, and Puck.

The difficulty was that the most natural choice for either of them was Tommy, and he clearly could not fill both roles. Given a choice, he wanted Bottom; he clearly lusted after the donkey's head worn by the character for the scene with the fairies. He had already tried the papier-mâché creation on so often that not even the much-amused servants were startled to see him cavorting about in it anymore. But in Nan's opinion there was no one else clever and lively enough to play Puck—

Memsa'b, the girls, and the birds had ensconced themselves in that overgrown summerhouse (which Memsa'b referred to as a "folly") to sort through the final cast options. And Memsa'b was growing a little frustrated, in an amused sense.

"I vow," she said in exasperation, after yet another sort-through of the boys, shuffling them into various parts to see if a new configuration would solve the dilemma, "I am tempted to play Puck myself at this point. There is not a single boy half as able to do Bottom as Tommy, he has most of the part by heart already. But there isn't anyone, girl or boy, as well suited to Puck either! Except, perhaps you, Nan."

"But I've already got most of Helena by heart!" Nan wailed, aghast at the notion of having to learn a different role after all that work.

"Ah, dear lady, and tender maidens," said a bright voice from the doorway, making them all turn, "Perhaps I can solve this problem for you."

There was a boy there, perhaps a little older and a trifle taller than Nan. He had a merry face, sun-browned, with reddish brown hair and green eyes, and wore very curious clothing—

At first glance, it *looked* perfectly ordinary, if the local farmers hereabouts were inclined to wear a close-fitting brown tunic and knee-breeches rather than sensible undyed linen smocks and buff trousers, but at second glance there was something subtly wrong about the cut and fit of the garments. First, they looked like something out of a painting, something antique, and secondly, they looked as if they were made of leather. Now, the blacksmith wore leather trousers, and the village cobbler, but no one else did around here.

And there was something else about this boy, a brightness, a spirit of vitality, that was not ordinary at all.

And that was the moment when Neville made a surprised croak, and jumped down off the marble seat where he had been pecking with great interest at a hole in the stone, to be joined on the floor by Grey. Both of them stalked over to the boy's feet, looked up at him—

—and bowed.

There was no other name for what they did, and Nan's mouth fell agape.

But this was not the only shock she got, for Memsa'b had risen from *her* seat, and sunk again into a curtsy. Not a head-bowed curtsy, though, this was one where she kept her eyes firmly on the newcomer.

" 'Hail to thee, blithe spirit!' " she said as she rose.

The boy's eyes sparkled with mischief and delight.

"Correct author, but wrong play and character, for never could I be compared to Ariel," he replied and swiftly stooped down to offer Neville and Grey each a hand. Each accepted the perch as Nan stared, her mouth still open. "How now, Bane of Rooks!" he said to Neville. "I think you should return to your partner, before bees see her open mouth and think to build a hive therein!"

With another bow, and a croak, Neville lofted from the boy's outstretched hand and landed on Nan's shoulder. Nan took the hint and shut her mouth.

Wordlessly, he handed Grey back to Sarah, who took her bird with round eyes, as if she saw even more than Nan did to surprise her. "So ho, fair dame, did you think to plan to play my play on Midsummer's Day and *not* have me notice?" he said to Memsa'b, fists planted on his hips.

"I had not thought to have the honor of your attention, good sirrah," Memsa'b replied, her eyes very bright and eager. "Indeed, I had not known that such as you would deign to notice such as we."

He laughed. "Well spoke, well spoke! And properly, too! Well then, shall I solve your conundrum with my humble self, and let your restless Tommy play the ass?"

Nan blinked hard, as a furtive glimmer of light that could not have actually been there circled the boy, and then her brain shook itself like a waking dog, everything that wasn't quite "right" shifted itself into a configuration she could hardly believe, and she burst out with, "You're *him!* You're *Puck!*"

The boy laughed, a laugh that had a friendly tone of mockery in it, but as much to mock himself as to make fun of Nan. He bowed to her with a flourish. "Robin Goodfellow at your service, my London daisy! Not often evoked these present days, but often in the thoughts of my good country folk, who care very little for the passage of time."

"And how am I to explain one extra boy to the others?" Memsa'b asked dryly, rising from her curtsy. "Not that I would dare to contradict your will, but we poor mortals must have our proper explanations."

"Ah, that," he waved his hand airily. "A simple thing. Say I am the son of a friend of yours, I have conned the part at my school and will come to fill it here. And in your practices, do you take my part as you threatened to."

Memsa'b smiled. "A sound plan, but what of those others in my charge who will see you for something of what you are and may ask questions I cannot answer without your leave?"

He laid his finger alongside his nose, and then pointed it at her. "Well asked. Well thought. Perhaps a touch of glamorie will not come amiss, with your permission. 'Twill do them no harm. They will notice nothing amiss, nothing that their minds cannot find an explanation for, and the explanation will seem to come from outside their minds."

" 'Ere!" Nan objected. "Not on us! Please!"

A "touch of glamorie" sounded to her as if Puck was going to do something that would make her and Sarah forget what he was— and she didn't want to forget!

"We'd like to know what is really happening, please," Sarah chimed in, as Grey bobbed in agreement and Neville shifted his weight from foot to foot on Nan's shoulder.

Puck cast a glance at Memsa'b. "And so what think you?"

"That both these girls can hold a secret," Memsa'b said instantly. "Certainly they already have done so many times in the past."

"Then I bow to your will, London daisy," Puck replied with a grin. "Let it be as you wish, and you will see me again, on Midsummer's Night!"

Nan blinked, as there was a sudden glare across her eyes, like a flash of sun reflected from water, and when she could see again he was gone.

Neville bobbed and quorked once. He sounded surprised.

"Cor!" Grey said, in Nan's voice. "Blimey!"

"That was . . . entirely unexpected," Memsa'b said, sitting down hard, and looking a little out of breath, as if she had been running. "Of all the things that could have happened here, this is not one I would have ever anticipated! To have so powerful a spirit simply walk in on one—I confess it has taken my breath away!"

'Was that really P— *him?*" Sarah asked, her eyes still round, as if she didn't quite dare speak the name aloud. "The same as in the play?"

"Ah, now . . . I hesitate to pin down someone like him to any sort of limited description," Memsa'b temporized. "And the Puck of Shakespeare's play is far more limited than the reality. Let's just say he is—old. One of the oldest Old Ones in England. As a living creature, he probably saw the first of the flint workers here, and I suspect that he will see the last of us mortals out as well, unless he chooses to follow some of the other Old Ones wherever they have gone, sealing the doors of their barrows behind them. If he does, it will be a sad day for England, for a great deal of the magic of this island will go with him. He is linked to us in ways that some of those who were once worshipped as gods are not."

Nan thought about asking what all this meant and how Memsa'b knew it, then thought better of the notion. Memsa'b had said that she and Sarah could hold their tongues, and this seemed like a good time to prove it.

Instead, she said, "Didn' you say that them barrows is burial mounds of kings an' such? So how can they be doors?"

Memsa'b chuckled. "And so they are. But you, Nan, are a little girl and Neville is a raven—yet at the same time, you are a Warrior of the Light, and Neville is your battle companion. Some things, and some people, can be two different things at the same time. Barrows can be both portals and burial vaults, and those who have no eyes to see the doors in the hills will not be troubled by the knowledge that they are both."

Well, that seemed sensible enough, and Nan nodded.

"Will we see 'im again afore the day?" she asked.

"Now that I cannot tell you." Memsa'b pursed her lips. "If you do, be polite, respectful, but don't fear him. He is the very spirit of mischief, but there is no harm in him and a great deal of good. You might learn much from him, and I never heard it said that any of his sort would stand by and let a child come to harm. His knowledge is broad and deep and he has never been averse to sharing it with mortals."

"But would he steal us away?" Sarah asked, suddenly growing pale. "Don't *they* take children, and leave behind changelings?"

Here, Nan was baffled; she had no idea what Sarah was talking about. But Memsa'b did.

"I don't believe he'd be likely to," she replied after a long moment of thought. "Firstly, I don't think he would have revealed himself to us if he was going to do that. Secondly, what *I* know of such things is that his sort never take children that are cared for and wanted, only the ones abused and neglected." She held out a hand, and Sarah went straight to her to be hugged reassuringly. "No one can say that about any of you, I do hope!"

With the casting problem solved, preparations for the play went on so well that it almost seemed as if there was a blessing on the whole plan. Tommy was, of course, in ecstasy at being able to play Bottom. Not only were the servants charmed by the idea of being an audience for such a thing, but the local vicar got wind of the scheme, and asked if they would be part of the church fete, which was also to be Midsummer's Day. Now that was something of a surprise for all of them, but a welcome one, at least for those who, like Nan and Tommy, felt no fear at performing before larger audiences. So far as both of *them* were concerned, they'd get right up on stage at Covent Garden without a qualm.

With the new venue in mind, further touches were made on props and costumes. Permission was granted to rummage through selected attics and use whatever they could find there; a happy discovery was that at some point in the past, the inhabitants of the manor had engaged in amateur theatrics and had held many fancy-dress parties. While much of the costuming was sized for adults, there was enough for children, or that could be cut down to fit children, to make vast improvements in the wardrobe.

Memsa'b commented on none of this, but Nan had the shrewd notion that they were the benefactors of someone's subtle Magics. Not that she cared. She and Sarah were the beneficiaries of this bounty, for Grecian garments (or at least, Grecian-inspired costumes) were the sorts of things easily adapted to child size, and they were now the proud wearers of something that looked entirely professional, rather than something cobbled up from old dust sheets.

Sarah looked utterly adorable, to tell the truth, like something off a Wedgewood vase, with her draped gown and a wreath of wax orange blossoms in her hair. Most spectacular though, were Mary Dowland and Henry Tailor, as Titania and Oberon, respectively; the most amazing, fantastical costumes had been found for them, and if they looked a bit over the top by daylight, in evening rehearsals under dimmer light they looked very magical indeed and nothing like a pair of schoolchildren.

There were enough bumps in the road of production to ease Nan's fears that things were going entirely *too* well. There were plenty of forgotten lines, fumbled speeches, and places where it was all too apparent just how amateur this amateur production was. But the closer they got to The Day, the more excited Nan became, and so was everyone else, right down to the servants, who fell over themselves to help.

Rather than cart everything to the church grounds, permission was granted for the audience to come to them. That meant that there would be no need to move anything so far as the players were concerned.

The performance for the servants was set in and around the folly, which would serve partly as stage setting and partly as prop room and changing room, since children able to remember several parts were taking several minor roles at once. The semiclassical structure suited itself well to the purpose, and it was surrounded by picturesque faux "ruins" that removed most of the need for scenery.

The day before the performance, since the weather bid to stay fine (more of Puck's magic at work?) most of the preparations were done in advance. On Midsummer's Day the fete was held at the church, and the servants got half days off to attend in shifts. The children also had leave to go, but since it was not a true fair, and the entertainments were entirely home grown, no one really wanted to do anything but final walk-throughs and a full rehearsal. So the fete went on without their attendance.

The final rehearsal was—a disaster. Dropped lines abounded, nerves were everywhere, and even Sarah was reduced to frustrated tears at least once.

At the end of it, Nan was exhausted and discouraged. She felt wrung out—and their Puck had not appeared, so Memsa'b had once again read his lines. She poked at her dinner without any real appetite, until Memsa'b noticed and had it taken away in favor of cucumber soup and buttered bread. That went down easier, getting past a throat tight with nerves.

After dinner, Memsa'b drew her aside before they all got into costume again. "Don't worry," she said, with a hug. "The tradition in the theater is that the worse the final rehearsal is, the better the performance will be."

"But what about our Puck?" Nan asked, forlornly.

"Don't worry," was all Memsa'b said. And Nan had to leave it at that, because it was time to climb into their costumes and troop down to the folly, where the servants were already stringing up fairy lights and improvised stage lights, laying out rugs and cush-

ions to sit on for themselves. Wagonloads of people had been ar-
riving since before supper, and people had been picnicking on the
lawn in anticipation of the performance to come. There was a
steady buzz of talk audible even from the manor itself, and the
sound of all those people made Nan's stomach knot up. It didn't get
better when she heard the couple of hired musicians playing to en-
tertain the crowd—a fiddler, a flute player, and a fellow with a gui-
tar. They had been making dance music for the Morris dancers at
the fete, and vicar had arranged that they would also be providing
incidental music during the play. They were *good*. It seemed impossible that even with the desire of the audience to be pleased,
the children could pull off a performance to compare favorably
with the musicians.

And yet—

Suddenly, between one breath and the next, all of that changed.

The moment Nan set foot in the folly, she felt a change come
over her. A curious calm overtook her, curious because she felt
tingly and alive as well as calm, nor was she the only one. A quick
glance around showed her that everyone had settled. The nerves
and restlessness were gone from the rest of the cast; the edge they
all had was of anticipation rather than anxiety—

And not one of them mentioned the lack of the promised Puck.

And at the moment when they were all milling about "back-
stage," waiting for Memsa'b to announce the play, Nan felt a tug
on her tunic and turned to find herself staring into those strange,
merry green eyes again. This time the boy was wearing a fantastic
garment that was a match for those Titania and Oberon were
wearing, a rough sleeveless tunic of green stuff and goatskin
trousers, with a trail of vine leaves wound carelessly through his
tousled red hair.

"How now, pretty maiden, did you doubt me?" he said slyly.
"Nay, answer me not, I can scarce blame you. All's well! Now, mind
your cue!"

With a little shove, he sent her in the direction of her entrance
mark, and as she stepped out into the mellow light of lanterns and

candles, she forgot everything except her lines and how she wanted to say them.

Now, Nan was not exactly an expert when it came to plays. The most she had ever seen was a few snatches of this or that—a Punch and Judy show, a bit of something as she snuck into a music hall, and the one Shakespeare play Memsa'b had taken them all to in London.

But the moment they all got "onstage," it was clear there was real magic involved. All of them seemed, and sounded, older and a great deal more practiced. Not so much so that it would have been alarming but—certainly—as if they were all well into their teens, rather than being children still. Everything *looked* convincing, even the papier-mâché donkey's head. Lines were spoken clearly, with conviction, and the right inflection. Nan and Sarah even made people laugh in all the right places.

And as for Puck—well, he quite stole the show. From the moment he set foot on "stage" it was clear that the play was, in the end, about *him*.

Yet no one seemed to be in the least put out that he took the play over. Not even Tommy. And perhaps that was the most magical thing of all.

Lovers human and faerie quarreled and reconciled; the rustics put on their silly play with a great deal of shouting and bumbling about. Puck made mischief, then made all right again. The stage lights somehow put out far more illumination than they should have, and the twinkling little fairy lights looked genuinely magical. In fact, there seemed to be a kind of golden, magical haze over it all.

It ended all too soon, with the cast being applauded wildly by an audience on its feet, and all of them—except Puck—carried back bodily by the servants to be treated to a late-evening treat of cakes and ices and tea.

Somewhere, between the folly and the manor, he had vanished again. And no one said a word about his going.

Oh, they remembered him, all right, but no one seemed to find it at all strange that he wasn't here, sharing in the triumphal treat, basking in the admiration of the servants. As Nan devoured lemon ice and cake with the single-minded hunger of someone who did not eat nearly enough dinner, she found herself in awe of that—

Because it was one thing to work a bit of magic on a couple of people. But Puck had worked a very subtle magic on a great many people; he'd done it flawlessly and invisibly, and in such a way that, as she listened, she realized he had somehow managed to implant in everyone's mind that the boy who had played Puck was always somewhere on the premises, but in a place other than where the person talking about him was him- or herself at that moment.

Out of sheer curiosity, she finally asked Tommy as she got another helping of lemon ice, "Hoy, seen that lad Robin?"

"Went to change out of his costume," Tommy said around a mouthful of cake. "Said the leaves itched."

Nan listened with astonishment to the talk going on. No one doubted that it had been *him* at all those rehearsals, rather than Memsa'b reading his part; memory had been altered, clearly, in everyone except Memsa'b and Nan and Sarah. There were even stories about how he had done this or that in rehearsal! And later that evening, as the servants cheerfully collected costumes and the children prepared for bed, she asked one of the maids where Robin had gone, and was not greatly surprised to hear that, allegedly, his parents had come to collect him at some point while the rest were finishing off the treats.

"Taking the last train back to London," the maid said cheerfully. "I suppose, a big boy like that, he's used to staying up late—but it is a pity he couldn't stay. Still! Your Memsa'b said she didn't like inviting them to stay without permission of the Master, and that's only right and proper, since he don't know them."

And that seemed to be that.

❄

Memsa'b made it a point to come say good night to every child, every night. Sometimes Nan was already asleep by the time Memsa'b got to them, but not tonight. As their mentor entered their little room, Nan was sitting up in bed hugging her knees, Sarah was beside her, and even both birds were still awake and waiting.

Memsa'b held up a hand, forestalling the volley of questions Nan wanted to fire off before they could be launched.

"No, he didn't give me any message for you. Yes, that was his 'glamorie' at work, and no, I have never seen anything quite like that in my life." She shook her head. "It was quite amazing. I stood there and *watched* as peoples' memories changed, and I could not for a moment tell you how it was done. All I can think is that this is how his kind have protected themselves over the centuries."

"I thought you said it was wrong to meddle with peoples' thoughts," Sarah said, her eyes narrowed.

Memsa'b pursed her lips, and sat down on the bed beside them. "I still think it is wrong—but it would be a greater wrong, and very dangerous for Robin, to have left their memories alone." She grimaced. "Even I have meddled, now and again. Sometimes you have to balance wrong against wrong and choose the one that does the least harm." She patted Sarah's hand, as Sarah looked very troubled. "It's a hard lesson that you learn, growing up, that you can't always answer 'yes' or 'no,' that something is entirely right or entirely wrong. Most of the time the answer is somewhere in the middle."

"You think we'll see 'im again, Memsa'b?" Nan asked softly, hoping that the answer was going to be "yes."

"I don't know," came the reply.

And with that unsatisfying answer, she had to be content. That—and their own, unchanged memories.

10

David Alderscroft had no intention of having any more to do with the Harton School or Frederick Harton. While the man did have a high level of native intelligence, and while he did not have the advantages of a public school education and had clearly worked hard to rise above his plebian origins, he was still, when it came down to the matter, common. He was certainly not in David's social set. While David considered himself to be free of snobbery, he also regarded himself as a practical man, and practically speaking there was nothing that a man like Frederick Harton and one such as himself could possibly have as mutual interests.

Nevertheless, he decided that it behooved him to do some investigation of the man. After all, frauds abounded in psychical circles, and it was wise to make sure that Harton was not of that ilk. The man's insinuations that someone among the Elemental Mages of London could be ultimately responsible for the attacks on his charges had been subtle, but exceedingly unwelcome, especially since such insinuations implied that David did not know enough about the Elemental Mages around him to be able to completely refute such a charge. And since when was *he* supposed to be responsible for the actions of all the Elemental Mages in this part of the world anyway? Wasn't that like implying that Frederick Harton was equally responsible for the actions of all the psychical Talents in the city?

Yes, whispered a tiny voice inside, *but you are the Lodge Master of the Master's Circle here. You were the one who organized it and runs it. Doesn't that make you responsible?*

As if it wasn't perfectly obvious that it *must* have been someone in Harton's own circles who was responsible. Who else would have had the knowledge and the motivation?

Today he had the results of his investigation on his desk, from the private agent he had employed to delve into the Hartons and their school and small importation business. He should have been pleased to discover that both Hartons had a sterling reputation, but somehow this only irritated him. He knew this irritation was irrational, and that irritated him even more, as he turned the closely-written pages over and read them with care.

Drat them both.

I will forget about this, he vowed. *It is a dead issue. Neither of them will trouble me again.*

He decided to take refuge from unwelcome thoughts by immersing himself in the round of summer entertainments organized by Lady Cordelia, arranged to introduce him gradually into political circles. Tennis-parties, afternoon teas, dinners—all were designed to make him visible, but not intrusive. Lady Cordelia took a Thames-side summer home for the purpose; something where a wide, spacious lawn suitable for croquet and picnicking al fresco, and the proximity to London were the most important features. Ministers who lived in London had no difficulty in getting to these entertainments, and yet the contrast between the bucolic suburb and the hot, noisy city could not have been greater. In such pleasant surroundings, in an atmosphere in which Lady Cordelia laughingly forbade all talk of politics, it was possible to make a good impression without ever actually saying anything.

Though truth be told, he was finding his acquaintance with

these lions of Parliament a bit disappointing. If he had followed his inclinations, they were not the folk he would have been spending these pleasant summer hours with. None of them had much in the way of interests outside of politics. All were devoted, more or less, to the arts of manipulation. They were facades, like stage scenery, implying a substance and solidity that was in reality nothing more than paint on canvas. They did not read; they did not think much past the needs of themselves and their select circle. When they attended plays or concerts, it was not to pay attention to the performance, but to be seen attending the performance. Their wives were pleasant nonentities, chosen for their ability to adorn a dinner table and play gracious hostess—and for the ability to smile and meekly accept whatever their lord and master decreed. Outwardly respectable, the pillars of society, they stood four-square for Moral Behavior, Propriety, Virtue, and Values, and there wasn't one of them that did not have a mistress tucked away in Mayfair, shared the attentions of a London courtesan, had at least one maidservant who did a bit more for her master than dust, or visited a discreet brothel on a regular basis. And that was merely the tip of the proverbial iceberg.

That they were venial was not what bothered him so much; it was the hypocrisy. All men had their failings, and he was no more a bastion of personal rectitude than the next fellow, that he should go casting stones. The problem was that these men set themselves up as the models of rectitude while secretly and deliberately choosing the opposite path.

He knew these things—and other personal failings—because Lady Cordelia kept him informed of them. Not that he was supposed to do anything with the information, no, nothing like that. He was supposed to hold it close against the day when a subtle hint would convey a tacit warning that cooperation was better than opposition. And that bothered him, too. It felt somehow wrong.

It was a chess game on a grand scale, hunting for weaknesses, not exploiting them yet, but having the knowledge ready if it needed to be used. He liked chess. He wished he could take the same pleasure in this game. Certainly, the major pieces on the board were as bloodless as the white-and-black marble pieces of his favorite set.

The trouble was, it was always the pawns that were sacrificed, and the pawns were anything but bloodless. Wives, children, associates—people who would probably suffer more than the major players if everything went badly. You thought about these things, the innocent bystanders, when you were the Chief Huntsman of a Master's Circle. You had to. In Magic, things were different; when you did something knowingly wrong, when you hurt people who did not deserve hurt, it came back on you later. The scales were evened a great deal faster for a Mage than for an ordinary man, who might wait until the day he was called before the Almighty to answer for what he had done.

He consulted his calendar to discover that this evening's excursion would be a concert on the lawn of Lady Cordelia's summer residence beneath the stars—taking the cue from the much-less-genteel church fetes and outdoor entertainments of London, and making it acceptable for the set to which she and David belonged. As usual, the word "concert" was something of a misnomer. Yes, there would be music—tonight it would be a string quartet on the terrace—but the number of people actually listening to the music would be low. Most would be there to be seen—to display new frocks and jewels, to be seen speaking to the "right" people, to make one's presence known or reinforce one's standing in this particular group. Miss too many of these social outings without an adequate excuse and people began to talk, to question if you had been invited at all, and if not, why not—

As he was assisted into his evening dress by his valet for another one of these dreary mock-festive occasions, he found his mind drifting back to summer parties when he had still been in school, when he had spent one week after another making the rounds of week-long visits to estates in the country and had not considered those simpler pleasures beneath his dignity. Then he and the others had *gone* to the church fetes, and bought useless embroidered cushions and tatted antimacassars and eaten ices and listened to village musicians and actually enjoyed themselves. . . .

And with a curse, he flung himself into his carriage for another evening of pretense and empty smiles.

But, he reminded himself, this was the life of an adult. It was more than time to put away childish notions, to settle into the serious business of life. Life was not church fetes and ices. Life was doing things one did not want to do with the goal of getting things, great things, accomplished.

Besides, Lady Cordelia had assured him that eventually he would come to take some sardonic amusement in these occasions, as he watched the facades strut about pretending to be substance.

But in the back of his mind he couldn't help feeing this was all very inferior to honest laughter and the taste of a lemon ice beneath the stars of a country night.

❅

With the excitement of the play over, a languor settled over the children for the next couple of days or so. There was, alas, no further sign of Robin Goodfellow either, though Nan looked in vain for him everywhere she went. It was Memsa'b who roused them all out of it by proposing a contest.

"We have gone over a great deal of the history of this house," she said over breakfast, three days after the play. "But there is a great deal more here that can be discovered. I want each of you to find out all you can about the history of some particular place or object in this house, and link that to the greater history of England. The one with the story that is best will be allowed to come with me to select a school pony at the Horse Fair."

Now, since the mere existence of a "school pony" had been the subject of much rumor for two days—originating with Tommy who had sworn he had overheard a conversation between two grooms suggesting that some unknown benefactor was going to field the money for such a thing—the news caused a sensation. Every single girl knew exactly what she wanted—a gentle, fat white pony with a soft nose and big eyes, who would willingly be hitched to a cart for rides all over the estate. And every single boy knew what *he* wanted—a lively black pony with white socks and a blaze, and an eye full of mischief, who would willingly run at breakneck speed beneath his rider, and take fences even a tall hunter would balk at. Never mind that no more than two of the girls knew how to drive, and of the three boys who had been taught how to ride, none of them had been on a member of the living equine species in more than a year. The lines were drawn, the camps set up, and a grim rivalry ensued.

Now Nan, who was still in charge of helping the ayahs with the littlest children, was at a distinct disadvantage on two counts. One, that she had to wait until her chores were over that morning before she could go in search of her research subject. And two, that while she enjoyed history, her knowledge of it was extremely patchy.

So by the time she got to looking over the grounds and manor house, all the obvious choices had been spoken for. Sarah graciously offered to give up her own choice—the set of African tribal weapons she found in the gun room—but Nan was determined to find her own mystery to unravel.

But it seemed that every time she went to Memsa'b with a choice, it was only to discover that either she had misremembered and they had already learned about it as a group, or that someone else had already spoken for it. She didn't want to try and ferret out anything like the stories behind portraits or bits of furniture or books, Memsa'b had ruled out things that were clearly nothing more than hunting trophies, like the chandelier of stag horns or the heads of dead animals in the gun room, and the boys had all straightaway bagged things like suits of armor and heirloom swords.

It was with a sense of frustration that Nan began poking around the building, looking now for anything that gave her the least little stirring of interest. There was nothing inside in the areas that they were allowed to explore, and not even for the privilege of going to a Horse Fair was she going to dare the wrath of the house-keeper to venture into forbidden zones. Some of the other girls could get away with that, but it seemed that the housekeeper had dire expectations of Nan's ability to stay out of trouble, and kept Nan's leash extremely short.

The knot garden and the tiny maze (so small even the toddlers could find their way in and out of it) had already been taken. The other gardens were "too general" according to Memsa'b, "Unless you can find a specific plant that is unusual or clearly imported." The folly had been taken. The false ruins were spoken for.

At this point it was late afternoon, and there didn't seem to be anything that was going to be interesting to look into, which meant things that were difficult, dull, or both. At that point, Nan was kicking a round stone along the path in front of her in frustration when the stone smacked into the side of the dry well. She made her usual aversive detour—and then stopped.

Surely, if she felt a sensation that was *that* strong, there must be something there worth looking into. . . .

She went to Memsa'b, who raised an eyebrow at her. "It is old enough, surely. If that is what you want—"

"I'm about run out of things, Memsa'b," Nan confessed. "Dunno what else to do now."

Memsa'b rubbed the back of her right hand as if troubled. "There is something I do not like about that well," she said slowly. "I do not know that it is dangerous, but the place troubles me profoundly. I would prefer that if you really want to pursue this, you do it without spending too much time at the well itself. There is something not quite right there."

"Unhappy memories, mebbe?" Nan ventured shrewdly.

"It could well be. Well, if this is what you want, then by all means, use it as your project." Memsa'b looked down at her own hands for a moment. "But Nan, be careful about that place. It might be that there is nothing there, but it might very well be that we both sense something dormant there; something asleep. Don't wake it up."

Nan had figured that the best place to begin in her hunt for information was with the groundskeeper, but to her surprise he neither knew nor cared about something that was not only useless, but a nuisance, since occasionally things got dropped down it that he had to fetch back up again.

Not by accident, of course. No, it was generally deliberate, at least as far as Nan could make out from the man's grumbling. He didn't like the well. No one liked the well. But Master wouldn't brick it over because there was something historical about it.

Excited now, Nan tried to pursue the question further but the old man refused to talk about it anymore.

Frustrated, she began canvassing the rest of the servants, but most of them had no idea what she was talking about, except that few of them cared to go near the well. Most of them simply said that the well was ugly and there was no reason to spend any time around it. Three of them, however, said that the well made them uneasy and wouldn't even discuss it.

Dejected, she flopped into a chair at dinner between Sarah and Tommy and spent most of the meal interjecting heavy sighs between their excited comments. Sarah began looking at her curiously, and finally even Tommy noticed that she was being glum.

"No luck with your project, then?" he said, sympathetically. "Come on, Nan, tell us what it is, and maybe we can help."

"Even if we can't help, we can try and make you feel better," Sarah offered.

With another heavy sigh, Nan explained her idea, and that she had come up dry. Sarah shook her head—she was doing the history of a Cavalier-era portrait, and having no difficulty, for the artist was quite a famous one, and there were lots of books even in the manor library that talked about it. "I don't think I've seen anything in the library about the well," she said doubtfully.

But Tommy looked thoughtful.

"Maybe Gaffer Geordie can help," he said.

Nan blinked at him. "Who's that?" she asked

"He lives down in the pensioners' cottages," Tommy explained.

"He used to work in the stable, oh, a long time ago! Before the last of the old family died and the cousins inherited."

Well, that sounded promising. But if he was that old—

"He ain't dotty, is 'e?" Nan asked dubiously.

Tommy shook his head vigorously. "Not a bit! Whenever there's something wrong with a horse or a dog, they go to Gaffer before they call in the farrier or the horse doctor. Most times, he sets it right. And when they do call the horse doctor, he won't do a thing unless Gaffer is right there."

That sounded even more promising. But it didn't answer the question of why Tommy thought this Gaffer could help. Before she could say anything though, Tommy answered that question.

"Gaffer Geordie knows everything that's ever happened here right back to his grandfather's day," he explained. "So if there's anything about the well going back that far, he'll know."

The next day, armed with the information that Gaffer lived in the cottage "with all the dogs," Nan and Neville trudged down to the row of cottages that had been built to house Highleigh servants too old to work who had been pensioned off. And very shortly, Nan realized that the seemingly vague directions were not vague at all, for it was obvious which cottage was the Gaffer's.

Dogs—all of them old, maimed, or both—lay in the sun along the wall of the cottage on either side of the door, sat quietly watching the street, or attended to doggish business around the grounds. There were probably thirty of them; most were foxhounds, though there was a three-legged wolfhound, and a cluster of pretty little spaniels with various imperfections. The Gaffer himself, like a king enthroned among his subjects, sat on a stool beside his doorway, smoking a pipe, and watching the world pass by.

He was an astonishing sight in Nan's eyes; she had no idea just how old he was, but his hair and beard were snow-white, and two bushy white eyebrows overshadowed a face that was a mass of wrinkles, in which his eyes appeared like two shiny black currants. He certainly looked a lot older than her gran ever did, and gran had been the oldest person Nan had ever known. He wore a linen smock and buff trousers, a pair of old, worn boots, and a floppy hat.

He gave Nan a friendly nod as she approached, and grinned at Neville. She half expected to hear some sort of country dialect she'd only half understand when he opened his mouth, but instead, out came, "So, raven lass, come to see old Gaffer Geordie, have you?"

Nan nodded, distracted by the dogs, which came up to sniff and inspect her. Neville eyed them with disdain, even contempt. It was pretty clear that Gaffer Geordie saved the dogs no one else wanted. Even the spaniels at his feet, while pretty and charming, were not perfect specimens.

"So what can old Geordie do for you?" the old man continued, eyeing her with curiosity. "I don't know much but dogs and horses, lass. If there's aught wrong with your bird, I probably can't help you."

Neville quorked, and shook himself. "Neville's right as rain, sir," Nan said, as politely as possible. "I heard you knew a lot about Highleigh Park, an' I wanted to ask you 'bout something. That dry well by the kitchen garden—"

"Oh, now, that's an uncanny spot that is," Gaffer Geordie said instantly, and shook his head. "Had a bad reputation. Some said it was a cursed place, and some said it was a curse on the master of Highleigh. Very uncanny, and no surprise, seeing them bones as was pulled out of it."

There could not have been anything more likely to spark Nan's interest than that sentence. "Bones?" she repeated, as Neville bobbed his head.

"Oh, aye, bones. A full skellington, it was, and chains, leg chains and arm chains." Geordie nodded wisely. "Summun dropped that feller down and clamped the lid on the top, leavin' him to die. Master of Highleigh that *was,* back when I was no more bigger than you, reckoned to clean out the well, maybe use it for summat, but after the bones was found, he gave up on the notion of usin' it for anything. Vicar took charge of them, gave the poor fellow a proper Christian burial. Spot's been a bit quieter since then." He scratched his head. "Used to be, there was noise in that well, of a night, now and again."

"Moaning?" Nan asked, shivering.

But the old man shook his head. "Curses."

That was all he could tell her, but it was more than she had until that point. The next person to approach seemed to be the local vicar who was, in any case, coming to take tea with Memsa'b. Unfortunately, he could not shed light on the matter either. "That was long before my time, dear child," he said, shaking his head. And that seemed to be that.

Until, however, someone unexpectedly approached Nan the next day, rather than the other way around.

Called out of the nursery by one of the ayahs, she found the estate manager waiting in the hallway with an enormous ledger under his arm. She knew he was the estate manager only because she had seen him consulting with Memsa'b over some matter and had been told who the lean, slightly stooped, middle-aged man was. He was smiling slightly and pushed his glasses farther up his nose with one finger.

"You would be Miss Nan, investigating the mystery of the dry well?" he asked, making it sound far more intriguing than it had been up until that moment.

She nodded, and he handed the large and heavy book to her, bound in brown calfskin. "The Lord of Highleigh of those days was an amateur antiquarian and archaeologist, although they would not have put it that way back then. In his own writing, he referred to himself as a Student of Natural Sciences. He took notes on everything he found and did in and around the estate, so if there is any record of anything to do with the well, it will surely be in this book."

Flabbergasted, as well as astonished, Nan took it from him. "Thankee!" she exclaimed. "Thankee kindly!"

He waved her thanks off, peering at her benignly from behind his spectacles. "On the whole, having you children here has been no great work or inconvenience and has been quite amusing. This project of your schoolmistress' is teaching you all valuable lessons in conducting research, and I am happy to be able to assist."

With that, he went on his way, leaving her clutching the oversized volume to her chest.

After luncheon, she, Sarah, and Tommy—who, having completed his own history of the suit of armor in the library, was eaten up with curiosity about Nan's project—took it to the dining room, opened the book on the big table, and began looking through it. The three of them knelt side-by-side on dining room chairs so they could all get a good view. The neat, copperplate handwriting was surprisingly easy to read, and the three of them, with the birds looking on from Nan and Sarah's shoulders, perused the pages with interest.

This self-professed "Student of Natural History" was more of a dabbler in anything and everything, it seemed to Nan. There were notes on chemical experiments, on stellar observations, weather observations, but what clearly intrigued him most was the far past. It was when he was digging the foundations of the folly that he first encountered some Roman artifacts, and the discovery of the few coins, the bits of pottery, and the old dagger changed his life.

While he did not go wholesale into digging up his estate, he used every new construction project as a reason to excavate. When he was not digging, he was finding other places where he could indulge his hobby.

And that brought him around to exploring the past through the records of his own family, and trying to link what he found to the papers and diaries in the family archives.

He wasn't often all that successful, and some of his notes seemed to be stretching the facts even to Nan. How on earth could he determine that a coin was Roman, for instance, when it was so worn that there wasn't anything to show it even was a coin except that it was round and bronze?

Eventually, though, he had built all that a reasonable man could, and he turned his attention to other places he might go looking for bits of the past.

That was when he hit on the idea of clearing out the old well.

The children leaned over the book intently as they realized that they had struck gold at last. The first few entries, mostly the general dates Lord Mathew had uncovered telling him who had ordered the well built and why it had gone dry, interspersed with observations about the weather and the implications for the harvest, were rather boring. One very small man had to be lowered down to the bottom on a rope, and dug the debris out, shovelful by small shovelful, dumping it into buckets to be sent up for examination and disposal. Then it all got sifted once it arrived at the top of the well, and anything not dirt, rocks, and plant life were set aside for Lord Mathew to look at in detail. It had been difficult finding someone willing to go down into the well; it had a bad reputation, and according to Lord Mathew's notes, the servants claimed that on certain nights one could hear moaning and vile curses coming from the bottom.

Then the digger found the skull and nothing would persuade anyone on the estate to go down into the well. Lord Mathew, now afire with excitement, stripped to his shirtsleeves and had *himself* lowered down into the hole. With the aid of a lantern held over his head, he meticulously excavated until he uncovered the entire body.

Whoever it was, there had been manacles about his wrists and ankles, with chains on them. Clothing had not survived, but there had been silver buttons on his coat and trousers, and he had worn fine leather boots with silver buckles. Another buckle might have been an ornament on a hat. Lord Mathew tentatively dated these objects to the time of Charles the First. Since this was the time of the Civil War, and many records were lost then when the manor was invaded by Roundheads and many things stolen or burned, Lord Mathew despaired of finding any answer.

Still, he tried—and erring on the side of compassion, turned the remains over to the vicar of the time for a Christian burial.

Nothing else of note was taken out of the well, and that ended the tales of moaning and cursing coming from the well. Lord

Mathew's researches were in vain; because so many people died or vanished during that time, there simply was no telling who it could have been.

They closed the book and looked at each other, the odd sourish smell of an old book still in their nostrils.

"Well," Sarah said finally, "you have enough to write that report for Memsa'b now." And it was true that she did, but the results were less than satisfying.

Nan nodded. "But it don't solve the mystery," she added, feeling obscurely disappointed.

"Crumbs," Tommy said, clearly disappointed. "It doesn't. Maybe Memsa'b will have some ideas where to look next."

Nan sighed, and went to fetch pen and paper to write her report. She had no illusions about her report winning the coveted place at Memsa'b's side, but now she was far more interested in getting to the bottom of this than going to the Horse Fair.

❄

She had to wait until she was alone with the headmistress before she could bring up the topic. "I wonder," Memsa'b said slowly, after she and Nan had finished another of her "special" lessons. "I wonder if there isn't a way to find something out about the mysterious body in the well directly." And she looked straight at Nan.

The implication was obvious, since Nan had just completed another lesson in psychometry, one in which she had learned to tell how far back in time a particular reading on an object had taken place. They were sitting in the parlor, and Nan had just "read" one of the old vases there, a huge blue-and-white monstrosity that was always full of fresh flowers.

"Wot? *Me?*" Nan said, startled. " 'Ow? We 'aven't got the skellington, or even them silver buttons." Whatever had become of those objects was a mystery, though Nan figured they had been buried along with the remains. They weren't novel enough, nor old enough, to have entered Lord Mathew's collection of artifacts and souvenirs.

"The well, Nan," Memsa'b pointed out. "You can 'read' the well itself."

"Oo-eck." Nan could have hit herself for not thinking of that solution earlier. " 'Course I can! Mind, there's been a lot 'uv people gone and touched that well since, things'll be a bit dimlike."

Memsa'b gave her an admonishing look. "Don't you think that's all to the good? Considering that we are discussing the circumstances that led to a man's perishing there, laden with chains? This is not something that I would care to experience at first hand."

Nan shrugged. Sometimes Memsa'b forgot how little Nan had been sheltered from. Murder in Whitechapel was a way of life, so to speak. " 'Sides," she continued, "I got Neville now. He stood down that nasty thing in Berkeley Square. I don't reckon something that never did wuss than swear 'ud bother him none."

From the back of the chair beside her, Neville bobbed his head, fluffed his feathers, and uttered a short "quork."

"I am more than willing for you to try this, or I would not have suggested it in the first place," Memsa'b said, interlacing her fingers together in her lap. "However, there are some things we should consider first, and discuss, you and I, and things that I should research myself. I don't want you plunging headfirst into this, and especially I do not want you doing this without me. Do I have your word?"

With a sigh, and with a glare from Neville that suggested that if she did *not* promise, he might well give her a good peck, she gave her word.

"First of all, although the memories are old and the remains are no longer physically present, a spirit *could* still be bound to the place of its death and you could awaken it," Memsa'b said thoughtfully. "That could be good—we might be able to convince it to go on its way—or bad—because it might attack. So at the very least, I need to be there, and most of the children need to be kept away. I would prefer it if Sahib and possibly Agansing could also be present. Agansing's people have a great deal of experience with Ancestor Spirits, both good and bad, and that might come in handy."

"Most of the others—you're thinkin' Sarah ought to be there, too?" Nan hazarded.

Memsa'b nodded, but reluctantly, keeping her eyes focused on Nan's. "Yes and no. Yes, because if there is a spirit, she is the one most likely to be able to speak to it. And no, because if there is a spirit, it may attempt to take her."

"There's Grey—" Nan pointed out. "She's Sarah's protector. Right?"

"Ye-es," Memsa'b agreed, but with some doubt. "I simply don't know how powerful a protector Grey is. And there is also the possibility that you could be harmed by this as well. These are all things that need to be balanced."

With a sigh, Nan agreed. By this point, it was pretty obvious that Memsa'b was not going to march straight down to the well and have Nan try her power of seeing things in something's past right soon. It was going to wait until the weekend, at best, which was when Sahib would be coming.

She did, however, go tell Sarah about Memsa'b's idea that night at bedtime. Both Sarah and Grey listened attentively.

And Sarah, who was sitting in bed clasping her knees with her arms, shivered when she had finished. "I'm not very brave," she said quietly. "Not like you, Nan."

Nan snorted. "Brave enough," she said roughly. " 'Ow brave is brave, an' when does it spill over to daft? Eh? I done plenty daft things some 'un might say was brave."

Sarah had to laugh at that. "I don't like to think of anything trapped or in pain, or both," she went on. "But that horrible thing in Berkeley Square—it scared me, Nan. I don't ever want to see anything like that again."

"No more do I, but this thing, the well, it don't *feel* like that thing in London," Nan pointed out. Then she sighed. "Really, though, we ain't got a choice. We'll get to do what Memsa'b says we can."

"That's true, and Memsa'b won't let us do anything that is really dangerous," Sarah replied, brightening, and changed the topic to speculation on who was going to win the coveted expedition to the Horse Fair.

But Nan stared up at the ceiling after the candles were out with her hands behind her head, thinking. It was true that Memsa'b would normally not let them do anything dangerous. . . .

Not knowingly. But even Memsa'b was concerned that there were hidden dangers here she could not anticipate.

That factor alone was enough to give Nan pause, and she tried to think of things that maybe Memsa'b would not, only to decide that this was an exercise in futility.

Oh, well, she decided finally, as she gave up the fight to hold off sleep. *Things'll 'appen as they 'appen, like Gram used to say. Let t'morrow take care of itself.*

11

MEMSA'B, Nan decided, looked worried, but was hiding it well.
Nan was more excited than worried, and Neville looked positively
impatient to get things started.

Sarah, however, was showing enough nerves for both of them.
And *she* wasn't even the one who was going to be investigating the
well and its haunt in the first place!

"Glaah," said Neville, and Nan got the sense of *"of course she's
nervous, she's nervous for you!"* And immediately she felt a little
ashamed of herself. Besides Sarah had said herself she wasn't
"brave like Nan," and it wasn't nice to be scornful of her for something she had admitted to herself!

And with that thought, she shook her head at how strange her
life had become. Not that long ago, would she have cared what
anyone thought? Would she have cared that she herself had
thought things about someone that weren't very nice?

No, of course not. It wouldn't have mattered. When you were
going to bed hungry every night, nothing much mattered except
finding a way to scrounge another bit of food. When you got
thrown out in the street in the middle of winter, all that mattered

was that you could find the penny for a place under a roof that night. Whether or not you thought something about someone that might hurt their feelings if they found out was so far from being relevant to how you lived—

It struck her for a moment how much her life had changed, and in her heart she apologized to Sarah for belittling her. Neville rubbed his beak against her cheek.

Beside Memsa'b were Sahib and Agansing, the latter looking entirely serene. That gave Nan heart; for Agansing was the one person she thought likeliest to sense incipient trouble before it became a problem.

Excluding the other children would have been tricky, except for one thing. The new pony had arrived, and all of them were down at the stable, being introduced, and taking their turns with him. There had been neither black ponies nor white at the Horse Fair, only varying shades of brown, which averted that particular crisis— the chosen beast was an affectionate little gelding with two white feet and a white blaze. Tommy—who had won the coveted position—immediately named him "Flash," but Flash's main pace was an amble, so he wasn't likely to live up to it. He had been advertised as being trained to ride or drive, so presumably everyone was going to be reasonably satisfied with him.

But with that sort of a draw down at the stables, probably no one was going to notice that Nan and Sarah weren't there. And even if they did, it was reasonable to assume that Sarah, raised in Africa, and Nan, raised on the London streets, hadn't ever had ponies, and probably didn't know how to ride or drive.

Which was, of course, true.

Nan had, in fact, encountered the pony and had not been impressed. In comparison to Neville, it came off a poor second in her opinion.

It was no hardship to either Nan or Sarah to be here, rather than at the stables with the rest.

They were all waiting for one thing: Karamjit to return from the stable, with word that the rest were all now fully involved with the pony and unlikely to take it into their heads to come back to the manor and go looking for Memsa'b, Sarah, or Nan.

And at length, Karamjit did appear, stalking around the corner of the hedge like a two-legged panther, taking his place beside Sahib. With that arrival, Memsa'b nodded at Nan, who braced herself, approached the well, laid both bare hands on the stone coping, closed her eyes, and slowly let herself "see" what was there.

There was an *immediate* surge of terror, but she had expected that and pushed past it. It was the reaction of that long-ago worker to discovering a corpse, and she had suspected this would be something she would sense very strongly. It was relatively recent in the life of the well, and it was powerful. With it came panic, the sense of being stifled and trapped, fleeting images of rough walls and above all, the need to *get out*. It didn't last long, and she moved beyond the moment.

Then, there was nothing, for a very long time.

Well, not *nothing*, precisely, but only vague whispers of a thousand passing personalities that hardly left an imprint at all; merest hints of emotion, piled one atop another in a confusing heap, and nothing much in the way of images. She was used to this sort of pattern emanating from a very old object, but the well was so public a place and it was so easy for people to brush a bit of themselves on it in passing that it was like pushing her way through endless, ghostly branches in a haunted forest without an end—

Then—

A force hit her like a runaway wagon.

Damn you!

Words—oh, yes—definitely words, but impact that shook her and made her fall forward against the stone wall of the well.

The anger, the fear, the despair struck her with all the immediacy of a physical blow.

Immediately, she felt Neville push himself into her neck, as her hands clutched the rough stone, and her body reeled along with her mind. She reached for his mental presence even as she managed to raise a hand to touch his neck, and the feelings receded.

But not so far that she could not read them.

She had images now, a dark-clad body curled into a fetal ball, chained hand and foot. A man, dying of thirst, knowing he was dying, and such rage in him that the rage itself took on what was left of his life force.

I know this part, she thought. She pushed past the images and the rage. This was the ending, the last bitter moments of a life. She needed to see where it started—

More images flooded her; she let them come. She knew that the best way for her to decipher the past of an object was to allow all the images to flood in at once, and sort them out after she had taken them in.

The well had "seen" the man, but the well had no eyes, so she would never know what the man had actually looked like, other than that he was lean, and his clothing was dark and quite plain. . . .

Another surge of emotion, more sustained this time; outrage rather than anger, and fear. Disbelief. Horror. Each of these in turn, all linked with a thought: *they're not coming back!*

Who was not coming back? No answer there; only the long-ago press of emotion as a man realized that he had been forgotten, abandoned, left to a fate that had only one ending.

" 'E can't believe this. Whoever put 'im in there either forgot about 'im or somethin' happened," she heard her own voice saying dreamily. "He's hearin' commotion an' 'e reckons it's the whole household packin' up an' leavin' and not knowin' 'e's down 'ere. 'E's been yellin', but nobody 'erd 'im." More images, and then, not images at all, but the things that had happened were happening to *her*; being lowered carefully into the well, head ringing from the blows, licking swollen lips and tasting blood, unable to see out of one eye. Anger at being defeated, at being caught. No words now, only feelings, emotional and physical.

There was a kernel there that was Nan, that knew it was a little girl, that the country was ruled by a Queen and not a King, that none of this was real. There was the sense of an anchor, a protector, who sheltered that kernel of herself. She had to just let it all wash over her, and not try to fight it, because fighting would only wear her out and thin her hold on herself.

She closed in on herself, made herself like a hard little stone, the kind you got in your shoe and couldn't get rid of. This wasn't an attack, any more than the foot in the shoe was an attack on the stone. There wasn't even a person behind it. This was all just idiot emotion, left behind by the trauma of long ago. Maybe there had been a ghost at one time, howling to be found, cursing those who passed by. If so, Christian burial, even though no one knew what name to put on a marker, had probably put an end to the haunts.

Finally, the little stone that was Nan dropped out of the swirling chaos of left-behind emotions. She had come through it. She was on the other side.

She opened her eyes, blinked twice, and sat down quite suddenly on the ground.

❋

Isabelle shook her head. "A mystery still," she mused. "From Nan's description, I would guess that the man was a Roundhead, perhaps a spy? For whatever reason, someone here decided he was a menace and imprisoned him in the well."

"And didn't tell anyone else," her husband pointed out. "That was where it all fell apart. We know why no one came to let him out—there was no one here."

Now that they knew what to look for, they knew that as the Royalists lost ground to Oliver Cromwell's troops, the family here had abandoned their manor, taken all the portable wealth they could muster, and fled across the Channel. As it happened, they had a great deal of "portable" wealth, and they had been able to get across the countryside and into France with no real difficulty. Others who had waited longer had not been so lucky. . . .

Frederick stretched, accepted a cup of tea from Isabelle, and looked to Agansing. "You're certain that this wasn't deliberate murder?" he asked. "Clearing that well of the taint of something like murder—"

Agansing shook his head. "The man's captors were hardly kind, but there is no trace in the original thought patterns that he anticipated such a thing here."

"Besides, dearest, why would anyone go to the trouble of binding and chaining him, then lowering him carefully into the well, if they intended to murder him?" Isabelle pointed out. "It would have take far less effort to simply knock him on the head or shoot him and throw him in the river. If he was found at all, it would be assumed he was another casualty of the war. It's what I would have done if I had wanted to murder someone at that date."

Agansing, for all that he knew her well, looked a little aghast. Frederick reached across the distance between their chairs and patted her hand affectionately. "Sometimes, my love, you make my blood run cold," he said fondly. "I'm glad you're on my side."

She sniffed. "Really, Frederick, I am only saying what I would have done, had I a wicked nature and been inclined to murder someone during the Civil War, *not* that I would countenance doing any such thing."

He chuckled; he'd been teasing her, of course, but she was a little irritated at him. It was not the sort of teasing she enjoyed.

Well, perhaps her nerves were irritated by being in proximity to the negative emotions in that wellhead for so long. She sat on her irritation and went on. "We definitely need to cleanse the place, or something might well take advantage of the situation. You saw for yourself how readily little Nan became absorbed; there is a great deal of energy there, and if we still have an enemy to Nan and Sarah, that place could be used to feed and hold a truly dangerous entity."

Frederick nodded. "I completely agree." He rose, cracked his knuckles, and held out his hand to assist her to rise. "And there is no time like the present."

❄

Cordelia was angry.

The servants sensed it, and stayed as far out of her reach as possible. She would have taken her anger out on David, but *he* had gone off to a country house party for the next several days. She had been invited, but she had turned the invitation down; the host bored her, the hostess was worse, and it would have been one stultifying round of lawn tennis and croquet in the afternoons, and rubbers of bridge and politics in the evenings. Except she would have been excluded from the politics, relegated to gossip and amateur theatrics with the ladies, and the politics were the only part of the house party she would have found interesting.

But several important men had been invited, which meant that David had to go. So he was not here to suffer the sting of her anger either.

She sat in her exquisite parlor, and after long, hard consideration, she leveled her gaze on an extremely expensive porcelain vase David had given her, full of water and white lilies that were nearly as expensive as the vase. She stared at it; obedient to her will, the little cold Elementals that looked like white, furred snakes wrapped themselves around the lilies and began to freeze them.

Within moments, they were solid enough to hammer nails with. They were lovely in this form, but as soon as they began to thaw, they would turn into a blackened mess that the maids would have to clean up. It would take them hours, especially if any of the ruined, rotting blossoms dropped on the tabletop and marred the finish. They would be waxing and polishing half the day.

The gesture didn't appease her wrath, but it did vent some of her feelings.

For the quarry had escaped! Before she could do anything about those wretched children, someone *else* had the unmitigated gall to invite them to his estate for the summer! She had no idea who, nor where it was. Her agents had been unable to get anything out of the few reticent servants left, and efforts to follow Frederick Harton had all ended in failure. She hired different agents, to the same end. It was immensely frustrating. The man was utterly ordinary, a commonplace soldier-turned-merchant. To be sure, he had *some* occult power, but it could not possibly be a match for that of an Elemental Master!

She was left to pursue the quarry through the only route she had left: Isabelle Harton's friends among the female Elemental Masters. She was forced to be extremely circumspect about it, for she did not want Isabelle to get wind of the fact that she was hunting for her and wonder why.

Her rage, like all her emotions, was icy and calculating. It was a force to be conserved and put to good use. And it occurred to her suddenly that there might be one more way of finding those wretched children. She could use her rage to best effect with it right now. But it would take exceedingly careful work if she was not to tip her hand.

She closed her eyes and took several long, slow, deep breaths, then rose, and went to her workroom.

She closed and locked the door behind herself, and sat down before her worktable. No Ice Wurms to be summoned today . . . but she left a single gray feather on the table in front of her.

She sat in her crystal throne, folded her hands in her lap, and began to still her body.

Her heartbeat slowed, her breathing became shallow and almost imperceptible, and within the half hour, anyone looking at her would have thought her dead, or near it.

In this state, it was easy to slip across the barrier between the living and the dead. Not far, but enough across the line to shadow-walk. Enough to talk to the ghost she herself had created, though she could not speak to nor see any of the others that she had no hand in making. Enough to be able to call one of her little servants to her, or to see them, enough to travel to a limited extent herself, in spirit, though she could not move far from her body.

She had a particular child ghost in mind, a dream-raptured little thing who in life had been mute, and in death was just as mute. If Isabelle caught the ghost, she could interrogate it all she liked; she would learn nothing from it.

The waif actually knew she was dead, but did not care. She had never seen the inside of church or chapel in her entire life, and so had no expectation of any sort of afterlife. What she did know was that she was no longer hungry, thirsty, or cold. This was a distinct improvement over her lot when she had been alive. While it was true that spirits saw the living world but dimly, as if they wandered about in a London "pea-soup" fog, this did not seem to trouble little Peggoty in the least. She had never owned a toy, she had never slept in a bed, she had never had a permanent roof over her head, so the lack of them did not trouble her either. She had been brought to one of Cordelia's "shelters" dying of starvation and tuberculosis, and while it might have been possible to prolong her life, Cordelia had simply taken advantage of the situation by putting the mite out of her misery in the usual way. Since then, she had been useful for simple tasks that did not require much thinking.

As nearly as Cordelia was able to tell, Peggoty passed her days as a ghost in the same way that she had passed them as a living child—wrapped in some strange dream world, half-awake and half-asleep. What it was that she daydreamed about, no one would ever know, for she lacked the means to tell them.

Whatever it was, she seemed content to "live" there in her daydreams between times when Cordelia needed her.

In that half world of mist and shadow, Cordelia moved, cutting through the mist to wherever it was in the townhouse that Peggoty had put herself. She could have summoned the child to her, of course, but she knew from past experience that would frighten the waif, who associated being "called" with punishment. Normally, this would not be a problem, but if Isabelle's pupil was somehow able to see and interact with Peggoty, the last thing that Cordelia wanted was for Peggoty to cling to that little girl for protection.

No, Cordelia wanted Peggoty to be her usual dreamy self, with nothing to cause alarm in her behavior. That way, the worst that would happen if she were discovered would be that Isabelle would succeed in sending Peggoty on to the next world—

Wherever, whatever the "next world" was for Peggoty. She was such a passive little spirit that "the next world" might only consist of a brighter version of the fog of dreams she moved through now.

Passing through the real world in her ghostly equivalent, Cordelia found Peggoty physically haunting the attic of her town house. The child stood dreamily at the window staring at what to her must have been a sea of gray, marked only by vague, shadowy forms, appearing, disappearing, looking more like ghosts to her than she did to the world of the living. Even here, halfway into the spirit world as Cordelia was, the child was nothing more than a wispy wraith, a sketch in the air of transparent white on dark gray. Although her head, hands, and chest were detailed enough, the rest of her was blurred, as if the drawing was incomplete and unfinished.

"Peggoty," said Cordelia, in her sweetest, gentlest voice.

The child turned and looked up at her mistress with large, dark eyes in a colorless face, a face thin with years of constant near-starvation, and as expressionless as a tombstone. Those eyes seemed to look *through* her, and Cordelia, although she was used to that look, still felt just a fraction or two colder than she had a moment before.

"Peggoty, I need you to go and find someone," Cordelia continued. "It is another little girl."

There was one thing that the Berkeley Square misadventure had produced; a handful of small feathers, gray and black. Peggoty could not touch them, of course, but she could get a kind of "scent" from them, and follow it the way a bloodhound would follow an actual scent.

Of course, Cordelia could have used the feathers to locate the girls with magic—had they not been protected by Masters of all four Elements. Cordelia made no mistake in underestimating her opponents just because they were women. They were, in fact, rather more likely to be supremely competent than not.

Any magical probe would be met by alarms, and if she was very unlucky, the instant response from whoever was responsible for setting up the Fire Wards. Cordelia knew that she was good, but she was not good enough to erase her tracks before another Master could identify her. Her magical "signature" was quite unique.

But a spirit, especially a harmless little thing like Peggoty, could slip in and out without ever being noticed.

She led Peggoty to her workroom, drifting through the walls, where she had left one of the tiny feathers on the table, and Peggoty's big eyes rested on it. "The little girl I want you to find has a bird, and this is one of its feathers. If you find the bird, you'll find the girl. I want you to go and find her, and when you do, come back here and show me where she is. Can you do that?"

Peggoty nodded, slowly, her eyes fixed on the tiny feather as she "read" whatever it was that told her where it had come from. Then, without looking again at Cordelia, the wraith turned in the air and floated silently through the wall.

Cordelia sighed, and with a mental wrench, brought herself straight back into her own body again.

This would take time, but Peggoty did not need to sleep, did not even tire, and was not easily distracted once she had been set a task. Perhaps the children enjoyed being given tasks as a change in the unvarying condition of their lives. It was difficult to tell, especially with one like Peggoty, who had never been a normal child.

Of course, the annoying thing was that none of this would have been needed if Cordelia had just been born a man.

She rose carefully from her chair—carefully, because after a session like this she was rather stiff—and left her workroom. After the chill of that room, the summer warmth felt like the sultry breath of a hothouse in July, and she winced. Burgeoning growth . . . meant burgeoning decay.

There had been another tiny line in her face again today, near the corner of her eye. She had preserved her beauty for so long—but even magic could not hold time back forever, it seemed.

Soon people would stop wondering if David was her lover and start wondering if David was her son.

It was enough to make her break into a rage, but rages were aging, and she had already indulged in one today.

If she had been born a man, no one would think twice about wrinkles and gray hair. In fact, such signs of aging would have been marks of increased wisdom and she would have more respect, not less, for possessing them.

Galling, to have to depend on someone else for the power she should rightfully have had on her own. And doubly galling to see David making his own decisions, without consulting her, as he had been doing more and more regularly of late.

She hated summer. She hated the heat, the unrestrained growth of nature. She hated being forced to relocate to that wretched house on the Thames just so she could continue to attract the right people to her parties. She hated the relaxation of etiquette that summer brought, although the relaxation of conversation was useful, very useful—but the same relaxation could be brought about with the proper application of fine spirits and a warm room.

It was far, far more difficult to collect children to make into her ghostly servants in the summer. Sleeping in alleys and staircases, even on rooftops and in doorways was no longer such a hardship in summer. It was easier to find food; things spoiled by the heat were tossed out all the time. Haunting the farmers' markets brought plenty of bruised and spoiled fruit and vegetables. They didn't come to her recruiters, and it was harder to summon the cold to kill them.

She stood at the window, looking out unseeing at the street just beyond her walls.

It was such a waste, too . . . those lives, those years that she could use, that youth she needed, all going for nothing. There was no way to capture that youth and transfer it to someone else, and even if she could, there still remained the insurmountable barrier of her sex. As long as she was a woman, she would never be taken seriously enough to achieve any kind of power in her own name. She breathed in the scent of summer life, green and warm, and hated it. *From hour to hour we ripe and ripe, and from hour to hour we rot and rot, and thereby hangs a tale,* Shakespeare had said. Ripe turned to rot all too soon, but sooner for women than men.

And it was a bit too late now to try masquerading as a man. Even if she wanted to. It would take far too long to establish that male persona in the position to which she had gotten David. The door of opportunity was slowly closing.

Her hand clenched. Unfair, unfair!

If only she could somehow *become* David, to control him directly instead of in this maddening, roundabout fashion! After all, what had he done with his life on his own? Reorganized that silly little Master's Circle of his! And of what use was that?

If only—

And at that thought, her mind stopped.

She mentally stood stock still to examine that thought again.

If only she could become David.

Was it possible?

Was it desirable?

The answer to that second question was an unequivocal *yes*. It was very desirable. It wasn't as if she had gotten any great use from her femininity in ages. Rather, it was something to be suppressed, as was evidence of her intelligence. If she was a man—if she was David—in order to masquerade as a man she would have to sacrifice what was amusingly called a "love life." There was no way she would be able to simulate lovemaking as a man. But she would be living a life no less chaste than she was now. It was no great sacrifice to give up something she wasn't "enjoying" in the first place. And in its place, she would get that access to power she craved, and the respect of those to whom she could display her full and unfettered intelligence.

Oh, yes, definitely desirable.

Was it possible?

She turned, unseeing, and sat down on the fainting couch at the window to think.

There was a moment when she collected her ghostly servants that the body was still alive, but soulless. The cold kept it preserved at that moment. If, while the body was still in that state, she could transfer her own self to it—

No one had ever done such a thing. As far as she knew, no one had ever tried. But she felt herself trembling with excitement at the very idea that it could be done at all.

She should not try this herself, not yet. She should try it with two of the children. None of her existing spirit servants, no; they were too useful and she needed most of them where they were. But perhaps, if she could find two children, very much alike so that they themselves would not be aware that the bodies had been switched, she could test it out without risking anything. Because she should try a switch first, before trying a substitution.

Then if a switch worked, she could try disposing of the first spirit before inserting the second. It would probably be useful if she could find a child with a fierce will to live, unlike her usual recruits whose hold on life was already tenuous. Yes . . .

And then, when she was certain she had the method honed and refined—

She could even picture it in her mind's eye. Inviting David to a late supper. Wine and brandy and perhaps a dose of opiates. Sending him up to bed—then slipping into the room when he was too deeply asleep to feel the cold, opening the window, and calling the Wurms just to be sure that it was cold enough.

The real trick would be to warm up the body quickly enough after she inhabited it; if she did not, she would die. That would require some physical means. Tricky, tricky. Perhaps—yes. The timing would be crucial, but she could do all this just before the maid was to enter the room to awaken her guest and ask how he wanted his breakfast. The maid would find the cold room and the cold body—but still breathing—and summon help. Only later would they find Cordelia's shell. Yes, indeed, tricky, but it could be done.

Yes, that would be a good plan, further made valuable by having witnesses that nothing worse than a mania for cold, fresh air had "killed" Cordelia herself and imperiled David.

And then there would be no more troubles over controlling David. She would *be* David. She could rewrite her will, leaving everything she owned to David as well, so that when her old body was found, she would lose nothing of what she had gained.

And then, when age caught up with the David body, she could find another protégé to school, and repeat the plan. Perhaps a girl this time; perhaps by that point it would be possible for a woman to wield power in her own right. But if not—look far enough and she could find a naïve young male Fire Magician, probably among the disadvantaged, hopefully without the inconvenient burden of parents, with whom she could repeat the process. Why not? Childless men took on protégés all the time. If anything, people would think how wise she was to have done so. The estate would have to go to some collateral line, of course, but the bulk of the money and material goods that were unencumbered could go to anyone. Herself, of course.

She would be immortal. She would have all the benefits of age, and none of the drawbacks. David's Powers were different. Instead of the weak Power of Air behind the Power of Ice, she would have the immense strength of Fire.

If it worked.

And that was the first step. She must find out if it could work, then perfect the procedure until it was faultless.

And this would be all the more reason to find those children and eliminate them; David knew about them now, and knew what they could do. If she made him into a wandering spirit, he would certainly go straight to them to expose her.

There was a great deal of work ahead of her. Fortunately, she had never been afraid of work.

Fortunate for *her,* at least.

12

SARAH had an unfinished daisy wreath in her lap, but she wasn't working on it. Nan, whose talents did not run to making wreaths and flower chains, had been splitting grass stems into strings, and by now had more strings than Sarah could ever possibly need.

Nevertheless, she kept splitting, because it was a way to help her concentrate. She and Sarah were having a "discussion," and Sarah was winning.

"I think we should try it," said Sarah. Her normally sweet face was set in an expression that Memsa'b would probably call "mulish."

Ever since they had helped to determine that the old well had been haunted by nothing more sinister than bad memories, Sarah had wanted to investigate the bridge, which had given off the same sort of unpleasant aura. Nan was not so sure this was a good idea, and the oddest thing was, this was a complete reversal of their normal roles. Usually, it was Sarah who was the cautious one.

Then again, it hadn't been Sarah who had been the one to experience those old memories either. Maybe that was what was making the difference this time.

An' I don't get too sympathetic 'bout her havin' ghosts move in. . . .

It was no use turning to the birds for advice either. Both Grey and Neville had responded with the mental equivalent of a help-less shrug. Nan got the feeling that neither of them felt as if they had enough information to give a good answer. Like Nan, they didn't like the idea, but they had no good reason to oppose it.

Still, on the other hand, Nan was also tempted. It felt as if this was something she ought to be doing. They were only going to in-vestigate. If there *was* anyone or anything bound to Earth there, surely Memsa'b and Sahib ought to know about it. And if there wasn't, then the nasty feelings ought to be cleaned up and Mem-sa'b and Agansing ought to know about it. Nasty feelings could af-fect people that were sensitive to them, and might cause a mischief.

There was a third aspect to this, which was that somewhere deep inside her, Nan felt as if there was a grown-up person chaf-ing to be out and doing things. She couldn't explain this feeling, but it was definitely there, and growing stronger all the time.

She had to wonder if Sarah wasn't feeling the same. Maybe that was why Sarah was so adamant about doing this.

"What can it hurt to just go and *look?*" Sarah asked at last. "We went and looked before and nothing happened. We won't do any-thing, just look! I want to fix it ourselves if we can, but not this time."

Nan grimaced, but she had to think that Sarah was right. "No touching the bridge and reading it, then?" she asked cautiously.

Sarah shook her head. "No. Just going there and getting the feeling of things without touching anything. Maybe we can take care of this by ourselves and maybe not, but we won't know until we look it over."

Nan sighed. She had been losing this battle since it began, and there was no point in pretending otherwise. She might just as well give in now as later.

"All right," she said, shrugging. "We can go and look. But nawt more!"

To her credit, Sarah did not lord it over her friend as some might have. "Then let's go now, today," she urged. "Before anyone thinks we might and tells us not to."

Nan raised her eyebrow at that. Sarah meant "Memsa'b," of course; there was no one else they had told about the bridge. And Sarah was sounding just a touch rebellious. That was a change. Sarah? Rebellious?

"I'm tired of waiting for things to happen *to* us," Sarah added unexpectedly. "I don't see any reason why we have to sit here and wait for trouble to find us, when we can go scout it the way a hunter would and know what's coming before it gets here!"

Nan blinked. Put that way—She brushed the grass stems off her skirt and stood up. "Let's go," she said decisively. "Memsa'b ain't convinced more trouble ain't comin' an' I don't know as buildin' up 'igh walls and sittin' behind 'em is such a good notion."

Now Neville finally roused from his own indecision and quorked enthusiastically. Grey just sighed. But she didn't seem inclined to want to stop them, so Nan took that as tacit assent. She followed Neville as the raven flew ahead, in their usual pattern of going to a tree within calling distance, waiting for the girls to catch up, and going on to another tree.

It didn't take them nearly as long to get to the bridge as it had the first time they had wandered out that far—but the first time, they had been doing just that, wandering, with no set purpose and no real hurry to get anywhere. As they approached the structure, it seemed to Nan that the uneasy feelings began at a point much further away than the first time.

"Was it like this, this far away before?" Sarah asked, in an uneasy echo of Nan's own thoughts.

Nan shook her head. "Dunno," she replied dubiously. "Could be 'cause we're expectin' it this time. Could be 'cause we know what t' look for. Could be misrememberin'."

They stood on the road, in the shade of a giant oak tree, and regarded the bridge carefully.

When you shut off those bad feelings, there was nothing about the bridge to give anyone cause for alarm. It was a perfectly ordinary structure made of yellowish stone, arcing over the river. It had three low stone arches, and ended in four squat, square pillars, two on either side of the span. The river was smooth and quiet, flowing by lazily. There were no sinister shadows in the bright sunlight shining down on it.

But when you let yourself open to those feelings, it seemed as if there *ought* to be sinister shadows everywhere, and dark forms lurking behind the pillars. Now even Sarah began to look dubious and uneasy, as if she had just decided this had been a bad idea, but wasn't going to say so.

Nan, on the other hand, was now determined to get to the bottom of all of this. Never mind that she'd been against it before, now she wanted to know just what it was that was at the root of all this.

"I'm getting' closer," she said shortly, and whistled for Neville to come to her. He landed on her outstretched arm and jumped to her shoulder.

She kept her eyes wide open, and pictured herself peering cautiously through a hole in a wall as she approached the bridge one slow step at a time. It was at the third step that she began to make something out.

It wasn't just memories. There *was* something there!

The feelings came first, with the sense of a presence.

It wasn't like the horrible thing in Berkeley Square, though— this was hunger, a great void of *need* and of loneliness, but not anything that Nan would have called "healthy." The closest she could come was to those few times when her mother had gotten maudlin drunk and had hugged her too tight and cried about what an awful mum she was, when all the time she wasn't so sorry that she wouldn't go right out and spend supper money on gin as soon as she sobered up. And this was to that experience as the sun was to a candle.

Another step, and Nan saw what it was, or saw something, anyway. Woman-shaped and shadowy, draped in veils, and a vast pit of greed and despair so deep that Nan knew if you fell into it you'd never get out again.

And she had something.

She had a little girl.

Not a living little girl, but another shadow shape, like a sketch made in white mist, a little ghost girl. The shadow woman held the girl ghost, who struggled soundlessly against the shadow arms that held her, eyes wide open in panic, mouth open too, and no sound emerging though it looked as if she was shrieking in terror. The shadow woman, horribly, was crooning a lullaby to the ghost girl, and even as Nan watched, the ghost girl began to fade into the shadow woman. It looked as if the shadow woman was devouring it or absorbing it and the ghost girl grew limp and stopped struggling a moment later.

"*No!*" Nan shouted. She reached down blindly for a stick, and came up with a sword in her hand. As she brandished it, she saw that Sarah had come to stand beside her, with both hands raised over her head, white light coming from them. Neville had flown down to land on the ground between the girls and the shadow, and Grey, grown to four times her natural size, was beside him, feathers fluffed and growling.

The white light from Sarah's hands lanced out, not to touch the shadow woman, but the ghost girl. The fading outlines of the ghost girl strengthened, and she renewed her struggles.

"You let 'er go!" Nan shouted again, flourishing the sword. "She ain't yours, you let 'er go right now!"

The shadow woman, who had until this moment, ignored the girls, now turned her attention on them. Eyes like coals burned in the midst of her veils, and a terrible wail burst from her, a sound that brought with it fear and anguish that battered against Nan until she could hardly stand.

Sarah *did* drop to the ground, and the light from her hands went out—but when the wailing stopped, she struggled to her feet again and held her hands above her head, and the light once again shone from them.

Still holding the struggling girl ghost, the shadow woman took one menacing step toward them. Freeing one hand, she made a casting gesture, and Nan felt as if there was a hand seizing her throat, choking the life from her. Neville and Grey shrieked with anger, and flew at the shadow woman, but could not touch her, while Nan tried to shout, and could get nothing out.

She dropped the sword/branch, and clawed at the invisible, intangible hand, as her lungs burned and she tried to get a breath. Her vision began to gray out—

"Not so fast, my unfriend, my shadow wraith!" cried a fierce young voice that brought with it sun and a rush of flower-scented summer wind—and blessedly, the release of whatever it was that had hold of Nan's throat.

She dropped to her knees, gasping for breath at the same time that she looked to her right. There, standing between her and Sarah, was Robin Goodfellow. He wore the same outlandish costume he'd worn for the play, only on him, it didn't look so outlandish. He had one hand on Sarah's shoulder, and Nan could actually see the strength flowing from him to her as she fed the ghost girl with that light, which now was bright as strong sunlight.

The ghost girl thrashed wildly, and broke free of the shadow woman's hold, and that was when Robin made a casting motion of his own and threw something at the shadow form. It looked like a spiderweb, mostly insubstantial and sparkling with dew drops, but it expanded as it flew toward the shadow woman, and when it struck her, it enveloped her altogether. She crumpled as it hit, as if it had been spun out of lead, not spider silk, and collapsed into a pool of shadow beneath its sparkling strands.

The ghost girl stood where she was, trembling, staring at them.

"She's stuck," Sarah said, her voice shaky, but sounding otherwise normal.

Grey waddled over to the ghost girl, looked up at her, and shook herself all over. Neville returned to Nan's shoulder, feathers bristling, as he stared at the shadow woman trapped in Puck's net.

"She doesn't know where to go, or how to get there, or even

why she should go," Sarah continued, pity now creeping into her voice.

"Oh so?" Puck took a step or two toward the ghost girl, peering at her as if he could read something on her terrified young face. "Welladay, and this is one who can see further into a millstone than most . . . no wonder she don't know where to go. Hell can't take her and heaven won't have her, but there's a place for you, my mortal child."

His voice had turned pitying and welcoming all at the same time, and so kindly that even Nan felt herself melting a little inside just to hear it. He held out his hand to the ghost girl. "Come away, human child, or what's left of you. Come! Take a step to me, just one, to show you trust your dreams and want to find them—"

Shaking so much her vague outlines blurred, the ghost girl drifted the equivalent of a step toward Robin.

He laughed. Nan had never heard a sound quite like it before. Most people she'd ever heard, when they laughed, had something else in their laughter. Pity, scorn, irony, self-deprecation, ruefulness—most adults anyway, always had something besides amusement in their voices when they laughed.

This was just a laugh with nothing in it but pure joy. Even the ghost girl brightened at the sound of it, and drifted forward again—and Robin made a little circle gesture with his free hand.

Something glowing opened up between him and the ghost girl. Nan couldn't see what it was, other than a kind of glowing doorway, but the ghost girl's face was transformed, all in an instant. She lost that pinched, despairing look. Her eyes shone with joyful surprise, and her mouth turned up in a silent smile of bliss.

"There you be, my little lady," Robin said softly. "What you've dreamed all your life and death about, what you saw only dimly before. Summerland, my wee little dear. Summerland, waiting for you. Go on through, honey sweetling, go on through."

The ghost girl darted forward like a kingfisher diving for a minnow. A flash, and she was into the glow—and gone. And the glow went with her.

Now Robin turned his attention to the shadow woman, lying motionless under his spiderweb net. "Heaven won't have *you* neither, and you're not fit for Summerland," he said sternly. "Nor am I the one to call hell to come and take you. But you're too much mischief in the world, my lady, and I can't leave you free."

Neville suddenly made a sound Nan had never heard him make before. Something like a quork, and something like a caw, it made Puck glance at him and nod.

"Right you are, Morrigan's bird," he replied. "That's all she's fit for. It's the Hunt for her, and well rid of her this middle earth will be."

He turned to Nan and Sarah. "Close your eyes, young mortals," he said, with such an inflection that Nan could not have disobeyed him if she'd wanted to. "These things are not for the gaze of so young as you."

She kept her eyes open just long enough to see him take a cow horn bound in silver with a silver mouthpiece from his belt, the sort of thing she saw in books about Robin Hood, and put it to his lips. Her eyes closed and glued themselves shut as three mellow notes sounded in the sultry air.

Suddenly, that sultry air grew cold and dank; she shivered, and Neville pressed himself into her neck, reassuringly, his warm body radiating the confidence that the air was sapping away from her. All the birds stopped singing, and even the sound of the river nearby faded away, as if she had been taken a mile away from it.

She heard hoofbeats in the distance, and hounds baying.

She'd never heard nor seen a foxhunt, though she'd read about them since coming to the school, and it was one of those things even a street urchin knew about vaguely.

This, however, did not sound like a foxhunt. The hounds had deep, deep voices that made her shiver, and made her feel even less inclined to open her eyes, if that was possible. There were a lot of hounds—and a lot of horses, too—and they were coming nearer by the moment.

She reached out blindly and caught Sarah's hand, and they clung to each other as the hounds and horses thundered down practically on top of them—as the riders neared, she heard them laughing, and if Puck's laugh was all joy, this laughter was more sorrowful than weeping. It made her want to huddle on the ground and hope that no one noticed her.

The shadow woman shrieked.

Then dogs and riders were all around them except that, other than the sounds, there was nothing physically there.

Feelings, though—Nan was so struck through with fear that she couldn't have moved if her life depended on it. Only Sarah's hand in hers, and Neville's warm presence on her shoulder, kept her from screaming in terror. And it was cold, it was colder than the coldest night on the streets of London, so cold that Nan couldn't even shiver.

Hoofbeats milling around them, the dogs baying hollowly, the riders laughing—then the shadow woman stopped shrieking, and somehow her silence was worst of all.

One of the riders shouted something in a language that Nan didn't recognize. Robin answered him, and the rider laughed, this time not a laugh full of pain, but full of eager gloating. She felt Neville spread his wings over her, and there was a terrible cry of despair—

And then, it all was gone. The birds sang again, warmth returned to the day, the scent of new-mown grass and flowers and the river filled her nostrils, and Neville shook himself and quorked.

"You can open your eyes now, children," said Robin.

Nan did; Neville hopped down off her shoulder and stood on the ground, looking up at Robin. There was nothing out of the ordinary now in the scene before them, no matter how hard Nan looked. No shadow woman, no ghost girl, no dark emotions haunting the bridge. Just a normal stone bridge over a pretty little English river in the countryside. Even Robin was ordinary again; his fantastical garb was gone, and he could have been any other country boy except for the single strand of tiny vine leaves wound through his curly brown hair.

"What—" Sarah began, looking at Puck with a peculiarly stern expression.

"That was the Wild Hunt, and you'd do well to stay clear of it and what it Hunts, little Seeker," Robin said, without a smile. "It answers to me because I am Oldest, but there isn't much it will answer to, not much it will stop for, not too many ways to escape it when it has your scent, and there's no pity in the Huntsman. He decides what they'll Hunt, and no other."

"What *does* it hunt?" Nan asked, at the same time that Sarah asked, "What *is* it?"

Robin shrugged. "Run and find out for yourself what it is, young Sarah. And go and look to see what it hunts on your own, young Nan. There's mortal libraries full of books that can tell you—in part. The rest you can only feel, and if your head doesn't know, your heart can tell you."

"Well," Nan replied, stubbornly determined to get *some* sort of answer out of him, "What was that thing at the bridge, then?"

"And I need to tell you what you already know?" Robin shook his head. "You work it out between you. She's not been here long, I will tell you, and I should have dealt with her when she first appeared, but—" he scratched his head, and grinned one of those day-brightening grins, "—but there was birds to gossip with, and calves to tease, and goats to ride, and I just forgot."

Nan snorted at the evasive answer, but Sarah smiled. "You never will answer anyone straight up, will you?" she asked with a sidelong glance.

"It's not my way, Missy Sahib," Puck replied, and tickled her under the chin with a buttercup that suddenly appeared in his hand. "Now go you back and not a word of this to your schooling dame. Just your bad luck that two things came together and you as the third made some things happen that might not have, otherwise. That was bad for you, but good for the little mite. Then came your good luck, that it all made a mighty big stir-up of the world, and that got my attention. And me knowing you, that called me. An hour one way or the other and this would never have happened. The shadow would have claimed the mite, and no doubt of it."

Nan could well believe that. And she also had no intention of telling Memsa'b about it.

But she was going to find out what that shadow lady had been, and why she was at the bridge.

No one had missed them by the time they got back, and evidently there was no sign of their misadventure clinging to them either. Nan and Sarah stood in the garden doorway for a moment, assessing the mood in the manor, and exchanged a look.

"Think I'm gonna talk to th' kitchen maids," Nan said thoughtfully. "If there's gossip about, they'll know it."

"I'm going to see if Robin was right about the Hunt being in books," was Sarah's answer. "There are a lot of oddish things in the library here."

With a nod, they separated, and Nan ensconced herself, first in the kitchen on the excuse of begging toast and jam and milk, then in the laundry, then in the dairy as the two dairymaids finished churning the butter out of the second milking, and turned the cheeses as they ripened.

By that time, the bell had rung for dinner, and it was too late to talk to Sarah about what she'd found out. She could tell that Sarah was bursting with news, though, and so was she—

The news had to wait. After dinner came the nightly chore Memsa'b had set Nan to doing, helping put the littlest ones to bed. And Sarah went to help Tommy catch fireflies—he had a scheme to put enough in a little wire cage he'd made to read under the covers by, but he couldn't get the wire bars close enough and they kept escaping, much to the delight of the bats that flew in and out of their open windows at night—

That had been something that had shocked Nan the first time it had happened.

The children from India were all used to it; the same sort of thing happened in their Indian bungalows all the time. But Nan hadn't ever even seen a bat before, and the first time one had flitted in the open window and fluttered around, she hadn't known what it was. A lot of the maids hated them, and shrieked when they were flying around a room, pulling their caps down tight to their heads (because bats allegedly would get tangled in your hair). The bravest of them whacked at the poor little things with brooms, and all of them kept their bedroom windows shut tight all night long. But Memsa'b told the children that sort of behavior was silly, so they kept their own windows open to the night air. The children all rather enjoyed the tiny creatures, and eventually even Nan got to liking the way they swooped around the room, clearing it of insects, then flitting out the window again.

Tonight the little ones were full of mischief, and each had to be put to bed half a dozen times before they actually *stayed* in bed. Weary, but relieved, Nan trudged up the stairs to the room she and Sarah shared, to find Sarah, Neville, and Grey already waiting for her. Nan changed into her nightgown and hopped up to sit cross-legged on her own little bed and looked at her friend expectantly.

Sarah laughed. *"You* first," she said.

Nan coughed, because a great deal of what she had heard was not the sort of thing that you told a "nice" girl like Sarah. Country folk were earthy sorts, and they had no compunction about calling a spade a spade, and not an "earth-turning implement." The maids had certainly filled Nan's ears, particularly when the cook was out of earshot.

"There was a gal down to the village that put on a lot of airs," she said, heavily editing out a great deal. The whole truth was that this particular young lady was a lot like Becky Sharpe in *Vanity Fair*; she wanted a husband with money who would let her buy whatever pleased her; if she could get one, she wanted a husband with a title too, and she was perfectly willing to use any and every means at her disposal to get it.

"She set her cap at this feller, this captain, what showed up here at one of them hunting parties," Nan continued. "Friend of a friend, the maids said, not some'un the master invited himself. Man didn't make himself real popular; I guess he broke a lot of shooting rules right from the start." The maids had been vague on that score; they didn't understand the shooting rules either. What they hadn't been vague about was that the shooting parties started forming up and leaving without the captain, as the guests tacitly organized themselves to be off when he was busy doing something else. Part of that "something else" had been to flirt with the ladies, and the maids had no doubt that if he'd had his way, there would have been more than just flirting going on. "There weren't no single ladies at this party, an' when he made himself unwelcome, he'd take himself down to the pub in the village sometimes, an' that's where this gal saw him and decided she was gonna get him."

And she hadn't scrupled as to means either. According to the maids she had brazenly hopped into bed with him practically from the time he first appeared.

"So she's canoodling with this feller, an' wouldn't you know, next thing he's caught cheatin' at cards up here at the party. There's a big to-do, an' he disappears in the morning, an' his friend don't feel too comfortable here neither, so he leaves early, too, that same afternoon. Gal at village don't find out about this till they've both been gone two days."

According to the maids, there had been a "right row" about that, too, complete with the abandoned girl in question storming up to Highleigh, demanding to see the master, claiming the captain had promised to marry her and insisting that the master of Highleigh make it all right.

Except, of course, she never saw the master. The butler handled it all with an icy calm that intimidated even the girl. He had made it clear to her that the man in question—"no gentleman, young person, I assure you"—was neither a friend nor even a casual acquaintance of the master, and that the master had no idea where the cad was, or even if he had a right to the name and title he had claimed. "She got sent away with a flea in *her* ear," the dairymaid had said maliciously. Nan had a feeling there had been some bad blood there. . . .

"So come Christmas, seems the gal has another problem, an' by spring, she's got a baby an' no husband."

The maids had been full of stories of how the girl had tried to seduce her way to a marriage license with *anyone* at that point, but of course, everyone in the village knew by that time that she had a big belly and nothing to show for it, and not even the stupidest farmhand wanted himself saddled with a child that wasn't his and a wife that wasn't inclined to do a bit more work than she had to. She had the baby, and though her family didn't disown her, they made it clear that she was a living shame to all of them and really ought to show her repentance in quite tangible ways. . . .

She hadn't cared for being a housemaid. She hadn't cared for the fact that the baby was the living badge of her disgrace, not to mention a burden of care that no one would help her with.

"So the baby disappears, an' everyone figgers she took it to th' norphanage or the workhouse and left it there, an' she gets to tryin' to find herself a husband again—"

"But she didn't take it to the orphanage, did she?" Sarah asked somberly.

Nan shook her head. "No. 'Cause after some whiles, she was actin' pretty peculiar, like she's got somethin' weighin' on 'er, an kept comin' back to the river at the bridge. She'd come there in dead of night, an' just stand there, starin' at the water. Pretty soon she's actin' real strange, askin' if people can hear a baby cryin', an' then before Christmas, she drownded herself. So they reckon she drownded it in the same place she done herself, poor mite."

"Real strange" was a gross understatement. She'd been caught once or twice trying to take babies out of cradles when the mothers in question stepped out of their cottages for a moment. She had covered herself in a set of tatty, head-to-toe black veils she found somewhere. And she had all but haunted the bridge. Everyone knew by then that she had murdered her own child, but without a body or a confession it was hard to do anything about her. There was some tentative movement by the village officials to get her sent to an insane asylum, but before anything could be done, she had already killed herself.

Sarah shivered all over, and her eyes got a little teary. "Poor baby!" she said finally. "What a nasty, wicked woman."

"But it does pretty much account for what we saw," Nan replied. She felt obscurely sorry for the baby—but in her part of London, so many babies died all the time, that it was hard to get all worked up about one. Even the ones that were wanted died so easily that a mother was likely to bury four for every one she was able to raise. "So. Your turn."

Sarah nodded, and her sorrowful expression cleared. "There's more than one version of the Wild Hunt," Sarah replied, licking her lips thoughtfully. "I looked through a lot of books and Robin was right, there were several in the library here that talked about legends and magic and things like that. Had you noticed? There are a *lot* of odd books in that library."

Nan scratched her head. "Well," she said finally, after a moment of consideration, "The feller what owns this house is somebody Memsa'b kind of knows. I don't reckon he's one of her toff friends from before she went to Indja. You know, mebbe he's like one of us, and mebbe that sort of thing runs in the family? So the library'd be full of that kind of books."

Sarah nodded. "I think you're right. In fact, you know I thought it was a bit odd that a house this old *wouldn't* have a ghost, but maybe it doesn't because the family that lives here has always made sure that ghosts moved on."

Nan nodded, and hugged her knees to her chest. "I reckon you're right. So you found some books. What'd they say?"

"Well, one says that the Wild Hunt is—like Robin's people." She lowered her voice to whisper, as if she didn't like to say the words too loudly. "Elves. The Fair Folk. It says they come out of barrows at night to hunt the mortals that drove them out of their circles and groves. That one made it sound like these were bad Elves, though, and that they hunted people down at night for the fun of it."

Nan mulled that one over. "I don't see how that can be right," she said judiciously. " 'Cause they took that ghost. But Robin *did* call 'em, so mebbe it is."

"Another couple of books said it was made up of ghosts, people who had lived violent lives and died violent deaths." Sarah unconsciously pulled her covers a little closer around her. "And some of those books say that they're trying to make up for what they did by going after bad people. Like they are getting a second chance to keep from going to the Bad Place."

She meant hell, Nan knew, though she couldn't imagine why Sarah wouldn't just come out and say the word.

"But some other books say that they're wicked people who are keeping themselves from going to the Bad Place by hunting down people and scaring them to death or chasing them until they die. And some say they are already from the Bad Place, and it opens up to let them out." Sarah shook her head. "I just don't know, because none of those seemed quite right."

Nan sucked on her lower lip. "Don't seem quite right to me neither," she said at last. "Like somethin' is missing."

"Well, the last book I found said that they weren't any of those things, it said they were gods." Now Sarah's eyes were bright with excitement. "It said the leader was a very old god, the Horned God of the Hunt, from back before the Romans came, and that being Hunted used to be the way they chose their kings and the way they punished criminals. So when he wasn't being worshipped anymore or making kings, he just went on punishing criminals by Hunting them when he could. The things that ride with him are the souls of those that the Hunt caught."

Nan felt a sudden conviction that this was exactly the answer they had been looking for, though she could not have pointed to anything but feelings. "Well, Robin said he was the Oldest Old One, so it stands to reason he could call 'em," she said, thinking out loud. "An' he said that he couldn't call hell to take that ghost, an' heaven wouldn't have 'er, an' she couldn't go to that place 'e sent the little girl, but I reckon riding with that Hunt could be as bad as hell."

Sarah nodded soberly, her eyes gone very large and solemn. "If the book is right," she said, "it could be worse. Because you get to see the living world, but you can't do any of the things you want to do. You're just stuck riding whenever the Hunter feels like taking the Hunt out."

"So what happens to you the rest of the time—"

"The book didn't say, except that it called them 'tormented souls.' Maybe just being able to see and be in the world you used to live in and never be able to touch it again is bad enough." Sarah shook her head. "It also said the worst of them get turned into the Hounds, which would probably be horrible."

Nan thought about how the Hounds had sounded, and shivered. "I think," she said aloud, "whatever happened to that ghost, she's gettin' what's comin' to 'er now."

Sarah took a long, shuddering breath. "I'm glad Robin made us close our eyes," she said finally. "Some of the books say that just the sight of the Hunt and the Huntsman is enough to drive you mad. Some say that's not true, but that the Hunt is horrible to look at and is sure to frighten you to where your hair turns white. I'm glad Robin kept us from looking."

"Reckon he'd 'ave let Memsa'b watch," Nan said judiciously, "But I reckon he figgered we're too young."

"Then I want to be too young for a long, long time," Sarah said firmly, and got a bow from Neville and a soft "Yes!" from Grey.

And Nan could not possibly have agreed more.

13

THE first experiments had been a success.

Difficult as it had been to achieve the proper depth of cold to hold the bodies in suspension, Cordelia had succeeded in exchanging the souls of two children.

She had acquired them from an orphanage, where they had been two of the scant ten percent that survived infancy and emerged into childhood. That had been an interesting visit in and of itself; she had never considered orphanages as a source of her little servants, but since she intended to let these two actually live so that she could continue to switch their souls from time to time, she had decided to create the persona of a fictional housekeeper looking for two little boys to serve as errand runners. Usually it was factories that came recruiting to the orphanages—very few couples were actually interested in adopting these waifs. After all, who would want a child whose mother was probably a whore, or if not, was without a doubt fallen from virtue? Such a child would have her bad blood, and possibly the equally bad blood of some drunken laborer, or good-for-nothing sailor, or—worst of all—a foreigner. No one ever considered, of course, that the fathers of such abandoned children might be their friends, their neighbors, or the sons of the well-to-do. . . .

Not, of course, that it mattered.

The director of the place had trotted out the best he had to offer, and she had taken two little boys about eight years old, but small and looking five at most, with thin, half-starved faces and dull, incurious expressions. In height and weight, they were virtually identical. The main difference between them seemed to be that one hummed breathlessly and tunelessly to himself constantly and the other did not. They were not very intelligent and altogether incurious; this, too, was probably the result of being starved all of their lives.

This was not what the director would have had her believe, but Cordelia knew better, both from scrying on these places from afar in preparation for selecting one, and from the stories children who had run from the orphanages into the street had told her.

Food was scant, and poor. Generally as little as the directors of the places could get by with. Cordelia suspected that they were pocketing the difference between what they were allotted to feed each child and what they actually used to feed each child. Meat was practically unheard of, the staple diet was oatmeal porridge, thin vegetable soup, and bread. Infants were weaned onto this as soon as possible. The infants in orphanages were generally wrapped tightly in swaddling clothes and laid out on cots, as many as would fit on each cot, so that they looked like tinned sardines. In this orphanage, they were lucky, their smallclothes were changed twice a day; in many other places, once a day was the rule. They were fed skimmed milk, or the buttermilk left after butter had been churned out of it; this was cheaper, much cheaper, than whole milk. They didn't cry much; crying took energy, and these infants did not have a great deal of that to spare.

It didn't take very much to kill them either. A bit of the croup, a touch of fever, being too near an open window—nine out of every ten died, and were unceremoniously buried without markers in potters' fields. They had entered the world noisily; they generally left it silently, slipping out of it with a sigh or a final gasp.

Older children fared little better, though by the time they reached the age of three or four, all but the strongest had been winnowed out. And orphanages would have made fertile ground for Cordelia to hunt for ghostly servants without ever having to kill the children herself, except that these children were either wild creatures or so utterly passive that they made Peggoty look lively by comparison.

However, with a bit of feeding, perhaps the passive ones could be enlivened to the point of becoming useful. It would be interesting to experiment with these two.

She had been told their names were "Robert" and "Albert." Virtually every other boy child in an orphanage was named "Albert," in homage to the late Prince of Wales. Presumably, this was in an effort to get the children into someone else's hands by appealing to their patriotism or sentimentality.

Well, as of this morning, Robert, who was the one that hummed, was silent, and Albert, who had been the silent one, was humming. Proof enough that the transfer had been successful.

She decided that she would wait to see which of the two developed the stronger personality over the next few days, with proper feeding and access to some second-hand toys and worn picture books she had indifferently purchased from a flea-market stall. Toys were supposed to be educational, and she didn't want to be bothered with actually sending them to school. That would be the one she would use in the second experiment to displace the spirit of the other. The displaced ghost she would make into her servant if it looked as if there was anything there worth the saving, the other she would feed for a while longer to see how he turned out. Orphanages might well prove to be an additional source of servants, when her own efforts on the streets dried up.

Provided, of course, she could keep people from noticing that all of the children she took to work for her died. The problem with using orphanages as a recruiting ground was that the people who ran them were generally busybody nosy-parkering sorts.

Well, she would deal with that difficulty later. For the moment, her experiment was going well, and she might not even *need* any more ghostly recruits if she could act in her own person as a man.

David was deep in the countryside at the moment. This was annoying, because she could not keep her eyes directly on him—but it was also something of a relief, because she was free to do whatever she chose without having to have him under her supervision.

And the cause was good. A "weekend"—which really meant a week or more—house party, at the estate of a very influential MP. Commons, rather than Lords, but in this case, that was all to the good. It was time for David to move a little out of his own social circle and into the circle that lived, breathed, and ate politics.

Not that the man was crude; it was his grandfather who had actually made the money. His father had undertaken the more genteel path of investing it prudently and skillfully. The son was a solicitor, with the specialty of estate management, and never saw the inside of a courtroom. Actually, he seldom saw the inside of his law offices; he had lesser solicitors and an army of clerks to do most of the work for him. The sole reason for becoming a solicitor, both in his and his father's minds, was so he could go into politics, the taint of Money having become cleansed and purified by contact with the Law.

So David was there this weekend, under the Great Man's prudently-extended wing. This would be a purely social occasion; the selected male guests would be examining him for any potential flaws, such as a weakness for dabbling in art or poetry, or a tendency to drink too much in public—or a too-flamboyant manner when drinking. The female guests would be probing his suitability as a husband—not that any of them would have a chance at him. Left to himself, he would marry in due course, but only within the ranks of the Elemental Masters.

Or at least, that was probably what he would do, though there were the odd marriages outside those ranks. It would make things difficult for him, of course, unless his wife was the sort to wish to play Lady of the Manor in the country, while he attended to his business in the city and his position as the chief of his Master's Circle—

Cordelia blinked at that thought, her attention distracted from assessing the two boys as they ate.

"Graves," she told the maid assigned to care for them, "Give them the toys when they have finished. And at luncheon, see to it that they not be allowed the jam and cakes until after they have finished the nourishing meal Cook will make for them."

The girl bobbed a curtsy. "Yes'm," she said deferentially. She had been an under-housemaid, chosen by Cook because she professed to have looked after her younger siblings until going into service. She seemed competent. She would scarcely have done as a nanny, of course, had these been anything other than what they were—pale, passive little specimens unlikely to give trouble. But she was certainly up to watching them, seeing that they were kept clean and neat, and teaching them how to play with the toys they had been provided with.

Cordelia retired to her parlor, but to think, not to conduct business or attend to social obligations.

The Master's Circle! How could she possibly have forgotten that? It was David's obsession, and if he suddenly "lost interest" in it, his friends among the Elemental Masters would certainly take note and begin to wonder.

But at the same time, if Cordelia were to continue to preside over it, there would be very little time before she was unmasked. The Masters often performed so-called "out of body" work; the moment she entered into such a work in the presence of others, it would be very clear who she was. You could not mask the soul self—

—or could you?

Was it possible to disguise the persona that your spirit assumed when out of body?

If it was—it would take time to learn. If it wasn't, she had better find out now.

Another delay! It seemed that every time she found a solution to the problems that beset her path, yet another problem arose! It made her furious, and that was bad; she had to control her anger, to make it icy, rather than fiery, or it would make problems for her. But it was difficult not to be angry. First, that wretched child medium had come to England—the one person who could uncover the ghost servants—

And at that thought, she mentally cursed. The child—somewhere in the country—was potentially within her grasp if only she could be found. She had started the hunt days ago—so where was Peggoty?

Surely, the wretched little girl wasn't *that* difficult to locate! There were only so many places near enough to London that it was possible for Harton to travel there and back on the weekend!

Peggoty must have gotten distracted, or gone off into one of her dreams again. It would be the first time she had done so while engaged in a task for Cordelia, but like many spirits, the child was becoming more detached from the world as time went on. That was a flaw she had to constantly battle against, and was one of the reasons why she had to keep making more servants.

Well, it was time to reattach her, and throw a good fright into her as well.

Cordelia retired to her workroom, pausing in the closet that led into it to take three strands of hair from a tiny drawer, one of fifty in a handsome little cabinet meant to hold pills. Each drawer was marked with a name card; only twenty were filled in. Each drawer held hair clipped from the living head of the child in question before it had lain down for its last sleep.

She locked the door of the workroom behind her, and placed the hairs on the table in front of her crystal throne. Sitting down on her throne, and raising her hands, she called three Ice Wurms to her.

A breath of cold mist drifted down over the table, and three of the tiny, exquisitely detailed creatures coalesced out of it.

Like Salamanders, they were sleek lizards. Unlike Salamanders, they were nearly transparent, and looked as if someone had animated a series of three sculptures carved from the purest quartz.

Each of them went to the three hairs lying curled against the stone; each inhaled one.

And sat there, doing nothing.

Cordelia stared at them in growing disbelief and outrage. "Well?" she finally snapped. "Go get her! Fetch her back here!"

The Ice Wurm closest to her looked up at her with colorless, transparent eyes. *She is not there to be fetched,* it said shortly.

What?

Cordelia felt as if she had suddenly run up against an invisible barrier; stunned, and still in disbelief. "What do you mean, she is not there?" she demanded, with just a hint of uncertainty in her voice.

She is not there to be fetched. Not in this world. The Ice Wurm curled itself indifferently on the table, and its two brothers did likewise. *If she is in another, we cannot tell.*

For a moment Cordelia contemplated the notion that the creature might be lying to her. But—no, it had no reason to lie. She had other means of verifying the truth, and it knew very well she would mete out punishment if she thought she had been deceived.

So it wasn't lying. Peggoty was gone—elsewhere. The Other World, whatever thing that might be. And there would be no fetching her back either, despite the claims of so-called necromancers. No one who had ever *gone* to the Other Side ever could be pulled back by mortal intervention.

The Harton woman. It had to have been her. She was the only one with the power to send a spirit on who would also have had any contact with Peggoty. Cordelia wanted at that moment to have the interfering cow's throat in her own two hands—

Still, there was always the possibility, however remote, that it had not been the Harton woman. It might even have been the wretched children. It was best to be sure.

"Who did this?" she demanded of the Ice Wurms, knowing that they would be able to sniff out the least trace of whoever had last intersected with Peggoty's being.

But the answer brought a chill to her heart that nothing she had ever encountered before could match.

It is best that you do not know, Master, came the cool, sibilant voice. *And it is best that we not tell you.*

※

The endless rounds of empty conversation alternating with the endless rounds of polite scrutiny finally got to be more than David Alderscroft could bear. Perhaps it was the sultry days, and the warm nights that made it so hard for him to keep a cool, calm demeanor. It seemed much more difficult here than in London. And of course, a little talk with Cordelia always put things in perspective.

The trouble was, it was her perspective. The longer he was away from her, the more impatient he became with some of her obstinate opinions.

Another remedy to restlessness and unhappiness was in order. A polite inquiry to his host gave him permission to make free of the contents of the stable; his reputation as a good rider must have made its way even into these circles.

He did not consider himself to be so good a rider that he was willing to mount anything under a saddle, however.

He consulted with the chief stable hand, and soon found himself atop a steady, if unexciting, bay gelding. Unexciting was roughly what he wanted right now, anyway. He needed to be away from the watchful eyes, the endless gibble-gabble, the tiresome matchmaking games. Time alone, that was the ticket. He'd be able to think once he was alone.

He had studied the map, so he knew where he was. His host's guests had permission not only to ride the grounds of this estate but the far more extensive lands of the neighbor's. Highclere, was it? Highleigh? Something like that. The owner was away, scarcely visited the place except in hunting season, according to what he'd been told. That was good; the last thing he wanted was to meet up with anyone.

With that in mind, it seemed like the best solution (if he wanted to avoid more of the guests from this party) would be to ride over to the other property. He would be harder to find that way.

The dividing line was a hedge that must have been centuries old, and was far too tall to jump. He rode along it until he came to a gate in the hedge. The latch was at the correct height for a rider. He rode alongside it, opened the gate without thinking, and sent his horse through it.

And his horse suddenly shied violently back, just as a childish voice full of indignation piped, " 'Ere! Pay 'eed to where you're a-goin'!"

It took him a moment to get his horse under control. When he finally did so, it was to stare down into four sets of indignant eyes; two sets of bright, beady birds' eyes, and two sets changeable and human.

"What are you doing there?" he exclaimed.

One of the two children, for children they were, stood up, arms akimbo. "Might ast you the same thing now, mightn't I?"

Her accent branded her as a Londoner, and from the streets. Her bold manner, however, was all her own.

And the bird that perched on her shoulder was easily three times as bold as that. The sight made him start. That was a raven. And if it cared to, it could probably take his eye out.

"Little miss," he said cautiously. "You know that—"

"Neville is an uncommonly large rook," the child said instantly, and turned to the bird, which ruffled his feathers and stared up at him, as if daring him to deny what the child had claimed.

It quorked derisively at him, proving it was no rook. The girl put her hand up to scratch the nape of its neck. He had once seen what one of those beaks could do to a bare hand, when a Raven-keeper at the Tower was a little too slow in feeding one of his charges. The bird had nearly added the finger to the menu for its dinner that day.

The girl looked at him as if she could read his thoughts, and her expression hinted at her amusement with him. He felt himself getting angry, and warned himself not to do anything nor say anything. These were only silly children. He gathered cold calm about himself, and looked down on them.

The other child had a Grey Parrot on her shoulder; the bird looked at him measuringly, then, without warning, barked a laugh so full of contempt it could have come from a human throat.

It stung, so much so that his next words were a challenge. "Who are you," he asked icily, "and what are you doing on this property?"

"We're guests, which is more'n you can say," the first girl snapped at him. "Don't you fret, we got permission to be here! Hev you?"

"Nan!" the second girl hissed warningly. The first turned to her, and the two went into a whispered colloquy. The ruder of the two kept looking suspiciously at him as if she expected him to mount his horse and ride them down.

He had never encountered children quite like these two—well, truth be told, he had never encountered a child quite like the one that kept glaring at him. The other seemed tractable enough, but this one! He was accustomed to street children who, at worst, offered to sweep a crossing for him, and if glared at, skittered away. This one challenged him outright, and acted as if *he* was the one who was the intruder here. Part of him noted that she *looked* like a little London sparrow, too, with her brown hair and brown frock.

Finally, the whispers ceased, and the rude one planted a fist on either hip and looked him up and down. "Sarah sez I hev to call you 'sir,' even though you come through from the other side of thet door, an' I ain't niver seed you 'ere. So, *sir,*" she somehow made the word a title of contempt. "We got permission t' be 'ere. We're a-stayin' at th' Big 'ouse. You got permission t' come ridin' through thet door onto this land?"

"Actually, little girl," he said, carefully coating his words in ice, "I have. By mutual agreement between the gentleman with whom *I* am staying, and the master of these lands, the guests of my host may ride here whenever they choose."

Not that it is any business of yours, his tone said, though his words did not.

The little girl snorted. "Awright, then," she replied ungraciously. "You kin go."

She and her little friend cleared off to one side; he mounted, but was no longer in any mood to ride. Instead, he made a show of a brief canter in the meadow beyond the door in the hedge, cleared the brook a time or two, then trotted his horse back through the door, shouting as he did so, "Shut the door behind me!" and giving it the force of an order.

The little girl slammed the gate so hard the hinges rattled.

And it was only at that point that he reined the horse in and realized that those had been no ordinary children. Ordinary children did not have ravens and parrots perching on their shoulders and acting like playmates.

They'd had no hint of Magic about them, but in that flash of understanding, he had no doubt that they had some sort of psychical gift.

The second girl hadn't spoken loud enough for him to hear her voice, but the first girl had been a plain street-sparrow Cockney. And how did that come about?

David's host had said that the master of Highleigh was "an odd duck," though he had given no details. Now David wondered if that was a simple description of eccentricity, or if the man was part of one or more esoteric circles. He could think of no other reason why a Cockney child of dubious ancestry and obvious psychical gifts should be on that property. . . .

There was one way to find out, certainly.

He rode back to the house, to ask his valet to make inquiries.

An hour later he was possessed of interesting—and disturbing— intelligence. Interesting, because it seemed that the master of Highleigh was also the owner of that dangerous property in Berkeley Square that his own Master's Circle had been forced to cleanse.

Disturbing, because the gentleman in question had turned over his home and land to the pupils and teachers of a school for the children of British expatriates for the summer.

Now, David knew of only one school likely to harbor psychically gifted children in London. He knew of only one reason—guilt— why a well-to-do London gentleman would have allowed the mas-

ters and children of that school to make free of his property for the
summer. And he also knew that two children—two little girls—in
that school were the keepers of pet birds.

The conclusion was inescapable. Isabelle Harton was living just
on the other side of that hedge, along with her pupils.

All other considerations, all other concerns vanished in the ap-
prehension of that knowledge.

She was here. She was, if not alone, without the oversight of
her husband. He could go and speak to her if he liked.

He could. And in so doing, he could make an utter and complete fool of himself.

Or he might rid himself of the memories that continued to in-
trude on him, no matter what he did.

A dozen times he made up his mind to go back down to the stable and ride over and be done with it. A dozen times he reconsid-
ered. And in the end, the silver chime of the first dinner bell,
warning guests that it was time to dress, rendered it all moot. He
had been able to escape his obligations for the afternoon, but he
dared not shirk them further, and to abandon his place at dinner
with no good excuse would be a *faux pas* he would be months in
living down.

He permitted his valet to enter and dress him for dinner, in the
stiff evening shirt, formal black suit, and tie that was considered
necessary here, even in the midst of summer. The ladies of the
party glittered in their jewel-tone gowns of satin and lace, orna-
mented (since none of them could even be remotely considered
ingénues anymore) with small fortunes in gems. And as he made
polite conversation and worked his way through the extensive
menu, memories kept reintruding, of those times that seemed a
world and a lifetime removed now. Times when the dinner menu
was restricted to simpler fare than caviar and quail's eggs on toast,
roast pheasant and baked salmon, and a dozen more courses before the end of it all. Times when no one dressed for dinner, or if
they did, the young men wore light-colored linen suits, loose and
casual, and the young ladies in their muslins and flowers looked

far happier than these prosperous dames in satins and rubies.
Times when the after-dinner entertainment would be to gather
around the piano or read aloud to each other, or for engaged couples, to stroll hand-in-hand in the garden—not for the men to split
off in one direction to smoke cigars, drink brandy, and talk into the
night while the women went off (again) to their own parlor to do
whatever it was *they* did while their husbands conversed about
"important business."

Suddenly, a feeling of intense dissatisfaction washed over him.
But oddly enough, it was not a vision of Isabelle that accompanied
that emotion, but the contemptuous eyes of the little street urchin
he had seen this afternoon.

He knew instinctively what she would call him, with her voice
dripping with scorn. A "toff," a "guv'nor," a "stuffed shirt." Someone who did nothing and consumed everything; who deserved
nothing and helped himself to everything. Who had never actually
earned anything he had gotten in life—

He wanted to protest that he had, in fact, earned this place at
the table, this glittering company, and the promise of power to
come.

Oh, yes, said those eyes in his memory, glittering with their own
malicious pleasure. *You've earned them, right enough. Enjoying
them?*

Well, no—

He could hear her laughter, and the raven's contemptuous and
dismissive quork.

In fact, in a kind of ghostly echo, he heard them all night, whispering under the important conversation, a counter-melody of
disdain.

❋

"I feel sorry for him, whoever he was," Sarah said, as the two of
them slipped into their nightdresses and turned down the bed-
clothes.

They had been discussing the pompous and self-important man

who had nearly ridden them both down this afternoon. Nan was still of the opinion that he had no right and no invitation to ride the meadow of Highleigh Court; that he had merely pretended to it. She had not liked him, not at all, and neither had Neville. It wasn't just that he was an arrogant toff, it was that there was something very cold, something not right about him. As if someone had taken away his heart and put a clod of frozen earth where it should have been. He'd nearly trampled both of them, and not one word of apology! No, he was too busy showing two poor little girls how important a fellow he was.

Never even asked if we was all right, she grumbled to herself.

"Well, I don't," she replied, climbing into bed. "Not even a little bit. Hope that fancy nag of his throws him inter a mud puddle."

"Nan!" Sarah replied, but giggled.

"Better yet," Nan continued, starting to grin, "Inter a great big cow-flop. A fresh one. Still hot."

"Nan!" Now Sarah could not stop giggling, and that set Nan off, too. The thought of the fellow with his dignity in rags was just too much for her sense of humor. And once she started laughing at him, some of her anger at him cooled. Not that she was going to forgive him for almost trampling them *and* being rude, but she wasn't quite as angry at him anymore.

"So why d'ye feel sorry for 'im?" she asked, as Sarah blew out the candle and the soft, warm darkness enveloped both of them.

"Because—because he's unhappy, and he knows why, but if he actually admits that he's unhappy and why, he'll have to admit that he's wrong and he's been wrong about everything," Sarah said softly, as Nan heard the first soft whirring of bat wings from up near the ceiling.

"Ev'thing?" Nan said, surprised. "That's a lot."

"It's his whole life," Sarah said solemnly. "He made a wrong turn, and he's never going to get it right unless he gives up most of what he's done."

Whatever Sarah knew or had sensed that led her to that conclusion, it hadn't been granted to Nan. Still, she didn't doubt her friend. "Money?" Nan asked, not able to imagine anything in a grown-up's life that was more important than that.

"Not money, but—" Nan could almost hear Sarah groping for the words. "—I can't explain it, but it's all things he thinks are important and really aren't. It's like he's throwing away real diamonds for great big pieces of glass."

"Huh." Nan considered this. "Must've been some'un convinced 'im those chunks uv glass was wuth something."

"It's very sad, because he's never going to be happy," Sarah whispered, then sighed.

"Well, he ain't our problem," Nan replied resolutely. "He ain't our problem, and he ain't gonna be. He ain't no ghost and he ain't no bad thought."

"No, he's not," Sarah agreed, sounding sad. "I wish I knew of a way I could help him, though. It kind of feels as if I ought to."

Crickets outside sang through their silence, and a moth flew in the window, wings white in the moonlight.

"Why d'ye reckon yon Robin he'ped us out, ye think?" Nan asked.

She figured by changing the subject, she would be able to get Sarah to talk about something other than that so-dislikable man, and she was right.

"I think Robin likes us," Sarah said at last, after a long moment of silence. "I'm not sure why. I think he likes Memsa'b too."

"I think ye're right," Nan replied, and sighed happily. "It's a nice thing, 'avin' some'un like that like ye."

"I think *he* admires you, Nan," Sarah replied, admiration in her own voice. "I know he thinks you're brave."

"Eh, 'e thinks you're pretty brave, too!" Nan countered, but couldn't help feeling a bit of pride at the thought. "I mean, you stood right up t' that shadow lady! Not many would 'ave."

"They would if they knew it was the right thing to do," came the soft reply out of the darkness.

Nan thought about that as she drifted off to sleep. Sometimes it was hard being Sarah's friend—because she would say things like that, things that part of Nan knew weren't really true—or at least, that everything Nan had ever learned in her short life told her weren't true. But then, just as she had made up her mind, another part would at least hope for the opposite, for Sarah's words, and not Nan's feelings, to be the right one. So part of her wanted to contradict Sarah, while the other part wanted to encourage her.

Eh, what's it hurt to let her think it? she finally decided, as sleep took her. *She's a queer little duck, and mebbe if she believes it long enough, it'll ac'chully happen someday.*

A comforting thought, and a good one to carry into the night.

14

CRICKETS sang outside the window, and a bat flew into the room, patrolled for insects, and flew out again. Isabelle Harton relaxed in the embrace of her husband's arms. While she was deeply enjoying this sojourn in what was the next thing to a castle, with far more servants than she could ever dream of employing herself, the pleasure was flawed by not having Frederick with her for most of the time. "Good gad, I have missed you," she said, contentedly, and yet with some sadness, knowing that on Sunday night he would once again take the train back to London.

She felt him smile in the darkness. "What a scandal!" he replied, contradicting his own words by pulling her closer. "Wives aren't supposed to miss the carnal attentions of their husbands. They are supposed to endure them for the sake of children."

She chuckled. "And what idiot told you that?" she responded. "Not the Master, that's for certain."

He laughed. "Something a well-meaning clergyman told a young officer a very long time ago, in an attempt to persuade the young officer that his pretty wife would be happier living in England. He swore that women would rather, on the whole, be left alone by men, and that she was merely being dutiful when she told him she didn't want to leave."

"And what young officer was that?" she asked, curiosity piqued.

He chuckled deep in his chest. She felt the sound vibrate through him and smiled. Of all of the things she loved about him, hearing him laugh was one of the best.

"Myself, of course," he said. "Who else?"

She arched an eyebrow, though of course he would not be able to see it in the dark. "I was never pretty." It was an old "disagreement."

"I thought you were. And I think you are beautiful now. Since I am the one who looks at your face more often than you do, I think I should be the one allowed to make the judgment." The usual argument.

She wasn't going to win it. She never did. "I wish the business would run itself." She sighed.

She felt his hand stroking her hair. "And I wish the school would run itself, or that you and I could build a little hut on the beach of a tropical island and raise goats like Robinson Crusoe. But goatskins make dreadful gowns, or so I'm told."

"Smelly, anyway." There were many things she could have talked to him about, but none of them were as important as simply being here in his arms, and luxuriating in the feeling that this was the best, the only place in the world for her, and that she would never have felt like this about anyone else. This was the still center of the whirling universe, where everything was at rest. In its own way, the jewel in the heart of the lotus, the place where love was, had been, and always would be. Buddhists, of course, would argue that point, preferring their way of detachment from the world. But on the whole, she preferred hers.

So she would not spoil the moment with anything other than things that would make him smile. So she told him about Tommy's latest misadventure until the bed shook with their laughter.

❄

Cordelia wished there was a way to look at "herself" in a mirror.

It turned out that there *was* a way to turn the face of your soul-self into something other than a reflection of the real-world "you." She'd had to search through some excruciatingly boring manuscripts to find it, plowing with determination through things that ranged from absurd to outright duplicitous, but she had found it. She thought that she had done a creditable job, given the cryptically worded instructions. Fortunately she had done enough out-of-body work with David that she knew what his "self" looked like. It would have been a dreadful mistake to have appeared in something other than the chainmail and surcoat he habitually wore in that semblance.

Perhaps it would be a wise choice to gradually have him wear a helm as well. That way she would have less chance of losing hold of the likeness of his face.

Yes, that would be a good idea. It should be easy enough, a little suggestion that if out-of-body work was becoming hazardous, a helm might be in order, to remind the soul-self to keep its defenses up. It was a very good thing that what the avatar *wore* was often as variable as the personality within. David, the most conservative of mages, had been known to vary the outfitting of his own avatar to suit the occasion, now and again. No one would wonder that he had assumed a helmet, and he himself could implement the change without much thought.

So the next part of the experiment could proceed as planned; to discover if one living soul could be used to push out another. The child that was silent was a weaker personality than the one that hummed. A dose of laudanum mixed with other drugs and a great deal of honey in its bedtime milk would ensure that its hold on its body was weaker still. There was a distinct advantage in that the second child's spirit would be drawn more strongly to the body that rightfully belonged to it. That would simulate her own will driving her to inhabit David's shell.

After watching the two children sharply for an hour or so, she was satisfied that she had set up the best possible conditions. It did

appear that the child about to be un-housed was another of the
Peggoty sort, however. Unlike the other, which was at least learning to play with toys in the manner of a normal child, the boy just
sat there staring vaguely at whatever object his nursemaid put in
his hands, now and again turning it over and over and studying it,
but otherwise showing no signs of real interest in it. And it was
getting fat, in a pale and puffy sort of way, from inactivity. Clearly
only the scant rations at the orphanage had kept it so slender.

Useless in every way. Best she get rid of it now, as one would
dispose of an unwanted puppy.

But she also wanted to eliminate every thought of suspicion,
so she went in and exclaimed about the child's lassitude to the
nursemaid.

"Yes'm," the little nursemaid agreed, bobbing a curtsy. "He don't
look right, and that's a fact, Mum. But he being a foundling and
all, they sometimes are sickly."

As if your brothers and sisters weren't! Cordelia thought with
amusement, knowing, as the maid did not know, that her mistress
knew everything of note about her family, including her mother's
three miscarriages and five dead children. One in every two poor
children died in infancy, and it was just too bad that Cordelia didn't
have a way to harvest or use those spirits.

Ah well, perhaps the answer lay in her researches. Now she had
more than one lifetime to look into it, and she no longer felt quite
such a sense of urgency.

But for a show of concern, she sent for the apothecary—not the
doctor, that would have been an excess—who shook his head and
opined that he did not know of too many orphanage children able
to thrive even in the best of situations. "Bad blood, My Lady," he
pontificated. "Mothers and fathers both usually addicted to gin,
opium, hashish—bad blood there and no mistake. Sometimes it's
just as well that they don't thrive."

She nodded and the nursemaid nodded, as he prescribed a
tonic, a bottle of which he produced with such readiness that she
knew he had brought it here on purpose to sell it to her. As was

appropriate, however, he did not offer it to her, nor did he name a price. He gave it to the nursemaid, who thanked him. A bill would be forthcoming, of course, and the housekeeper would deal with it.

There. The stage was set for tonight.

When the apothecary had left, she waited for the nursemaid to take the boys off to their bath, and confiscated the tonic, which might be good or ill, might even be the same ingredients as her own potion, only weaker, but did not suit her purposes. She poured the contents down a drain, and substituted her own mixture. The strength of what she poured in there would have put a grown man to sleep, much less a small child.

Then she waited.

She had been forced to make do now that it was summer and she could not expect an ice-laden wind to do her work for her, replacing the cold of winter with drugs and powerful magic. Instead of arranging for the window to be opened, when the nursemaid was safely asleep (thanks to a heavy dose of laudanum in *her* tea) she made her way quietly into the nursery where the two boys lay on their cots.

With her arms outstretched, and hands cupped upward, she silently mouthed the words of invocation, and felt power drain from her in response. A chill, white mist formed slowly over the two cots, and settled over the two boys. This was called "The breath of the snow dragon," and was the opposite side of the "breath of the dragon" invocation used by Fire Mages. That brought a furnace heat; this summoned the wind off the glaciers itself.

When she was satisfied that both boys were chilled to the bone and to all intents and purposes very near death, she closed her eyes and reached with spirit hands toward the strong one's body.

The spirit already drifted a little above it; now she had to detach it altogether.

The incantation she used was one that would have made any good and decent Elemental Mage cover his ears in horror. She had found it in an ancient book that allegedly contained spells dating from the time of Atlantis. Whether that was the truth or not, this was the only one that actually accomplished what it was said to do.

The silver cord connecting soul with body shattered. She snatched up the spirit and shoved it toward the second boy's body, at the same time repeating her blasphemous words.

The first child was already trying to reestablish a connection with a physical body, the end of the "cord" drifting about like the groping tentacle of a cephalopod. As she had hoped, because his spirit was the stronger of the two, it made the connection with the body that had originally belonged to it before the second boy re-anchored himself. The soul-self sank into the body, as the displaced ghost drifted toward the empty husk.

But before it could reach its former home, she had summoned a shield around it, preventing it from entering, and making it into one of her servants; this was a bit of magic she had long been familiar with and had used innumerable times. The glow of the shield surrounded the spirit and shrank, forming a kind of "skin," then faded.

Now it was hers. It could neither move back into the vacant body, nor go anywhere else. The spirit was sealed to the earthly plane, unless someone could be found to open a passage into the Other Side for it, or until it willed one open for itself.

It looked very like Peggoty had, a gray-white sketch in the air of an androgynous child figure, as it opened its hollow eyes to stare at her. "Go and play," she told it, and it turned away from her and drifted off, through the wall. It would linger somewhere about, just as Peggoty had, until she summoned it. Unlike Peggoty, it probably could be summoned by whatever means she chose without frightening it unduly.

And then she felt it, the triumph, the glee. It had worked! By heavens, it had worked!

And she allowed herself the indulgence of a feral smile, unconcerned, now, for its effects on her face, the possibility of wrinkles or creases. Because very soon now, it would not matter.

Not at all. Not when she could discard this useless body like the outworn thing that it was, for a fine new replacement, a replacement that was in all senses superior in every way to the original

❋

David Alderscroft could not sleep.

It had been a productive, but profoundly boring day. He knew that he should feel pleased about it, but all he could manage was a weary and resigned sense that he had accomplished what he had come for. Although the eminent politicians here were unclear as to why he wanted a new minister appointed to the Cabinet and exactly what the minister would be representing, it was a virtual certainty that he would get to be that minister.

A Minister of Magical Sciences, although that, of course, was not what he would actually be called. And no more than a handful of people would ever know that this was, in fact, the purview of the office.

It was more than time for such a Ministry, however. More than time for the Elemental Masters to step forward and put their hands on the reins of government. Too much secrecy had been going on over the decades, and at some point, without the cooperation of the government, that secrecy was going to fall apart.

He paced the length of the terrace in the darkness as he considered the night's work. None of the men here tonight would ever know that this "Ministry of Esoteric Sciences" was in fact about magic. Only the Cabinet and the Prime Minister would be told this. But revealing the knowledge at a high level virtually ensured that it would never be revealed at a lower level.

At this point, in David's view, such protection was absolutely vital. There had been too many near misses already, moments when he thought for certain some enterprising soul would uncover the Elemental Masters along with the proof to convince the skeptical. And then what?

Well, in worst-case scenario, there could be a kind of latter-day witch hunt, a crusade of the ordinary mortals against the extraordinary magicians among them. People did not like the notion that there were those who, by accident of breeding, had some powers or abilities that could not otherwise be attained. At bottom, even the lowest of day laborers swilling his gin was certain that nothing separated him from a baron of industry except luck. To discover, that there were people who had abilities he could never dream of having would certainly inflame tempers to the raging point.

And of course the government could not know of such things without wanting to have some form of control over them. There would be lists and registries, and fines for "practicing magic without a license." No, it would be a nightmare.

But if the government already knew—if, in fact, it was complicit in covering up the existence of magic and magicians—then it would have every reason to continue doing so. Incorporating the service of magicians into, say, the intelligence services, the "Great Game," as it were—that made a great deal more sense.

And it would give added impetus to keeping the existence of mages a secret. After all, there was no point in allowing that secret to leak out if a great deal of foreign intelligence was coming in by means of magic.

David already suspected that other governments had come to the same conclusion, although he had no direct evidence. The French of course—bah! Secretive and with logic as convoluted as the new ornamental balustrades of the Metro stations! They had probably been employing Elemental Mages since the time of Napoleon! And the Italians, of course, most probably in the Vatican. The Prussians were a bit more straightforward and the idea might not have ever occurred to them—but then again, they were ruthless and would use any tool that came to hand. The Balkans, thank the good Lord, were so disorganized that it was unlikely there was any concerted effort to use magic by the various factions of Anarchists and the like.

The Americans . . . unlikely. They simply did not believe in what they could not see, weigh, measure.

The Spanish, perhaps, given their mystical bent, but they were nonplayers so far as the world stage was concerned.

Who did that leave? India, China, inscrutable and of all nations, they were the most likely to be employing magical agents.

He grew tired of hearing his own footsteps on the terrazzo, and decided to stroll down into the garden instead. Maybe his thoughts would slow in the sultry, rose-scented air, and he would be able to get some sleep.

His own muffled footsteps on the turf, slow and deliberate, were the only sound around him. Insects stilled their chatter as he passed, so that he moved in a circle of silence. It seemed a little odd, but not unpleasant, so he merely noted the fact as he passed on, attempting to empty his mind so that he could, eventually, sleep.

But restfulness eluded him, and he let his feet take him farther, out of the manicured gardens and toward the "wilderness." This was a part of the grounds that differed from the lawn mostly by virtue of the fact that only the paths were mowed; or at least, so far as he could tell in the darkness. He had just stepped under the shadow of the ancient trees there, when a voice from behind startled him.

"So, son of Adam, you venture into my territory at last."

He turned. No Elemental Mage, much less a Master, would ever have mistaken the creature that stood on the path, arms folded over his chest, for anything other than what he was: a powerful Primal Spirit. Some might have said, a godling, as it was not of any one Element, but of all of them, though Earth held primacy in his makeup. In form, it was an adolescent boy, in antique costume, with a strand of vine leaves tangled in his long, curly hair, and the moonlight seemed to gather itself around the Spirit so that it was as easy to see him as if he stood in broad daylight. There was an impression of veiled Power there, a great deal of it. In this case, the very fact that this power was concealed from David's normally acute perception told him that the creature was not the usual sort he was likely to encounter.

"I beg your pardon?" he said politely. No point in beginning a confrontation—not that he had any doubt of his ability to handle the situation. It was only some Nature Spirit, after all. True, he had never yet met one this powerful, but still, he was no peasant, to be terrified by such a thing.

"I come to give you fair warning, son of Adam," it replied calmly. "Had you ventured here in the proper season, I would have no issue with the source of your power. But you come, out of skew with what is right and proper, and I will not have it. Wield your might unduly, and bring blight, and I will remove you—and at need, from this mortal coil entire."

Well, he might not have intended a confrontation, but there was no mistaking the challenge there! Insolent thing . . .

He suppressed his outrage, however, and merely said, coldly, "I am afraid I do not take your meaning."

The seeming youth snorted. "You lie, you do; you lie and feign you do not understand. But I will be plainer, then. You bring winter into summer, you take the Element that should be your companion and twist it to bitter usage. And I do warn you that you tread now on *my* ground, and I will not abide this thing. Use your breath of ice and bring blight here all out of season, and you will suffer the consequences. I do not meddle in the quarrels of mortals, but I will not permit *you* to meddle in my affairs and with my charge. Use what you have on your fellow fools, but do not o'erreach yourself."

David's temper flared. "And you, sir, dare to threaten me!" He gathered his own power about him like a cloak,

The spirit laughed mockingly. "I do more than threaten, son of Adam. You hold no sway over *all* that walks the Earth." And he raised only his eyebrow.

But the moment that he did, David was driven to his knees— literally—by fear. Fear so overwhelming, so crushing, that there was nothing he could do, for his knees gave way and his thoughts collapsed and although every fiber of him urged flight, his body was so paralyzed with terror that he could not move so much as a fingertip.

It lasted a lifetime, that fear. He could hardly do more than breathe, and even that brought with it more fear with every intake of breath.

Then, as suddenly as it had overcome him, the fear was gone. And so was the spirit.

❊

Sarah and Nan should have been in bed, of course. They should not have even considered setting a single toe on the floor now that the rest of the household was asleep.

But Nan had long ago discovered what—though they did not know it—generations of young maids who had been assigned to the room they were now in had discovered. There was a simple way to leave the house when they wanted to meet their swains in the moonlight. The window gave out onto a piece of roof that was nearly flat. That, in turn, led to a series of bits of ornamental stonework as easy to descend as a ladder, and from there to the top of a wall one could walk along until that, in turn, led to the roof of a shed that sloped down to within a mere four feet of the ground. Any girl sufficiently sturdy and willing to tuck up her skirts could get out. Again—although they did not know this—the housekeeper was well aware of this means of egress, and this was why there were no young maids ever given that room. But she had not considered that two little girls, strangers to the manor and mere children after all, might also discover and use this means of egress.

In fact, Nan had worked it out within days of their arrival. She just didn't bother to use it all that often. There was no real reason to; they hadn't transgressed so far in mischief as to have been confined to their room, and they were usually so tired at the end of the day that even when they tried to stay awake, they couldn't. But Nan had lived her entire life in rat-infested tenements that often had fires, and she had early learned to find an escape route in case the normal one was cut off. She had shown this one to Sarah, then both of them had mostly forgotten about it.

But not tonight.

There was something about the air tonight that had made both of them restless. Long after the lights had been put out, Nan had been lying in her bed, staring at the ceiling and listening to the bat make his rounds, and knowing from the sound of her breathing that Sarah was doing the same. And she felt, more and more strongly, that something wanted her to be awake, wanted her to come outside. She could practically hear it calling her name. Finally she threw off the covers, and got out of bed.

"I'm goin' outside," she whispered.

"Me, too," Sarah said immediately, doing the same. "Do you feel it, too? Someone wants us."

"Somethin' like," Nan agreed.

The two of them groped for their clothing and fumbled it on in the dark, helping each other with fastenings neither could see. Then Nan eased herself over the window ledge and out onto that bit of roof, and from there it was easy to feel her way down with her toes on the stonework. The wall top was broad and Nan felt no fear in walking it; moonlight shining on the stone made it as clear as any path. Sarah followed, and they both dropped down to the turf side-by-side.

Nan looked around, squinting, as if that would make any difference in seeing better in the darkness. She missed Neville, who was asleep, and hadn't stirred even with all of their moving around; he could see things she couldn't with no difficulty whatsoever. But Sarah acted as if she had the eyes of a cat, taking Nan's hand and tugging at it.

"The Round Meadow," she said, which wasn't round at all, only an approximation of round, but it wasn't that far from the manor, just a little ways into the "wilderness," which was a poetical way of saying that the only things mowed or trimmed in there were the paths for horseback riding. It wasn't very big either; more of a pocket-sized meadow, in which sweet grasses grew waist-high and flowers bloomed all the time. Sarah and Nan liked to play there, because you could trample down a little "room" in the grass and be quite private but still get to bask in the sun and watch the clouds go by overhead.

That was where they had spent most of the afternoon today, in fact. It had been a very lazy, sleepy sort of day, and no one had wanted to do much of anything. Memsa'b had let them all be somewhat lazy, and not do any lessons. Sarah and Nan had gone to Round Meadow with rugs and books and a picnic basket of tea things. Sarah had made daisy chains and crowns, then they'd both made flower fairies and set them up around their little grass-walled room, creating a village in miniature, with houses, a fairy pub with acorn cups and bowls, and a shop selling new flower frocks and hats. All very silly, of course, but then they had gathered up their "fairies" and divided them into "audience" and "players," and put on *A Midsummer Night's Dream* with Sarah and Nan dividing up the parts between them.

Nan could not help but think about that, and about how the first planned performance of the play had somehow called Robin Goodfellow. Was that why the two of them felt so restless tonight? Had the play once again worked its magic?

But when they got to Round Meadow, it was not Puck that they found.

There was something four-legged and white standing in the middle of the meadow where their grass-room had been. At first, all they could see was its back and part of its legs and its neck, all gleaming silvery in the moonlight, head down and grazing. They could both hear the sound of the grass being torn up and strong jaws munching it. For one moment, Nan thought it must be a small horse, perhaps gotten loose from that Great House on the other side of the door in the hedge. But then it raised its head and looked at them.

It was a deer. A doe, actually, as luminous as moonlight itself, watching them with gleaming silver eyes. Now, Nan knew how to tell a boy beast from a girl well enough, and this one was definitely a doe, and yet, crowning its graceful, great-eyed head were silver antlers.

"I thought only stags had horns," Sarah whispered to Nan, who only shrugged. That's what she had thought, too.

"Ah, but that is no common deer, daughter of Eve," said Puck, who had materialized out of nowhere beside them, wearing his outré fairy garb again and looking perfectly natural in it. "That is a Sidhe-deer."

"I c'n tell it's a she-deer," Nan responded.

Puck laughed. "'Tis spelled s-i-d-h-e, sparrow, and 'tis an old, old word for the Good Neighbors."

The "Good Neighbors," as they both knew, were another name for the fairy folk. So this must be some sort of animal out of those strange lands where the fairies still walked.

" 'Tis said," Puck continued, rubbing the side of his nose with one finger thoughtfully, "That they can become maidens when they choose. I've never seen it, but 'tis said."

They watched the deer in silence as she lowered her head to the grass again. "Why is she here?" Sarah whispered at last.

Puck shrugged. "Ask the wind why it blows where it will," was his enigmatic reply. "She is here because she chooses to be, and she will go because she has decided to. Perhaps your making your games in a round place, and your playing of the play made the spot into a fairy ring. And perhaps it is that you should be wary of the hard man who rode through the hedge the other day."

Neither of them had any doubt who he was talking about, nor did Puck's abrupt change of subject give either of them a moment's pause. The incident was still fresh in Nan's mind. And besides, there hadn't exactly been a lot of men riding through the doors in the hedges around the girls.

"I don't like 'im," Nan said flatly. "There's summat cold about him."

"And there you put your finger on it, my pretty London sparrow," Puck responded, with a nod. "Cold. Cold he is, cold out of season, cold at the heart, and there's an end to it. A man that cannot feel, be he mortal or fey, is a man who may do anything."

The Sidhe-deer raised its head again and looked at them. Was it nodding?

a barn, with four round faces peering at them out of it, and he spoke to the mother owl when she came with a mouse, so that she allowed them to stay and watch her feed the hungriest. It made Nan giggle to watch, as the mouse tail hung out of the owlet's beak, and it gulped and gulped and the tail slowly disappeared. She would have thought that Sarah would have been revolted, but Sarah found it just as funny.

He also took them to a fox den, and let them play with the cubs while mother watched benignly, though he warned them after, when he was taking them home, that they must never try such things when he was not about. "I have the speech with the wild things," he said. "And they know me. They will abide much from me that they will never tolerate elsewise."

"Well, of course!" Sarah replied, matter-of-factly.

It was a good thing he was along; he showed them a better way of scrambling up to their window. "I mind me," he said reminiscently, peering in through the open casement, "when there was a bright-eyed lass a-living here had a farmer's lad all head-tumbled and heart-sore, because he thought she'd set her cap on the steward's son. But when the banns were posted, it was the farmer lad who won the day. Of course," he said, with a wink, "it might be that *I* had a hand in that."

"With the little purple flower?" Sarah replied archly, referring back to the Shakespeare play.

"Now that would be telling, and I never tell."

And he was gone in an instant, and they got back into their nightdresses and crawled into bed to fall asleep the moment they got under the covers.

And in the morning, they might have thought it was all a dream—except that when Sarah stuck her hand into the pocket of her pinafore, she pulled out, much to her surprise, an owl feather.

"But what if he could change and feel again?" Sarah
quickly. "I feel sorry for him. I think he is very lonely. Wh;
could thaw?"

Puck shrugged. "I warn about what is, not maunder abou
could be. I do not meddle in the affairs of mortals, except
affairs of mortals affect what I have charge over. May be I
and may be he can't and it matters not at all. But his cold, hi
now that matters, and cold and ice are death and I will no
death in the season of life." He nodded at the deer. "It may
is here because of it. The Sidhe-deer will not abide death
season either."

Sarah set her chin in the expression that Memsa'b called
ish." "I think there is good in him," she said.

Puck shrugged again. " 'Tis not mine to say nor mine to d
thing about," he replied. "That's the affairs of mortals."

Sarah said nothing aloud, but Nan could almost hea
thoughts—*then I will.*

She sighed, but not loudly. If Sarah had made up her mi
do something, then it would be up to Nan to guard her in it.

Not that she was likely to get into too much trouble. The
was only a toff, maybe one with a bit of magic about him, bi
wasn't *bad* evil, he was only the sort that would meddle bec
he thought he had a right and he thought he was stronger
anything he meddled in. So up to the point where he fell into
hole he hadn't seen, he was safe enough.

"Well," she said aloud. "If we're gonna meddle, we best c
afore he gets himself into somethin' worse nor he is, an' bring
home."

Puck gave her a wry little bow. "And there's wisdom; to kr
when to run and when to hold fast, and when to stand by y
friend."

But his smile in the moonlight was warm with approval, a
when the Sidhe-deer moved on like a drift of mist, glimmerin;
moment among the trees and then gone, he took them off or
strange, wild walk in the night. He showed them an owl's nest

15

THE strange Spirit had rattled David as nothing else had in many, many years. He longed for someone to discuss the incident with, but Cordelia was in London, and he did not think there were any other Masters living near this place.

Which left only Isabelle. After all, she was no expert on these things. He didn't even know if she could see the Elementals and nature spirits.

But on the other hand, there was only one name for that terror that had overcome him. Panic—named for the Great God Pan . . .

Surely, that had not been—surely not. It had worn the guise of a mere boy, not the Great Goat-footed One. Why would the Sylvan Faun do such a thing?

For that matter, what would he be doing in England? This was not his place, he belonged in Greece!

And yet, David had seen with his own eyes lesser Fauns in England, little boyish earth spirits that haunted the gardens of Earth Masters. They had come, so why not Pan?

But why should it be so?

Perhaps Isabelle was no Elemental Master, but she did know of the Elementals, and other such creatures, too. Perhaps she had even seen this one herself. . . .

A dozen times David made up his mind to ride over to talk to Isabelle, and a dozen times found an excuse not to, until the day after his encounter when he was very nearly run to earth by a lady determined to have him for her daughter, to the point where he seized on any reason to go riding alone again.

"My dear woman," he said insincerely, "I would be charmed to speak with you, but I have an appointment to pay a call at High-leigh Court."

Mrs. Venhill stared at him. "A call?" she repeated. "I was not aware that you had any acquaintances in this part of the county." Her mouth tightened. She knew exactly what he was doing. But he had no intention of giving her a way to disprove his statement.

"I do not," he said calmly. "But an acquaintance of mine, a Mrs. Isabelle Harton, is a guest there. I have not seen her in many years, and she was quite eager to renew her acquaintance with me."

That last was the only lie; the rest was absolute truth, and carried the lie like froth on the top of a wave. And since he did not mention a *Mister* Harton, this would, he hoped, lead her to think that Isabelle's husband was no more, and she was a young, lonely, and presumably attractive widow.

And in a case such as this, an acquaintance out of one's youth was going to trump just about any cards a matchmaking mama could lay out. She was beaten, and she knew it. She retired gracefully from the battle lines, murmuring, "Ah! Well, of course you must go, it would be insufferably rude if you did not!"

Of course, now he had done it; he had to go, or at least appear to go, or Mrs. Vennhill would be very well aware that he had been putting her off. Do that too many times and one found one's invitations no longer extended or answered.

So he found himself on horseback again, riding off into a day that threatened rain. Not the cleverest idea he could ever have had, but it was too late now.

And he might just as well follow through with the putative visit.

After all, if it *did* rain, he would have to have shelter somewhere until it passed, and as a visitor he could at least claim that much even if the visit proved to be awkward.

He had no doubt that although he was not expected, he would be received with the proper respect, and so he was. The horse was taken around to the stables, and he was shown to the library, that being a proper and reasonable place for a gentleman to amuse himself when the lady he has come to see might be busy.

He did amuse himself by looking through some of the titles of the books there, and as he had half expected, a good number of them were occult or esoteric in nature. So the owner of the house *was* in Isabelle Harton's circle of acquaintances, or at least, presumably knew many of the same practitioners of psychical magic that she did.

He took one down and began to leaf through it, but it was heavy going, and he was having a difficult time untangling the sense of it, when light footfalls heralded the arrival of a newcomer, and he looked up to see Isabelle stepping into the room. She walked briskly over to him, and boldly tilted the book up to read the spine.

"Blithering idiot," she said, without preamble, and waved at the shelves. "Our host collects any sort of occult writing, but if you examine the shelves carefully and know some of the authors, you will soon determine that he has grouped his books according to their usefulness, or lack thereof." The half-smile she produced had more than a hint of irony in it; it was the smile of a knowing, worldly-wise woman, not the pretentious irony of a girl. "His categories—and I apologize in advance—are Useful, Moderately Useful, Nothing of Note, Idiot, and Blithering Idiot. I fear that the Blithering Idiots number twice as much as all the rest combined, but he takes some amusement in having them about. I am told, though I have not actually attended such a function myself, that one of the entertainments for his close circle of friends is to take down a book from those shelves and read it aloud as portentously as possible without cracking a smile or laughing."

He looked from the book to Isabelle and back, and felt something constrict in his chest. The woman of the photo was, in person, so much more.

The Isabelle he had known had been quiet, a little shy, diffident. Her attractive qualities had been shaded by that diffidence. If you knew how to look at her, she was quite pretty, and he had taken a certain amount of pleasure in knowing that nine hundred and ninety-nine men out of a thousand would never see her true beauty. Unlike Cordelia, of course, who was so strikingly handsome that even a dolt knew how attractive she was.

The woman that Isabelle had become was like Cordelia in that she left the impression that she was completely self-confident. It probably did not matter to her that the frock she wore was a trifle out of date, nor that it had never been in high mode. She wore it with an air that made what she wore irrelevant.

And there was beauty there, for those with eyes to see it. She had never been beautiful before, but she was now.

It was not the sort of beauty that would make her into a subject for photographic postcards, or cause artists to beg her to pose for them. But it was a beauty that would outlast those whose features made them into public icons.

It was the sort of beauty that would look good on the arm of a public official, and presiding at his dinner table. And the confidence she exuded would make her at home at any gathering of Elemental Masters though she did not share their gifts.

This could have been his—and he had thrown it away.

"You are looking well," he said, making his words formal, a barrier between them.

She inclined her head, graciously, with no sign that she shared the emotional turmoil that racked him. "And you, though I confess that when your card came in, I was rather nonplussed. We attempted to have an interview with you about the threat to my two pupils a few months ago, in which a foreign Elemental Master was involved. Is this the cause of your visit?"

Pupils? What pupils? An Elemental Master attacking children?

Belatedly, he recalled the business in Berkeley Square, and suppressed irritation. This was the last thing in the world he wanted to talk about. "I thought that matter had been adequately closed," he replied.

"Not in my opinion." The inflection was of mild rebuke. "But then, I am responsible for them, and you are not. I believe steps have been taken to ensure their safety that do not require the approval of the Master of the Hunt, nor the Wizard of London."

He felt himself flushing with embarrassment. Something about the way she said those two titles—especially the latter—made them sound overblown, like something a child would give himself in a game of "I Conquer The Castle." But he endeavored to sound casually dismissive. "Is that what others are calling me, the 'Wizard of London'? There is no accounting for gossip even among the Elemental Mages." He shrugged. "As for Master of the Hunt, that title and the duties that go with it have nothing to do with what others outside the Master's Circle do or do not do. No one needs ask me permission for anything one gets from another Elemental Mage so long as it does not interfere with their hunt duties. If they choose to squander their power, they may do so in whatever fashion they like."

It was an insult, he realized that a moment later. But she didn't even blink an eye in reaction. The insult simply slid past her, not as if she did not understand she had been insulted, but as if it simply did not matter to her.

But it was very clear that she was going to extract whatever guilt she could from him before she let him go. "If the safety of two helpless little girls has not brought you here," she said, "then to what do I owe the pleasure of this call?"

And now he found himself at a loss for words. There were many things he could say, and none of them were entirely the truth. Would she sense that? He had to wonder about that. Just what were her psychical abilities?

"I am visiting Mansell Hall," he prevaricated, doing the only thing he could, which was to set it aside. "I understood that you were visiting here, and since it had been many years since we parted, I wished to pay a courtesy call."

The moment the words were out of his mouth he could have hit himself. Of all the things to say, this was, perhaps the one with the least truth in it. And she would certainly sense that.

"Oh?" She raised an eyebrow. "I was not aware that our social stations were compatible enough for a courtesy call."

Now there, at last, she showed her claws. Not that he didn't deserve it—

But the fact that he deserved it made him feel resentful. She was not going to get the better of him in this situation.

"Social graces are never misplaced," he replied, in a swift parry, "And I have paid a call on Mr. Harton at the school already."

But she riposted just as quickly and to better effect. "In that case, would courtesy not have dictated that you pay the call when my husband was also in residence, and not when I was here alone? Especially as you have already made his acquaintance?"

Hit and hit again. She was right. This was—despite that there were servants all around in this place, not to mention the teachers and pupils of her school—ever so slightly improper *as* a courtesy call. "Alone" she was, in that her husband was in London and pre-sumably not expected here for several days. Had he come to see the schoolmistress about her pupils, it would have been one thing; that would have been proper and reasonable, and as he was the one of more social importance, the call would have been appropri-ately made at his convenience, not hers. Had he really come to see an old friend, it would have been another case, for long friendships dictated a relaxation of formal manners, and their differing social stature would not have mattered, nor would it have mattered that Frederick Harton was not present. Had he come to see the Hartons socially as a couple, that, too, would have been appropriate.

But to come here when her husband was absent and refer to it as a "social call" implied something else. That he wanted to renew more than just "the acquaintance," and not as one of "friendship."

And the damnable thing was, now that he had seen her, he realized that there had been something of that sort in the back of his mind, a thought that though she was married to someone else, it might merely be a marriage of convenience on her part. One of the reasons why he had never been able to warm up to any of the young women of his circle was that none of them had struck that particular spark within him that Isabelle had.

And none of them had aroused much interest in him either. There just had been nothing there, no moment of connection. Beneath young Isabelle's diffidence had been the banked fires of passion, and the promise that the man who could arouse them would have a precious gift indeed.

Beneath the mature Isabelle Harton's serene competence, those fires of passion blazed for those who could read such things. The promise had more than been fulfilled, and it was the foundation for her attractiveness.

But they did not blaze for him, though they might have had he taken a different path.

There it was: what he had lost, written plain.

And in some forgotten corner of his mind, he knew that he had hoped, with the knowledge of how many of his peers had kept women, that he could get it back, so long as she had not given her heart to Frederick Harton.

Somehow he would have cut her free and married her. Though in that dark corner the baser part of him might have toyed with the notion of making her his mistress, he knew now that he would never have settled for such a tawdry solution. No, if it had been possible to have this woman, it would have been aboveboard.

Oh, it would have caused some difficulties. A man married to a divorcee was unlikely to be made Prime Minister—*if anyone knew his wife was once divorced.*

And even though he knew the cause was lost, he couldn't help tracing out those ways in his mind, as if he was probing at a sore tooth. There were ways around that, trivial for someone with the Power of an Elemental Master and the money of an Alderscroft. Records could be destroyed, memories altered. No one need ever know—not even she; with certain spells he could erase the memory of Frederick Harton entirely from her mind. Paying off Harton himself to go lose himself in the wilds of Canada or the fastnesses of the Himalayas would have not even made a significant dent in the Alderscroft fortunes.

But it would not happen. A marriage of convenience could be erased. A marriage of hearts, minds, and souls could not be.

And such a marriage did not allow for any other parties nor any other ties. He had lost her for all time.

There was only one way to retrieve his dignity; to tell a part of the truth, before she guessed at that other, hidden truth.

"Actually, the truth of the matter is that this is not a social call. It is one esoteric colleague calling upon the expertise of another. I encountered something curious, and you were the only person near enough that might be able to explain it," he said, gathering his dignity about him and allowing her veiled slur to slide past his own icy calm. "Besides paying a courtesy call, I wished to call upon you as a consultant of sorts."

Her expression did not change as he described the nature spirit to her—though he took care not to describe the circumstances under which it had appeared, nor the creature's threats.

Her face turned grave. "You would be wise not to meddle with him," she replied. "He is older than you can guess. The country folk call him Robin Goodfellow—"

"Good gad!" he exclaimed, startled. "Surely not!"

"Surely, for I have encountered him, too," she replied, with warning clear in her tone. "And Shakespeare did not do him any kind of justice. He is to this land what Attic Pan was to Greece and Sylvanus to Rome. You meddle with him at your peril—"

Now, this made him angry, though he held his anger down firmly. "You meddle with him at your peril," indeed! It was like something out of a poorly-written novel. What nonsense!

He had been so fixated on his conversation that he must not have noticed that the threatening storm had become actuality, for suddenly, Isabelle's warning was punctuated, as with an exclamation point, by a bolt of lightning striking an ancient oak immediately outside the library windows, with a simultaneously deafening crash of thunder.

They both jumped; Isabelle clutched at the bookshelves, and he dropped the book he had been unconsciously holding, his heart racing.

His first thought—which he immediately dismissed—was that it had been a warning to echo Isabelle's. It wasn't. It was purest coincidence. There was no reason, no reason at all, to think anything otherwise.

It took him a moment to recover; another to pick up the book he had dropped. By that time he thought he knew what he was going to say.

But the conversation was interrupted by the intrusion of—of all things—that wretchedly defiant little girl child, easy enough to identify even in the storm gloom by the raven that rode on her shoulder and glared at him with bright, shining eyes.

"Memsa'b, the lightning frighted the babies half to death an' they won't stop cryin' and the ayahs tol' me to come get you." He felt the force of truth behind the words, but he also felt the force of something else. The girl really disliked *him* and was fiercely happy to be the cause of interrupting the conversation he was having with her schoolmistress.

Nor did Isabelle seem at all displeased by the interruption. "You'll pardon me, I am sure," she said, with absolute formality. "But my duties to my charges in this case are something I cannot leave to anyone else. I am sure I can extend the hospitality of Highleigh to you for as long as the rain lasts. You may find research into the books on that shelf—" she pointed, "—to be fruitful, especially in light of what you just told me. You'll forgive me, I am sure, if I do not make a formal farewell and leave you in the hands of the servants."

And with that, she turned and followed the infuriating little girl out of the room.

Once again, he found himself struggling against anger, and

only by invoking the disciplines that Cordelia had taught him was he able to regain his self-control.

That, too, made him angry. Oh, this was the first *and last* encounter with Isabelle Harton that he was going to have! He should have known better than to come here in the first place. There was a reason, a good one, why he had broken off the nascent relationship with the woman. Cordelia had been right. Anyone who could invoke such strong emotions in him potentially had a hold over him that he did not need nor want. No, what he needed was control, absolute and complete. He had been an idiot to even think about having any connection to a woman that went past mutual regard and a calm and rational assessment of how each could supply what the other required for a reasonably comfortable life. Marriages of convenience—much better, much more logical than marriages of emotion. Emotion sapped control and self-control and no Elemental Master had any business in allowing that loss of control to happen.

He had no choice but to remain while the storm raged—but he did not have to follow her suggestion to do further research into the nature of the creature that had accosted him. He already knew enough, now. His suspicions had been confirmed, and as irritating as it was to be challenged, then beaten by a Nature Spirit, this one had millennia of power behind him, and he knew, intellectually, that to pit himself against Robin Goodfellow was as foolish as going out and howling defiance at the storm outside. And really, why should he? There was no profit in it. No sense in any sort of confrontation.

He did not, however, have to like that revelation. But he needed to keep his emotional reaction to a minimum, or that, too, would cause a loss of control.

Nor did he have to like the fact that Isabelle Harton had also had an encounter or encounters with the spirit, and presumably had not gotten a similar warning.

So, petty as it was, he did the only thing in his power at the moment. Instead of researching among the books Isabelle had indicated, he selected a novel and set himself in a chair at the window to read it. Or at least, pretend to read it.

And the moment the sky cleared, he summoned a servant to fetch his horse, and was gone.

✳

With her experiment a success, Cordelia had no further need for the second orphan. She was, in fact, debating what to do with him when fate itself presented the solution in the form of a tap on the door of her study by the housekeeper.

"Beggin' your pardon, milady, but I'd like to know if you've got any plans for the future of that boy," the woman said, without preamble. No need to ask "what boy," since there was only one on the premises.

"Well, I had originally thought to make him a page. . . ." She allowed her voice to trail off, leaving it for the housekeeper to determine that Cordelia now had some doubts about the wisdom of that plan.

The housekeeper jumped on the opening, and shook her head. "You're kindness itself, milady, but that boy—there's only so much polish you can put on a lump of coal, milady. Might be shiny, but 'tis still a lump of coal, and that boy is never going to make a good page, and I don't need another head in the household that does naught but run errands. He's simple, milady, and that's a fact. Not so bad to have a simpleton boy about, but a simpleton *man*, that's another kettle of herring."

Cordelia smiled benignly. "Mrs. Talbot, you would not have come up here to speak to me about one little boy if you did not already have a solution in hand. What is it?"

The housekeeper relaxed visibly. "The sweep's here," she said—which statement did not precisely follow, but Cordelia waited for elaboration. "Seems he's not got an apprentice. Boy's been following him about, does what he's told, and he's small and likely to stay so. Sweep asked where the boy was from and wants to know if you'd 'prentice him out."

"Ah." Cordelia nodded. It made perfect sense. Chimney sweeps' apprentices had shortened life spans; between falls and the unhealthy effects of crawling through tiny, soot-and-tar-laden chimneys, the number of apprentices that actually made it as far as becoming full-fledged chimney sweeps was exceedingly small. Sweeps were always looking for nimble, undersized boys.

The housekeeper had been more than a bit shaken by the death of the first boy, and was also getting a bit tired of having the second underfoot as well as losing the services of a perfectly capable housemaid for as long as the boy required a nanny. She had already registered one or two mild complaints with Cordelia on the subject. Now, if ever, was the opportunity to tidy up.

"I believe you have hit upon the perfect solution, Mrs. Talbot!" she said, earning a smile of relief from her housekeeper.

And that brought the household neatly back to normal. The boy was taken away, his nanny returned to her normal duties, and afternoon quiet settled over the town house.

Now was a good time for Cordelia to retire to her workroom. Perhaps the Ice Wurms would be able to do something about those little girls . . . in any event, it was time to put her plans for David into motion.

She lit the lamps—magically, of course—shut the door and sealed herself inside. With a word and a breath, she called up the chill, and the water in the air condensed into a mist, and she waited for it to settle into the forms of her Ice Wurms.

But it didn't.

Instead, it spread itself in a single even layer on the marble top of the worktable and then—

Then there was ice. A thin film of ice that turned the surface of the table into a mirror, which reflected her face for an instant, and then reflected something else entirely.

She stared, mesmerized, into colorless eyes that took up the entire surface of the worktable, and which stared back at her in some amusement.

So, said a voice she had not heard in a very long time in her head. *You have found a way to achieve your desire. Your dream of power. Congratulations.*

She shook herself loose from the fascination of those eyes. "And if I have?" she replied. "I can't see that it would matter to you."

Oh, but it does, said the voice. *Very much so. As a mere female you were vaguely interesting, even amusing, but as a man you will have the reins of power in your hands. That makes you more than interesting, it makes you worth bargaining with in earnest.*

Bargaining? Now her curiosity was more than merely piqued.

But the first step in successful bargaining was to never show any interest.

"What do you want?" she asked.

Mostly an agent, a foothold. An opening into your world, and freedom from this cage in which I have been confined.

Aha! So the creature *had* been imprisoned where she found it! "And what could you offer me that I would want?" she replied.

It laughed. *Let me show you—*

16

SHE had not wanted to see David. Not ever again. She had thought that it was all over and done with when he appeared at the school and Frederick spoke to him.

She had thought that she had all her resentment, her hurt, and her anger over and done with, too, long ago. It should have been. She should have been past all this. There was no reason why he should still have been able to affect her.

She had been wrong. And she wasn't entirely sure that the lightning strike right outside the windows had been "accidental." Give the amount of wild magic in play here, the number of arcane entities simply appearing, and the feeling she had that this was both a nexus for powers and a place where they manifested easily, that bolt from the heavens might merely have been her reaction to David's presence.

Which meant that truly, her anger was not under control, it was merely being locked in place.

Not good. Not for a Warrior of the Light.

She could not afford to have uncontrolled anger. She could not afford to let this man unbalance her.

She thought, given the circumstances, that she had comported herself well. No longer the tongue-tied teenager when confronted with conflict, she had remained at least outwardly composed. Her words had been civilized. Her manners had been impeccable. He was the one who had acted poorly, if anyone had. She had even given him good advice, not that she expected him to take it. The more she thought about it, the more certain she was that he had had no idea of just how angry she had been with him.

Which merely spoke for his blindness, not her ability to control herself.

She paced the confines of the small parlor toward the back of the manor overlooking the gardens that she tended to use as her own. The babies were all soothed, the storm had passed, and David's physical presence had been removed.

Mentally and emotionally, however . . .

The anger roiled inside her like those storm clouds had. She thought she had forgiven him. Clearly, she had not.

In fact, she wanted him to be hurt as much as he had hurt her.

This was also not good for a Warrior of the Light, whose will could become action if she was not careful. And then she would be subject to threefold retribution. How had he done this to her?

It was unfair and grossly unjust. Here she was, struggling to make a decent life for herself and those in her charge—unable to bear children of her own, which was a terrible and deep hurt she had revealed to no one, not even Frederick—trying with all her soul to protect and serve as she was supposed to do with the scantiest of resources—

And there he was, arrogant, cold, making demands of her. Offering no apologies for what he had done to her. Treating her like a menial, like a toy he could break, wait for his servants to repair, and pick up to play with again. Clearly coming here expecting that if, once the "goods" had been examined and he still wanted them, they would be free for his taking. Oh, she had not missed the allusion to his powerful friends, had not missed the impeccably-tailored and clearly expensive riding clothes, the aura of power, the arrogance of wealth that assumes that if it wants a thing, it shall have that thing. And he knew that she knew all about the estate, the money, and the title.

She had been glad—glad!—to hear of his discomfiting encounter with Robin Goodfellow! Time and more than time for him to realize that his wants were not the center of the universe, and that he was not the most powerful creature in it! She was glad it was Robin that had done it, too, spirit of mischief that he was. David had never been comfortable with teasing, nor with being made fun of, and Robin surely had taken the starch out of him.

Time for him to get a dose of what others felt like when he casually leaned his power, of rank, of money, of magic, on them to force them to his will. No one had ever rejected him, or made him feel inferior. It was a lesson it would do him good to learn.

And still, here in the place where she was a guest, he had done his best to make it clear to her how very much less a person she was than he—

She wanted, at that moment, to be able to actually call lightning out of the sky to strike him. Not lethally, but—

"Memsa'b?"

The small voice at the door to the parlor made her pause in her pacing. She turned.

It was little Sarah, looking up at her with a worried expression, bird on her shoulder. She wondered if Sarah had sensed her inner turmoil. If so, she owed it to the child to calm herself.

"Sarah," she said, with false calm. "If this is something trivial, I am rather preoccupied and I would hope we can deal with whatever it is later—"

Sarah looked up at her solemnly, her expression as sober as a judge.

"Memsa'b—that man that was here?" Sarah paused, and Isabelle waited for the child to tell her that he shouldn't come around here again. It was what she was expecting, when Sarah continued, "We need to help him."

Help him—help him? After endangering these children? After ig-

noring the corruption in his own circle? After coming here to lord it over me—to offer me crumbs from his table in exchange for the grace of his temporary attention—

She allowed none of this to show, and kept her psychical walls up to keep from disturbing the little girl more than she already was. "Sarah, dear, I am afraid that in this case, you really know nothing of the situation," she said carefully. She reminded herself that she was not angry at this child, she was angry, rightfully, at David. She should not unload her anger at David onto Sarah, who had done nothing to deserve it.

Two sets of eyes, the round yellow ones of the bird, and the round brown ones of the child, looked up at her solemnly.

"He is unhappy," Sarah said simply. "And you are unhappy, too. You're angry and upset and so is he. And you're so unhappy you feel dangerous. It's the kind of unhappiness that makes bad things happen."

Isabelle had been about to send the child off to play, when something about that last sentence chilled her anger and made her blood run cold. The words felt like a prediction. This was not good. . . .

"Sarah," she said instead. "Please, come sit with me."

She turned and took a seat on a spindly-legged divan and patted the hard seat beside her. Sarah did not hesitate a moment to carefully climb up next to her.

"Now," Isabelle said, "would you tell me what you mean by that?"

Sarah regarded her gravely, and Isabelle felt another emotion, but this time the opposite of the chilling effect of the child's words. Little Sarah had a wise old soul in her; Isabelle had learned to recognize such people in India. Normally, such old souls were content to enjoy their childhoods and not "wake up" until they reached a stage where it was appropriate for them to be active again. Nan, too, had an old soul, but it was clearly the soul of a warrior, not a wise man.

Sarah, however, had a spirit within her that was quite remarkable. It peeked out through those eyes every now and again, leaving whoever it regarded usually feeling warm and protected. And that wise old soul wanted to help Isabelle.

With a sigh, she knew she was going to have to set her anger to one side. Sarah nodded a little as Isabelle settled her hands in the correct position in her lap, and went into a light meditative trance. She visualized her anger as a fire raging out of control, and slowly confined it to its proper place on the hearth again, because even negative emotions like anger had positive uses. It wasn't easy, but she'd had good teachers in such discipline.

You must recognize that these things are within you and learn to use them, said the voice in her memory. *Otherwise they will use you.*

Yes, teacher, she said to the memory, and the fires crept back to their place.

She opened her eyes and looked down at Sarah, who was patiently waiting, and looked ready to wait forever.

"He's very unhappy," Sarah repeated. "I think he must have made some bad mistakes a long time ago. He thought he was being clever, but he was choosing a bad path. Now he's all twisted up and—cold. And that's bad, too. It's going to make trouble if he keeps on as he is."

Bad mistakes . . . The words took her aback for a moment. In the long view, which she was, for the moment, forcing herself to take, how important was a failed romance? It only really mattered to her, didn't it? How could David rejecting her possibly lead to something Sarah would call a "bad mistake"?

"He does have a great deal of influence," she said, thinking aloud. "What do you mean by saying he is cold?"

I know what I mean, but what is Sarah seeing?

"He doesn't feel anything anymore," Sarah said, her little face taking on an expression of deep sadness. "Or what he does feel he steps on right away. He thinks this is being clever, but it's like bricking up your windows so nobody can see inside your house. Then you can't see outside *or* inside yourself; you're all alone in the dark, and you just kind of wither. And when people don't feel anything anymore, they can do bad things without really thinking about it because it doesn't matter to them."

Isabelle felt shocked. *Out of the mouths of babes!* But then, Sarah was no ordinary child, "That's quite true," she acknowledged. "But if he doesn't feel anything anymore, just what exactly can you and I do? It would seem that he is so far down his chosen path that our influence is negligible. He is not inclined to listen to me, and he definitely will not listen to you."

Sarah frowned. "Well," she replied. "I don't know for certain if he really *doesn't* feel anything for true, or if it's only that he tries not to feel anything. But I think something bad is going to happen to him if we can't wake him up again. And when that something bad happens to him, he'll do a lot of bad around other people."

Then the child shook her head. "It's all hard to explain, and it's not like I know something is going to happen, it's just that I feel it is. I don't have a picture or anything in my head, and Grey just feels the same."

Too young to see the future, because she is too young to cope with needing to see it, and too young to cope with knowing what is to come. It would have been very useful if she and Nan had been in their late teens and fully into whatever powers and abilities they were going to get.

Well, perhaps Sarah could evoke more if Isabelle gave her more information.

Isabelle sighed. "He came here to tell me that he had encountered Robin. He wanted some information; I suspect he was not aware of Robin's true nature and thought that he could simply coerce or confine Robin if—"

"If he thought Robin was in the way," Sarah finished, with a decided nod. "Like Nan and me were in the way the other day when he came riding a horse through the hedge, and almost ran us down."

Isabelle felt another surge of anger, but this one was clean, simple anger at the careless man who would pay no attention to where he was going—not that she thought the children had been in any follow the advice of Lewis Carroll. "Begin at the beginning, go on until you reach the end, then stop."

And the beginning was forgiveness.

"You can go, Sarah," she heard herself saying. Obediently, the child nodded, and hopped down off the settle to walk quietly out of the parlor, leaving Isabelle alone.

I don't want to forgive him—

The mere idea made her angry, so angry she could feel a headache coming on.

Coming on?

She put her hands to her head and gasped as a lance of pain transfixed her, stabbing into her temple.

And it was that pain that finally awoke her to the reality of what she was doing to herself.

The child was right. The rancor she held for David Alderscroft *was* like a thorn in the foot that she refused to remove because she had not put it there. Nevertheless, it was stabbing deeper with every step she took. How long before it began to fester?

Judging by her strong reaction, not long at all.

"Bother," she said aloud. "I am *not* very good at this sort of thing—"

How to forgive when you really didn't want to?

Convince yourself that you do, of course.

With a sigh, she resigned herself to the inevitable. She went upstairs to the bedroom she had been given, and got a thick pile of foolscap out of the desk. Pen in hand, she sat down to make a list.

She was, by nature, a very methodical person. It was in her nature to approach a problem by writing a list.

She divided the paper in half with a line down the middle. On the one side she would write out all of her grievances; on the other, write the reasons why she should give the grudge up.

One: he broke my heart.

Broke it? Not really. Oh, it had *felt* like a broken heart at the time, and certainly she had been horribly unhappy, but with the perspective of time it was not—quite—a broken heart. She wrote

danger from David. First of all, few horses that were not actually vicious or panicked were likely to trample people. Horses hated soft things underfoot, and given the choice, would shy rather than run something down.

Nevertheless—it was careless, it was heedless, and it was certainly an example of the sort of arrogance that was making her so angry with him.

He certainly had not come to anyone here at Highleigh to report the incident, which was the least he should have done. Any responsible adult would have done so. A truly responsible adult would have made certain the girls were well, then brought them to the manor himself.

No, she was vexed, very vexed with him. That was twice he had endangered the lives of two little girls with no demonstration that he considered them to be as important as a pair of stray kittens.

"Obviously, since you are not sporting hoofprints, he didn't harm you," she said with calm she did not feel. "I trust he apologized."

That would have been the least that any decent man would have done.

"No. He shouted at us for being there, and Nan shouted back at him and he got angry. Nan said she thought he had no right being there, which got him more angry. So he just rode around the meadow, then went back." Sarah shook her head. "And that's why Nan's angry with him," she added. "He didn't treat us very well, but I know why. He was in the wrong, but he feels like he *has* to be right all the time. The more wrong he is, the more he acts badly in order to prove that he is right. So since he feels that way, he can hurt people quite easily." She looked thoughtful a moment. "I suppose," she said, in tones that suggested she was trying to find David's point of view, "if we had been crying and acting scared or hurt, he would have acted differently. But since Nan was being rude, he must have supposed that we were all right and he was free to be angry with us."

Isabelle clenched her jaw, then forced it to relax. And she thought about what her friend Bea had said about this circle of Elemental Mages David was putting together, and how he had political ambitions. And then her blood ran cold.

The one thing that had kept the practitioners of the arcane from meddling as much as they could if they chose, was that they had kept themselves out of "secular" life, so to speak. There was little or no interference on their part with the lives of those who were not so gifted, except, perhaps, the occasional rescue.

And thus far, there had been no one who was really willing to take that step into the lives of those who were not Elemental Mages. There was an unspoken accord between the Mages and the Gifted and Talented that they would not interfere with one another either.

But combine a powerful Elemental Master, the circle he had founded, political ambitions, and the absolute certainty in that Master's mind that he was right and what he wanted was what was best for all—

Add to that the unwillingness on the part of that Master to admit he could ever be *wrong*—

It would start small, of course. Such things always began small. First political contacts, and then, to a chosen man or two in very high places, the proof that magic existed and it could be used to produce real effects. Pointing out that using magic for the good of the Empire was the only patriotic way to proceed.

Then it would begin, with the Elemental Mages cautiously being given poltical and governmental positions and power. Perhaps there would be a special Ministry in charge of the Arcane. And at first, its work would be entirely benign. Renegade Magicians would be tracked down, rounded up, and possibly laws put through so that they could be made accountable for what they did. And in David's circle there would be a sort of policing force ready-made. They would all have official government sanction, and a certain amount of power. Power could be very addictive.

But then—how long would it be before all Magicians were asked to register with this Ministry? How long until any Magician that had elected not to register was deemed a "renegade" and reg-

istration was no longer voluntary? How long before it wasn't just Magicians, but all the Gifted and Talented as well?

And then, how long before the Magicians extended their hands over the ordinary people who had neither Gift nor Talent?

Then what?

There were many possibilities, and all of them were chilling.

All of this ran through her mind while the child sat there, solemn-eyed, watching her.

"Things could be very bad if his heart stays frozen, couldn't they?" Sarah asked quietly. "Your face went all still, Memsa'b. It only does that when you're thinking that things could be bad."

Isabelle sighed. "Yes, Sarah. Things could be very bad. The trouble is, I don't know how to put them right."

Sarah's eyes never left hers. "Mummy says that the way to st[art] putting things right is always to start with forgiveness."

Isabelle felt as if someone had struck her a blow. Forgivenes[s] was the one thing she did *not* want to give him! And yet—

"Mummy says not forgiving someone hurts you worse th[an] hurts him," the child persisted. "Even if he doesn't deserve [to be] forgiven. She says not forgiving someone is like not pulling [a thorn] out of your foot just because you weren't the one that put it [there]."

Isabelle regarded the child steadily, and the old soul [looked] back at her out of Sarah's eyes. Somehow she doubted tha[t] "Mummy" had said anything of the sort. No, this was a[dvice] from a source that Isabelle would be wise to heed.

"So, we start with forgiveness," she said, strugglin[g with her] own rebellious heart. "But where do we go from there[?]"

Sarah looked uncertain. "Maybe—Robin?"

Isabelle blinked. That was not a bad notion. Th[e worst that] would happen would be that he would tell them it w[asn't his] business.

And even if he himself declined to help them, [he was] going to give them some idea of which way to go.

Yes, it was a very interesting idea indeed.

How to approach this, however. Well, the be[st]

that down on the other side of the line, then something else occurred to her.

If he had not cast her off, she would never have gone to India and never met Frederick.

So *Frederick,* she wrote on the right-hand side of the page.

So if he had not broken her heart—*He hurt my pride.*

True enough, very true. And hardly the reason to carry a grudge. Pride got hurt all the time, it always went before a fall.

So *true,* she wrote on the other side, and added *and no harm done.*

He drove my friends away.

That was a lie. She had *run* away, and as she had discovered, her true friends had not been driven away, and had, in fact, only been waiting for her to approach them again.

So *false* she wrote on the right-hand side.

He's arrogant.

True, but if she began to hate everyone who was arrogant, she would soon be spending all her time seething in a self-made mass of anger, too tied up in knots to actually get anything accomplished.

He thinks no one is right except himself.

Also true, but—the same argument held.

Down the lists on both sides she went, until she had three full pages of reasons why she should not forgive him—and six pages of reasons why continuing to be angry at him was foolish.

She stared at her lists and began to chuckle.

She never could hold a grudge in the face of logic. The logic here was overwhelming, and with a mocking nod of self-deprecation, she acknowledged that.

She put down the pen and stared out the window at the neatly ordered gardens. "I forgive you, David Alderscroft," she said aloud. "I forgive you for being an arrogant ass. I forgive you for being cruel to the poor fool I was. Because if you had not been cruel, I would not have Frederick, and for that blessing I can forgive you just about anything."

She felt some of her rancor ease. Not all, by no means, not all—but she would repeat this vow of forgiveness as often during the day as she remembered to do so, and eventually—probably sooner rather than later—she would feel it unreservedly.

And in a way, it would be a better revenge than continuing to hate him, because the last hold on her he had would be gone.

She laughed, put the foolscap into a drawer, and went down to the kitchens. She needed to find out how long the house party he was attending would last. And the servants knew everything. This might not be a matter of any urgency, but she really dared not take that chance.

❊

Cordelia nibbled the end of her pen as she considered which of her social contacts would best be able to get her invited to the house party David was attending. Under most circumstances this would have been the very last thing she cared to do, but after due consideration, she had realized something quite vital

It had occurred to her somewhat belatedly that it would be better, far better, if the transfer of souls took place somewhere other than in her own home. If it was to occur during something like this house party, for instance, there would be no breath of scandal attached. But to have David here in her London town house overnight—people would talk. There was no reason for him to stay overnight. Even if he drank too much, which of course he never did, he would not be put to bed here. In a manor or a big country estate, such things were done, because of the distances, but in London? No. If he were to be sick enough to be put up in the home of a single woman, there had better be a doctor called and two nurses in attendance. A gentleman capable of going up a set of stairs to a room would insist on going home in his carriage.

She wanted no taint attached to David, since shortly she would *be* David.

But a country house party? Ideal. Any stigma would attach to the owner of the house, the host of the party. The usual difficulties of explanation involved when a lady was found wandering late at night near the room of someone who was not her husband would not come into play. Her magic would prevent anyone from seeing her going to and from David's room. Once she was in David's body, she could carry the lifeless corpse of Cordelia back to her own room to be found in the morning. It seemed like a flawless plan.

So her first step; find out how much longer the party was to continue, and her second; somehow contrive to get invited to it.

Both were trivially easy for someone with Cordelia's magic and social experience. To ascertain the first, she sent to David's housekeeper to find out when he was expected back. An unexceptional, perfectly ordinary question and one she had asked the housekeeper many times before. One's housekeeper was always the first to be informed of a prospective absence or return, often before one's spouse knew. Of course, she did not ask directly; her secretary took that task. The answer came within the hour: in about a week.

He had already been there a week at this point. It was an unusually long time for a house party, but this one was hosting a number of quite important politicians, but not all at once, since many of them were not on speaking terms with each other. Such were the ways of politics; one's deadliest foes were generally in one's own party. Still, at the moment David was both an unknown and someone to be courted, and David was staying on as an extended guest to meet all of them.

Now, since she did not know the host directly, she had to contrive an indirect means of getting an invitation. But she was the mistress of the art of the indirect by now, since no mere female ever got anything done directly. No, they had to sneak and cajole and bargain. Any direct approach was unthinkable. A man could pay a call on a successful host at his club and say "Look, old man, I need to be invited to your soiree this weekend." No one would question such a request. But a woman, particularly an unmarried woman—

Tongues would wag and people would speculate about lovers.

Surely nothing other than a lover could prompt such behavior out of a woman.

So she would have to go about this carefully, though there was nothing particularly complicated about what she needed to do, only tedious.

An hour in her workroom, scrying in her ice mirror, got her the names of those to be invited for the next week. She put on her walking suit, hat and gloves, her engraved card case, called for her carriage, and sallied forth to make calls with the determination of a Wellington planning a campaign. A set of morning calls for the least important, afternoon calls for the most, with tea reserved for the best target.

She loathed making calls. If there was a more useless waste of time she had yet to find it.

Normally this would not have involved the list of calls, but normally she would have had weeks or months for her little child ghosts to whisper in the ear of the intended victim and persuade said victim that she could not possibly go, but that dear Cordelia would provide the perfect substitute. The all-important matter of the guest list (or in this case, lists) were arranged very carefully at these parties. When guests were not accompanied by their respective spouses, an equal number of gentlemen and ladies must be arranged. When single ladies were required, they had to be above reproach in all ways. She certainly qualified on that score. No one had ever breathed a single word of scandal about her. She had never encouraged anything but the most restrained and polite of male attentions. Her pedigree was exceptional, her acquaintances wide and all of the best society, and she was, in public, neither too educated nor too ignorant. She made the ideal guest. She knew when to keep her mouth shut, when to amuse, and what topics were safe.

Your son and your husband were safe from her attentions. She could be relied upon to be seated next to a boring old man and appear fascinated, to play whatever game of cards you required a partner for, to shoot adequately if you wanted women along at a shoot, and to not complain if you didn't. She could not sit a horse, but she could help amuse her fellow females when the hunters went out. She had no sense of humor, but that was scarcely obligatory in a mere female. She could play badminton, croquette, lawn tennis, and lawn bowls without complaint. She had no history of attempting to curry favor.

After careful weighing and measuring, which was the point of all that exercise going from town home to town home, she knew which of the rest of her "friends" was the likeliest provider of the invitation. She found her quarry, a plain and uninteresting cousin of the host, who was being invited merely to "make up" the rest of the party. She paid a call on the cousin who was a timid thing and not inclined to make a fuss—and really did not want to go to this party anyway.

When she was done, the cousin was feeling really very ill, and not inclined to go off to a strange house in the country, away from all her creature comforts. Though London might be warm in the summer, it at least had the benefit of containing all that was familiar, and a few close friends who were just as plain and uninteresting as the cousin herself. She could spend her week in her usual round of pursuits or go off to the country to be bored and unhappy, and probably looked down upon.

And here was a substitute, sighing wistfully and saying that she was tired of both London and her own Thames-side house, and longed for the tranquillity of "true" country life for a week or so.

Cordelia watched with satisfaction in her ice mirror how the cousin sat down that very afternoon to write regrets and a suggestion.

And Cordelia's little ghosts stirred uneasily until she picked just one to do her bidding and whisper encouragement into the ear of the host as soon as he got that letter. They were not happy about being sent out now, not after the way in which Peggoty had been sent out and had not returned.

She considered sending the new one, and rejected the idea, picking instead a scraggly little boy who had been very reliable in the past. While not precisely fearless, he was certainly not as fearful as some of them.

With that particular task completed, she sat back in her crystal chair. There was no reason to leave the workroom just now, and every reason to stay. Not the least of which was that the temperature here was that of a brisk late-autumn day, with frost on the ground, and the temperature of her parlor, indeed, of the rest of the townhouse, was considerably higher.

Ah. Now you understand.

That voice again. She looked up from contemplating her hands and saw that the surface of the entire table was frozen over, creating a mirror an inch thick, in which she could only see a pair of enormous ice-blue eyes, blue as the light in the heart of a glacier. The eyes stared at her in amusement.

Now you understand. I wish to hold this place for myself and my kind. I wish to bring winter forever to this island of yours.

That actually startled her, because she had never guessed *that* at all.

"Why?" she asked it, as visions of a frozen London came and went in her extra mirror. The visions actually did not look particularly unpleasant, actually. The Thames was frozen solid and being used by a few hardy souls as a highway. Snow drifted up against most buildings as high as the second story, then froze hard, so that people had to either tunnel their way out or come and go through the windows.

There were remarkably few people about. Now that might have been because it was so difficult to get around in the Arctic landscape, but Cordelia didn't think that was the case. No . . . not when so few chimneys were smoking . . . not when there was no sign that any one was coming or going at the Houses of Parliament.

It certainly looked as if London had been abandoned—

And then an image of Hyde Park, and someone driving through it in a sleigh, a sleigh drawn not by horses, but in the Finnish fashion, by reindeer. Clever that; horses were ill-suited for running on snow and ice. A closer look—it was David Alderscroft in the back, being driven by a servant muffled to the eyes in furs. But something told Cordelia that it was *her* living in that body, not the original owner.

Better and better.

When I hold this island through you, you will need no longer fear discovery. You can collect your own circle of Elemental Masters to serve us. You will be the King—or Queen, if you so choose to revert to a female body—in all but name. Eventually, as the years pass, you will become the monarch. Have we a bargain?

"There is always a price," she said aloud. "What is it?"

Your heart will be mine.

She was startled for a moment. Surely the creature did not mean—

You will never again feel passion of any sort. That will be mine. No pleasure. No anger. No love, nor hate, nor grief, nor joy.

For a moment she was incredulous. This was all? "What," she asked mockingly. "Are you not going to require my soul?"

It only laughed. *Your heart will do.*

"Done," she said, without hesitation. "We will rule the boreal kingdom of Britain together."

It laughed. *So let it be written,* it said, in the ancient words of sealing. *So let it be done.*

17

CORDELIA realized within an hour of her arrival that her original plan was not going to work. David had brought his valet with him, and the man slept in a room attached to David's own. That was a complication she had not foreseen, although she had brought her own maid with her. She had intended to drug the girl to avoid an unnecessary expenditure of magic energies, which would be at a premium in the height of summer. There was no way that she would be able to also drug David's man. And even if she could—

Her room lay in the other wing of the place. To return her dead body to her room, she—in David's body—would have to carry a lifeless corpse from one end of the building to the other.

Not feasible.

As she smiled and occasionally murmured pleasantries over tea, her mind was abuzz with activity. There had to be a way to make this work!

David seemed rather surprised to see her when he joined the party for dinner, but a serene smile seemed to reassure him, and he nodded to her from his place nearer the head of the table than herself. She acknowledged the nod, then went back to her conversation with an elderly duke. It was surprisingly interesting, actually; the man had spent his active years as the ambassador to the Court of the King of Sweden, and she was able to ask him a great many questions about life in extremely frigid climes. He, in his turn seemed pleased and surprised that she had an interest in such things.

After dinner, some of the ladies of the party took a turn in the gardens, which had been illuminated for the purposes with Chinese lanterns and torches. She took the opportunity to view the grounds, which, she had been told, had been specially designed to be particularly attractive at night. There were many sorts of night-blooming plants here, and paths that were broad, with turf as smooth and soft as a carpet. There were tall hedges that divided the garden into a series of roofless rooms. and as she strolled with three other ladies, it began to dawn on her that she had found the perfect place for her plot.

She could slip out into the garden under the cover of the darkness. Then she could call *him* here, to some secluded spot. She could plant the suggestion in his mind via one of her little ghostly servants that he was too warm to sleep, and was coming out into the garden to have a solitary turn and perhaps a smoke. No one would ever see them meet. If anyone saw him or spoke to him, it was unlikely that anyone would connect David Alderscroft with the lifeless body of his mentor, who would be found the next day.

In fact, she would make it appear that she had gone out for a similar stroll, had sat down to rest, and simply—died.

The hardest part would be subduing him without drugs, for obviously she was not going to be able to slip any such thing into him in a strange household. She would have to call upon other powers.

There were spells to bring sleep, and while they were wildly expensive in terms of the power needed, it wasn't as if she was going to require that power later. Or, if she did, her ally could probably supply it.

Unless . . .

She smiled. Of course.

Instead of relying on her ghosts, she could tell him simply that she had uncovered some magical threat to him out here, and had come to warn and aid him. Obviously, they could not meet within the walls of a stranger's home for this; she would have him come to the garden and join her for spell-work. Once he had submitted to her as the mentor, she could do whatever she wanted with him.

Simple. As the best plans always were.

He would not even worry at first as the breath of the Ice Wurms wreathed him about. He was used to it, after all. And by the time he realized that this was not the usual cold spell-work, it would be too late. He had snubbed the normal Fire Elementals for so long that they would never come to his aid if he called them—and the Ice Elementals answered to her.

She smiled, and began to stroll the gardens looking in earnest for the most secluded spot. Not tonight, of course. But soon, soon.

There was nothing like seeing a plan finally come to fruition. And the fruit, when she plucked it, would be sweet indeed.

At last she found what she judged to be perfect. Far enough from the buildings that it might as well be invisible, with tall hedges on two sides, and a secluded bench. There were no lanterns or fairy lights in this part of the garden either, but the bench was overarched by a trellis of night-blooming jasmine, which made it just the spot for a lady to sit and enjoy the evening.

In fact, she tried it out for a moment, and was satisfied.

Do not be too satisfied.

The cold voice in her mind was accompanied by the bite of frost from a spot on the path just in front of her. There was a column of mist there, faintly glowing, and a suggestion of eyes at the top of it.

You are in enemy territory, and they will stop you if you are not prepared.

"What enemy?" she demanded sharply.

If you are wise, you will find a way to accomplish this on your own ground.

"Not in any timely fashion," she replied, in tones as cold as the mist. "The longer I delay, the likelier it is that Ashcroft will manage to drift away from me. He grows independent, and this is making me uneasy. And there is no way to accomplish this thing either in his home or mine without scandal."

If a column of mist could shrug, this thing did. *Then you will need my help,* the ice creature said. *We will begin with your child ghosts. Summon them now.*

She was about to protest that this was not a simple thing, when a chill of warning made her think better of it. She had thought that she was in control of this situation. The cold, collected voice in her mind and the power behind it gave her the first intimation she might have been mistaken.

It would frighten the children, making them useless for her purposes, but she didn't think that was going to matter to the Ice Lord, as she was now calling him in her mind. "I cannot do this at this moment," she said simply. "I must summon them by means of the things I have in my room." She never traveled without a needle case, a roll of small felt pockets, each of which held a small, labeled sample of hair.

Fetch it and return, the voice commanded curtly. *Time is of the essence.*

The tenor of the voice raised the hair on the back of her neck, and she began to realize that she might have made a very profound error.

It was, however, too late to correct that error now. The best she could do would be to ride out the storm that she herself had set in motion.

That she would survive this storm was not an issue. She knew that she would. The creature needed her. But she needed now to be on the watch for ways in which she could turn it to her advantage.

Carefully avoiding the other ladies, she slipped silently into her room and retrieved what she needed. As she passed the billiard room, it was clear that the political discussion was still in full swing, by the haze of tobacco smoke and the rumble of male voices. And she felt anger at that, anger that the women were excluded without a single thought—

But this was not the time nor the place. She slipped back out into the dark gardens with their softly glowing, colored lanterns, and paused to listen to the female counterpart to the male conversation. High-pitched, artificially cadenced nonsense punctuated by the occasional polite titter. That made her angry, too. The amount that could be accomplished if these women would not allow themselves to be made into powerless ornaments—

Well, they were fools, and their men with them. Most of the earth's population was as foolish and as useless, fit only to take orders and serve. Serve Cordelia, of course. The England that she ruled would be structured accordingly.

But for now, she must summon her ghosts and see what the creature did with them. She did not doubt that there was danger to her plans here, even if she could not see it. The creature had not failed her before, and it clearly had a strong incentive not only to tell the truth, but to keep her safeguarded.

She would not, however, make the mistake of expecting that condition to last.

❄

The next morning, she was amused to overhear the gardeners bemoaning the "patch of blight" that had appeared overnight in a remote part of the garden. It was not blight, of course, but the direct result of the Ice Lord's work with the child ghosts. The gardeners were scrambling to replace the patch of turf and the plants, to trim back the frost-killed branches of bushes. The children now stood as arcane sentries, guarding the house and grounds, not only from immaterial threat, but from anyone with any sort of power, Elemental or psychical. They might not be able to stop all intruders, but they could certainly delay and damage even the most powerful, and they would give a warning.

They were no longer vague little sketches of children either. The

Ice Lord had transformed them utterly, into feral, fierce creatures exuding menace. It would take a brave person indeed to dare to go past them, and a powerful one to be willing to try taking them on. It wasn't that they were strong individually—it was that they were now vicious as weasels, and would swarm anybody who tried to take one on.

After she had gone back to the manor, and engaged in some pointless gossip with the other ladies before retiring, she had made a point of enforcing slumber. Tonight was going to be difficult enough without fatigue. The day had dawned unseasonably cool and continued that way, which she considered either a good omen, or an evidence that the Ice Lord was already exerting his power.

She actually thought it vanishingly unlikely for it to be the latter. The Ice Lord had made it quite clear that the bulk of the action was to be in her hands. That he had interfered at all in the case of the ghosts was something he had done with great reluctance. There was someone or something out there that he considered to be a great hazard to them and to their enterprise.

So the unseasonably cool weather was just a coincidence, but one she could take advantage of. She rose and her maid dressed her while she thought long and hard about what her next step would be.

But the opportunity to speak privately with David came sooner than she had thought.

"We must talk," he said under his breath, as he passed her on the stairs, she going down to breakfast, he returning from it.

"Now is as good a time as any," she replied, "I am not so enamored of grilled tomatoes that I cannot take the time to speak with my pupil when he looks so distressed. Let us take a turn in the gardens."

Here, of course, was where she overheard the lamentations of the gardeners, and smiled to herself.

"I am not sure where to begin," he said at last. "I encountered a—a nature spirit here. It threatened me."

"Uncommon but not unheard of," she observed. "Clearly, though, this was no common spirit."

"No," he said grimly, and proceeded to describe his encounter in minute detail, while she grew more surprised by the moment. There was only one creature she could think of with that sort of power. And the fact that it had threatened to interfere now made her understand why the Ice Lord had taken direct action.

Her first thought was that the spirit—clearly one of the Greater Fey, those who had been, in their time, worshipped as gods—had somehow deduced her plan and the Ice Lord's. If that was the case, a few puny wraiths were not going to stop him.

But then she realized that all of the threats had been aimed toward David, and the warning specifically pointed at this part of the country. There had been an implication that the spirit did not care what happened in London, so long as no Ice Magic was brought *here*.

So it didn't know.

Just because a creature was very powerful, it did not follow that it was omniscient. And even if it had the capability to read the future, it did not follow that it would. The Greater Fey in particular had curious holes in their thinking. They tended to be "flighty." They had difficulty in concentrating on any one thing for too long. No matter how important something was, there was always the possibility that once it was out of immediate sight, it would also be out of mind.

Chances were, the creature had already forgotten about David. And by the time it realized that they were working Ice Magic, it would be too late. Nor would it occur to the Fey that there could be more to it than just Cordelia's plan.

But this fed directly into *her* plot.

"You were right to be concerned," she said earnestly. "This is a dangerous creature, capricious and unpredictable. I must safeguard you from it."

His lips thinned as he frowned. "Simply tell me what to do," he replied, once again showing an annoying independence. "I can handle this myself, I should think."

"Under normal circumstances, yes," she replied. "But these safeguards are against the Greater Fey and must be placed externally. Even if I told you how to place them—which I will, of course—you would only be able to place them on someone else. The subject must be unconscious in order for the protections to be invoked, or the initial disorientation as one is suddenly able to see the Fey realms is far too painful."

She congratulated herself gleefully at that stroke. Brilliant! Now she could do whatever she liked with him with absolute impunity. He would never even question what she was doing, because he already had had the experience of what happened when one first was able to see the creatures and energies of Elemental Magic. It was generally very disorienting and sometimes distressing. Children who were born into nonmagical families sometimes went mad, or believed they were doing so. He had no idea whether or not being able to see the Fey would be worse than that, although, in fact, the Fey realms did not exist, and the Fey were simply Masters of *all* the Elements.

"When can we do this?" he asked eagerly, as she regarded him with grave eyes.

"Tonight would not be too soon," she said soberly. "And if you meet me here in the garden, I will find a secluded place where we can work undisturbed."

※

Isabelle was just finishing her correspondence when the sound of a familiar footstep made her raise her head and swivel swiftly in her chair.

Just in time to have Frederick stoop over her and kiss her passionately, his arms including both her and the ladder-back of her chair, which was probably the only reason why he wasn't crushing her into his chest. Not that she would have minded being crushed into his chest.

As always, she closed her eyes and allowed herself a moment when all she thought of, felt, knew, was him; the moment of being completely *with* him, in love, surrounded by love, engulfed by love. As always, it was better than it had been the last time. She had never been more sure of him, never been more sure that no matter how things changed, the two of them would see that they changed in a way that only brought them closer.

Being together, in that way that stole her breath and stopped her heart and held them both in timeless time.

The moment passed, as such moments always did, leaving behind echoes that created their own kind of song inside her. She felt him stand straight and opened her eyes, smiling.

He looked down at her, chuckling, his eyes crinkling at the corners. "Once again, we scandalize the servants."

She laughed. "I did not expect you until tomorrow!"

He grinned and shrugged. "Doomsday Dainwrite sent me off with a half holiday," he replied, and his face took on the mournful expression of a bloodhound contemplating an empty food dish. *"You need to go to your wife,"* he said in sepulchral tones. *"Terrible things are about to happen, and she will need you."*

Isabelle laughed at that, because the head of the firm, called "Doomsday" even by his own wife (who he predicted would leave him, drown, catch fire, be struck by lightning, or die of some plague virtually on a daily basis), had never, ever been right in his predictions of disaster and mayhem. The only times disaster *had* befallen the firm or some person in it, Doomsday had been completely silent on the subject and had been taken as much by surprise as anyone else.

"Well, it is not as if you have not earned a half holiday and more," she replied, taking his hand in hers, and holding it against her cheek for a moment, then letting it go.

"And so have you. We are having tea on the terrace, away from the children, and then we are going for a walk on the grounds, you and I and no one else. And we are going to talk of nothing but commonplaces." He bestowed a look on her that told her he was accepting no arguments. But then, she was not inclined to give him one.

By dinnertime all was back to normal, except that she felt as rejuvenated by the afternoon as if she had spent a week at the seaside. Her good humor spread among the children; for once there were no quarrels, no outbursts of temper, scarcely even a raised voice when there was contention over the last jam tart. That pirate of a raven, Neville, was on his best behavior, and Sarah's parrot Grey did not even indulge herself in her own favorite bit of mischief of sorting through the bits in her cup and dropping what she didn't care to eat on the floor.

The children went off to baths and bed with scarcely a moment of fuss. The youngest, now at the "escape from the bath and run through the halls naked, shrieking," stage, for once did not indulge themselves. It was the perfect ending to a perfect day.

Until, as the oldest were settled into their beds, and Isabelle finished the rounds of "good night hugs," she and Frederick stepped out onto the terrace—

—and the perfect day shattered.

One moment, they were holding hands, gazing at the stars and listening to the nightingales and the occasional call of an owl.

The next, they were clutching each other, half-deafened by the thunderclap, half-blinded by the lightning bolt that had delivered Robin Goodfellow to the foot of the terrace. A very angry Robin Goodfellow, who was nothing like the merry lad who had strutted his way across their improvised stage, playing himself with gusto and glee.

No, this was a tall and terrible creature, dressed head to toe in black, features inhumanly sharp and feral, with a face full of wrath and a sword in his hand.

"Woe be unto ye, son of Adam and daughter of Eve!" he cried, in a voice that echoed hollowly. *"Your friend would not heed my warning, nor thine, Eve's daughter, and he and his leman seek to unleash that which has no place here!"*

And with another bolt of fire and explosion of thunder he was gone. But a cold, angry wind sprang up in his wake, sending storm clouds racing from east to west, plastering Isabelle's gown to her legs.

"—what—" Frederick began, having to shout to make himself heard over the tempest.

But Isabelle had no doubts. "Alderscroft," she shouted back. "David Alderscroft is—invoking something. I don't know what, but—"

"But we need to put a stop to it," Frederick shouted back, and as one they turned—

To find Nan and Sarah behind them, birds crouched down on their shoulders against the wind—and behind them, Agansing, Karamjit, and Selim.

The girls both wore expressions of fierce determination, and faintly glowing auras that looked incongruous on two youngsters dressed in schoolgirl pinafores.

Isabelle's entire nature went into revolt at the sight of the children. Whatever needed confronting, *they* had no place there!

The three men were overlaid with their aspects of Warriors of the Light; Agansing in the garb of the Gurkha, enormous *kukri* at his belt, Karamjit in the tunic and turban and bearing the sword of the Sikh fighter, and Selim, also in turban and tunic, but with a spear to Karamjit's curved sword.

"The avalanche has begun, Memsa'b," Agansing said eyes glinting. "It is too late to make a choice among what will fall. The children summoned us; they in their turn were summoned."

Isabelle looked down at the girls, and her heart sank.

Agansing was right as often as "Doomsday" was wrong.

✳

Nan was dead asleep one moment, and wide awake in the next.

She woke with the absolute certainty that something was horribly wrong. It was like the same feeling she'd had back in Berkeley Square, though different in that the threat was not directed at her or at Sarah. But a threat there was, a deadly one, and she had to meet it. She glanced up at Neville's perch above her bed to see the raven looking down at her. She felt him in her head, calling something; felt that "something" waking up.

She leaped out of bed, to find Sarah also scrambling up.

"Wot is it?" she asked, feeling shaky and scared, but also, another part of her, galvanized and energized and—eager?

"Don't know," Sarah replied, pulling her dress over her head, "—but it's—"

"*Bad!*" Grey cried, every feather sticking out so she looked like a gray pinecone. *"Bad, bad, bad!"*

That was all she had time for when the whole building shook beneath a cannonade of thunder.

And it was as if some uncanny telegraph connected them, for the same information flashed into both their minds.

"Robin!" cried Sarah, and "Puck!" shouted Nan at the same time, while Neville called alarm and Grey uttered a high-pitched, growling shriek.

"He's angry!" Sarah added, her face white in the light of the candle Nan lit.

"He's more'n that," she said grimly. "He's gone for killin'."

Difficult as it was to imagine friendly, funny Robin Goodfellow prepared to kill something, she had no doubt in her mind at all that this was what he was prepared to do. And she also had no doubt in her mind that it was her job to prevent it, if she could.

And not just for the sake of the potential victim, either—

"Oh, Nan—" Sarah turned round eyes on her. "If he does that—"

Nan nodded. She knew, and knew that somehow the knowledge came through Neville, that if Robin Goodfellow, the Guardian of Logres, was to spill human blood, he would be banished from the Isle for all time. And if that happened—much, if not all, of the magic would go with him. She sensed a future stretching out from that moment, bleak and gray and joyless, and shuddered.

Around them, the other children, startled out of sleep by the thunder, were calling out, the babies crying. The ayahs were busy calming them, and no one paid any attention as Nan and Sarah, with Neville and Grey clutching their shoulders, slipped out and downstairs.

No one that is, until they ran right into Agansing, Karamjit, and Selim.

A wave of dismay swept through Nan as she winced back, sure that she and Sarah were going to be rounded up and sent back upstairs.

But instead, Agansing held up his hand and peered at them. That was when Nan realized there was a kind of ghostly, glowing "other" version of Agansing superimposed on the everyday fellow.

"We will need these fellow Warriors, my brothers," he said solemnly. Karamjit peered at them and nodded. Selim sighed with resignation.

"I bow to your superior experience, brother," Selim said reluctantly. "But I cannot like it. They are too young."

"Younger than they have taken up arms, and they have unique weapons none of us can wield," Agansing replied, and turned to Nan. "We go to join Sahib and Memsa'b. We are needed."

"Yessir," she said, feeling oddly as if she ought to be saluting.

All of them moved swiftly in a group to the doors leading onto the terrace, the two girls having to trot to keep up. A vicious wind howled around the windows, and in lightning flashes from outside it was obvious there was a storm raging—wind, but no rain as yet.

They emerged onto the terrace and into the icy teeth of the wind just as Sahib and Memsa'b turned.

"The avalanche has begun, Memsa'b," Agansing said, eyes glinting. "It is too late to make a choice among what will fall. The children summoned us; they in their turn were summoned."

We summoned them? For a moment Nan was aghast at the lie. But then—then something told her it was not a lie, but the truth. Somehow she and Sarah *had* summoned the men, or at least, Agansing. She didn't know how, but—

That other presence within her smiled grimly; she felt it smile. Felt it tell her how it had summoned a fellow warrior with a mental trumpet call to arms.

The wind had begun to die, although eerily silent lightning still raged in the clouds above them. "It is David Alderscroft,"

Memsa'b was saying. "I don't know what he is trying to do, but Robin Goodfellow warned him off doing so, and I tried to echo that warning. He—"

She left whatever she was going to say unsaid, and merely shrugged, the gesture more eloquent than words of what she thought about men who refused to listen to sound advice.

"Then we have to stop him," Selim replied immediately. "By force, if need be."

"There's more nor that," Nan piped up, urged by that silent presence within her that felt strangely like some kind of version of herself, only older, stronger, tougher. "If'n Robin hurts a mortal, som'thin' bad 'appens. 'E gets banished."

Memsa'b's eyes grew wide in the light from the lightning. "Oh—" she said, "Oh—that would be—"

"Not only the end to magic in the Isle, but it would open the door to a great many things that would make life very uncomfortable for the rest of us," Sahib said grimly. "With the Guardian at the Gate gone—"

"Run," Memsa'b said, suiting her actions to her words, as she picked up her skirts in both hands and fled down the terrace like a racing deer. "*Run!*"

They followed her; she ran like that girl in the Greek myth Nan had just read—Atalanta, that was her name, or something like. Nan snatched Neville down off her shoulder and cradled him in her arms as Sarah did the same with Grey; the birds would never have been able to stay on their shoulders while they ran. It was a good thing Memsa'b was wearing a white summer dress; they were able to follow her, flitting along the paths of the estate like a ghost, with Sahib like a shadow right beside her.

After a little, Nan realized where they were going; the door in the hedge that the arrogant man had ridden through.

And that was where and when it all came together. The man that had nearly ridden them down and the man that Memsa'b was angry at and the man who was about to unleash all hell on them with his foolishness were all the same man, and his name was David Alderscroft. . . .

❄

Sarah was glad that she and Nan were used to playing hard. She would never have believed that a grown-up could run like that. Memsa'b had hiked her skirts clean up over her knees, and her legs flashed through the grass in a way that should have scandalized anyone who saw it. It was just a good thing that Memsa'b never did wear the kind of dresses people called fashionable; in fact, Sarah was not entirely sure Memsa'b ever wore corsets either. She'd never have been able to run in anything fashionable.

Sahib put on a limping burst of speed and got to the door in the hedge ahead of Memsa'b and wrenched it open. They all caught up to her and piled through the door and—

And they all stopped dead in their tracks.

Sarah felt a tingle, and knew that this was *her* moment, at the same time as Grey said urgently, "Go! Now!"

She shoved through the adults, and saw what it was that had them paralyzed.

There was a crowd of—creatures—lined up on the bridle path, standing as a barrier between them and wherever it was that Memsa'b was leading them. They weren't physical. They might have been the ghosts of children, once.

They weren't now.

They glowed a leprous white, and where their eyes should have been there were only empty holes with a dull, red gleam to them, as if old, dying embers lay at the bottom. Their unnaturally long fingers were crooked into vicious claws, and in place of fingernails, they had talons. Their mouths were agape, showing feral, pointed teeth, and a craving for fear and pain emanated from them in a way calculated to make any sane person turn and flee.

Except—

Except they *were* the spirits of children still. And under all that, they were lost, alone, afraid.

And that was what Sarah must reach.

She put Grey on her shoulder, and felt the parrot spread her wings, as if giving her shelter.

"Sarah—" Sahib began, but Memsa'b shushed him.

"Give her backing, my brothers," she said instead, and Sarah felt a steady, warm glow building behind her, a warmth of love and support, as Nan pushed through also and came to stand beside her. She cast a glance aside.

Nan—Nan was a warrior.

The transformation was complete. Instead of the little girl in the pinafore, what stood beside Sarah was a wild creature out of an old Celtic saga, a glowing golden fighting maiden in a short, red wool tunic with a short bronze sword and a slight smile on her face that was just the least little bit disturbing in its enthusiasm.

"I see what needs be done, sister," Nan said, with no trace of her usual accent. "This is old magic, and I know it well. I shall sever the soul from the rider, so you can set the spirits free."

And with no more warning than that, she leaped at the line of waiting creatures, then leaped in among them—

—and began to dance.

That was all that Sarah could call it. The creatures swarmed her, but seemed unable to touch her. With Neville making vicious stabs at weirdly transparent faces, battering them with his wings, Nan danced among them, feinting, leaping, whirling, never staying in any one place for long, until—

Strike!

The sword licked out, and there was a cry, and something with tattered wings and a terrible face separated from the seething mob, as the spirit of a small child, faded and frightened, dropped out of it.

"Come!" Sarah called, holding out her arms to it, casting her heart toward it. It fled to her, and as it neared, with a cry, Grey stood on her tiptoes and spread her wings wide, and a bright light surrounded them both. The child ghost flung itself at them, touched the light—and vanished.

The thing that had separated from it uttered a scream of mingled rage and fear, and popped like a soap bubble, just as Nan made another of those lightning strikes, and severed another "rider" from its victim.

Sarah lost track of what was going on; it took all of her strength and concentration to help Grey keep opening that "door" to the beyond and persuade the children to pass through it. But eventually, Grey settled down on her shoulder again, shook herself and uttered a soft, tired sigh. The light around them faded, and she blinked, to see that the golden warrior was gone, and there was only Nan standing on the path with Neville at her feet, looking disheveled and tired—but triumphant.

But there was no time for congratulations. There was a cold, ominous glow beyond the trees, and the clouds were swirling in a whirl over the spot, lightning firing almost continuously from them.

"Run!" Memsa'b called again. And they ran.

❊

David Alderscroft was beginning to feel misgivings about all this.

It didn't *feel* right. He couldn't put his finger on why, it just didn't. Maybe it was the strange storm that had sprung up. Wind, clouds, and more lightning than he had ever seen before, but no rain.

Maybe it was the oddly eager light in Cordelia's eyes.

Maybe it was an uneasy feeling that he did not know nearly enough about what she was going to do—or said she was going to do.

Or that he sensed an invisible, icy presence lingering somewhere nearby. It was not one of the Ice Wurms he was used to using. It was a lot—larger. And it was able to conceal itself from him almost entirely.

Why would it want to do that?

The longer he stood here in the lightning-lit garden, watching Cordelia set out her preparations, the more his instincts were overriding his control. From nagging doubt to insisting, from insisting to screaming, they were telling him that despite all appearances, this was a bad idea, that he should leave—

Except that his instincts had told him this sort of nonsense before. He was more than instinct. He was a rational, thinking man. And all this fear *could* be the work of that very nature spirit that Cordelia meant to protect him against.

And yet—the spirit had been very specific. It had warned him against practicing his Ice Magics here, and no more. Or actually, it had warned him against practicing them against the countryside. As if there was any reason why he would do that.

So why was Cordelia so intent on protecting him from it? It wasn't as if he had any reason to practice any magic at all in this place. And the creature hadn't done anything worse than frighten him.

As he stood there uncertainly with a tempest overhead, and growing misgivings in his heart, the solitude of that corner of the garden was broken, not once, but twice.

And in that moment, everything changed.

A bolt of lightning struck the ground to the east of where he and Cordelia stood, blinding and deafening him for a moment. And when he could see again—

He felt himself go rigid. It was the nature spirit again, but

—different. Very different.

It was taller, its features were sharper, and it was dressed, head to toe, in black. Surrounded by a coruscating rainbow of all powers, it stared at him and Cordelia in a dark rage.

That was when the thing that David had only sensed until this moment made itself visible to the west of where he and Cordelia stood.

Or—more visible. There was something about whatever the entity was that made him struggle without success to keep his eyes on the spot where it stood, and he couldn't look directly at the thing at all. His eyes and his mind slid around the edges of it, without being able to concentrate on it.

And then—seven people strode into the garden as if they had every right to be there.

Two of them he did not know, but both were clearly foreign, probably from some part of India. One he recognized as the servant that had let him into Frederick Harton's home and school. The fourth was Frederick Harton himself, and fifth and sixth were the two little girls he had nearly run down. And the seventh—

—the seventh was Isabelle.

Cordelia drew herself up in surprise. "Well," she said. "I confess, I had not expected you to turn up here. Isn't it rather late in the day to be playing the rejected lover?"

Isabelle ignored her. The lightning made for a poor illumination source, washing out all colors, and it occurred to David then that she looked like a marble monument. Her hair had come down and tumbled in wild profusion down her back. "David," she called, her voice trembling a little. "You do not want to be here."

"Oh, indeed," Cordelia replied, her own voice utterly, coldly polite. "And why would that be, I wonder? Surely you are not going to claim that I have some nefarious designs upon him. Simple logic would show that if, indeed, I had wanted something of his power and position, I would have had it long ago."

Isabelle ignored the jab, and concentrated on David. "You need to ask yourself why it was so needful that you be here now, in the middle of the night, alone. This woman is not your friend."

"And you are." Cordelia did not laugh. "This sort of flummery was all very well when you were a girl, Isabelle, but it ill-suits a grown woman who should have better self-control and a more realistic view of life."

Isabelle continued to ignore her. "David, when has she offered you so much as a single moment of honest friendship?"

He paused; there was something stirring inside him at her question. "What do you mean?" he asked cautiously.

"Ordinary friendship," Isabelle persisted. "Spending time in one another's company not because you were expecting some sort of gain, but merely because you enjoy spending time there with him."

Friendship. David could remember having friends. He could recall hours spent playing parlor games, or having discussions on anything and everything long into the night. He remembered, dimly, the pleasure he had gotten from it. When had he stopped doing that?

"What nonsense." Cordelia's eyes glinted. "This foolishness is for children. Adults have no such need. Begone."

A rumble of thunder followed the word, but overhead the storm was dying, and the nature spirit was listening intently.

"I am not one of your familiar spirits to be banished with a word, Cordelia," Isabelle said sharply. "David, you cannot go through life in isolation, seeing others as objects to be manipulated and used, and watching for the same behavior in others."

And that was exactly what his life had become. He saw it in a stunning moment of clarity. He had not done a single thing he truly enjoyed in the last year, nor spent a single moment in the company of someone he would have sought out on his own. What had his life turned into?

"There are more important, and more lasting, things than power and position, David," Isabelle continued. "Power is ephemeral and can be taken away. Position is just as ephemeral. But no one can take love and friendship. You can lose them by your own actions or lack of them, or by neglect, but they cannot be taken away."

The clouds parted overhead, and bright moonlight shone down on them. The spirit moved closer, head tilted to one side. She glanced at her companions as she said that, and they moved closer to her. Her husband put one hand on her shoulder, and in another moment of clarity, David saw what he had not seen before. These people were not masters, pupils, and servants. They were also friends.

And what of his friends? He recalled their names and faces clearly and they were no longer in his "circle." He had told himself he had outgrown them, but that was not the truth. The truth was he had thrust them away, or ignored them, because Cordelia had told him that his precious time was too valuable to waste in their company. And so they had stopped calling on him, stopped issuing him invitations. And he turned from friends to those who were politically valuable. His life had become an unending round of work. He no longer even read things that were not in some way related to his ambitions. He looked back over the past several years and saw nothing but empty hours, gray and uninteresting. He looked ahead to the future, and tried to imagine what life would be like if he achieved those ambitions. Surely, it would be worth the cost.

But he realized with a sinking spirit and a feeling of nausea that it would only be more of the same. More empty, pleasureless years, punctuated by a few hours of fame, which would only bring him to the attentions of people who were just like him, who had ambitions of their own, and hoped to maneuver him to get something.

If he married, it would be to a woman who brought him more connections, perhaps more wealth, who would spend as little time as possible in his company. She would be too busy exercising her own ambitions to become a notable hostess in the most exclusive of sets. Even if she felt some dim stirrings of affection, she would have no time for anything other than bearing the "heir and a spare" required of her, and furthering her own social climb.

"What was the last moment of simple pleasure you remember having, David?" Isabelle asked quietly. "Something you enjoyed for its own sake."

With a plummeting heart, he realized that the only simple moment of pleasure he had experienced in the last several weeks was sitting down to dinner in his club and enjoying a well-cooked meal.

Weeks! He had gone weeks with the only memorable moment being a meal!

Cordelia glanced sharply at all of them, and must have sensed that she was losing him. "Enough," she barked.

But he was too deep in despair at his situation now to pay any attention to the author of his misery. He looked at Isabelle, who had one hand resting affectionately on the shoulders of each of the children—at her husband, whose very posture proclaimed that he would quite cheerfully and publicly take her into his arms for a loving embrace at any moment, and know it would be returned with equal fervor. He looked at the three "servants," whose protective posture said that they would lay down their lives for these friends—

These children were not even Isabelle's by birth, and yet he could see they loved her unreservedly. If he had children of his own, they would grow up in the company of nannies and nursemaids, tutors and governesses. They would be sent away to school, return home only for a few days at a time, and over the course of twenty years, if he was in their presence for a grand total of six weeks' worth of time it would be amazing. They would call him "Pater," and they would respect him, but they would not love him, and when he died he would go to his grave with their dutiful attendance and concealed pleasure that he was gone and they could now enjoy his wealth and property unfettered by any rules or constraints of that stranger who had been their father.

The Hartons were surrounded by servants who loved and protected them. He was surrounded by servants who probably resented and definitely cheated him. Frederick had a wife who so clearly adored him that nothing made her unhappy except to be separated from him. He lived in a lonely empty house, a condition that would not change even if he took a wife of his own.

"I would not exchange a single moment of my life for all of your wealth, David," Isabelle told him, as Cordelia seethed. "Your power cannot buy me peace. Your position cannot bring me friendship. Your estates cannot give me hope. And your wealth cannot purchase love." Her voice took on tones of remote pity. "What you have is worth nothing to me. And this is what Cordelia has brought you to."

Bleak, black despair settled over him like a blanket. If he could have gotten himself past the shame of it, he would have wept. By now, he was a cold, heartless, ruthless creature. He had lost the friends he had once had, and no longer knew how to make new ones.

And as for love—

He had driven it away.

He stared at Isabelle numbly, wanting to howl his grief to the moon.

The little girl with the parrot looked up at him solemnly, and paced forward until she stood a mere foot from him. And she held out her hand.

"I'll be your friend, Mister Alderscroft," she said soberly. " 'Cause sometimes the reason you are friends with someone is that they need one."

Something broke inside him—or perhaps, it was better to say that something melted. Tears burned in his eyes as he took the child's hand; they overflowed and trickled down his cheeks. The child tugged on his hand and drew him to stand beside her friends.

Cordelia's cheeks flamed, and she made a summoning gesture. "You flout me at your peril!" she exclaimed. "You—"

"They have the protection of Robin Goodfellow, sorceress," said the earth spirit, coming to stand on the other side of Isabelle. "The Fey do not take sides in mortal quarrels—but I am a law unto myself and I say they are under my protection—and have my friendship."

Undeterred, Cordelia voiced the Words of Power to bring her creatures to her.

But David, with a little shock of surprise that he still recalled the words, called upon the allies of his true Element of Fire to come to his aid. After the way he had shunned them, he would not have been surprised that they did not answer.

But they did.

A rain, a stream, a river of Salamanders, greater and lesser, of Imps and Lyons and Firebirds and even a Phoenix, all came crowding about him at his summons, as if they had only been waiting for this moment.

They stood, shoulder to shoulder, in a compact group of solidarity, surrounded by creatures of Fire. And at last, the near-invisible Ice Lord spoke.

"You have failed, woman," it said. *"You are mine."*

In the blink of an eye, it somehow surrounded her, and before she had a chance to scream or cry out, they were both gone.

Epilogue

DAVID Alderscroft surveyed his quarters with melancholy satisfaction.

He had closed and sold his town house, and moved into rooms at his club. Men in general were not so exacting of the requirements of friendship as women were. Some weeks and months of careful tending, and he would soon be living among men who considered themselves his friend. And at that point, he would begin renewing his acquaintance with those old friends he had thrust aside. They would take some more careful cultivation, but eventually he thought he could win them over again. And he would never make the mistake of losing them twice.

But there was no point in keeping up his town house, because he knew, deep inside, that he would never need it, for he would never marry. He had rejected love once. Unlike friendship, that sort of chance never came again. In the moment that his heart had thawed, it had also broken.

And it was his own damned fault.

Still. In the midst of heartbreak—there were the little compensations. He glanced affectionately at the pasteboard square in his hand.

Dear Uncle David, it said. *Please come to the school this weekend. We want to show you the new ponies and take you riding on the paths we have been cutting, and we have decided to make September 12th Nan's official birthday. There will be cake and ice creams. Love, Sarah.*

David's old estate was no longer empty and hollow. It rang with the happy voices of children—the children of Elemental Mages, the children of the Talented and Gifted, and the children of expatriates. It was now the home to the Harton School, and, he trusted, would provide a harvest of fine young men and women for decades to come.

It was a good legacy.

And he planned to create a second as well; his Circle would work not only for the protection of Mages and Masters, but for the protection of all of England, so that another creature like the Ice Lord could never slip onto the island without someone noticing.

Good legacies, both of them.

He set down Sarah's invitation, picked up a pen, and began to write out his acceptance when a second piece of paper fluttered to the ground. Without his prompting, a Salamander manifested, darted to the floor, and retrieved it, returning it to the desk only slightly scorched.

Isabelle's note, attached to Frederick's accepting an honorary chair in the London Circle as spokesman for the Talented and Gifted, in response to his addenendum that he was sorry he could not invite her, but that as the Club was exclusively male—

Dear David, if I wanted to prance around in fancy dress, I would join the Order of the Golden Dawn. Their robes are just as ridiculous, and they serve a better tea. Affectionately, Isabelle.

The Salamanders danced as the room rang with laughter.